RETURN
TO
BEAUTY

RETURN
TO
BEAUTY

A HISTORICAL NOVEL

ERNEST L. SCHUSKY

SUNSTONE
PRESS

SANTA FE

Sunstone books may be purchased for educational, business, or sales promotional use.
For information please write: Special Markets Department, Sunstone Press,
P.O. Box 2321, Santa Fe, New Mexico 87504-2321.

Printed on acid free paper

Library of Congress Cataloging-in-Publication Data

Schusky, Ernest Lester, 1931-
 Return to beauty : a historical novel / by Ernest L. Schusky.
  p. cm.
 ISBN 978-0-86534-700-7 (pbk. : alk. paper)
 1. Navajo Indians--Fiction. I. Title.
 PS3569.C55546R48 2009
 813'.54--dc22

                          2008054717

Published in
Santa Fe

WWW.SUNSTONEPRESS.COM
SUNSTONE PRESS / POST OFFICE BOX 2321 / SANTA FE, NM 87504-2321 /USA
(505) 988-4418 / ORDERS ONLY (800) 243-5644 / FAX (505) 988-1025

RETURN
TO
BEAUTY

ONE

1822   NUEVO MEXICO

"Stop grinding that corn, woman. I'm hungry. I have to leave soon."

Yahzi sucked in her lips to conceal a sneer but fixed the man with an icy stare until he looked at the ground. Neither her eyes nor her tongue ever failed to subdue him. He spat but not in her direction. She took a handful of corn from a basket, spread it over the metate and pounded the kernels with one end of the mano to crack them, then turned the stone to hold it with both hands. She tossed her shoulder-length, black hair behind her head before grinding the kernels into meal with a vengeance. A stray hair crept onto her long face that showed off a flawless complexion.

The cold seeped up through the worn wool mat that Yahzi knelt on. She pulled her poncho closer to her throat, brushed away frost glistening on the metate's edge. She looked at the tip of the rising sun, anticipating its warmth.

"It'll be noon before I get something to eat," Pablo grumbled under his breath. He leaned his rickety chair back against the outside wall of their one room adobe home. "I'll be frozen stiff before then."

From underneath the small cooking ramada in front of the hut, Yahzi glanced dismissal at Pablo, drooling onto his shirt. A shirt so stained with dirt that the saliva didn't show. If he ever scrubbed his face, he might pass for a Mexican instead of a Dinee. No doubt, he wished he were born a Mexican instead of a Navajo.

Yahzi stirred her cook fire to life, adjusted the thin, flat stone that served as her grill and let it heat. She brushed the corn meal from the metate into a pottery bowl and added water from the olla that hung from a forked pole of the ramada. She knelt to mix the batter, paying little attention. She stared into nothingness, recalling her childhood.

"You're daydreaming of your brother again." Pablo spat his accusation. "You'll never see him. Nor any of your Navajo relatives."

1

He was right about her daydream. Yahzi spent her daylight hours imagining her return to Dinehtah, her homeland. She had little hope that her parents still lived but her brother must. Her kind and gentle brother, Nakai. He had helped her drive the family flock to pasture and remained with her in grassy parts of the canyon while the two of them sprawled on their backs watching the clouds. He found shapes that she'd never imagined, then tell stories about them to bring deep laughs from Yahzi. Since Nakai was only a year younger, she never had to care for him the way sisters usually watched over younger brothers.

Nakai was a perfect companion except when his friend, Bahe, joined them. Bahe was a few years older than Yahzi, his constant smile foreshadowing his practical jokes. He delighted in teasing Yahzi and turning Nakai against her. She'd tire of Bahe but missed him when he failed to visit after a few days.

"You should be thinking of my son." The man looked at Yahzi's swollen belly. "How we'll teach him proper Spanish and custom. How to be a carpenter so he can live in Santa Fe instead of this rundown rancherita on the frontier." He scowled. "And you'll not be teaching him Navajo. We're Christians, not pagans."

Yahzi winced as she scooted closer to the fire because the baby kicked her. The thought that a tiny person lived within her alleviated the pain. She always wanted a child, but now she didn't. How could she escape burdened with a baby? She couldn't leave her child with Pablo. He couldn't care for himself, let alone an infant. She inhaled deeply, exhaled slowly, and felt the fetus calm itself as her stomach muscles relaxed.

She patted the corn meal into flat circles and dropped five onto the stone slab. As the tortillas sizzled, her mind wandered to her childhood home in Canyon de Chelly. How far to the north or to the west was it? Where would she find someone to lead her to her brother? Surely one or more of her sisters remained in the canyon, despite the tragedy that had happened. She imagined her sisters married and with children of their own. One was a toddler when Yahzi last saw her, the other she remembered strapped to a cradle board. Even swaddled, her large eyes and already thick eyebrows,

2

much like Yahzi's, foretold beauty. Indeed, neighbors said that the baby was as beautiful as Yahzi with her smooth skin and lustrous hair.

"Hurry up, woman. The señor needs me to help with the horses."

"Don't pretend importance. Any slave can do what you do." Yahzi was so disgusted with Pablo's currying favor with Diego Baca that she let her anger show. A rare event, spurred by Pablo's interrupting thoughts of her brother and sisters.

"I'm not a slave." Pablo sniveled. "I've been baptized, same as you."

"I'll never be the same as you," Yahzi snarled. "Gave up your language when they enslaved you. Won't learn it from me. You'll never be more than a slave. My son will never be more than a Spanish lackey, too." Yahzi choked on the thought, then mumbled under her breath, "If he remains here with you."

No, she'd take the child to Dinehtah with her. Somehow.

She'd be as glad to leave Pablo and the ranch as to see her brother and sisters. To snuggle in the warmth of their hogan. To bathe in the beauty of her canyon's walls. To walk in beauty, the phrase her grandmother used so often. The phrase that echoed in Dinee legends and prayers.

Yahzi had shaken out their sheepskin bedding and swept the floor before grinding more corn for the evening meal. She hummed a Dinee lullaby to alleviate the pain in her lower back. By late morning she had enough meal for the day that she could spend the rest of the time doing the señor's washing. Since her pregnancy had become obvious, half a day's work satisfied Señor Baca. She suspected his generosity had more to do with their past, however, than with her present condition.

With luck she could include a few of her own things in the wash. And if Auntie Dezba remembered they'd agreed to meet, the two would have an hour or two to talk while Yahzi labored over dirty clothes.

Yahzi hesitated at the ranch house door. She'd do anything to avoid contact with the Spaniard. The tingling of revulsion tightened the muscles in her neck, but the feeling was not exactly hatred.

Whatever the conflicting emotions were, they had to do with a complex past she and Diego shared.

"The clothes are just inside the door," a husky voice called from within the house. "If you aren't careful with the soap, you'll have to use soapweed. See if you can get my shirt clean without tearing it."

One small rip the last time—it had been ages since she had torn anything—and Diego wouldn't let her forget. Well, that's not the only thing he's held against me, Yahzi thought. At least I won't have to face him if the laundry is where he put it last time.

She half opened the door to see a pair of trousers, his shirt, and dingy underwear on a chair just inside. Outside, with the clothes in hand, she noticed another silver button missing from the row lining his pants. A worn place on the trousers' knee would soon need patching. The seat was equally worn. She wondered if he had enough money to buy another pair, smiled at the thought of Diego huddling in a poncho while she washed and dried his only set of clothes.

Behind the ranch house, Yahzi found the iron kettle she used for laundry. It smelled of rancid mutton. She wiped at a rim of grease midway down its side, shrugging her shoulders when she scrubbed it only half-clean with a bunch of dried grass. She winced as she bent over to pick up the unburned ends of wood that had been used the night before, then poured in two buckets of water from the horse trough. Bits of ice clung to the rim. She started a fire with tinder and a glowing ember she had brought from home. The cook had failed to replenish the firewood, so she went in search of more. Enough to warm the water, nothing more.

The water was luke-warm when Auntie Dezba came wheezing around the corner of the ranch house, wiping her nose with the back of her hand. Her smile danced across her round face in beat with the flashing of her eyes. It was hard for Yahzi to reconcile Dezba's name, meaning Goes to War, with her personality.

Dezba carried wood under one arm and a blue skirt and her only blouse under the other. A poncho kept her torso warm. Or half warm. Dezba looked like a Pueblo Indian although Yahzi had trouble recalling that Dezba was born in Jemez Pueblo. Dezba's Dinee words had little accent, and she had become like a true father's sister to

Yahzi. The old woman had almost convinced Yahzi that Dezba's Jemez clan was the same as Towering House, the clan Yahzi was born for, the clan of her father.

"I thought there'd be no firewood," Dezba said. "I heard those two vaqueros cooking up something last night. Did they leave us anything?" She added her wood to the fire and held her hands toward the flames.

"A scum of mutton fat in the kettle."

"No wine?" Dezba stood upright, turned her back to the fire, raised her poncho and rubbed her naked buttocks. Her smile danced even more. "I knew they were drinking because of their singing. If you can call the noise they made a song."

"Didn't it bother Diego?" Yahzi asked.

"He wouldn't say anything to them. No one else will come here to work since the Dinee began raiding."

"Did they talk about Dinee?" Yahzi's relatives could be among the war party. They could take her home any time now.

"Well, one vaquero claimed he saw two Dinee at that ranch west of here. He bragged how he chased them off."

"Are you ready to go off with a war party?" Yahzi said. Even if the warriors were only a scouting party, they could offer the opportunity she yearned for. Dezba didn't answer. The elderly woman seemed settled into their current life, no longer regarding herself a slave.

Finally Dezba replied. "Where would we go?"

"Back to Canyon de Chelly!" Yahzi's exclamation surprised herself. But, how could Dezba have forgotten home? Except Dezba seemed to be forgetting a lot.

Yahzi changed the subject. "We're almost out of soap. Use this last piece on your things."

The water was luke-warm while Yahzi finished Diego's laundry. She noted that his shirt was turning yellow, aging as he was. She scrubbed hard to remove the grime on the collar and a grass stain on an elbow. By the time she finished, little soap was left for her blouse. She took off her poncho and blouse, replaced the poncho before dipping the blouse into the kettle and rubbed the last bit of soap into the rough fabric. Perhaps she'd be on her way home before Diego required another laundry.

As she rinsed her blouse, a pain shot from abdomen to her hips. She straightened up, rubbing her lower back. Still stiff, she placed her hands on the warm kettle rim and backed away to straighten her spine. She ached all over, but the feeling was not as intense as the pain that stabbed her back. Now she had grease on her hands, rubbing her fingers together, knowing the last of the dirty water wouldn't remove it. She found more grass, rubbed hard with it, and got rid of the rest.

"Your hands are so rough from this soap." Dezba held up a sliver she had saved and turned up her nose. "They wouldn't look so rough if the rest of your skin weren't so beautiful." She reached over to run a hand along Yahzi's cheek.

Yahzi turned to her friend and grasped her hands, tears in her eyes. Dezba's gesture reminded her of the way Diego once fondled her face, praising her complexion, not allowing her to wash clothes.

She dropped Dezba's hands when the baby kicked and massaged the place where its foot had been.

Dezba reached over to feel Yahzi's stomach. She giggled. "She's going to be a strong girl. She'll make you comfortable when you're old."

"I feel old now," Yahzi said. "If I don't get away soon, I never will." She drew the back of her hand across her brow. "I miss Canyon de Chelly so much it hurts."

"I remember the first time I saw it," Dezba said.

It was a memory she had shared many times, but it always interested Yahzi. Dezba could recall events twenty years ago more vividly than things that happened yesterday.

"The Catholic priest at Jemez married us although we didn't think of it as a real marriage. After a while, my husband said it was time to go home. I agreed, but I was afraid. I didn't know anyone there." Her eyebrows arched.

"He had only one horse so I rode behind him. We took turns walking. He hadn't prepared me for the canyon's beauty. The bright red, with black streaks running down, some of them cutting across. Such shades of red and orange! I'd never seen beauty like that. Water running along the canyon floor. Everything so green. It reminded me of the Jemez River."

Yahzi wrung out Diego's shirt and pants while Dezba reminisced.

"When we got to his mother's hogan, everyone ignored me. I guess they were letting me get accustomed to them. They all surrounded him and asked what he wanted to eat. They didn't ask anything about me." She paused. "Well, everyone was speaking Dinee real fast. I didn't understand it very well then. I got confused when I tried to talk it."

Yahzi imagined the Dinee welcome. No one looking at Dezba, except everyone watching her from the corner of their eyes.

"After a moon or two it got better. We ate mutton all the time. Plenty of corn and beans, and dried peaches. The peach trees were better than ours at Jemez." Dezba licked her lips.

"Did his family build you your own hogan?" Yahzi asked her usual question.

"We used an old hogan nearby. I saw my mother-in-law often, but we didn't speak much."

"Do Jemez mothers-in-law talk to their daughters-in-law?" Yahzi had heard the answer before, but she knew how much Dezba enjoyed answering.

"Oh yes. I don't know where the Dinee got the idea to avoid mothers-in-law. Maybe from the Utes." She laughed so hard her cupped hand over her mouth failed to conceal yellowed teeth.

Yahzi couldn't remember how many times Dezba had teased her about Dinee borrowing Ute customs. It didn't strike her as funny, but Yahzi laughed her polite laugh.

Dezba returned to a story that was so familiar to Yahzi. "In those early days when I didn't speak the language well, my husband's brothers talked about how when I had a baby they would be fathers of my child." Dezba glowed at the memory, then giggled. "I thought that they intended to father a child by me. It took me forever to learn what they meant. I was so dumb." Dezba giggled in embarrassment. "But it was the same at Jemez. I called all my father's brothers, 'father.' Just like all my mother's sisters were my mother."

"You aren't dumb," Yahzi exclaimed, as she usually did. "You're smart to see how your mother's sisters are like mothers to you—and you are a mother to your sisters' children. The Spanish never understand how we're related. Once I tried to explain it to Diego, but he claimed it was the work of the devil." Yahzi took Dezba's hands again. "You're smarter than any Spaniard!"

"And you're so kind." Dezba chuckled, "Well, maybe that husband of yours doesn't think so."

"Pablo is my husband only by Spanish custom," Yahzi spat out the word "husband." She stuck out her chin. "I'd never share corn pollen with him. I only married him in the Spanish way because Diego's wife forced us to."

Dezba took Yahzi's hand, a tear in her aunt's eye.

"It's far from the worst thing that happened to me—or us." Yahzi wiped away Dezba's tear.

TWO

Yahzi nodded goodbye to her aunt as Dezba started down the path to her stone hovel, hidden in a draw behind the ranch house but within hailing range of it. Clay patches clung to the sides of the hovel, but more mud had worn away than remained. Yahzi admired how Dezba never complained when freezing rain pierced the warped boards in what passed for a roof or when the wind driven snow found cracks in the shack's sides. Somehow I must take her with me if I go, Yahzi thought. When I go, she corrected herself.

She hurried toward the ranch house, grateful to leave the clothes where Diego had put them. But he stepped to the door before she could put down his shirt and pants. "Good afternoon, Maria," he said.

Yahzi glanced around, pretending she did not recognize her Christian name.

"Don't play dumb with me, Maria," Diego emphasized "Maria."

Yahzi shrugged. "Your clothes aren't dry, señor."

"Bring them inside. You can put them over a chair."

"My husband is expecting me." She turned to go.

"Your husband can pick his nose another two hours if I need you, Maria." Diego raised his voice. Yahzi didn't budge. Diego stepped forward and put both hands on her shoulders. "My wife died more than a year ago. After your baby is born, I want you to return to the house, Maria."

"Will you call me Yahzi?"

"That's not your name." Despite a years-long tan, red flooded Diego's face. "Maria is a sacred name."

"Is that why you people give it to every slave woman you take?" No one could miss the bitterness in Yahzi's voice.

"Yahzi," Diego responded with the softness that Yahzi recognized as Diego cunning. "You are one of us, no longer a pagan. You're a Christian." Diego searched Yahzi's face for a sign of agreement. He found none. He sighed in exasperation. "We can consider Yahzi a Christian name if that's what you want." He paused. "But Maria is a

9

beautiful name. I had a sister named Maria. That's why I had you baptized Maria."

Yahzi believed he might have been lying the first time he told her his sister was called Maria. Now, from the way he uttered the name, she was certain he lied. Nor was she fooled by his smile and the charm he mustered when he purred, "You should live here in the house with your baby. It will never go hungry. I can be the child's godfather."

"Then you'll be a *compadre* of Pablo's." Yahzi sensed Diego's degradation at being related to Pablo, even if only in ritual kinship.

"And be Pablo's compadre." Diego repeated, but his grimace told her the thought turned his stomach.

"I'm sorry about your wife, Don Diego, but I don't intend to take her place in your bed."

"Yahzi, remember the good times we had there." Diego was as suave as when Yahzi arrived at the ranch some twenty years ago.

"You took me to your bed only because your wife had gone to Mexico for the doctors there. Your *curanderas* here weren't good enough for her, were they?"

"She said she was leaving me to get an annulment. I explained that to you, Maria."

"Yahzi," she barked, then softened. "In those days you could have told me anything. I knew so little of life. I celebrated my *kinaalda* only a few months before you people took me prisoner."

"You never mentioned a kinaalda. What is it?"

"It's how we Dinee celebrate when a girl becomes a woman. When women can have children. Do you Spanish celebrate the event?" Yahzi had heard about the meaning and ritual of Confirmation. Before Diego could reply, she said, "No, you hide the wonder of sex. Your precious Maria has to be a virgin, or she wouldn't be a goddess." Her attempt at blasphemy sent a tremor down Yahzi's spine. Her face flushed, she wondered if the color showed as much as the red in Diego's.

"You take care, woman. I won't suffer sacrilege from you. After all, you're just a…"

"A pagan slave! Say it, Diego. You bastard." Even in her fury Yahzi chose her words with care. She used "bastard" with deliberation, knowing how Diego would react to the insult that his mother was less than perfect.

"A slave. Nothing but a pagan slave—until saved by baptism. Have you forgotten its glory, woman, like you have forgotten the Virgin's mercy?" His knuckles turned white from the way he gripped Yahzi.

"How can I believe in mercy when you enslave us? How, Don Diego?" She filled "Don" with scorn.

Diego reacted to his defeat. He dropped his hands from her shoulders, took half a step back and slapped Yahzi so hard she fell to the ground.

She got to her knees, staring into Diego's eyes with contempt. He started sobbing, took her by the arms and lifted her to him. "Maria, my beautiful Maria. Hair black as ever. It's kept the sheen of its youth, just like your skin." He ran his hands along both cheeks. "Forgive me. I'll never hit you again. Tell me you'll come to live with me."

"I'll come to you," she murmured. She could lie to him as readily as he lied to her.

As soon as Yahzi returned to her adobe hut, she rubbed both cheeks to conceal the outline of Diego's fingers so she wouldn't have to recount the confrontation to Pablo. She kindled the fire and boiled what remained of the morning's corn meal. Pablo would complain that he'd rather have tortillas, but she'd ignored his complaining for years. The green wood she'd used was enough of a problem without the endless patting that tortillas required. As she put her small clay pot on the fire, the acrid smoke caught her nostrils. She half sneezed, half coughed.

Pablo came down the path from the corral, dragging a bridle in the dust. The smell of a stable accompanied him. "Is dinner ready, woman? I have more work to do this evening."

"You mean more groveling to your master?" Yahzi kept her face averted.

"Don Diego is your master, too," Pablo said.

"Don Diablo," Yahzi hissed. Her loathing for the Spaniard blocked the usual calm she reserved when dealing with Pablo.

"You watch your tongue, woman. Or he'll knock you down again." Pablo scrutinized her every move, studying her reaction.

Yahzi put a hand on the cheek that Diego had struck but guessed Pablo could not see the mark. Was he guessing that Diego had hit her? Perhaps Diego had cuffed him as well. She paused only a moment. "Is that why you're in such a foul mood? He hit you again? I haven't seen him. Only his filthy clothes."

"Don't lie to me. I saw him knock you down. What did you say to make him so angry?" Pablo stepped closer to Yahzi, still dragging the bridle behind him. A wisp of dust trailed.

Yahzi wrinkled her nose. She'd never grow accustomed to the stench of stables. "It's no business of yours. Go back to shoveling manure. Maybe I'll have a meal ready for you after you've cleaned up Spanish horse shit."

Pablo drew the arm back that held the bridle, hesitated a second, and swung it at Yahzi. His hesitation gave her time to anticipate what he intended. She jumped back, out of range of the leather straps, then leaped forward and kicked Pablo in the groin. It wasn't the first time she'd taken advantage of his vulnerability.

He dropped the bridle, grasped his crotch, and gasped for breath, his muttering filled with curses. Tears ran down his cheeks. His face turned an ugly white. After a spasm of coughing, he gagged on the blood he spat. His reaction was like the time at Christmas when Yahzi guessed the deadly Spanish disease had struck him. The disease that dried up lungs.

Her scorn turned to pity as she imagined his tortured end, gagging on endless blood and sputum. She went to his side, helped him half-straighten up, and led him to his rickety chair by the door. "Would you like some water?" she said.

"Please," he mumbled.

At least Yahzi thought he said please. She couldn't remember that he'd ever used it to her before. She lifted the scrap of blanket that served as a door, found a clay cup, and returned to the ramada. She filled it from the olla, brought the water to him, and lifted it to his lips. He swallowed twice, then choked on a third try, spitting up more blood.

"I'm sorry, Yahzi." His tears continued. "I was watching from the corral when I saw him hit you. I wanted to kill him, but what could I do?"

Helpless. Hopeless. That's what makes a slave, Yahzi thought. Maybe that's why she seldom felt sorry for her so-called husband. When she had kicked him before, he'd at least had the strength to run off flinging a curse over his shoulder. Now he was helpless, bent over in the chair, tears running, only lifting his head when Yahzi took one of his hands in hers.

"What hurts most, Yahzi, is the thought that you might leave me. Now that his wife is gone, I'm afraid Diego will ask you to come back to him. That's why I spied on you, I swear," he sobbed his confession. "I was glad he hit you. He must not want you." He looked into Yahzi's eyes. "Tell me he doesn't want you."

Yahzi avoided an answer. "He complained about how I washed his clothes. Said I'd torn his shirt. I guess I didn't say I was sorry quickly enough. So he hit me."

"Did you love him when you lived in the big house?" Pablo's voice almost returned to normal.

"There's no word for 'love' in Dinee. I'm not sure I know what the Spanish mean by love." Yahzi congratulated herself on the evasion. She guessed, as an adolescent, she had grown to love Diego —in the Spanish way.

"Did he stop loving you after the baby?" Pablo whispered the question.

"I don't know. His wife came back. That's why he insisted I marry you."

"He didn't care that your son had a club foot?" Pablo sat up a little straighter.

"I'll never know. I kept Hokee on a cradle board. Diego urged me to use a cradle he built for our baby. He did call it 'our baby,' but I wouldn't use the bed he made. It rocked back and forth. It'd make a baby dizzy."

"Maybe that's why the Spanish get so crazy. All that rocking when they're babies," Pablo said.

Yahzi laughed. She guessed Pablo meant to joke although that was a rarity for him.

"His wife went crazy when she first saw Hokee," Yahzi continued. "He was no longer a baby. I kept him away from her because of how much he looked like Diego. No one could miss it." Yahzi half smiled.

"Did she take to her bed like she often did?" Pablo showed more interest in Yahzi's early life than he ever had.

"Diego convinced her that Hokee could not be his son because of his club foot. He said there had never been a club foot in his family, and he claimed it was males who passed it on."

"I never knew that." Pablo said.

Yahzi couldn't help thinking that her husband was as dumb as Diego's wife, but she resisted expressing her thoughts. "Diego was lying to her. She believed him because she wanted his lies to be true."

"Oh," Pablo said. He rocked his head back and forth, a gesture that Yahzi had never bothered to understand.

"Do you think Hokee will ever come back to us?" Pablo said. "I may not have been his real father, but I helped raise him like a father, didn't I?"

Yahzi sighed. Pablo had wanted Hokee to help him with his chores, but he had ignored the boy while he was a toddler. She recalled with bitterness the time they thought Hokee had smallpox. Pablo had fled to the stable, leaving the boy's care to her.

Nevertheless, for the moment Pablo had her pity. "He'll never come back," Yahzi said. "We should have stopped using his name long ago."

"So you think he's dead?" Pablo pulled his head into his shoulders, stifled a cough.

"He's dead, Pablo." Yahzi was tired of lying about her son. "I killed him."

THREE

Yahzi had never seen such deep furrows in Pablo's brow. Perhaps he really had loved Hokee. She patted his hand. His eyes reminded her of the way Diego's hound looked after it was kicked.

"What do you mean, my woman?" Yahzi had never heard such concern in his "my woman" before. "You could never kill your child."

"Do you remember the night he and I fled? You and Diego and that slave who died were herding sheep to Belen. Anyway, I told you a Dinee raiding party carried Hokee and me off."

Pablo nodded his head, nervously fingered the hairs below his nose that he called a mustache.

"There were six Dinee, not the twenty I said or whatever number I made up so Diego wouldn't go after them. They had come to kill him and other ranchers because so many sheep were being stolen from Dinehtah, and when the Spanish weren't stealing, they were grazing their cattle on our land. Dinehtah couldn't feed its own sheep." Yahzi placed a hand on Pablo's arm.

"I begged them to take me with them. At first they wouldn't, but I learned two of them were Bitter Water people. They couldn't refuse a clan sister."

"How about Hokee?" Pablo asked. "They didn't want him holding them back, did they?"

Yahzi looked at the ground, sighed at the memory. "It was night. I didn't tell them about his foot. So they let the two of us ride the pack horse. In the dark they rode slowly. We kept up with no trouble."

"But in daylight, what did you do?"

"There was only one ranch left to attack. It was north of here. That old man who lived on it is gone now. He didn't have many sheep, but most of the time he grazed them in Dinehtah."

"I remember," Pablo said. "Don Diego told me the Dinee killed him."

"Not the raiding party I was with. He and his Mexican Indian ran off. The two slaves he owned took the Spaniard's horses and sheep and came with us." Yahzi took a deep breath. "I was so sure I'd make it home."

"I'm sorry," Pablo said. "But I'm glad to have you here."

Yahzi looked askance but leaned against Pablo's arm.

"I was sure we headed toward Canyon de Chelly. On the way, I smelled pinyon pine, the way it smells on the slopes of Tsoodzil." Yahzi stared into the dying fire, fanning at smoke when the wind changed. She got up to add more wood, watched the flames, and savored a hint of burning cedar.

"Did the Spaniards catch you?"

"The cowards never would venture far into Dinehtah. At least not then."

"So what happened?" Pablo said.

Yahzi wanted to reach over and close Pablo's drooling mouth. "We had ridden into a canyon. Not steep, not beautiful the way home is. The stream bed had dried up. A party of Comanches was looking for slaves. They're no better than the Spaniards. There must have been fifty of them."

"I hear they get a better price for slaves in Mexico."

Yahzi sighed. Pablo's attention span was never long. She hesitated but her need to confess won out. "The wind was coming our way so we heard them first. By now the Dinee realized what a hinderance we were. A boy with a club foot and a woman."

Pablo rocked his head in a meaningless gesture, his mouth drooling.

"They led me to a side canyon, its entrance just wide enough to allow a horse through. They told me to ride to the end of the canyon and hide in a cave not far up the canyon wall. They promised to cover my tracks at the entrance."

Pablo shivered. His shudder made Yahzi aware of the night's approaching cold. At least there was only the suggestion of a wind. "We didn't have to ride far. It was colder than it is now. There were good footholds up to the cave. Once we reached it, I realized the horse would start back down the canyon. The Comanches were sure to find its tracks."

"Couldn't you go after it?" Pablo said.

"I was so cold." Yahzi shivered at the memory. "A wind came up. In the dark, I was afraid I'd miss the footholds."

"So what did you do?"

"In the morning the horse was gone. I was sure I heard Comanches. Of course, the canyon entrance was too far away for them to have found the horse, but my imagination ran wild."

Yahzi got up, went inside, and brought out a sheepskin to share with Pablo. "It was light enough for me to see footholds above the cave leading to the top of the canyon. It was steep, but not far, maybe the height of ten men."

Yahzi's throat tightened. She dreaded telling more but couldn't stop.

"When the sun came out, it shone into the cave. It seemed warm after the night. I rubbed Hokee's hands. When I told him about the footholds, he thought we should climb to the top. He said we could spy on the Comanches. He never showed any fear."

"I knew that about him. I taught him how to be brave." Pablo stuck out his chest and took a deep breath.

Yahzi ignored his boast. She continued with her story. "I went first. A couple of places the footholds had worn away. I helped Hokee along. We were at the top when I heard a Comanche war cry. But maybe it was my fear. I'll never know." A tear ran down her cheek. "I hurried up. There was a ledge where I could lie down to reach for Hokee. He had kept up so he must have heard the war cry, too."

Yahzi stared into the fire without speaking.

"Yes, my woman," Pablo voiced impatience. "Then what?"

Yahzi shook her head. Glanced at Pablo. "Hokee was almost up. I reached for him. He took my hand. Then he lost his footing. He was swinging, all his weight on me. I couldn't lift him." An icy chill filled Yahzi. "Why couldn't I lift him?" she cried.

She clutched her left hand. "How could I have let go?" Tears streamed down. Her voice cracked. "How could I?"

Her left hand began to tremble, then her arm, then her shoulder. Pablo leaned over and held her.

"He was a big boy. I remember how heavy he was." Pablo patted her back.

"Don't you understand," she said. "I let him go because he held me back. We'd never make it to Dinehtah." Her sobs were incessant.

Pablo didn't answer, but a tear ran down one cheek.

The next morning Yahzi's baby woke her with its kick. She wondered if it were cold. She'd never warmed up during the frigid night even after Pablo cuddled against her and shared a sheepskin.

She slipped from under the cover, tucked it around Pablo, and wrapped her arms around herself to stop shivering. She found a few embers from the night before, picked up some tinder tucked in the hut's ceiling, and blew a flame to life. She had sufficient twigs to get a fire going but scurried into a nearby gulch to retrieve wood. It was scarcely enough fuel to get her pot boiling. After Yahzi added her meal to make mush, she held her hands to the fire, wondering if the warmth would ever reach her.

Pablo stirred, shook off the sheepskin and used Yahzi's shawl in its place. He looked foolish huddled under the shawl, one hand holding the ends of the cloth, the other reaching toward the fire. At least his mouth was closed.

"No tortillas?" he whined.

"I promised I'd help Dezba this morning," Yahzi lied. She didn't exactly lie, her friend always needed help, and Yahzi was desperate to see her after the confession to Pablo.

She watched Pablo gobble twice as much corn mush as he left for her, hoping what she did eat went to the baby inside her. Yahzi set off for Dezba's. She felt compelled to share her secret with Dezba since Pablo had learned it.

Dezba was sitting cross-legged before a loom letting the sun bathe her face. The weaving was less than a finger's length longer than it was two days before. The smell of burnt dung hung in the air. Yahzi saw charred remains of horse droppings in the smoldering fire. She yearned to take Dezba into her own home, but Diego sent the old woman scraps from his kitchen so Dezba often ate better than she and Pablo did.

Yahzi knelt beside the loom. "You have a gift. It's going to be a beautiful blanket."

Dezba smiled. "Do you really think so? I only have brown and black yarn."

If one liked brown and black, the blanket might pass as beautiful. But then, the Spaniards cared only for the warmth that Dinee wool provided.

"Do you have one of your own blankets to keep you warm at night?" Yahzi said.

"There's a small one I wove when I first got here. It's pretty well worn. But Don Diego gave me a sheep skin last year."

"Wasn't it a little longer than a year ago?" Yahzi said. She recalled how ragged the skin was, doubting that it added any warmth to the scrimpy blanket.

"It doesn't matter," Dezba said. "We'll be going home soon, won't we?" A smile flickered on her lips.

"Is that what you want?" Yahzi said. Dezba rarely talked of going home any more.

"No. What I want is for Christmas to come. We had so much to eat then." Dezba swallowed. "It won't be long, will it?"

"Not long," Yahzi said. Under her breath she muttered, "Only ten months or so in the Spanish way of keeping time."

Yahzi rose, rubbed her stomach, and sighed.

"Your baby wants to see daylight," Dezba laughed. "I hope she can take the cold."

"So far, she seems content to stay inside," Yahzi said. "I can still ride." Yahzi hoped Dezba would talk more of home. The mention of home always cheered her.

Instead, the old woman said, "I'm surprised you're pregnant. It makes it hard to escape, doesn't it? I thought you didn't want another baby."

Dezba's frankness startled Yahzi, but it was getting hard to know what thoughts the old woman might express.

Yahzi looked around, "You're right, Auntie. I didn't want a baby. After Hokee went away, I was determined never to have another child.

At least, not here. Not where my child would grow up to be a slave and denied a real name."

Dezba fingered the warps before her, her lips moving as she counted, then turned to Yahzi. "I guess it's easy to refuse Pablo."

"Not easy enough." Yahzi wrinkled her nose. "Once in a while in the summer he bathed," she laughed. "He made a good match for me on the sheepskin when he didn't stink."

Dezba chuckled. "So sex made you forget home?"

"Well, I had taken precautions. There's a curandera in Cebolleta who has a medicine to prevent a baby, and I thought I was too old for babies."

"I guess that woman was pretty good with her magic. I've heard Don Diego claim the curanderas know so much. I've also heard him curse them for failing. I guess they're not as good as Jemez medicine people." Dezba counted her warps again. "Didn't she know how to get rid of the baby?"

"Yes, but she wasn't at Cebolleta when I needed her. I waited too long for her to return. Now look at me." Yahzi glanced at her swollen stomach in disgust. "A while longer and I won't be able to ride," she sobbed. "No one's coming to this out-of-the-way ranch anyway."

The crying left Yahzi exhausted, sparing the pain of telling about losing Hokee. She concentrated instead on imagining an escape to her homeland.

Dezba must have sensed the change. "We'll leave soon, my niece. Riders could come any day, now." Dezba looked into the horizon as if she heard the hoof beats. Yahzi looked, too. Dezba often knew things about the future. Or is it only my wishful thinking? Yahzi asked herself.

FOUR

A week or more passed with no sign of outsiders. Yahzi wondered if Dezba's gift to see into the future was failing along with her memory. She made her way to Diego's house to get his laundry, wondering how to cope without soap. She hoped he had left his clothes by the door again so she could avoid him.

However, Diego was standing outside scanning the southern horizon. Yahzi hesitated, dreading the confrontation. When her foot caught a pebble, Diego turned to stare at her. She wondered what the smirk on his face meant.

Before he could speak, the sound of horses coming from the south caught their attention. Two young vaqueros rode over the horizon at a trot. The lead rider waved his sombrero in salute. Even from a distance, Yahzi could tell that the two came from families of wealth. Silver buttons lining their leather trousers glistened in the sunlight. Saddle studs sparkled in the sunlight. Their fringed rifle cases looked as if Comanches had made them for the trade in luxury goods.

The first rider's black Arabian surely had won more than one race against other Spanish steeds, but Yahzi imagined it racing a Dinee pinto, outmatched in the rugged terrain of Dinehtah. The second horse, a roan, lacked the sleek beauty of the first but matched its pace.

When the riders dismounted at the house, a vision flashed through Yahzi's mind. Either horse would make a fine means for her escape. She saw herself being entrusted with their care, winning the animals' confidence with soft words and a handful of corn. Tonight she'd sneak back to the corral. The moon was full, but would rise late. She'd be on her way to Dinehtah with the help of a full moon. Surely, the first Dinee she met could point her toward Canyon de Chelly.

And, no one could pursue her on Diego's horses. The stallion was so close to being blind it balked at every shrub. The gelding was so lame it couldn't make up its mind which leg to limp on, and the mare was as pregnant as Yahze. The burro didn't count. It was as tough as Yahzi, but its short legs hardly outpaced hers.

21

After flamboyant greetings among the three men, Yahzi stepped closer to eavesdrop. Diego was insisting the two stay weeks with him, calling to the Mexican Indian cook to substitute Sunday's beef for the mutton planned for the evening meal. As the three men walked toward the corral, Yahzi sauntered behind.

"Can you believe your cousin is getting married?" the second rider said to Diego. "I never thought he'd give up his freedom."

"Is she rich?" Diego said to his cousin. "Surely, no beautiful woman would marry a man as ugly as you."

The second man answered. "So rich her beautiful blue dinnerware was brought all the way from China."

"Well, my cousin," Diego laughed. "I can always use a loan."

"I may need a loan for my bachelor's party," his cousin joked. "You're invited, of course. You'll be able to eat enough for a month. Drink enough for a year."

Diego helped the two men unsaddle their horses. Pablo ran from the stable to take the saddles, put them on racks inside the ramshackle structure Diego called a stable, and returned to take the reins from the vaqueros. He led the horses to a hitching post and rubbed them down. When the men turned toward the ranch house, Yahzi hung back, expecting Diego to send her away. But he was so engrossed with his two visitors that he failed to notice her. She sidled closer.

"Orofre has been courting this rich widow for a year. Your cousin claims he couldn't make up his mind, but everyone in Belen says the widow put him off, hoping for a better catch."

"Who's a better catch in Belen?" Diego said. "Orofre's father runs as many cattle as anyone, no? And I've seen the blue table settings his mother uses."

"His mother's dishes are from Puebla," Orofre's friend answered. "His father lost many cattle to the cursed Navajo this past year. On top of that, the Mexicans threaten to fine him, accusing him of loyalty to Spain."

"I don't understand?" Diego muttered. "Since when is loyalty to the Crown…?"

The two men laughed. "You haven't heard that Mexico won its independence, have you?" His cousin wrinkled his nose. "Those priests and intellectuals don't know the first thing about governing. They think they can control the peasants with religion and philosophy rather than an iron fist." He ground his right fist into his left palm. "They'll learn fast enough how Indians pay back kindness and generosity."

"It doesn't matter who rules Mexico," Orofre's friend said. "Belen and Santa Fe are so far away, the new government won't care what happens here. Any more than the old one did."

"We're not even sure the Crown has lost," Orofre said.

"One way or the other, we'll get even less help from Mexico." Diego shook his head in disgust.

"What help do we get now?" Orofre scoffed. "We've always sent them more than they send us. All of Sonora and Chihuahua wants our cheap blankets. The mines can always use slaves. Not to mention the hacienderos need for servants." Yahzi blanched. She'd never realized the Mexicans had enslaved so many of her people.

"You haven't come for slaves, have you?" Diego asked. "Just two of you can't risk a raid into Dinehtah."

"We won't go far," the friend said. "We're not looking for much. Only a woman to serve Orofre's new family—a wedding present to his bride. A young woman so your cousin can enjoy the present, too." He laughed harder at his insinuation than either Orofre or Diego. "If she already has a child, so much the better," the friend continued. "There's a good price for kids in Belen. In Sonora they bring more than a hundred pesos."

"Enough," Diego said, noticing Yahzi. "Let's go inside. You must be thirsty." He nodded to the horse trough. "You can wash up there."

"Bring a towel from the house, Maria." He scowled at Yahzi. "Quickly. You'll find soap with the laundry. It's the last, I swear! Save a little for the laundry, leave the rest for the guests."

Yahzi hastened to the ranch house, found a small chunk of soap with Diego's laundry, and waited until the three men entered the house. Orofre pinched her buttocks when she passed close to him. Outside, she dropped the dirty clothes, slowly gathered them, busied herself rearranging everything while she continued to listen.

"A young one like that would make a fine maid for my household." Orofre said. "Where'd you get her?"

"She's from Canyon de Chelly, a far way off. A Nuevo Mexicano volunteer with a large party of soldiers took slaves. I'd been lucky at Monte when we played. He paid me off with her."

"What kind of profit did the expedition make?" Orofre asked.

"Not much," Diego said. "But the soldiers taught the Navajo a lesson when we killed a whole cave full. Of course, the savages sought revenge." He shrugged. "I only profited from the raid when I won Maria."

"So that's how you got that one?" Orofre said. Yahzi understood he meant her. "How long did it take to break her?"

"That's a long story." Diego hesitated over his words.

The memory of how the Spanish slaughtered her people at the cave brought tears to Yahzi's eyes.

Yahzi fumbled her way to the kettle used for the laundry, found it reasonably clean, and gathered fire wood. She had forgotten an ember, went to Diego's kitchen, and asked the Mexican Indian for fire. He found a smoldering stick in his stove and handed it to her without a word. Yahzi wondered if they had exchanged a hundred words in the twenty some years she had known him. Now he was stooped and lame, his hearing likely gone. At least, Diego had not forced Dezba to marry him, a fear both held after Yahzi's marriage to Pablo.

Once the fire was going, Yahzi forced herself to stop thinking of how the Spanish had slaughtered her people. She set off to ask Dezba to join her. At her aunt's hovel, she cleared her throat. Getting no response, Yahzi called a greeting in the Spanish style.

"Who is it?" Dezba answered.

Yahzi wondered what Dezba could be thinking. She stooped to enter, pushed at the ragged cloth meant to keep out the cold. It was a moment before Dezba flashed her smile of recognition. The old woman sat before her loom, counting threads on one side of the warp, then counting threads on the other side. In the dim light Yahzi couldn't be sure, but Dezba's spindle appeared to be empty of yarn.

"I came to see how you are," Yahzi said.

"I'm fine." Dezba said. "Except someone keeps taking my yarn. It's so hard to weave without thread. And I've imagined a delightful design."

"What is it?" Yahzi knelt beside her aunt and looked around for more yarn.

"I'm going to put our four sacred mountains in the four corners of the blanket. You won't tell Don Diego, will you? He might think that's heathen."

"He'll never know." Yahzi patted the old woman's back. "They'll make a beautiful design. I can imagine Tsoodzil in this corner." Yahzi spotted a full spindle of brown yarn along the wall and reached for it. "Here's more thread so you can finish."

"Oh, good. A nice day to weave, don't you think? I can kneel here by my loom and watch the blanket grow. Don Diego has been angry at how little I weave." Dezba put the spindle down and counted again.

Yahzi left with a forced smile, wondering if Dezba would be better off in Dinehtah.

The water was warm when she picked up Diego's shirt to scrub the collar while the pants soaked. She wasted little time on his underthings, indeed paid little attention to what she washed as she listened to the newly arrived horses bray greetings to the others in the corral. She slipped away to them, found some corn, and rubbed their necks while they ate from her hand, confident they'd remember her in the evening. She returned to the wash, scrubbing away while picturing herself racing past Tsoodzil atop the black Arabian.

That night Yahzi plotted details of her escape. She recalled where Pablo put the vaqueros' saddles, knew the hooks where the bridles were hung, even recalled the location of one of Diego's less worn halters. She'd take both visitors' horses so there'd be no chance of pursuit. With two horses she could outrun anything from the run down ranches surrounding Cebolleta. In no time she'd be home with two horses for her brother's herd. She'd return with him to rescue Dezba.

Pablo's snores told her it was time. She rose half way, had to stop to rub her back, then straightened, her hands pressing on her waist.

25

For a moment she feared she couldn't ride. She shivered at the thought of not being able to mount until she recalled the beauty of the canyon and the spirit of her brother. And, if he'd moved from the canyon to live with his wife, Yahzi's little sisters would make room for her. The thought of home made her aches vanish.

She crept from the house toward the corral, stealing into the stable where she shouldered Diego's halter. She reached into the corn bin, took an ear and entered the corral. The Arabian eyed her, gave a gentle snort, and backed away a step. The second horse shook its head, staring at her hand. She held it out, the horse approached, and she haltered it while it munched the ear. She tied the halter rope to the fence, went back inside, selected the bridle with the most silver, and picked up more corn.

The Arabian was greedy for its treat and almost bit Yahzi's hand. It reared its head only once as Yahzi slipped on the bridle, patted its cheek, and whispered her hopes to it in both Dinee and Spanish. The horse nodded as if agreeing to help her escape as she led it into the corral. She went back inside, found the rawhide piece that went under the saddle, managed to lug it and the saddle to the corral. The Arabian hardly moved as she put on the rawhide, seduced by the way she rubbed its neck and chest. She led the two horses toward the gate, holding the Arabian close, whispering in its ear that they'd walk a while before she mounted.

At the gate a sudden movement caught her eye. She cursed herself for not being more alert.

"What are you doing, woman?" Pablo whispered.

Yahzi froze, fumbled for a lie that might be convincing. "Don Diego wanted me to saddle them so his friends could get away in the dark."

"You're lying, Yahzi. He would have come to me. You were going to run away, weren't you?"

Yahzi considered another kick to Pablo's groin, but it was she who hesitated this time. Pablo took a step closer and slapped her so hard she fell to the ground. The Arabian pulled free, turned and kicked Pablo. Its hoof caught him in the knee. He screamed in agony. Yahzi jumped up and caught the halter of the roan, but the Arabian pounded

26

its way around the corral, as if fleeing from a mountain lion. While Pablo limped to the gate, Yahzi pulled herself onto the back of the roan and chased the Arabian. She'd slowed both horses to a walk when Diego shouted a curse. Under her breath, she cursed Pablo for waking Diego.

Yahzi was reaching for the reins of the Arabian, so intent on fleeing that she failed to sense Orofre coming up behind her. He grabbed the reins, seized her hand, and jerked her around to face him, then pulled her to the ground. He raised his leg to kick her when Diego yelled for him to stop. Diego ran to Yahzi, yanked her upright, cursing her with words she'd never heard before.

"So this is how you repay my kindness?" he hissed into her ear. "I must repay you with Spanish justice."

FIVE

Yahzi's attempt to escape made Diego angrier than she had ever seen him. He gripped her arm and yanked her to the house. Orofre called to him that he and his friend would remain in the corral to calm their horses. Pablo slunk away.

As Diego shoved Yahzi through the ranch house door, he pointed to the far end, where he kept the bedding. She wondered if he'd attempt to rape her, swore under her breath she'd rip his face apart, then jerked her arm free. She glared at him. He spoke with a rasp. "Do you know how Señor Zaldivar punished the Acoma for rebelling against Spanish kindness?"

"No," Yahzi lied, recalling the horror she felt when Diego first told her. When she was young and naive. Now she needed time to scheme so Diego wouldn't tie her to the corral fence as he had done once before when she had fled, pregnant with their son.

"The Governor sent the Word of God to the Acoma through a priest who brought cattle and sheep. And what did the cursed Acoma do? They killed a dozen Spaniards the first chance they got." He seized her chin, forced her to look into his eyes. "When Zaldivar reconquered them, he had all the surviving men brought before him." Diego forced her face close to his, enunciating every word. "He cut a foot off every male over the age of twenty-five."

Yahzi stared into his eyes without blinking, hating him and all Spaniards, refusing to utter a word.

"You're over twenty-five, Maria. Shall I cut off your foot?"

"It's how you treat slaves, isn't it?" Yahzi never faltered in her answer.

Diego's face grew livid. "Oh Yahzi, what can I do with you?"

"Whatever you want. I'm your slave." She moved closer to him. He relaxed his grip on her chin.

"You're not a slave, Maria. You've been baptized. You're one of us."

Yahzi sensed Diego felt guilt. She searched for a way to play upon the feeling, anything to avoid confinement. "You told me I was

Spanish when you brought me to your bed. That I was civilized. I believed you. I even believed you loved me."

"Oh, remember those days, Yahzi. The discoveries we made in bed. We were the best of lovers."

"It was good, Diegito. Maybe we could recapture those days." She moved close enough to work one thigh between his legs.

Diego's face flushed. He put both hands on Yahzi's shoulders. "What about right now? I'll be careful. We mustn't hurt the baby." He reached behind Yahzi to pull her blouse over her head.

She took his hands in hers. "Not now, Diegito. You know what happened last time."

"What do you mean, Yahzi?" Diego dropped her blouse to stroke her arms.

"We made love after I felt the baby kicking."

"I remember. Afterwards, you let me rub my hands over your stomach to feel our baby kick." He continued to rub her arms.

"My people know that making love that late harms the baby," Yahzi lied. "The Dinee never do it."

"I've never heard that." Diego dropped his hands to his sides.

"That's what you told me then. That nothing could hurt the baby. Even though I warned you it was dangerous." Yahzi's mind raced as to how best to exploit Diego's guilt.

"I don't remember," Diego stammered.

"It's why Hokee had a club foot. You twisted our baby's foot when you claimed to be so careful."

"I don't remember." Diego looked puzzled. "I didn't know."

Yahzi pressed her advantage. "Even your curanderas know the risk. At least the one I talked to about it." She tried to remember the name of the curandera who had died in case Diego asked.

"I'm sorry." Diego stared at the floor. "Can you forgive me?"

Yahzi patted him on the cheek. "We must wait, Diegito. It won't be long. One or two months."

If I have to stay longer than that, she thought, I'll kill myself—or him.

Diego slouched and turned away.

Yahzi slipped out the back door in the kitchen, leaving Diego to invent his punishment for her when Orofre questioned him. She doubted it would take much cunning to deceive Orofre and his friend because they were unaccustomed to frontier ways.

Pablo was waiting for her at their home, wrapped in a blanket and tending a fire. His breath mixed with the smoke. She paused a moment, reluctant to share even the warmth of a fire with a Spanish lackey. If he hadn't interfered, she'd be well away from the ranch by now.

But Yahzi had learned not to dwell on what might have been. She'd get her revenge on Pablo as she had the Spanish. She ground a fist into her eyes to provoke tears, then half stumbled, half limped, toward the fire.

Pablo's lips quivered as he looked at her. "What did Diego do to you?"

"What do you think he'd do?"

"You're crying. Did he whip you?" Pablo's voice trembled.

"I've been whipped before. Did I cry then?" Yahzi stared into Pablo's eyes.

His jaw dropped. "Then what did he do?"

Yahzi held a hand to her groin, sucked in a breath as if in pain. "You don't want to know."

"Oh no, Yahzi. Curse him." Pablo stepped toward her, but she backed away from him. "But if you fled on a stolen horse, they'd have killed you when they caught you."

"How would they have caught me when I had both horses?" Yahzi's tone was bitter.

"But you're pregnant. Too pregnant to ride far."

"What horse does Diego have that could have caught me?"

Pablo stood with open mouth. "I hadn't thought of..." He stammered, "He would have used a neighbor's. It's too dangerous. You're my wife. I had to protect you."

"Some protector. Where were you when he dragged me to his bed? Away from his cousin's eyes."

"Oh, Yahzi, do you think he harmed our baby?"

"We can't know until the baby's born, can we?"

Pablo struggled for a way to show his sympathy but was unable to find words.

Yahzi said nothing. She slipped into their hut, sat in a corner rather than sharing their bed.

She dozed, half awake, but couldn't recall dreaming. Pablo sprawled on their pad of a bed, wrapped in the blanket. For a moment, Yahzi was tempted to join him, but disdain led her outside. At least Pablo had gathered some wood. She worked the embers into a fire and warmed herself. The sun rose in a cloudless sky, a windless day. Surely, it couldn't stay so cold for long.

Finally, the sun provided as much warmth as the fire. She thought about what to cook for breakfast. Pablo's snores kindled her contempt for him, and she set off to eat with Dezba. Pablo could think about his manhood while he prepared his breakfast. Or better yet, he could go hungry.

As she passed the ranch, a strange smell set off a rumble in her stomach. A mouth teasing but pungent smell, familiar but without a name that she could recall. A few more steps, and the heavy fragrance awoke her memory. Bacon. Some part of a pig if she remembered correctly. Orofre and his friend must have brought it. She guessed it to be a Spanish treat, but the odor was overpowering, repugnant, or was it? Her mouth filled with saliva.

No sounds came from the ranch house. She guessed the Mexican cook was the only one awake, but surely the three Spaniards would be eating soon. And talking. She wondered what Diego had told them about her punishment.

When she reached Dezba's, her mouth watered again, this time to the smell of beef. At least a hint of beef. She found her aunt heating a battered metal pot over her cook fire. Yahzi coughed to announce her arrival.

"Oh, niece. How good you've come. We can share a meal." Dezba stirred the pot as a few bubbles appeared along the edges.

"It smells like beef." Yahzi said.

"It is. Beef and beans." Dezba's smile spread across her face. "Diego and his friends didn't eat everything the Mexican Indian

31

prepared for their dinner. So the cook brought me this potful." Dezba pointed to the food with her lips.

Yahzi had two small chunks of meat, the first beef she'd had in moons. Dezba had only one tortilla to give her. Yahzi rationed it with care to sop up every trace of beef along with the dozen or so beans. Her stomach begged for more.

"It was wonderful, my aunt. But you must still be hungry after all you gave me."

"A little." Dezba used her finger to scoop up the last bit of juice from the pot. "Why don't I see if the cook has anything more?"

"I'll go," Yahzi said, picking up the pot to return it.

When she entered the kitchen, the cook gave her his cockeyed smile. Whatever he mumbled, Yahzi couldn't understand. Just then, Yahzi heard Diego and his two guests. She wrinkled her nose at their raucous laughs, never having learned to appreciate Spanish humor. Then their tone turned serious.

"You want to leave this morning? I deserve a longer visit," she heard Diego say.

"We've caused you enough trouble," Orofre said. "That servant trying to escape. She'd never have done that if it weren't for our horses being here."

"Nonsense," Diego protested. "She couldn't have gotten far. It's nearly twenty years that she's been here so she can't remember how to reach her home."

"But she set a bad example," Orofre's companion said. "How did you punish her?"

"You've got to know their customs," Diego said. "They value their hair more than their skin. She'd rather I whip her than cut her hair."

"It was a beautiful head of hair," Orofre exclaimed. "What a pity. I must see her bald." All three laughed although Yahzi sensed Diego's laugh was forced.

"I didn't want her bald," Diego said. "I only cut out a chunk of hair. That hurt her more than a beating."

A chair scraped the floor, and Diego called to the cook.

32

"Coming, señor," the cook answered. He forked slices of bacon from a frying pan full of grease onto a platter and rushed it to Diego. He came back, took tortillas and a pot of beans from the back of the stove and hustled into the large room.

When the cook returned, he fumbled in the back of a cabinet, found a cracked platter, and handed it to Yahzi. He spread two pieces of stale bread on it and turned to the frying pan.

Yahzi missed some of the conversation in the other room until she heard Dezba's name. She moved closer to the wall. Diego claimed the old woman knew the country they intended to explore, and he'd call her when they finished eating. Yahzi jumped when the cook touched her arm to get her attention. He motioned her to extend the platter with the bread, then poured the bacon grease over it. He smiled and pointed to Dezba's hovel. Yahzi hustled out the door and hastened to her aunt's.

The two women burned their tongues on the grease as they bolted the bread while Yahzi gasped out her plan to Dezba, insisting she say as little as possible. As they walked to the house, Yahzi convinced herself that Dezba could follow her lead.

Inside the kitchen, Yahzi took the cloth that the cook used to dry things and covered her head with it. The man looked at her mystified but said nothing. In minutes, the men's conversation indicated they had finished their meal.

"I'll have my cook get the old woman," Diego said.

When Diego came to the kitchen door, he was startled to see Yahzi and Dezba. His mouth dropped open at the sight of Yahzi's covered head, but his half smile told her that he approved of the make-shift shawl.

"We will help your friends if you'll have the cook prepare a dinner for us like your friends had last night," Yahzi said.

"All right," Diego said. "But you know you can eat like that every night when you come to the house, Maria." Diego did nothing to hide his leer. "How well does Dezba know the country? She's been away for years."

33

"It's been a long time, of course. But the best grazing places don't change much. She remembers where Navajo families graze their sheep. Fields that aren't too big so only a few people will be there."

Diego motioned for the two of them to follow him into the other room. They stood before the two seated men, their heads bowed. In subdued voices Yahzi told Orofre what he wanted to know. Orofre stared at Yahzi's head but then concentrated on her directions as she conferred with Dezba. Yahzi made up details of the countryside, relying on Dezba to describe its grazing potential.

On their return to Dezba's hovel, her aunt voiced concern. "I guess you didn't always understand what I said. Two of those places I told you about are only fit for goats. But you said sheep grazed there." The furrows on Dezba's brow deepened.

"Auntie, don't worry. You did everything right." And I hope I did, Yahzi thought. Orofre should run out of supplies before he finds anyone where I sent him.

SIX

The next day when Yahzi went to see Dezba, her aunt arched an eyebrow. "Do you think I fooled those two friends of Diego?"

"Auntie, I'm sure you did." Yahzi put an arm on Dezba's shoulder. "They'll not find anyone. They had only two or three days food supply when they left. Unless they steal a sheep, they'll be back soon. Without captives!" Yahzi didn't have the confidence of her words. She worried that her advice to Orofre and his friend might mean the capture of innocent Dinee. She couldn't help recalling how being in the wrong place at the wrong time led to her and her aunt's slavery.

Dezba laughed, followed by a fit of coughing. Yahzi pulled the woman close to her, wondered how much of a burden to her escape Dezba might be. "You need a warmer poncho."

"I'm alright," Dezba looked up. "There are no clouds."

"It's warmer but will get cold. This is a good day to plaster your home."

Dezba found four empty pots at the back of her hovel, and the two women made their way to an arroyo where they filled the containers with clay. By the time they got back, the sun yielded its congenial warmth. After putting down their loads, they basked in it a moment.

"I'll get water," Yahzi said. "You sit and decide where we start."

When Yahzi returned from the horse trough with two pots of water, Dezba was sitting with her back against the south wall of her home, dozing. Yahzi was reluctant to wake her. What if they were to escape on Orofre's horses? The plastering would be a waste of time. But if they didn't leave, Dezba needed the protection.

Yahzi nearly yelled. "Where would you like to start, Auntie?"

Dezba shook her head. "Have you got the water?"

"Yes. We can mix the plaster. We have enough for one or two walls."

"The wind gets to me from the north and the west."

"Let's start at the bottom of the north wall." Yahzi filled a long crack in the old plaster, shoveled clay between two large stones.

35

Dezba took a handful of the mixture and daubed at the other end. "I never realized how many cracks need filling."

More like gaps than cracks, Yahzi thought. Half way up, she saw they'd used half the plaster. "Let's do the bottom of the west wall."

Dezba looked perplexed. "Shouldn't we finish this wall." She cocked her head at Yahzi. "Don Diego won't like it. He's always telling me I never finish what I start."

"Diego doesn't have to sleep here. You do." When Dezba bit at her lips, Yahzi softened her tone. "We'll finish the tops tomorrow. You can be proud of your work."

After they used all the clay, the two women sat against the south wall soaking up sunshine. Yahzi breathed deeply. She'd rest a while before finding Pablo to look for a sick sheep.

"Do you think those two gentlemen will return today?" Dezba asked.

Yahzi frowned, didn't understand what two men Dezba meant.

"When we got that delicious grease—on that bread? Wasn't that because those two gentlemen are visiting?"

"Yes, Auntie." Yahzi thought of how close she had come to escaping, shrugged off the memory. "I expect them back today or tomorrow." Yahzi imagined herself on the black stallion, well into Dinehtah—if it had not been for Pablo. She forced herself to forget, thought instead of how they had misled the two newcomers. "I hope they found nothing."

Yahzi sat against the wall and patted the ground for Dezba to sit beside her. In moments the old woman was nodding. Yahzi half dozed. She imagined herself riding into Canyon de Chelly, bright sun bouncing off the red and orange canyon sides. Her brother had married a woman not far up the canyon. She saw a toddler in front of her sister-in-law's hogan. She looked for other nephews or nieces of hers.

In her dream, her sisters lived near their mother's place. She visited them after seeing Nantai. He owned a large herd of horses. With the Ute stealing sheep, and the Comanche savages looking for a fight, not to mention Nuevos Mexicanos on slave raids, Nantai would be a famous warrior.

36

Yahzi remembered how he loved to mold clay sheep and horses. Once, he'd made a corn husk doll for her with a face of clay so realistic that she named it. She half awoke to one of Dezba's snores, tried to return to her half dream, half reverie state.

Diego's shout awoke her. "Cousin, you've been successful."

Yahzi rose to one knee. She drew a deep breath to stand upright, hands pushing against the back of her waist. She recognized the horses before she could identify Orofre and his friend. A third person, a woman, rode behind him. As the riders drew near, she saw a girl seated behind Orofre's friend. Her heart sank.

When the two horses reached the ranch house, the men reined in their mounts. Diego laughed. "You've been lucky. A mother and child?"

"Indeed," Orofre said. "We thought your old woman had misled us. At first, we found nothing but poor grazing land, not a Navajo in sight. Not until we found this one spying on us from a ridge. I guess she'd chased a lost sheep."

"Young, strong, and a beauty she is," Diego said, pulling the woman from the horse since her hands were tied behind her.

She kicked him in the shin, hissed something in Navajo, and started to run. Orofre chased her on his horse, knocked her down, dismounted and grabbed an arm. "So you'd leave your child behind. What kind of mother are you?"

"Does she speak Spanish?" Diego asked.

"I think not. Hasn't said much in Navajo either."

Yahzi would have waited longer behind the ranch house wall in order to hear more, but Dezba blustered forward.

"Where did they find you?" Dezba asked the woman in Dinee. "I'm sorry I sent them," she added before the woman could answer.

The woman looked puzzled and frowned her response.

"She looks part Spanish," Yahzi said to Diego as she came forward. The woman's complexion was lighter than usual, but from her demeanor Yahzi believed the captive to be a full blood Dinee. "You wouldn't enslave a mestizo, would you?" she directed her question to Orofre as much as to Diego. "She could be one of you."

"She'd speak some Spanish if that were true." Orofre fumbled his words as if Yahzi had raised the possibility in his mind.

"Ask her how much Spanish she knows." Diego seemed to guess at Yahzi's attempt to aid the captive. "Have her talk to us in it, not to you."

Yahzi told the captive in Dinee that she might save herself if she spoke Spanish to the white men. She should tell them about a white father and say he was from El Paso, a place far enough away that the white men couldn't confirm her story.

The woman's face twisted in contempt. "I was born to Mud Clan. I'd never claim to be anything but Dinee. I hate Spaniards, and I hate their language."

"It's the only way I can save you," Yahzi said.

"Will it get me back to Dinehtah?"

"I don't know. But it may keep you from being enslaved."

"If I can't return home, I'd rather die." The determination in her voice left no room for doubt.

"What about your child?"

"I'll kill her!"

"Oh, no," Dezba exclaimed in Dinee. "We can care for her."

"That's enough, you two." Diego spoke like a master. "Is she going to speak Spanish or isn't she?"

"Say whatever you know in Spanish," Yahzi implored.

The captive sucked in her lips, glared her contempt at Yahzi.

That evening Yahzi sneaked up to Diego's house to eavesdrop. She heard men's rumbling voices but could not discern what they said. She was about to try another wall when a hissing sound came from behind her. The captive lay on her side, beckoning to Yahzi.

When Yahzi approached, she saw leg irons binding the woman to a tree. Diego had provided a sheepskin for her to lie on and a second one for cover. Yahzi had seen leg irons once on a Spanish prisoner but hadn't thought much about them except to realize Spaniards could be as cruel to each other as to Dinee. Her throat constricted as she leaned over the woman, thinking how hard it must be to break the iron chain.

"How will they get you loose in the morning?" Yahzi asked.

38

"They have an iron stick they put in that hole." The woman pointed to the lock. "They twist it, and it opens."

Yahzi's brow furrowed. "I don't know how to do it."

"Tell me where my daughter is?" the woman said.

"I think she must be in the house. There's one large room with a small kitchen to one side. They can watch her if she's in the large room with them." Yahzi sought to reassure the captive. "They won't hurt her. They've taken many young girls to make servants of them."

"Will they sell her away from me?" The woman's voice cracked from fear.

"The man who captured you is going to marry a rich woman. The family will keep you and your daughter together."

"If he is about to marry, why did he use me?" The woman's tone was plaintive. "He smelled so, I nearly vomited in his face."

"The Spanish are that way. They don't think we are human. You could have been a sheep for all they care." Still, Yahzi recalled Diego's frequent tenderness toward her.

"I guess he needed to practice his love making in order to marry. He didn't know anything about it." The woman wrinkled her nose. "His friend knew even less. He barely entered me when he finished."

"Did they beat you to make you lie with them?"

"No. One held me down while the other forced himself into me. They both growled and made such strange sounds that I think they didn't enjoy it. It was so different from what I've known."

"You may have to get used to the one they call Orofre. You'll be his slave. You and your daughter. At least you'll get enough to eat. Learn Spanish and your life won't be so harsh. They'll baptize you, and say you're Christian. It's a harmless ritual."

"I'll find some way to kill myself—and my daughter."

The woman covered her face with her hands and sobbed.

"I'm afraid I helped them capture you," Yahzi said. "My aunt and I sent them to a valley we thought would be deserted."

"It is," the woman said. "Someone took my son while my husband and brothers were away. I tracked the thieves to the valley where they captured me. I was so busy looking for my son, I only had seconds to hide after I saw them."

"Did you have to travel far from your home?"

"Not far," the woman sobbed again. "I've lived on the borderland a long time."

"What clan were you born for?" Yahzi asked.

"Mud," she said.

"But you said Mud was your mother's clan." Yahzi suspected for the first time that the woman might be lying to her.

The woman sighed. "You must think I was born in incest. Let me explain." Her words suggested that she had told her story before. "My father was a Nuevo Mexicano. A poor servant. When his master accused him of stealing, he fled to Dinehtah. He didn't know what to expect." Her voice trailed off.

"How did he ever become your father?"

"My mother's people took him in. He learned Dinee quickly, became one of us. Except he didn't have a clan. So we adopted him. So now I have to say I'm Mud, born for Mud."

Yahzi grinned. "It's odd. I told the Spaniards you looked part white, but I thought that I was lying." She turned serious. "Your father must have taught you some Spanish."

"No. He loved the Dinee so much he'd only speak our language."

"Did he help name you?" It was Yahzi's way of asking the women's name.

"My mother and father named me Nascha before my kinaalda. They never told me why they chose to name me for an owl." Nascha's look was pensive. Yahzi guessed the woman wondered if she'd ever see her parents again.

"I was taken captive just after my kinaalda," Yahzi said. "Today, I don't know anything about my family. My parents might be dead, but my brother must live. I hope to see him again." She breathed deep. "I will see him again!"

Nascha raised an eyebrow at Yahzi's decisive tone. "How will you do that?"

"This man," she gestured at the house, "can't keep me. I'll escape to Canyon de Chelly." She paused for a moment. "Have you heard anything about a Dinee warrior from the Canyon?"

"I've heard talk about a warrior named Ganado Mucho. I think he's from there."

"Does he have many horses and sheep?" Her brother had never shown much interest in owning anything, but that was years ago.

"I guess he must. Why else the name?"

"You don't know where he's from?"

"He could be from Canyon de Chelly, but I'm not sure where that it. He leads many Dinee since the Spanish threaten us from the east and south. We're banding together, no longer fighting each other," She paused, "Except some Dinee in the east fight along side the Spanish."

"What else can you tell me of Ganado Mucho?"

"He came to our camp one day. Told us how to contact him when the Spanish raided us. I'd guess he's about your age. He had a fine complexion like yours." She whispered, "I thought he was more handsome than my husband."

Yahzi took a deep breath. Surely, Ganado Mucho must be her brother. "Don't you have any idea where Canyon de Chelly is from here?"

Nascha frowned. "If you're from there, why don't you know?"

Yahzi realized why the woman must be suspicious. "When the soldiers captured me, they tied my hands behind me and blindfolded me. I don't know what direction we took from the canyon. I'm not even sure how many days we traveled."

Nascha shrugged. "I've never been there. I don't know where it is."

Yahzi despaired. She had little chance to win Nascha's confidence before she'd be taken away.

SEVEN

Yahzi tossed and turned, torn between memories of her brother, and thoughts about the fate of Nascha. At least she had stayed with Nascha long enough that the men hadn't raped her that night.

Still, she felt a failure not to have freed the captive nor to have learned the location of her home. But as the sun brightened everything around her, she remembered where Diego kept a box of iron sticks. When he told her never to touch them, she realized how valuable they must be. If she had just remembered earlier, she could have sneaked into the house when the men slept and used an iron stick to free Nascha. Now it was too late. The men would be awake, the Mexican cook making breakfast. They'd leave soon, taking Nascha away to be a slave.

Yahzi rose and hastened toward the house, leaving without eating. Pablo complained as he rolled over and saw her go. He'd have to make do with scraping the bean pot. At the house Yahzi found the Mexican cook taking a clay pot to Nascha. She caught a whiff of mutton. When she reached the tree that imprisoned Nascha, the woman was sitting up. The cook handed the pot to Nascha, saw Yahzi, grinned at her and offered a tortilla. "I'll get more. Diego and his guests celebrated last night. He told me to cook a large breakfast."

Yahzi guessed the cook must have enjoyed a good part of the meal he prepared. She couldn't remember the last time he had smiled at her. She turned to Nascha. "I said you'd have plenty to eat. Even meat when you get to Orofre's home."

"Is this food poisoned?" Nascha sniffed at the pot. "Or is it how they bewitch people?"

"You are too valuable for anyone to hurt you. I've never heard any Spaniard speak of witchcraft." She shrugged her shoulders. "There is so much they don't know."

Nascha dipped a finger into the pot and scooped up beans and bits of mutton fat. She took a small bite, waited, licked her fingers. Then, she used three fingers, gulping down the food. After another

42

mouthful, she stopped. "You must be hungry, too." She offered the pot to Yahzi.

Yahzi's mouth watered. Her stomach rumbled its distress, but she said. "No, I've eaten. You finish it."

At that moment, Diego stepped from the house to look at the sky, then at the prisoner. When he saw Yahzi, he frowned. "Stay away from her, Maria. She's no relative of yours."

Yahzi took a few steps toward Diego, pretending to obey. She smiled at his poor judgement about Dinee relations but realized priests had misled him. She'd overheard Diego explain to his wife how clans were the basis of Dinee society, and the Nuevo Mexicano ranchers had been advised to take advantage of clan divisions.

"I was telling her how life can be good among the Spanish. Especially in a family rich with sheep and cattle."

Diego raised an eyebrow. Yahzi decided not to pursue her lie.

"I want you and Pablo to go to that wash north of the hills. My cousin saw a couple of sheep there when he was returning."

Yahzi nodded that she understood. But before she went in search of Pablo, she whispered to Nascha not to give up hope. Warriors were raiding even the largest Spanish towns to free Dinee prisoners.

Pablo sat with his back to the fire, picking at yesterday's beans encrusted in a clay pot. When he heard Yahzi approach, he asked with a growl where she had been.

"I had to see if Dezba was all right. Yesterday, she was feeling sick."

"You should take care of your husband before running after an old woman like that. I'm already late reporting to Don Diego."

"I saw him already. He told me we're to go up north to look for lost sheep."

"Is this another lie, woman? Yesterday, Diego said we would ride out to see if Esquipulo and Ricardo have moved the sheep to better pasture. You know what careless shepherds they are."

"Go ask him yourself, then. I'll fill a gourd and start toward the hills. You can catch up."

Pablo burped before he scurried away toward the ranch house. Yahzi packed her corn meal in a small-mouth jar and sealed it against the hungry mice, also suffering from a long winter. She filled a gourd flask from the ramada olla and slung it over her shoulder. She walked slowly so that Pablo could overtake her. For the moment, it was better to talk with him than to contemplate Nascha's fate.

A day that started cold turned warm when the sun reached its peak. Pablo swallowed half the water at noon despite Yahzi's warnings to conserve. She satisfied herself with a quarter of the flask despite the sweat she endured from traversing one gully after another, finding no trace of sheep.

The rest of the search amounted to nothing more. Pablo, for once, saw a rattlesnake before it saw him. Yahzi twice scared rabbits. The first time no stone was near at hand. The second time she was ready with a rock but missed the bounding animal by an arm's length. If only my brother were here, she thought, he'd carry a throwing stick and never miss.

She and Pablo sat for a long time, not caring if two or three sheep remained lost. Yahzi hoped some poor Dinee had found them and were feasting. She imagined the butchering and could almost taste the heart and liver. When living with Diego, she had tried to persuade him to taste the organs, but he insisted they be reserved for the sausages that Spaniards made from other parts of the sheep.

Pablo rose first. "It'll be dark when we get back. Just time enough to care for the horses. I'd eat their oats if any were left." He reached out a hand for Yahzi, but she struggled to her feet before he could help her.

"There's a little corn meal left," Yahzi said. "But not enough firewood to heat the cooking stone for tortillas. All I can do is boil mush."

Pablo's lips quivered. It looked as if he were about to complain, but he said nothing.

Yahzi reached home before Pablo because of a thorn in his moccasins, and he took a long time to massage his foot. Yahzi drank all the water in the olla and built a fire with an armload of wood she

44

picked up on her return. It was enough to boil a pot of meal. She heard Pablo swearing after he returned and lifted the olla to drink. Yahzi would have left his ill temper for the evening, but hunger drew her to the mush.

"I guess you're happy," Pablo growled. "You make me go for water, do woman's work. What kind of wife do you think you are?"

"One who's spent the day doing your work. What kind of husband are you to need a woman to find lost sheep?"

"I didn't ask for your help. Don Diego ordered you to come with me." Pablo put his hands on his hips. "And it's me that'll have to face him when I tell him we didn't find anything. I'm the one he'll slap around."

Yahzi almost felt sorry for Pablo, but when she saw the corn meal about to boil over she forgot him, lifting the pot to the side of the fire, scalding a finger in the process. She sucked on the burn, turned the pot to boil on the other side.

"Isn't it ready yet?" Pablo's stomach grumbled louder than his words.

"It has to cool." Yahzi used the bottom of her dress to move the pot from the fire.

The two didn't speak while the mush cooled. Once they could dip their fingers into it, they raced each other to fill their stomachs.

"Why can't we get along?" Pablo whined.

Yahzi shrugged. She thought her disgust with Pablo so clear that the answer was obvious.

Pablo studied the embers, added a piece of wood, and stood. "Let's go face Don Diego."

Yahzi rose, her hands kneading the back of her waist.

"Remember the last time we stood up to him together? He didn't hit me once."

Yahzi nodded as if remembering but couldn't recall any time that Pablo ever stood up to Diego even with her beside him.

When they reached the ranch house, Yahzi's mouth dropped. Nascha was still chained to the tree. She'd been sent off to keep her away from the prisoner. She suspected Diego had taken his cousin to check on the shepherds, two hapless Nuevos Mexicanos who needed as much watching over as the sheep.

She halted, grabbed Pablo's arm. She needed time to think.

"What is it?" Pablo said. "Are you afraid?"

"I need a moment." She almost confided the scheme she hatched but decided against it. Pablo could only be trusted with protecting his own interests. "I must convince Nascha to accept Baptism. You must keep Diego and his friends away from the house because he doesn't want me talking to her."

Pablo's brow furrowed. He shook his head. "I don't know what to tell him."

Yahzi took a deep breath. "Go to the stable to care for the horses. Get the mare to lie down. Then run to Diego and say she's foaling. She's about to anyway. He'll believe you."

"But what happens when he finds out she isn't?" Despite all the grime, Yahzi could see the blood drain from Pablo's face.

"He's been mistaken about the mare before. He can't blame you." Yahzi struggled to remember a time when Diego had misjudged an animal's giving birth.

"Well, I hope you convince that woman to be baptized." Pablo went to the barn, returned, and trotted to the house to knock on the door. Yahzi hid at the side of the house. She admired Pablo's out-of-breath deception, hearing him lie almost as convincingly as she did. Diego called to his guests, and the three raced to the stable, Pablo at the rear.

Yahzi stole into the house, went to the shelf where Diego kept his precious iron tools and a box of the iron sticks. She shook the box. About ten sticks of finger length rattled, some longer than others. She took a long one and a short one.

A hoarse voice whispered from a corner. A Dinee girl with her hands tied behind her back asked Yahzi where her mother was. Yahzi smiled at Nascha's daughter. She would be as beautiful as her mother. Her slim figure promised to fill out. Yahzi went to the girl and struggled with a knot. While she untied the ragged rope, the frightened girl asked if the men were going to eat her. Yahze assured her they wouldn't.

"Are they witches?" the girl asked in a frightened whisper.

"No. They won't hurt you. I hope you'll go home with your mother." Yahzi sucked in her lips. "If I can free her."

"Are we going soon?"

"I think so." Yahzi put an arm around the girl's waist and led her outside. The girl burst into a run when she saw her mother. The two embraced.

Yahzi was right behind. She bent over the leg iron and fumbled with the longer iron stick when she found the hole for it. She poked at the opening, but nothing happened. Just then she heard Diego yell a curse at Pablo, and the three Spaniards came out of the stable. Yahzi grabbed the girl, ran with her to the house and wrapped the rope around her wrists warning her to pretend she was still tied up. Then, she fled out the back door.

EIGHT

Yahzi glanced over her shoulder as she crept toward Nascha. She could free her while waiting for the Spaniards to sleep after their game of Monte. The way they shouted when they threw down their cards made it unlikely they could hear Yahzi from inside the house. When she got close to Nascha, the woman asked about her daughter. Yahzi explained she was untied and prepared to flee once the men slept.

"We'll get you out of these chains, first," Yahzi whispered.

Nascha stretched out her legs, holding the chains to prevent their rattling. Yahzi bent over the leg irons to examine the hole in the lock. She selected the shorter stick and poked it in the opening. Nothing happened. When she inserted the longer one, it hit something. She twisted the stick but to no avail. She pried at the hole from various directions. Sweat broke out on her forehead despite a chill in the air.

Footsteps froze her fingers. She heard Spaniards calling out curses over their cards, but one of them must have come to check on the captive. She licked dry lips. She fought for a reason to explain her presence, unsure how to deal with Orofre or his friend.

"My woman, what are you doing?" Pablo's whisper startled Yahzi.

"My husband," words Yahzi rarely spoke. "We can't let them take Nascha away. Think of that child inside the house, if not of Nascha."

"It's not my concern." At least he whispered.

It was a better answer than Yahzi expected. It meant Pablo might not warn Diego of what she was doing. She poked again with the iron stick, holding her breath while waiting for it to open.

"Why are you sticking that nail into a keyhole?" Pablo asked.

"Nascha says an iron stick will open the lock."

"You have to have what they call a key." Pablo straightened up. For once, he knew something that Yahzi didn't. Then his lips trembled. "Where did you get the nails? Diego will be furious if he finds out you have them."

"Where is this thing they call a key?" Yahzi's tone demanded an answer.

48

Pablo fingered his chin. "I don't know. The Spaniards hide their keys."

"Where would Diego hide this one?" Yahzi insisted.

Pablo shook his head. "I've never seen leg irons on the ranch. Orofre must have brought them." He nodded, smiled at his cleverness. "That's it. Orofre must have the key."

Yahzi turned to Nascha. "Did you see where the Spaniards hid the iron stick?"

"No. They used the stick only once, that night when they raped me. I don't remember much of that night." Her voice cracked.

Yahzi poked one last time at the keyhole. Her shoulders slumped. She raised her arm to throw away the iron stick, thought better of it, and handed the two nails to Pablo.

Pablo winced. "What do I do with them?"

"You put them back when Diego's gone. They go in a box next to the iron things he calls his tools."

"You'll get me whipped, woman. I'm not staying here any longer." He shuffled off, clenching the nails with both hands.

"What do we do?" Nascha asked.

Yahzi fought back tears, said nothing.

"I'll go off to be a slave in the morning. At least, I'll have my daughter." She paused a minute. "They will let my daughter stay with me, won't they?"

"I'm sure they will."

"Did they tell you that?"

"No. But when they took me as a slave, they kept my aunt with me."

"It must have been good to have a relative with you. What happened to her?"

"She's the old woman who lives over there." Yahzi nodded to Dezba's hovel. "You must have seen her yesterday."

"Once. But she stayed away from me. One of the men spoke to her a long time before they went off."

"He told her to keep away from you. She's getting old and losing her spirit."

"My great grandmother is like that. All she does is spin wool."

"It's odd," Yahzi said. "Dezba was born a Jemez so she never used a loom as a girl. But when she married a Dinee, she became one of us and learned to weave.

"Her husband brought her to his home in Canyon de Chelly. Their family lived close by mine so I knew her well. I helped her learn our language."

"That must have made her feel better."

"Her mother-in-law taught her to weave. That woman wove ponchos so tight they could hold water." She nodded her head in approval. "You know," she continued, "it's pueblo men who weave. Never the women. So Dezba joked about how she had to become a man." Yahzi smiled. "Jemez men wove beautiful sashes. One of the first things Dezba did was to weave me a white sash. No other girl in the canyon had one like it." Her voice dropped. "The sides were crooked, but she spun very fine thread. I wore that sash at my kinaalda."

"Did you marry a Dinee after that?" Nascha asked.

"No. My mother moved to a new hogan near the canyon mouth. After we built there, I went back up the canyon to visit Dezba. There was a man there I liked, but he was off hunting. It was then that it happened." Yahzi choked on "it happened" and stopped.

Nascha urged her to continue.

"I was wearing my sash. With a new buckskin dress. Not like these rough goatskins." She fingered her skirt. "We'd had a feast. I had a leg of lamb that I took to Dezba's family. Everyone was so happy." She stopped.

"And?" Nascha said.

"A few days later Dezba came back with me to my home. We ran into Dinee warriors on horseback. They were leading many women and children to escape a Spanish army. At a steep part of the canyon, they led the women and children along a secret path close to the top where there was a large cave. It was hard to get to. A few children and an old woman stumbled along the way, but a warrior grabbed them each time."

"Did you and your aunt hide with them?"

"No. Dezba didn't recognize any of those people so she took me to a cave on the other side. We couldn't see the big cave entrance, but we heard kids crying and mothers telling them to keep quiet."

"Did the men stay with them?"

"No. They came down and rode their horses all around the canyon floor to cover the tracks. All I could think about was my mother and father, my brother and sisters. The Spanish might have surprised them." Yahzi swallowed.

"Have you heard anything from them?"

"Nothing. But my heart knows that my brother lives, and I'm sure some of my sisters must be alive."

Nascha nodded in agreement, but her lips turned down.

"Finally, the Spanish approached. Probably a hundred. Many were on horses. One carried what Dezba called a lance. At the top of it was the head of a Dinee."

Yahzi trembled. Nascha's whole body shook.

"What makes the Spanish so blood thirsty?" Nascha said.

"I guess they're born that way," Yahzi said. "The head was so bloody, I couldn't recognize the face.

"They were just about past the cave where everyone hid when an old woman called them names and cursed them. She kept yelling insults in Spanish. She'd been a slave. She must have thought the Spanish could never get to her."

"You mean they did get there?"

"The Spanish dismounted, and we heard the women throwing stones at them. We could see Spaniards climbing the walls of the canyon." Yahzi bit her lip. "One of them found us when he was looking for a way to fire his gun into the cave."

"What happened?"

"Dezba kicked and hit him. I bit his ankle. We almost shoved him down the cliff, but three others came to help him. They knocked Dezba down. I thought they'd killed her so I scrambled to the canyon floor and ran as fast as I could, but one of them got on a horse and chased me. He dragged me back by my hair. My sash was all covered with blood, but one of those soldiers took it, anyway. At least, they didn't kill Dezba. She was bleeding all over but sitting up."

"Did you think they would kill you?" Nascha said.

"I thought so. Until they tied us up. Our hands tied to our feet behind our backs. They left us on the canyon floor while they found places to shoot into the cave. We saw everything that happened." Yahzi held her face with both hands. "Soldiers climbed high enough to shoot into the cave. Their shots hit the ceiling and ricocheted around. We heard children screaming, women wailing. I still hear the screams. The smoke from all that gun powder made it seem like dusk. Every time I smell gun powder, it reminds me of that day." Yahzi half gagged.

"I guess they took a lot of slaves," Nascha said.

"Not from that cave. It was so well protected that even a girl could shoot anyone trying to get in. The Spanish just kept firing until they killed everyone." Yahzi bit at her trembling lip. "After they climbed in, we heard a couple of girls scream, but no Dinee came out."

"What good did all that killing do?" Nascha asked.

"Nothing. Except they had us. They untied our feet and marched us down the canyon. They found a few more Dinee along the way. I was so scared they'd find my family."

"You mean they didn't?"

"By the time we got to the canyon mouth, there were thirty- three of us—women and children. They had to guard us so closely the soldiers couldn't look for anyone else. After that they tied our hands behind us and blindfolded us. It was a terrible ride out of there." Yahzi didn't realize she was wiping tears from both cheeks.

Nascha pulled Yahzi to her and the two lay in each other's arms, sobbing. Exhausted, the two women fell asleep on the sheepskin.

The morning star woke Yahzi. She struggled to remember where she was, tussled with the sheepskin wrapped around her and Nascha, freed herself, started to comb her hair with her fingers, then shook it loose instead. When she saw Nascha's leg irons, she tugged at them, tried to break a link in two, then bit it. The rust taste mingled with dirt and grime.

"What are you doing?" Diego screamed from behind her.

Yahzi had been so intent on the chain, she failed to hear Diego leave the house.

"Take these off her," she begged. "Let her go. What help can she be? Burdened with a child. Not knowing any Spanish."

"Not nearly as defiant as you've always been," Diego snapped. "She's worth a lot. The child, too."

"Why don't you buy her? Keep her here." Yahzi seized Diego's leg, her eyes implored his help.

"I don't have the money, Yahzi." Diego kicked his leg free. "My cousin will take good care of her. She and her daughter will be Christians in no time. The girl is her daughter, isn't she?"

Yahzi nodded. She translated what had been said for Nascha whose face was downcast.

Orofre and his friend came up with their horses saddled, Pablo trudging behind them.

"Go saddle the stallion, Pablo, and bring him here. Stop at the house and get the food the cook has prepared."

Pablo trotted off. Orofre stood over Nascha and asked Yahzi to find out how old the woman and her daughter were. Further questions reminded Yahzi of Diego bargaining over a horse.

When Orofre inquired about Nascha's health, Yahzi conferred with her, explaining the symptoms of venereal diseases. After Nascha replied, Yahzi repeated her description of the symptoms, leaving no doubt in the Spaniard's mind that Nascha was infected. Yahzi felt certain her ruse worked when the two men cursed their luck in the crudest Spanish Yahzi had ever heard.

Pablo came up with Diego's stallion and two saddle bags over his shoulder. Diego threw the bags onto the horse's back, apologized to his friends that his horse would delay them, then glared at Pablo. "Go in the house and bring the girl out." Pablo ran inside and reappeared with the daughter, struggling to tie a knot. Diego glared at him. "I'm going to my cousin's fiesta. Be sure your wife is here when I get back. You'll get fifty lashes if she's gone. Do you understand?"

Orofre mounted. His friend helped Nascha up behind him, he mounted, and Diego lifted Nascha's daughter to him. Diego swore at the stallion as he mounted. They left at a walk, his horse bumping into the water trough.

Yahzi pictured Diego in a frenzy when he returned. Fifty lashes would leave Pablo as helpless as the stallion. Pablo's health was not Yahzi's problem. She'd take the mare or walk.

NINE

The first thing Pablo did was order Yahzi to accompany him to their hut where he retrieved the nails she had stolen. He led her back to the ranch house so she could show him where the two iron sticks went. Yahzi gave up hope of talking Pablo into returning to Dinehtah with her, but various schemes went through her head.

"You're not getting out of my sight, woman," Pablo growled. "Not until Don Diego returns." He shoved her ahead of him toward the kitchen. The cook stared at them. "Diego said you'd give us some chili since he'll be gone on our ration day."

The cook glared at Pablo but filled a small clay container with red powder. He handed it to Pablo with a half smirk.

"Do you have any onions left?" Pablo said. "It's been months since we've tasted onion."

The cook shook his head.

"Could we have our corn and beans for the week?" Pablo used the same whine that he employed when entreating Diego.

The cook shook his head even harder. "It's not the day."

Pablo led Yahzi to the stables and handed her a pitchfork. "We can take turns cleaning out this shit. I know how much you like the smell."

Yahzi sneered her contempt while her body struggled with loading the manure on a sled. The day warmed and the odor became hard to endure. She had helped Pablo before, tugging the refuse to a pile that the cook used for compost. The chilies, onions and garlic that he grew rarely lasted past Christmas. Diego and the cook ate the other vegetables that struggled through the dry summer. Only the chili peppers seemed at home in the rugged lands of northern Nuevo Mexico, yet they, too, often had to be helped along with pots of water.

"You've done your share, my woman." Pablo reached for the pitchfork.

Yahzi lifted a heavy load on to the pile she had already pitched. "Diablo," she cried. "This handle's full of splinters."

"Is that all you have to complain about?" Pablo said. "I get them all the time."

Yahzi pinched at the dark point in her thumb. She could see what looked like an end. The splinter had entered straight on, so embedded she had little hope of retrieving it. She sucked at it, tried to feel the end with her teeth. Nothing.

"I had a splinter that stayed in my hand more than a week," Pablo said. He propped the pitchfork against a wall to point into his palm. "I didn't think it would ever come out."

"Are you going to finish loading the sled?" Yahzi said.

Pablo picked up the pitchfork and threw two more loads onto the sled. "That's enough. We don't want any slipping off."

Yahzi grimaced at the half load, then decided it wouldn't matter if they finished cleaning the stable. By tomorrow, she'd be gone forever.

While the two scattered the manure on the garden, Pablo complained how thoughtless the cook was to refuse them their next ration of corn and beans. With Diego gone, he'd have more than usual.

Yahzi said she'd ask the cook for an extra serving and left Pablo to return the sled. She knocked at the kitchen door in the Spanish manner. When the cook opened the door, Yahzi showed him the splinter. He invited her in, searched through the knives on the counter, took the smallest, and tested its edge. He wiped the blade on the front of his shirt, and sliced a gap of skin along the splinter. Yahzi winced, sucked at her thumb, tasted blood, and felt the sliver of wood with her tongue. She pinched it out with her teeth, thanked the cook profusely in her most formal Spanish, and told him how she worried for the health of her baby. He patted her cheek and went to a sack of beans, hoisted it and poured out what her blouse would hold as she lifted it to make her own sack.

While the beans soaked that night, Pablo and Yahzi recounted the meal they had at Christmas when Diego provided a chunk of mutton for stew along with a few onions. The memory added nothing to the watered corn mush they ate.

The lack of food made Yahzi think she might convince Pablo to leave the ranch. "Come with me to Dinehtah, Pablo. The Dinee share their food. We'll have plenty to eat."

Pablo's mouth dropped open. His upper lip trembled. "This is our home, Yahzi. What's there for you or me in Dinehtah? None of your relatives may be alive. Where would we live?"

Yahzi knew from his expression that he would never leave the ranch. He was too scared even to try life in Santa Fe.

"You're right, my husband. There's no life for us there. I'd miss Dezba and you. It's a hopeless dream of mine."

Pablo burped, rubbed his stomach. "I'm glad you understand. We can enjoy life here. Raise our son to be Christian." He smiled, staring at Yahzi's stomach. "To help us in our old age."

When Pablo yawned, Yahzi shook out the sheepskin they sat on and took it inside. Pablo lifted his goatskin shirt and scratched his sides before following her. As soon as Yahzi spread out the sheepskin on the dirt floor, Pablo laid down. Within minutes his snores echoed in the room. Yahzi pictured starting her escape on the mare while leading the crippled horse.

As she readied a water gourd and her few possessions, she heard horses' hoofs. She wondered what Diego had forgotten, shook Pablo awake, and told him he'd be needed. He cursed her insistence, then asked what Diego wanted when a horse whinnied.

A sliver of moon light allowed Yahzi to see six men leading horses toward the ranch house. She rushed off without Pablo to see if they were Dinee. One had broken open the door to Diego's house and stood pointing a gun inside. The others circled the door with guns drawn. Yahzi took a deep breath and stole closer. The first one stepped inside the house. She imagined the Mexican cook fleeing out the back door.

Four more men went inside; the fifth held the reins of the horses. A man from inside called in Dinee that the house was empty. Yahzi rushed forward calling a greeting in Dinee, telling the men that the Spanish rancher was gone and they had nothing to fear.

The man holding the horses leveled his gun at Yahzi. She ignored the threat, screaming that she was of Bitter Water, born for Towering

House. The five men came out to circle Yahzi, their guns pointing at her.

She glared at each one in turn, then asked who was Bitter Water or Towering House. Silence greeted her until the tallest of the men cradled his rifle. He pointed with his chin to a man with a ripped shirt that matched a ragged scar down his left cheek.

"He's been promised to a Bitter Water, but the woman thinks he's too ugly."

The others snorted. One said, "He'll never have enough sheep to marry her. His relatives think he's too lazy."

More guffawing. Yahzi felt assured by the joking. The men had accepted her as one of them. She joined in. "Have you come to find him a wife among the Spanish?"

The men didn't laugh. "Maybe a woman to attack, the way the Spanish do." The tall man jeered.

Yahzi hesitated, unaccustomed to Dinee men on a war party. "I'm the only woman here, besides another old Dinee. The Spaniard has gone to Belen."

"What are you doing here?" the tall man asked.

"They enslaved me just after I arrived at womanhood. I've been here almost twenty winters." The tall one studied Yahzi's face. She returned his stare. She guessed he must be the oldest one, five or six years younger than she. His erect posture added to his height.

Torn shirt squinted at her. "You're close to Dinehtah. Why haven't you fled?"

"Many things happened to keep me here," Yahzi said. "I'm ready to go with you now."

Just then a seventh man appeared nudging Pablo along with a knife. Yahzi knew Pablo must be trembling, maybe his lip bleeding from biting it.

"Do we cut him open to eat his heart?" his captor said.

"He's Dinee," Yahzi said. Her mind raced. "The Spaniards cut off his tongue when he talked back to them." In Spanish she hissed at Pablo not to say a word. "I told him he need not fear you. When he's frightened, he forgets our language. He's never been quite right in the head since they cut his tongue out."

58

"Who else is here?" the tall one asked.

"My aunt, the old Dinee. A Mexican cook. He probably fled when he saw you ride up. Two shepherds are with the flock, a day or two ride away." She pursed her lips toward the south.

"No one else?" the tall one asked.

"No one," She looked at the seven. "I've told you who I am. Who are you?"

"We're all Mud Clan." The tall one's tone left no doubt he led the war party. "We've come in search of a clan sister. Spanish dogs took her three days ago. We've tracked her here."

"Oh, no," Yahzi wailed. "Nascha. Your sister's Nascha?"

The seven moved closer to Yahzi, glaring suspicion. The tall one asked, "How do you know Nascha?"

"A Spaniard called Orofre captured her. A present for his bride. He, his friend, and the rancher rode out this morning. With Nascha and her daughter. They'll be in Albuquerque or close to it, on their way to Belen."

The men muttered among themselves, acknowledging that they could not overtake the Spaniards. The man with the ripped shirt wanted to attempt an ambush between Albuquerque and Belen, but the others argued it would be impossible.

"Then we kill these slaves, track down the cook, and burn the house." The scar on torn shirt's face was livid.

More muttering. The tall one refused to kill a fellow Dinee. Others rumbled agreement. Yahzi felt a consensus grow.

She spoke up. "Not much to burn in the house. You could break up his things. They mean much to him."

"Those things aren't worth a sister," torn shirt growled.

"I'll lead you to the rancher's flock. You can kill his two shepherds. They're Spanish," she spit. "And take his flock."

The tall one stepped close to Yahzi, glanced at her protruding stomach, studied her face a second time, but only for a moment. "When we kill, it will be Spanish. His flock may be worth the effort to drive them north." Several of the men agreed. Two argued that they could raid more ranches around Cebolleta if they were not hindered by sheep.

Yahzi claimed the two shepherds had been with Diego a long time. Their deaths would be a blow to him, and without them he'd be unable to operate the ranch even if he got more sheep. The place would go deserted. Her argument proved persuasive.

The Dinee handed their reins to her and went into the ranch house. She heard furniture breaking, pans being banged around, and sounds she couldn't identify. Pablo started shaking. She explained her lie about his tongue. Three men brought bedding and other things that could be burned and dumped them outside. One man struck flint and steel to ignite the pile.

Yahzi jumped at the sound of a gun shot. She couldn't tell where it came from, but Pablo stared at the stable, and three of the Dinee looked that way. A second shot followed. Torn shirt came from there, his rifle smoking. "Two horses. We can feast on them before we ride."

How will I ever get away? Yahzi thought. One of the Dinee handed her a knife from the kitchen. She realized he meant for her to butcher. She went to the stable and started with the mare, cutting her open for the heart and liver. The unborn colt kicked at her. She cut its throat, then took its heart and liver, wondering how they would taste. She decided its haunches must be tender and sliced one away. She finished with the other horse's organs. As she hoisted the meat to her shoulder, a whinny from a far corner of the corral caught her ear. She smiled. Pablo probably hadn't bothered to feed the burro. His carelessness had spared its life.

By the time she returned, Pablo was bending over a fire made with Diego's furniture, tending a pot of boiling corn meal. Beans were boiling in a second pot. Tears ran down Pablo's cheek from an onion he cut. Yahzi couldn't recognize it from its color, but the shape was right. As she got close, the smell was far from right. She guessed it wouldn't deter Pablo.

Yahzi dumped the meat and organs at his feet and dashed to Dezba's hovel. The hut was empty. She called in all directions but got no response. Then she spotted a bean on a path leading toward Cebolleta. She followed the trail, finding a few more beans. Dezba must have fled toward town, taking what few provisions she had. She probably thought the raiders were Comanche or Ute.

When Yahzi returned to the cook fire, she found the Dinee roasting meat and passing around a pot of corn mush. A few were bedding down around the fire while jesting about the cloth they'd salvaged. Ripped shirt wore Diego's old poncho, flapping it in exaggerated gestures. One of the youngest had found a shawl of Diego's wife and wore it as a sash. The tall one had tucked Diego's hammer into his belt.

"Nataalith will have to get in close to use his new war club," one Dinee whispered behind his back.

Nataalith sought out Yahzi. His cold look matched the tone in his voice. "Where did the Spaniard keep his money?"

She shrugged. "What little he had, he must have taken with him."

"Where'd he keep his money?" Nataalith turned to Pablo.

Pablo shrugged. Nataalith eyed him sharply.

Yahzi spoke up. "Diego never trusted him because he's dim-witted." Pablo glared at Yahzi, but his open mouth contributed to a dim wit's look.

"How'd he keep the ranch going?" Nataalith asked Yahzi.

Yahzi explained how she and Pablo managed around the house, how she and Dezba provided an income with their weaving, how Diego traded sheep for other food and a few clothes.

The Dinee sniffed his disdain.

"It's a terrible life—being a slave of such people." Yahzi gestured her suffering. "Now you've freed me. My home is in Canyon de Chelly. Can you take me there?"

She didn't expect a war party to burden itself with a pregnant woman, but she refused to give up hope.

Nataalith's eyebrows leaped. "We have only one pack horse. Even if you could ride, we can't spare it."

Yahzi's heart beat fast. None of the men would allow her to ride behind them, not on a war party. She clenched her teeth. She'd do anything to leave with them. "There's another mount in the stable your man overlooked. I can ride it."

"What about the dim-wit?"

"No need to take him. Most times he forgets he's Dinee." She swallowed hard before begging Nataalith to take her.

The man scoffed.

She fought back tears at the thought of leaving Dezba, but she couldn't let her child grow up to be like Pablo.

"Let me ride with you until I can't keep up. Then point me in the direction of Canyon de Chelly."

The tall one spoke to his comrades to explain how Yahzi yearned to return home. He told them about his brother-in-law who traded at Canyon de Chelly. He could lead her home on his next trip. Yahzi's heart raced at the news.

Two of the men argued that a pregnant woman would slow them down. Yahzi countered as to how she could lead them directly to Diego's flock and the two shepherds. Her argument proved persuasive.

"We'll go after the flock in the morning—as soon as we finish the meat and beans," Nataalith said.

Yahzi's mouth went dry at the thought of what might happen when the war party saw that her mount was a burro. Her upper lip broke out in a sweat.

TEN

Yahzi woke before any of the men. The stench of burnt cloth overpowered the roast meat smell of horse flesh. She went behind the kitchen for firewood, returned, and started a fire from the embers of a smoldering rug. Smoke made her sneeze. Two of the Dinee woke, grabbing their rifles. One yelled at the pox-marked man to ask why he wasn't on guard. Nataalith sat up and berated pox-marked.

"The beans are ready." Yahzi sought to humor the men. "I'll warm up the meat that's left. Do we butcher more?"

"He'll do it." Nataalith jabbed his chin at pox-marked who hustled toward the stable.

While Yahzi busied herself with the fire, Nataalith asked, "Where are these two Spaniards and their flock of sheep?"

"There are no landmarks to guide you. I'll show you the shortest way." Yahzi didn't add that the last time she'd been there was three or four years ago.

"The pack animal carries a full load. She can't ride behind any of us with that swollen belly." Torn shirt shook his head while he spoke. Yahzi wondered if she had done anything to offend him.

"I told you I have my own mount." Yahzi didn't speak with the same conviction she had the night before.

The next moment, a braying caught everyone's ears. Pox-mark came from the corral leading the burro. "Should I butcher him by the fire?" he looked at Nataalith.

The Dinee started joking about what burros must taste like. Only one of them had eaten the flesh before.

Torn shirt turned to Yahzi, a knowing grin on his lips. "Is this the mount you're going to ride?"

"Yes." Her answer was close to a whisper. But then she spoke up. "He couldn't win any races against your horses, but he can go farther with less food than any of your mounts." Yahzi didn't know if any of what she said was true, but she had heard men tell stories about a burro's endurance.

63

"The mount's so skinny he's not worth butchering," a man with half an ear laughed.

"How do you ride 'mount' without scraping your feet on every cactus in sight?" another called out.

Yahzi knew the Dinee would tease her endlessly about her "mount."

"Finish eating what's left," Nataalith commanded. "We'll feast on mutton tonight." He turned to Yahzi. "Where's the dim wit?"

"He's likely hiding in the hills," she said. "The old woman ran off too. You don't have anything to fear from them. The rancher will kill Pablo when he returns and finds his ranch in ruins. My aunt headed to the desert. She won't last long there." She hoped her lie had no truth to it.

Nataalith shrugged. "Get your mount saddled, or whatever you do to ride him. We're going."

Yahzi led the burro back to the stable. The saddles were all too heavy, but she heaped on two hides and a ragged blanket. They'd keep her warm at night as well as make the ride bearable. She remembered a worn bridle that would serve her better than the burro's halter.

The sun had passed overhead, and Yahzi still had no idea where the two shepherds might be. An uneasiness crept into her stomach. She wondered how Nataalith would react if he believed she led them astray or into a trap. Her mind raced for excuses when Nataalith turned his horse sharply to the left. In moments, Yahzi was beside him as he pointed out sheep tracks.

Yahzi rode a little farther until she came across two sets of footprints. They were left by home-made sandals that gave feet less protection than moccasins. But Esquipulo and Ricardo were too proud of what they believed to be Spanish heritage to wear anything Indian.

"The tracks were made today," Nataalith said.

"Looks like this afternoon." Yahzi bluffed. Tracking skill might be a useful asset to Nataalith—if he didn't see through her ruse.

Nataalith raised an eyebrow. "How do..." His sentence was interrupted by the bleating of sheep.

"If just you and I rode on, the two shepherds won't suspect anything. I'll tell them you're interested in trading ponchos for a ram." Nataalith looked at Yahzi from the corner of his eye. For the first time she studied his features. His lustrous black hair framed a narrow face with rugged features. "The others can surround the flock to keep it together while we kill the shepherds."

Nataalith half grinned. "How are you going to kill anyone?"

Yahzi's nostrils flared. "Give me your new war club. While you shoot one, I'll strike down the other."

Nataalith laughed. "I'll shoot them both. Maybe you'll want to scalp them—like the Comanches do."

Yahzi insisted she had no use for anything Comanches did.

Nataalith held up his arm and signaled the other warriors to circle the flock but to keep hidden while he and Yahzi approached the two shepherds.

He handed Yahzi the hammer. "You can club them after I shoot them. Make sure they're dead." His eyes sparkled. He failed to hide his grin. Yahzi didn't think much of his humor.

She kicked the burro, and it jumped ahead of Nataalith's horse. He was laughing when he caught up.

As they passed over the brow of a hill, Yahzi saw Esquipulo sitting in the shade of a pine tree. What looked to be half of Diego's flock was grazing on dry winter grass. Ricardo was nowhere in sight.

"Where's the other man?" Nataalith's question was filled with suspicion.

"They must have split the flock because the grass is so scarce around here." Yahzi sounded as if she were familiar with the terrain.

"What if he calls to the other one." Nataalith glared at Yahzi.

"I can convince him he has nothing to fear. He won't suspect a thing." Yahzi sucked in her lip, wishing she'd been friendlier with the shepherds the few times a year they visited the ranch.

Esquipulo stood. He held his shepherd's crook with both hands as if it were a weapon. Yahzi noticed a large knife at his side, something she'd forgotten. Nataalith blew out a breath.

Yahzi halted a few paces from Esquipulo and slid off the burro. "Don Diego sent me with this trader. He's got top grade ponchos that he wants to trade for sheep. Diego knows you and Ricardo need ponchos. He says you can trade a ram or three ewes for whatever you can get. But it'll be your last ponchos for the year."

"Does the Navaho speak Spanish?" Esquipulo asked.

"No, I'll translate for you."

"Let me see your ponchos," Esquipulo said. He shifted his crook to one hand and stepped toward Nataalith's horse.

Yahzi called to the Dinee to show him the poncho he had strapped behind his saddle. Nataalith dawdled with whatever he had strapped back of him. Esquipulo walked close to the horse to see better, his back turned to Yahzi. She took the hammer from her belt, raised her arm and rushed three steps forward. Her momentum and full swing crushed Esquipulo's skull. He was dead before he hit the ground.

Yahzi was surprised at how little blood flowed from the wound, but the hammer was covered with a grayish, sticky mess with splinters of embedded bone. She wished she hadn't known Esquipulo as well as she did. She felt nauseous until Nataalith guffawed.

"You have been with the Spanish a long time," he said. "You know how to use their war clubs." This time he snorted.

Yahzi wiped the hammer with some grass and handed it to him. "Now that I've shown you how to use it, you can kill Ricardo."

"Where do we find him?" Nataalith asked.

Before Yahzi could answer, torn shirt rode up. "The other flock is in the next valley."

"How many shepherds?" Nataalith said.

"Only one."

"They found only two small grazing areas and divided the flock." Authority filled Yahzi's words.

"Or they could no longer stand the smell of each other." Nataalith held his nose while he laughed.

"Let's go get the rest of the herd," Yahzi said.

"Will you club the other Spaniard?" Nataalith offered the hammer to Yahzi.

She turned to mount her burro. "You have your rifle. We don't have to worry about a gun shot being heard."

Two of the Dinee rode up and dismounted. They stripped Esquipulo of his pants and shirts. One took off his sandals and examined them. He snickered in disgust and tossed them back on the body.

All the Dinee returned to Nataalith. He pointed to three and told them to follow with the flock. He nodded to torn shirt to lead the way to the other shepherd. The man started at a trot, and Yahzi was soon left in the dust, barely keeping ahead of the flock.

Before she reached the valley, she heard a gun shot and knew it was over. Ricardo would have started to run at the sight of the Navajos, but one of the Dinee no doubt was waiting for him. When she caught up, she glimpsed a naked body sprawled alongside the wash. The Dinee were regrouping the sheep into one herd. The bleating animals would be reluctant to leave the water and the patches of grass that the stream nourished.

Nataalith suggested that they get the flock moving. At first, jokes about the intelligence of sheep flourished but quickly died out as sheep broke away to remain in the valley. Yahzi was surprised that the Dinee showed such impatience. They must have herded stolen sheep before, but they took little interest in the present task.

Once they had all the sheep out of the valley, the herding went better. Even so, Yahzi had no trouble keeping up. A lamb broke away and headed for a patch of grass. Its mother bawled for it, then ran after it when it did not respond. The Dinee pressed on, leaving the ewe and her young. Yahzi could not. She kicked her burro and went after the two. Nataalith called for her to come back. She ignored him and kept going. When she reached the lamb, she dismounted, grabbed it, and threw it atop the burro. She struggled up behind the kicking ball of wool, the ewe sticking close to her lamb.

When Yahzi reached the herd, Nataalith joked about how clumsy a burro must be to ride. Other men joined in the joking. One claimed the lamb did a better job at getting the burro to trot than she did. Their joking reminded Yahzi of how her father had teased his sisters-in-law.

Nataalith stopped early for the night when they reached a stream bed with a trickle of water. The sheep gave him little choice. They descended on it like a coyote on a lamb. The men watered their horses along with the sheep, then found a pond upstream where they drank and filled their water gourds. Yahzi drank until she thought she would burst.

Nataalith handed her a water gourd. "I thought you'd bring one of those Spanish canteens of metal."

"In the rush, I forgot," Yahzi admitted. "I can't take yours."

"I wouldn't give you mine." Nataalith laughed. "This is a spare from the pack horse. Don't break it. It's the only one left."

Yahzi slung the gourd over her shoulder. She found her burro still drinking, tethered it, and collected firewood. Two of the Dinee were also gathering wood. One used his flint and steel, and a fire soon roared.

"Shall I kill a ewe?" Yahzi asked Nataalith.

"The men will find one without a lamb. They'll bring it here to butcher. Did you forget a knife, too?"

Yahzi bit at her lip. How could she have forgotten a knife? She stared at the ground.

Nataalith handed her the hammer. "You can use this to butcher."

Yahzi's jaw dropped. She wondered if Nataalith could be so impressed with Spanish iron.

He started laughing before drawing a large scabbard from inside his deerskin shirt. "Maybe this will do?"

Yahzi recognized Esquipulo's knife, took it from him, and felt its edge. Esquipulo had plenty of time to sharpen it. Before she could return the knife to its scabbard, pox-mark rode up with a ewe across his saddle. Without a word, he tossed the dead animal in front of Yahzi. She soon had it skinned, doing her best to impress the Dinee with her skill. Pox-mark joined her to hold joints apart while she sliced through them. Torn shirt found green limbs to make roasting sticks. Soon the smell of cooking meat filled the air. The half an ear man claimed he could eat more than anyone else.

The meat was far from done when they ate, but Yahzi's empty stomach failed to notice. She couldn't compete with the men, but she ate the most she ever had since being enslaved.

While the men spread out ponchos around the fire, Yahzi relieved her burro of the hides she'd used for a saddle. She'd sleep warmer than she had for a long time.

A couple of the men burped. Others followed as if they were competing to see who could burp the loudest. When they quieted, one of them said to Yahzi, "We know you are Bitter Water Clan from Canyon de Chelly, but we don't know much else. Tell us more."

"I've been a slave so long I hardly know who I am. But now that I'm free, I'll go to my family and discover myself."

Murmurs of assent flowed from the Dinee.

"I had a brother almost my age when I was captured. My sisters were babies. I must find my brother. I know it's not likely, but maybe one of you know him."

"He could have married a Mud woman, come to live with us." Pox mark spoke on impulse. "He has a brother-in-law from Canyon de Chelly." He pointed at Nataalith with pursed lips.

"He's too young to be her brother," Nataalith said.

"My brother must be famous. I feel it. Maybe a medicine man, but I bet a warrior chief."

"It could be Ganado Mucho," pox mark said. "He's from the Canyon. About your age."

"Tell me about him," Yahzi pleaded.

"The Spanish raids are more than we can endure," Nataalith began. "They move onto our lands from the east and south, encourage the Utes to raid us from the north. Pay the Comanches to take Dinee slaves."

Yahzi could feel Nataalith's anger.

"What's worse, they have turned Dinee against Dinee. The Dineehanaih fight alongside the Spanish. What traitors!"

"But why?" Yahzi asked.

"They live too near the Nuevos Mexicanos," torn shirt said. "The white men made them promises, but their treaties are worthless. The traitors will find out."

"What are the true Dinee doing about it?" Yahzi said.

"Many chiefs are emerging among us," Nataalith said. "We need war parties everywhere. This Ganado Mucho is cunning. He's killed Spaniards. Took their livestock. He's given away most of what he's taken, yet he has many sheep and cattle."

"Have you ever heard his childhood name? Is it Nantai?" Yahzi asked. "He could see sheep and cows in the clouds, herds of horses. He made up stories about them that made me laugh out loud."

"I heard Ganado Mucho talk once," torn shirt said. "He told how the Spanish took slaves, how they killed so many women and children in a branch of Canyon de Chelly, it's now called Canyon del Muerto."

"I was there." Yahzi exclaimed. "That's when they took me prisoner. My brother would have known about it. Ganado Mucho must be my brother!"

Torn shirt nodded his agreement. Nataalith looked away, his forehead furrowed.

ELEVEN

Half the Dinee war party were stirring when Yahzi awoke. She hustled to prod the last of the embers, thankful she had put aside firewood the night before. Two men chewed at half raw mutton while others sliced meat to fit roasting sticks. Nataalith said he could use help bringing in stray sheep while the mutton warmed. He and three others mounted. The cooperation reminded Yahzi of the order in her childhood home when everyone knew what was required of them, so unlike the ranch where Diego commanded everyone's work.

It wouldn't be long until Yahzi was home, at least to Nataalith's hogan with a brother-in-law to take her to Canyon de Chelly. Eight days had passed since they started north, more time than what the Spanish called a week. She didn't remember which day of the week it was, and relished the idea of never again thinking of days of the week. She no longer had a need to count time or save time or spend time the way the Spanish did.

Torn shirt interrupted her reverie. He claimed he smelled roasting mutton before he saw the camp. A lamb bawled in front of his saddle, its mother trotting beside him, bleating peevishly.

"We should've butchered this kid last night instead of that ewe. It's going to cause us trouble all the way."

"It's your teeth that cause the trouble. How do you bite off anything to chew with no front teeth." All the Dinee laughed at half an ear's quip.

Yahzi had wondered how torn shirt lost a front tooth ever since she noticed one was missing.

Torn shirt dismounted, lifted the lamb from his horse and tossed it to the bleating ewe.

"You keep your daughter close to you from now on," he said to the sheep. "Else she'll be roasting on the fire. It if were your son, I'd be butchering him right now."

The lamb ran to the ewe and tried to nurse. The ewe bleated and headed to the flock, the lamb at her heels.

The Dinee squatted around the fire. Even with their mouths full of meat, they continued to jest. It reminded Yahzi of the way her young uncles and her father kidded each other during the long winter nights. She choked as she realized the years she had missed of Dinee humor. A tear gathered in the corner of an eye when she recalled her grandmother telling of how Dinee walked in beauty, how they sang in beauty, how they rode in beauty. She realized that when her grandfather implored the gods, he had prayed in beauty.

Nataalith and two others finished eating at the same time. They wiped their hands on the bottoms of their buckskin tunics and rose to look around at the sheep and their horses.

"What if half of us herded the sheep home while the others raided that ranch we scouted on the way down?" torn shirt said.

"We've killed two of the white men, besides taking their sheep. Isn't that enough?" Nataalith said.

The other Dinee voiced their opinions. Yahzi saw that most of them felt justice had been done, though doubtless they wouldn't give up plans to rescue Nascha. A clan sister couldn't be kept enslaved for a few sheep and the deaths of two Nuevo Mexicano laborers.

"We should get these miserable creatures home before we think of more revenge." Torn shirt joined the consensus.

Yahzi picked up her worn blanket and ragged hides and headed for her burro. She intended to do her share of herding even if it meant being exposed to more joking about her "mount."

Toward the end of the day, Yahzi found herself bringing up the rear of the herd, sneezing dust, chewing dust. She had rounded up three strays which was as much as anyone else had done. Nataalith dropped back. His presence was all that Yahzi needed to feel part of the war party.

"Did you herd often as a slave?" he asked.

"At times. When one of the shepherds couldn't. Otherwise, I worked around the ranch."

"Where did you learn how to use a hammer?" Nataalith used the Spanish word for hammer. His grin exposed his even, white teeth.

"Is that what you call your iron war club?" Yahzi's burro halted to chomp at a clump of grass, a few green blades at its center. She let it bite off a mouthful before she jerked his head up and prodded its sides.

"Yes. We use some of their tools these days. Hammers are good whenever we have nails."

"They also make good war clubs." Yahzi's laugh was quiet.

Nataalith chuckled. "Not nearly as good as our war clubs." He rubbed his hand along the iron head of the hammer. "You saved my life when you killed that shepherd. At least you made things easier for everyone."

They rode for a while in silence, Yahzi recalling how easy it was for her people to enjoy each other's company without speaking. She put words out of her mind and basked in the thought that Nataalith's brother-in-law would guide her home.

Left hand rode up to interrupt the silence. "There's an old man on foot with three sheep. He looks to be one of us, but he's wearing Spanish pants."

"Did you speak to him?" Nataalith asked.

"No. Just watched him. He gave no sign that he saw us. He kept shading his eyes and looking around."

"Let's go see what he's doing out here. There's been no sign of anyone since we killed those two Nuevos Mexicanos."

The two men rode off at a trot. Yahzi felt compelled to stay with the sheep even if her burro had been able to keep up with the horses. It wasn't long before the other Dinee were shepherding the flock into a dry creek bed where the stranger stood with his sheep. He raised an arm and called a greeting in Dinee.

From a distance, Yahzi watched while Nataalith and two others dismounted and talked to the stranger. Two other Dinee took a machete from the pack horse and dug in the stream bed. Yahzi licked at parched lips. She guessed the sheep sensed water. They moved toward the digging men. She hoped the two would be quick to start the hole for their own drinking water.

Torn shirt used flint and steel to ignite a handful of dry grass. Others brought in a little firewood. Yahzi hastened to gather more.

She prepared a few roasting sticks when she heard squeals from a lamb. She turned just in time to see left hand slitting its throat. She licked her lips. Blood wasn't as good as water to quench thirst, but it would do until the second water hole was dug. She added wood to the fire and made her way to the lamb. The men there had their faces smeared with blood. Soon hers was just as bloody.

When Nataalith and the stranger approached the fire, Yahzi stared at the newcomer longer than was polite. He was obviously Dinee, his weathered cheeks and forehead as wrinkled as the land around them. He'd been tall, but his wiry frame was now bent forward. His teeth were all in place but as yellow as an old ewe's.

The man went to where the lamb was being butchered, perhaps to feast on her liver or heart or at least to have whatever blood could be drained from it.

"The old man is from up north." Nataalith announced in a low voice. "I met him once before. Right now he's visiting Jemez. Guess he got lost looking for sheep. He'll tell us more after we eat."

Yahzi felt at ease with the Dinee men. They gathered their share of firewood, did most of the butchering, and didn't expect her to watch their skewers of lamb. She prepared meat for the stranger while she cooked her own. He joined her at the fire, looked at her through squinting eyes, then licked his lips at the smell of roasting lamb. A milky film over his eyes failed to hide a sparkle that belied the wrinkles surrounding them.

"I hope that lamb belonged to a Spaniard," he said. "Spanish lamb always tastes better than Dinee lamb." Yahzi joined the laughter of those around her. "These Jemez sheep I have. They're ready to eat, too. Taste better than Dinee mutton but not so good as Spanish mutton." Polite laughter followed.

"What are you doing out here with Jemez sheep? Did you get lonely for a flock?" Left hand joked.

"We heard the Comanches are raiding. My nephew and I came out to bring in the flock. When I went after three strays, I got lost. I just discovered a landmark when you rode up. Good to talk Dinee again. I been stumbling along in Jemez. They got words that never end coming out the mouth."

"What relatives do you have at Jemez?" Nataalith asked.

"My first wife was from Jemez. Good woman." He stared at the roasting sticks near him, rubbed his mouth with the back of his hand.

"Why didn't you bring her so she could visit?" Yahzi asked.

"Spanish captured her. When I didn't hear anything about her for three winters, I married again. Two sisters that time."

"Better marriage." Left hand's exclamation left no doubt what he thought of women who were not Dinee.

"Well, in some ways," the newcomer said. "But those two ganged up on me all the time. I caught it from both of them when one thought I hadn't treated her the same as the other. They'd throw me out of their hogan. I didn't have no place to go."

The Dinee roared. One said it must be good to have two wives but only one mother-in-law. Another asked why Dayish didn't go back to his mother's hogan. Dayish explained that his mother lived far to the west. He joked, too, that with his poor eyesight he was forgiven when he failed to avoid his mother-in-law.

"She ought to wear a bell to warn you." a man chimed in.

"She tried that but I mistook her for a goat." The stranger kept a straight face while the Dinee howled with laughter.

Yahzi hid her laugh with her hand. The diversion gave her time to study the newcomer, certain she had encountered him somewhere.

"What about your Jemez mother-in-law? Did you avoid her?" Nataalith asked.

"Whenever I could," he answered with a chortle. "Ahh, she was alright. A good woman, like my wife. After we lived at Jemez for a year, she agreed to come with me to Dinehtah."

"Your mother-in-law agreed to go home with you?" left hand said, provoking more laughter.

"My home was a long way from Jemez," the stranger continued. "She—my wife—learned to speak real good Dinee. She didn't mind much when my unmarried brothers teased her. She kept telling them she'd find wives for them so they'd move out."

The Dinee smiled. Several took meat from their roasting sticks. Yahzi held out a stick to the visitor, its slices thin, dripping juices. She took one with thicker pieces. No one spoke much until they finished eating. Then, a young Dinee asked Dayish why he had returned to Jemez.

"The people are getting tired of war with the white men. I wanted peace as much as any one. So when one of the chiefs asked me to come along, I was happy to do it. They said they could use someone who spoke Jemez and a little Spanish." He lowered his eyes and his voice, lost in thought. "They were good men."

"Why do you say they 'were' good men?" Nataalith asked.

"The Spanish have built a fort at Jemez. It gives them a lookout for what's happening west of Santa Fe. The sons of dogs!" he used Spanish, then stopped speaking.

"We're waiting," Yahzi whispered her encouragement to him.

"There were twenty-four leading men with me. We were only going to stop at Jemez to learn what was going on in the pueblos and to tell them we wanted peace. The Spaniards invited us in. They talked of nothing but friendship. I went to visit my nephew. The white men didn't pay any attention to an old man like me." Dayish swallowed hard. "Sons of dogs!"

"Take your time," Yahzi said.

"They feasted the chiefs. A Jemez woman who served them told me about it. A white man sat in between each Dinee. Spaniards behind them. When they started eating, the Spanish seemed cheerful. The Dinee suspected nothing. The captain, or whoever led them, gave a signal. Those white men sitting behind grabbed the arms of the Dinee while the men in between stabbed them. That woman said she'd never seen so much blood."

The war party growled in anger.

"Then the Spaniards made the Jemez people throw the bodies over the wall of the pueblo to let the dogs eat them."

The men stopped growling and sat with heads bowed.

"That was about two moons ago. A moon ago another five Dinee chiefs arrived on their way to make peace. The Spanish invited them in, feasted them, and killed them the same way. They can never get enough blood."

"Was one of the leaders Ganado Mucho?" Yahzi couldn't contain her anxiety that her brother might have been among the chiefs. Torn shirt scowled at her for the interruption.

"No. I met him once. He wasn't one of them."

"He's safe, then?"

"I guess. But who knows what will happen when Dinee try to make peace again."

"We should raid their fort," torn shirt snarled. "We must show them we aren't afraid."

"There are too few of us." Nataalith looked at the other men. "We could raise a war party at home. Dinee everywhere would join us."

"I could find men at Canyon de Chelly," the stranger said.

The men didn't react, but Yahzi exclaimed, "Is that your home?"

"Yes. I took my first wife there to my mother's hogan. She said she'd never seen anything so beautiful."

"Is her name Dezba?" Yahzi shivered. "Did the Spanish take her captive when all those women and children were massacred in a cave, a branch off Canyon de Chelly?"

"Yes." the man said. "What they now call Canyon del Muerto." He stared at Yahzi his head half cocked. "How do you know her?"

"I am Yahzi. I was visiting you before the Spanish came. Your wife was coming home with me."

Dayish squinted at Yahzi, bent his head closer to her. "I remember. You came to our hogan after your kinaalda, didn't you?"

"That's right. When Dezba and I were returning to my hogan, we met Dinee hiding their women and children in that cave. We hid on the other side of the canyon. The Spaniards found us and took us as slaves. We ended up on a ranch near Cebolleta." Guilt for abandoning Dezba flooded through Yahzi. She sat speechless.

"And?" Dayish prodded.

Yahzi turned to him, her face a blank.

"What happened to my wife?" Dayish said.

"We tried to escape. I mean…She's alive! She'll be so happy to know you're alive." Tears flowed down Yahzi's cheeks. Her insides burned because she had deserted Dezba.

Dayish's face showed no emotion.

Won't he be happy to see her? Yahzi asked herself. She also wondered, after so many years, if her aunt would want to reunite with Dayish.

Yahzi's next thought was of herself. She had been on her way home. Dayish could return with her to rescue Dezba, and the three could go on to Canyon de Chelly.

TWELVE

Yahzi felt as close to Dezba as any of her own father's sisters. She owed it to her aunt to unite her with Dayish.

Yet, a return to the ranch would end her escape. And how could Dayish help Dezba escape if they returned?

And she didn't know what awaited her at Diego's ranch. What had he done when he returned to find the house ransacked, his flock killed or stolen, and his shepherds killed? No one would come to a hostile frontier to herd sheep for him. Could he entrust Pablo to herd? Yahzi would have to help Pablo—if Diego found sheep. He had nothing to trade for them nor any money. She enjoyed the thought of Diego working as a ranch hand.

Yahzi wondered for a moment about Diego's threat to thrash Pablo if he didn't find her at the ranch. The sight of Pablo tied to a fence post getting fifty lashes aroused no sympathy from her. Instead, she thought of how she'd be saddled with him as a husband if she returned. Shackled to the ranch once again, how would she ever walk in beauty?

A picture of Dezba scavenging the kitchen for food, foraging the desert, turning to Pablo for help, made her heart race. She'd have to return, to forget living in beauty.

But how could she? Her burro's ribs had shed any flesh they once had. It couldn't survive the return trip without forage and rest. Besides, Dayish was on foot. Even if they dared go to Jemez while the Spanish were massacring Dinee, no horse was to be had because the Spanish forbid Pueblo people to own horses.

She also asked herself how Dezba would receive Dayish. He hadn't made any serious attempt to rescue her when she was taken prisoner. What kind of husband was he? More important, she recalled that Dezba never spoke of Dayish without prompting. She had mourned his loss the first few years they spent with Diego, but after that she talked only of her brothers and sisters.

When Dezba realized she'd not have children of her own, she'd recall her sister's children and the ones she was sure were being born while she was in captivity. They were her sons and daughters as surely as if she had given birth to them. In her later years, Dezba pestered Yahzi to assure her that the Dinee custom was the same. No matter how often Yahzi told her that it was only the Spanish who failed to call their sister's children "sons" and "daughters," Dezba's face lit up whenever Yahzi assured her that a multitude of sons and daughters would welcome her home as one of their mothers.

Yahzi was so intent on her thoughts that she failed to notice two lambs straying from their mothers to graze on a few green stalks of grass. Nataalith rode to her side to joke about how she must be daydreaming of Canyon de Chelly. Before she could kick her burro into action, Nataalith rode to the two strays and drove them back to the flock.

"There's little for them to eat here and not time to let them find what there is," Nataalith said.

"Is it much farther to your hogan?" Yahzi asked. When she got no reply, she corrected herself. "...much farther to your wife's hogan?"

"One more night before we reach home." He looked at Yahzi's swollen belly. "You've done well to keep up. To help herd the way you did."

Yahzi acknowledged the praise with a smile.

"I've not had any children by my wife," Nataalith said.

"You haven't been married long. You're often away protecting your homeland." Yahzi's statements were questions as much as assertions. She welcomed Nataalith's talk. He had told her little of himself, and it was pleasant to converse in Dinee.

Nataalith assured her he had been married longer than it took to father children, and while he often accompanied war parties, he spent more time guarding his wife's livestock and his horses. Yahzi asked about his herd, and he described each of his ten horses. He suggested that his wife's wealth in sheep and goats exceeded his in horses.

Yahzi arched an eyebrow. "So much wealth for someone so young?"

"Not so young," Nataalith said. "About thirty winters."

"Oh," Yahzi said. "I thought less."

Just then her burro stepped in a hole and stumbled. Nataalith jerked his horse to her side to hold her in place.

"Is it much trouble?" he said.

"What?"

"Carrying the baby. You work as hard as any of us, but we're not burdened with child. How do you do it?"

Yahzi shrugged. Her laugh was rueful. "I don't have much choice, do I?"

Nataalith grinned in reply. "I like a strong woman. You know what you want. I bet you think every day will get better than the last one."

"There's no sense in looking back. I'll find beauty where I'm going."

"Eh," Nataalith uttered in a long breath. "*Hozho*. I knew it."

Hozho. Yahzi hadn't heard the word since her capture. She wasn't certain she remembered all that composed hozho. Beauty of course. What else? Harmony and balance were basic. How out of balance she'd been as a slave. Now she felt in harmony with a raiding party. If she recalled rightly, hozho included peace, but since the Spanish invaded Dinehtah how difficult to find peace, except within. And, she'd kept her health, somehow. Even with all the Spanish sickness that they called diseases, she remained well—a vital part of hozho.

"Do you truly think I've managed to value hozho?" She hoped to hear confirmation from Nataalith.

"I'm certain."

"That's kind of you. Then I can go with your brother-in-law to Canyon de Chelly."

"When he sets out on his next expedition."

"How often does he go?" Yahzi tried to hide her anxiety but knew it must show.

"He may have just left. It depends on what trade goods he has and the weather." He shrugged. "You know."

Yahzi didn't know, but nodded her head as if she did.

The next day Yahzi pictured how she'd be received in Nataalith's hogan. His wife's relatives would shower him with concern while saying little to her. At least, she'd understand everything that was said, not like poor Dezba on arrival at her husband's Dinee hogan.

The memory of Dezba sent a shiver down her back. She'd turned her back on Dezba for the chance to walk in beauty. Her aunt might be starving now, or Diego might have taken her to Santa Fe to sell. Then Yahzi realized Dezba was too old and feeble to be of any value. She bit at a finger in shame but could think of no way to have persuaded the war party to take Dezba with them. She swore to herself that once she found her brother, she'd persuade him to rescue Dezba.

"On the right!" The cry startled Yahzi. It sounded like torn shirt's voice, but Yahzi couldn't imagine what he meant by the words. Then she guessed Spaniards from Jemez had challenged the Dinee. It meant the pueblo was close, and the Spanish would accuse the Dinee of stealing the sheep they herded. She wondered how Nataalith could explain what they were doing with the flock or if Dayish would convince the white men that they came in peace.

What if the Spanish had heard of the deaths of Diego's shepherds? But how could the news have traveled so quickly? No, the Nuevos Mexicanos were the same ones who had massacred Dinee coming in peace. They'd stop at nothing. She kicked her burro's flanks and charged the sheep. They ran but not for long. They were too tired to do anything but walk.

Yahzi's fears were confirmed by a shot. Followed by two more. Yahzi halted her burro. Her impulse was to head for the firing, but reason told her she'd be in the way. She kicked her mount and yelled at the sheep before her. If she could get the herd north while the men held off the Spanish, she might help.

Left hand and a second Dinee rode by her, kicking at their horse's flanks. "Drive the sheep north," one shouted while the other pointed.

She felt reassured she'd made the right decision to head the flock north. Farther on, she saw Nataalith talking to a figure standing on the ground. He was motioning with his arm. When she heard more shots, Nataalith jabbed his finger to the north. As she got closer, she saw the man on the ground was Dayish. He was shielding his eyes with both hands, looking from Nataalith toward where the shots came from.

"Find an arroyo and hide in it," Nataalith said to Dayish.

"Perhaps I can help you with the Spanish," Dayish said. "They might listen to me."

"It's not white men. They're Comanche. They'll kill any of us they find. Hide while we hold them off."

Dayish turned and fled toward an arroyo.

"Yahzi." Nataalith's tone made it clear he was giving a command. "Forget the sheep. Go back to the ranch where we met. I'll come to free you when I can."

"I'm coming with you. I can use a rifle."

Nataalith looked almost ready to accept her offer. Then he frowned. "How did a slave learn to use a rifle?"

Yahzi couldn't think of an answer so she used the tone that Nataalith had. "Show me. I can point it as well as any man."

"It's not that easy. Besides, we'll have to ride hard to escape the savages. Your mount could never keep up."

"But I don't know the way back," She'd paid no heed to the landmarks on their way north, so delighted to escape from the south.

"Ride south a day, then east. You'll come to the Rio Puerco. Plenty of water. Feed your mount!"

Yahzi started to protest, but Nataalith cut her short.

"The river flows southwest. Follow it until it bends to the southeast. Continue southwest until you find landmarks."

Yahzi nodded in agreement.

"Remember! I'll come for you," Nataalith turned his horse and dug his heels into its sides.

She'd head for the river, confident she'd find her way to the ranch. This time she'd flee with Dezba. But she couldn't imagine what awaited her at the ranch.

THIRTEEN

Yahzi gave up guessing what awaited her at Diego's ranch, but knowing that Nataalith would come for her and Dezba made the anxiety bearable. In a moon she'd be to Canyon de Chelly. Maybe two. She hated that she was measuring time. It jumbled her thoughts. She should be thinking of what she'd need to escape with a baby.

Yahzi turned her thoughts to Dezba. She wondered how her aunt had survived after the Dinee raid, how much better off she'd be reunited with Dayish. For a moment she considered Diego seeing the ranch in ruin, his sheep and horses gone—except for the burro.

Her thoughts of impending doom were forgotten when she rode to the top of a ridge and looked southeast onto a verdant valley. Its green promise of nourishment looked as welcoming as her memory of Canyon de Chelly. The cottonwoods were beginning to leaf and grassy underbrush of green carpeted the forest floor. Mount—she had named the burro—stopped to sniff and look, then picked up the pace. If a priest had ever told Mount of paradise, the valley must look like his reward for the journey he had endured.

Yahzi had gone three days without food. She imagined trapping a rabbit or a bird, guessed she'd be lucky to find roots. Mount plodded to the river without pause. She scooted off his back while he drank his fill. Her feet never felt such relief as they did in the cold water. She scooped up handsful of water, splashing Mount at the same time. She laughed as she dipped her arms in the water, undressed, and bathed herself.

The baby twisted, she put hands on lower back and pushed inward, lifted her stomach before kneeling to revel in the stream. She drank again wondering if she could swallow enough to satisfy her thirst. When she could drink no more, she splashed herself, then wrung out her buckskin dress.

Farther upstream a thick growth of cattails lined the bank. Yahzi and Diego once made love beside a pond filled with the plant. Diego had pulled up stalks to show her how good they tasted. They must be even better roasted, she thought. She put a hobble on Mount and hastened to the cattails. Two frogs jumped into the water at her approach. She chided herself for not being quiet, would have eaten them despite the Dinee tabu on their flesh, but forgot the frogs while pulling up a dozen cattails. The roots were more delicious than she remembered. She selected a dozen more for roasting before remembering she had no way to light a fire.

Yahzi nibbled on cattails while contemplating the leafing willows as a sign of warmer spring nights. Mount brayed his appreciation of the lush grass. She'd have to restrain his feasting or he'd suffer colic.

Yahzi wondered what kind of hunger her baby experienced the last three days. Perhaps all the mutton she'd enjoyed with the Dinee had kept it nourished. The thought of meat made her mouth water. Already the roots were losing their appeal. She tugged at strings of cattail caught between her teeth.

She looked for seeds, knowing it was too early to find any. A pack rat scurried from its home, hindered by pregnancy. Yahzi stepped on it, scooped it up and twisted its neck. She broke a fingernail prying at its skin, but managed to strip it clean. She bit at the flesh trying to avoid the rat's innards. The taste of blood and the raw flesh set off her appetite for meat.

She sat down to think, her legs stretched in front of her.

Her mother's brother had once shown her how to make a trap for rabbits. It wasn't hard with a piece of string, but all she had was Mount's hobble. She struggled to her feet and went to the worn blanket that served as part of her saddle to work at its ragged end. The threads she secured were small and worn, but she rolled them together on her thigh. Soon, she had the right size and strength.

Yahzi searched the grass, noted two more pack rat nests, and found what looked to be a rabbit trail. A young willow tree provided a springy branch and a couple of sturdy sticks. She wasn't sure she'd remembered how to set the trap, but it looked as if it would work. She rolled a clump of grass through the circle of string, and the trap sprung into action. She laughed aloud at the thought of a rabbit suspended in the air.

When Yahzi finished resetting the trap, she remembered Mount would overeat if left to himself. When she found him, she tugged at his bridle to lift his head. He jerked and brayed, but Yahzi held tight and led him away from grass while singing a Dinee lullaby.

As they crossed a rocky patch, Yahzi remembered how her grandfather would break stones, using the flakes to shave his scraggly beard. She knelt and smashed one stone against another. Nothing like a sharp flake came from the effort. She tried again and got two flakes but neither sharp. She picked up another rock and slammed it against a large stone. Three more flakes with a cutting edge flew off. She ran a finger across their edges. They'd serve to skin a rabbit.

She led Mount to the river, used the hobble to tie him to a tree, and gathered grass for a bed. The night was warm; even in early morning her blanket kept her on the bed of grass until Mount brayed his hunger a third time. She untied him and used the rope as a hobble.

When she straightened up, pain jolted her back, but she forgot the ache when a rustling sound erupted from the grassy carpet. Apprehensive, she edged toward the sound. A rabbit struggled in her trap, suspended in the air. She dashed toward it, wrung the rabbit's neck, but not before a flailing paw scratched her arm. She ignored the cut while she used two of her blades to skin the catch. She drank the rabbit's blood before slicing pieces of the flesh small enough to chew. The creature had little fat, but she sucked at every bit of it. How delicious rabbit stew would be if only she had fire.

After five days of rabbit, pack rat, and cattails Yahzi wondered if she could live in the valley forever. The diet sustained her. Mount did even better. His ribs were as well covered as she'd ever seen them. This valley must be like the Garden of Eden that Diego claimed was where God made First Man and First Woman.

However, thoughts of meeting Nataalith drove her to leave for the ranch. She dried a few day's supply of rabbit flesh for the trip and wrapped as many cattail stalks in a hide as it would hold. She bundled grass for Mount and left not long after sunrise.

By late afternoon she arrived at the bend where the river turned from its southwest course to the southeast. Mount had to be prodded to enter the desert, but she kept him on course the rest of the day. She didn't bed down until nearly dark, didn't find much comfort on the rocky desert floor. Mount snorted in disgust as he chewed at a prickly pear cactus.

Yahzi hadn't gone far the next morning when she sighted a mountain that had to be Tsoodzil. She could find the ranch using it as a landmark. Again, fears sprung up as to what awaited her, and she doubted that Nataalith would come for her despite his promise. She asked herself why he should risk so much for a poor slave. She decided to flee at the first opportunity.

In late afternoon she recognized a landmark not far from Diego's ranch. She camped early, reluctant to reach the ranch. Her nose wrinkled. She thought she smelled Pablo's sweat and grime. Yahzi's head drooped. She gnawed at the last cattail stalk. She unrolled her sheepskin and blanket to enjoy one last night of freedom.

The morning light showed she was closer to the ranch than she thought. She rode Mount up to her shack and dismounted. The place didn't smell of Pablo as much as usual, but unwashed pots suggested he still lived there. She found a few beans she'd secreted for an emergency, but mice had gotten into her reserve of corn. She shrugged and tried to picture Nataalith starting south for her.

She led Mount to the stable, sniffing in disdain at the smell of bacon. It took moments more to identify the scent of coffee. It had been ages since Diego could afford coffee. From the smells Yahzi guessed the cook must have come back which meant Diego had returned. She intended to leave Mount in the corral and slip by the house to see Dezba. As she left the corral, Diego and a young Spaniard stepped from the ranch house.

"So, you have come back," Diego called.

Yahzi nodded but said nothing. She walked toward them with her head down until she reached them. Glanced at both before bowing her head. The Spanish stranger wore a well trimmed beard, his hard eyes arched by eyebrows that ran together.

"This is Maria," Diego said. "Pablo's wife."

"You didn't tell me she's pregnant. How the devil do I use a dirty Indian too swollen to bend over?"

"She's a hard worker, Armando. Once she's had her baby, you'll see."

"How do I feed another mouth for a month or more?" Armando glared at Yahzi. "When is your baby due, woman?"

Yahzi shrugged.

"Answer your mast...," Diego caught himself, "your new haciendero."

"Don't call me an haciendero," Armando snarled. "This hell hole never qualified as an hacienda even before the savages destroyed it."

"They couldn't destroy the land," Diego said in an oily voice.

"How could they? There's nothing here to destroy." Armando spat.

"It's good for sheep. Orofre assured you it supported a flock before the Navajo raid."

"My uncle knows little of herding sheep," Armando wrinkled his nose. "Only how to woo rich women."

"So he has sent us, er..., sent you, a fine herd. Pablo and the Nuevo Mexicano shepherds will be here any day."

"If the savages haven't killed them. And if that dirty, fat Indian hasn't eaten all the lambs," Armando snarled.

"Let's get this straight." He glared at Yahzi. "This woman is Pablo's wife." He turned to Diego. "Is that right?"

"Yes," Diego nodded. "They both have been baptized and married by a priest. He recorded them as upstanding Christians. Civilized Nuevo Mexicanos. Pablo doesn't even speak the language. Maria prefers Spanish."

"Let her tell me what language she prefers," Armando said. He addressed her in rapid Spanish, asking which language she liked best.

Yahzi sucked in her lips, feeling utter contempt for the young Nuevo Mexicano.

"Tell him, Maria. I know how well you understand Spanish." There was a whine in Diego's voice.

"My name is Yahzi!"

"And you'll give a devil's name to your child." Armando slapped Yahzi so hard she tasted blood. He scowled at Diego. "You failed to break her, didn't you?"

"Yes. No! She's a good Christian and a loyal servant, I swear."

"Didn't Pablo tell me that she ran off with the Navajo who raided the ranch? That she went willingly. Is that what you call loyalty?"

"Tell him, Yahzi." The whine was clear. "I mean Maria. The Navajo forced you to go, didn't they?"

"No." Yahzi's eyes flared defiance. "I went willingly. I'll go again when I get the chance."

Armando's face reddened. "The penalty for running away is a flogging. In your condition, I can't give you what you deserve, but you'll get a taste of what's to come for your treachery." He grabbed her by her hair and yanked her toward the corral. She stumbled but stayed upright. At the corral, Armando grabbed a hobble and lashed her wrists to a fence post, then went inside the stable. He'd tied her wrists so tight that she thought the pain might be her punishment.

Yahzi's mind raced, wondering what more to expect. She'd heard Diego threaten flogging often but had never seen him use the whip except on animals.

Armando returned with a riding crop. "Go to the kitchen, Diego, and get a chili pepper."

Diego stood with open mouth.

"Go! Or get off my ranch."

Diego trotted toward the house.

"I'm only going to lash you once, Maria. That is your name, isn't it?"

Yahzi didn't answer.

"But first I'm going to rub your skin with chili so the whip will work it into the flesh. Two stings for the effort of one." Armando's laugh was unlike anything that Yahzi had ever heard.

He pulled her buckskin dress atop her head. Yahzi gasped. She hadn't expected to stand naked before Armando. She tried squeezing her legs close together. Armando laughed at the effort.

"After you've given birth, you get eleven more lashes, Maria. This is only a taste of what's to come." Again the strange laugh. "But if you compose a poem of praise to the name Maria, perhaps I won't use the chili pepper. A poem in excellent Spanish, of course. You do prefer Spanish to Navajo, don't you?"

Yahzi hung her head in silence, gritted her teeth. She could endure.

FOURTEEN

Yahzi took deep breaths. The baby was writhing in anticipation of the flogging. She willed it to be calm while she vowed not to cry out. Armando looked at the ranch house and swore under his breath.

"What's taking you so long, Diego?" Armando called. "I'm not going to stand in this sun much longer."

Diego didn't answer. Yahzi had to look over her shoulder to see him coming. He walked with a slouch.

"Where's the pepper?" Armando demanded to know. Diego held out his hand. "Is that the smallest one you could find?" Armando's words rang with sarcasm. He fixed Diego with a scornful look.

Diego offered the chili to Armando, his chin dropped to his chest. Armando refused it.

"Wipe her back with it," Armando ordered.

Diego swiped the chili across Yahzi's back.

"Not like that." Armando's face grew red. "Break it first. Then rub the juice in. Have you never felt the sting of chili?"

Diego broke the chili with his fingers, rubbed it hard across the top of Yahzi's back, then stepped in front of Armando to wipe the rest of her back gingerly.

"No wonder you failed to run a ranch." Armando grabbed Diego's shoulder and pulled him away. He raised the riding crop and struck Yahzi with all his might.

She gasped but held in the scream that needed to be released.

Diego hastened to untie her wrists.

Yahzi tightened her facial muscles to keep tears from flowing. Thoughts of a hammer in her hand, smashing Armando's skull, lessened the throbbing in her back.

"The Indians are above animals, Diego. They may be Christians, but you must never allow them to forget their place. They'll never be civilized."

Diego stood with bowed head, massaging Yahzi's wrists.

"Do you understand, Diego?" Armando shouted in Diego's ear.

"I understand," Diego muttered, dropping Yahzi's wrists.

"We'll see." Armando was shaking his head, a snarl on his lips.

Yahzi backed away with a half smile. By suppressing her scream, she felt victorious once more—although thoughts of more lashes brought bile to her mouth. She started toward her adobe shack, until remembering Dezba, then headed to the stone hovel instead.

"Where is she going?" Armando asked.

"Never mind," Diego answered. Armando let the matter drop.

When Yahzi reached Dezba's stone shelter, she cleared her throat. Dezba hurried out.

"Yahzi," Dezba nearly shouted. "I've been looking everywhere for you." She embraced her niece. Yahzi flinched.

"What is it?"

"Armando flogged me, but only once. I'll be alright."

"Come in, my niece." She lifted Yahzi's dress and examined her back. "I don't have any herbs."

"He rubbed my back with a chili. Do you have some water?"

Dezba ran outside to the olla, brought it in, and sat it beside Yahzi. She soaked a rag and gently dabbed at Yahzi's back. Yahzi flinched once or twice when Dezba touched the lash mark.

"Did Diego do this to you? I thought Diego liked you."

"It was Armando."

"Who's Armando?"

Yahzi hesitated. Dezba had to know him. "He's the new ranch owner."

"You mean Diego's friend?" Dezba glanced around. "I don't think he's a nice person."

"You're right, Auntie, not nice."

"He comes every morning to see how much weaving I've done. I've never done enough." Dezba shrugged. "He says I won't get my rations if I don't do more." She studied her fingers. "I'm already hungry."

"Has Diego helped you at all?"

"He brings me a few beans. Makes me promise not to tell his friend. Diego does all the cooking now." Dezba sucked in her lips. "I don't know what happened to the cook."

"He ran away when the Dinee came." Yahzi studied Dezba's face to see if she remembered the raid.

"Was that when you went away?"

"Yes. The Dinee forced me to go with them." Yahzi couldn't bear to tell her aunt that she had fled without her.

"Why did you come back?"

"Comanches attacked us. I had no where else to go"

"I'm glad you came back. It must be dangerous away from the ranch." Dezba's hands trembled. "It was hard to find enough to eat. I'd forgotten so much about the desert. Which cactus is easiest to peel. I got thorns in my hands." Dezba looked at her palms. "I guess I was meant to live here on the ranch."

Yahzi took her aunt's hands. "Auntie. When I went north with the Dinee, we met Dayish."

"Dayish?" Dezba squinted. "I knew a Dayish. It's a Dinee name, I think."

"You remember Dayish." Yahzi rubbed her friend's hands and wrists. "Dayish!"

"I liked Dayish—I think."

"Think hard, Auntie. Dayish."

"Dayish and I shared corn pollen." Dezba sucked in her lips. "We were married at Jemez, but he was Dinee. He took me to his hogan." Dezba's look of consternation frightened Yahzi. Before she could speak, Dezba continued. "It's coming back. Dayish taught me to walk in beauty. His mother and sisters were good to me." A look of contentment replaced the consternation. "I'd like to go home to Dayish." A tear ran down one cheek.

"Come," Yahzi said. "Let's sit at the loom. I'll help you weave."

Yahzi noticed that Dezba had a full spindle of wool. She squirmed into a comfortable position before the loom and started weaving. The motions brought back memories of her mother's hogan. She imagined a design but knew she couldn't execute it. It didn't matter. The Mexicanos were satisfied with simple patterns as long as the blankets were warm. The joints of her fingers tightened. She flexed them but that did little to relieve the tension. The burning of her back struggled with her determination to weave. A dizzy spell overtook her, and she collapsed beside the loom. The last thing she felt were Dezba's hands, bathing her back, her tongue clicking its solicitude.

Yahzi awoke to sunlight, blinked her eyes before recalling where she was. Dezba held her head in her lap, rocking gently, singing a Jemez lullaby. Yahzi's back felt on fire. She wasn't sure if the lash mark hurt more than the chili. She had no time to contemplate the matter because Diego appeared at the door with a pail in one hand.

"Here are beans for you two. I guessed you'd spend the night here." He looked at Yahzi. "I added a little meat. It'll help your back heal."

Yahzi refused to answer. Dezba acknowledged him with a thank you and a nod of her head.

"Armando wants to see you at the house in half an hour. Clean yourself up after you eat." He looked around the hovel, shook his head at the cracks in the walls. "Keep working on the blanket, Dezba. Armando complains that we're feeding you and getting nothing from your labor. He'll send you to Santa Fe if you don't do more."

When Yahzi finished her half of the beans, reserving the sliver of meat for her aunt, she went to the horse trough. She bathed her face in the end free of greenish slime.

She knocked at the kitchen door and called for Diego, heard him scurry to the door.

He explained. "Armando will be sitting at his desk. You stand before him. Don't look him in the face. Don't speak until you're spoken to."

"I suppose, now, you don't want me to come live with you after the baby is born?" Yahzi didn't bother to hide her scorn.

"Things have changed so much, Yahzi. I'm sorry. Perhaps, one day…"

Not before I've fled with Dezba, Yahzi thought. She went to the other room where Armando sat behind a few crude planks resting on a wobbly support. He studied a paper before him, letting her stand a few minutes.

When he looked up, he said, "We must all do more than our share until Pablo and the two new hands get here. Don Diego has been

93

doing the cooking. You'll take over for him. It means cutting the firewood and cleaning up. Once you get a fire going in the stove, empty the night jars by our beds and get on with breakfast. You'll have plenty of time to launder, as you did before. In your free time, you can help Don Diego in the stables." He fixed Yahzi with a glare. "And the old Indian woman—I understand she's your aunt?" He went on before Yahzi could answer. "Help her with her weaving. She's not earning her keep. I'll have to take her to Santa Fe if she can't earn her keep."

"And our wages?" Yahzi asked. Diego had never paid them anything, but he had explained how the Spanish denied they kept slaves.

Armando smirked as if anticipating the question. "The ranch pays you in food and clothing. At Christmas, there'll be centavos so you can tithe to the Church." His lip curled. "That's all, Maria. You'll need wood for the evening meal. Don Diego will show you where things are in the kitchen. I personally supervise the rations. Don't take anything that doesn't belong to you. You've felt the lash. You don't want more than what's coming to you after your child is born, do you?" He glanced at her swollen belly, looked away in disgust.

Yahzi shrugged. "One more thing," Armando said. "When the flock gets here, the real work begins. The sheep will need shearing, and there'll be more hands to feed. You will still find time to help with the shearing." He raised the riding crop he kept on the desk and slammed it on the boards. "And you'd better not be having the baby in the midst of shearing."

Yahzi turned to leave. Before she reached the door, Armando called, "Maria, you work hard with the shearing, and you'll get only half the lashes I've promised you."

Yahzi gritted her teeth and swore to herself that she'd be gone before the shearing began. She and Dezba.

The next morning after Yahzi brought firewood to the kitchen, she lifted her breasts. They hadn't been so heavy during her first pregnancy nor had the small of her back ached the way it did now. She rubbed her waist with both hands, wondering if this baby would ever come. As soon as giving birth, she'd leave, somehow managing with the baby.

Armando called from the other room that he was dressing and expected breakfast. Yahzi fed the fire and stirred the beans. Water boiled in another pot to make the corn mush that Armando preferred in the morning. She'd learned his preferences for keeping house, but she still could not satisfy him with her cooking. Finding and cutting firewood took more time than cooking, keeping the stove going was as troublesome, and Armando's demands for how he wanted his food cooked were so unreasonable she came close to dumping a frying pan of grease on him.

This morning, she had forgotten to add the dried meat to the beans soon enough, but it would have a little time to soften. Armando insisted on having his mush before his beans. Diego came in from outside, drying his face with a tattered towel, tossing it to Yahzi when he finished.

"Things will be better when the two new men come," Diego said. "In the meantime, don't forget the night jars. I emptied them for you yesterday." Diego wrinkled his nose. "Perhaps Pablo will help you with those."

Yahzi almost laughed at the thought of Pablo helping her. Dezba was more of a help, but Armando insisted she stay at her loom.

"What size flock are the shepherds bringing?" Yahzi asked.

"Nearly a hundred." Diego lowered his voice. "I'm not sure there are enough rams." He stepped closer to her and whispered. "I don't think the ranch can support so many sheep."

Diego seemed ready to tell her more, but Armando stalked into the kitchen, looked at the table and demanded breakfast. Yahzi hustled to set out bowls and pour the corn mush. She stirred the beans and hoped the meat had softened while Armando and Diego blew on their mush.

"I expect the shepherds today, tomorrow at the latest." He looked at Diego. "Make sure the corral is ready for the sheep. Get that burro out of there."

"What should I do with him?" Diego said.

"You might butcher it so we'd have fresh meat." Armando glared at the chunk of dried meat on his fork. "I'm sick and tired of jerky. How am I supposed to chew this?"

Yahzi's heart beat faster. She couldn't cook Mount. Maybe she could chase him off.

"But he's too valuable to eat," Diego protested.

"Of course. What kind of fool do you think I am? Tie him to a tree somewhere until the shearing is over." He looked at Yahzi. "You see that the burro's fed, woman. Surely there's a little pasture close by your home where you can hobble him."

"Yes, Don Armando." It was the first time Yahzi had used the title of respect to address Armando. He cocked his head in her direction.

Later, Yahzi finished cleaning up from the evening meal and prepared what she could for morning. She meant to look in on Dezba although her body pleaded for rest. She'd started for her aunt's hut when a dust cloud appeared on the southern horizon. Armando was standing in front of the house and called to Diego that the shepherds approached. Yahzi stood in near paralysis. If she went to her hut, Diego would be yelling for her help before she could lie down.

She stood, not knowing what to do until Armando yelled. "Open the corral gate, Maria. Diego, make sure the fence poles are secure. If they're not, we'll spend all night and tomorrow chasing sheep."

Yahzi lifted the top latch of the gate with ease. The lower one gave her trouble. As she struggled with it, she realized that the gate hinges were so worn they were about to pull loose. Her exhaustion gave way to elation.

"Get the old woman, Diego. We'll need everyone to drive them into the corral. Maria, stay close to the gate. Once they're all in, shut it." Armando slapped his riding crop against his leg, paced endlessly. Muttered to himself, "How many have they lost?"

Yahzi wasn't sure which of the figures at the back of the flock was Pablo because they were so soaked in dust. She didn't care. She'd rather not see him at all. And if her plan worked, she wouldn't.

"Is that you, Don Armando?" a herder called.

"Down here. Bring them to the corral. Have you lost many?"

"Not many, sir. No thanks to the dirty Indian you assigned to help."

"He'll make up for it when we start shearing, or he'll feel my whip." Armando slapped his leg twice with the riding crop.

Dezba trailed behind Diego to take up a position between the corral and the house. Even Armando positioned himself to make sure the flock entered the corral. The bawling of the animals was as overwhelming as the dust they raised. Yahzi spotted two rams vying for leadership with their bellowing. The noise from the ewes suggested the flock was more interested in water than in settling down. The sheep shied away from Dezba when she flapped her shawl, Diego and Armando waved them on, and they headed into the corral. The two herders and Pablo dropped beside the corral, desperate to open their canteens. Armando and Diego slapped each other on their backs after seeing the sheep corralled. They headed to the house. Dezba shook out her shawl before folding it and refolding it.

Yahzi kicked loose the bottom hinge of the corral gate, tore away the worn leather hinge at the top, and shoved the gate onto the ground. She pushed past several ewes to reach a ram, struck him on the backside. He kicked the sheep around him before heading for the opening. Once he bellowed, another ram reared and bucked at ewes around him. The flock bolted for the opening. Within minutes sheep were heading in all directions. Armando's shouts from the ranch house door were incomprehensible.

Yahzi dashed to Dezba, took her by the hand, and led her to the adobe hut where Mount was tethered. "Untie the burro, Auntie, while I get my flint and steel."

"Are we gong after the sheep?"

"No, Auntie, we're going home!"

FIFTEEN

"My home is back there," Dezba pursed her lips to point inward her hovel.

"Home!" Yahzi hissed the word into Dezba's ear. "We're going to our real home. Your home with Dayish."

"Who's Dayish?" Dezba looked frightened.

"Your husband. You want to spend your life with him!"

"Yes." Dezba's smile showed through her dust covered face. "My husband, Dayish. I love Dayish." Even in her haste, Yahzi wondered for a moment how Dezba had learned about what the Spanish called love.

She put Mount's reins in Dezba's hands. "Hold him tight, Auntie. I'll be right back."

Yahzi rushed into the hut. She shuffled through shards of adobe plaster on a roof beam to find the small knife that Diego had given her when they became lovers. She took flint and steel from a corner, a present from Diego when she gave birth to Hokee. She grabbed a worn belt of Pablo's and a frayed pouch, dumped in the knife and fire making tools, tied the belt to her waist. The need for food struck her. She could slip by the chaos around the corral and make her way to the kitchen. She pictured where the beans were stored beside the corn meal, plus a metal pot that would hold them both. She knew exactly which peg held the canteen that Diego treasured.

Armando was perched on top of the corral fence shrouded in dust, screaming directions. Diego shouted an answer from somewhere beyond Dezba's hovel. Yahzi hoped he'd fall into the pit she and Dezba had dug for clay. She hoped Armando had been right—that he would spend all night and the next day searching for sheep.

She slipped into the kitchen. Although it was dark, Yahzi had no trouble locating the pail she wanted. She scooped up beans from a barrel and grabbed a handful of chilies. A scent of dried meat tempted her. She threw the largest chunk in the bucket and dashed to the corral. The confusion in the dust cloud was as great as ever. She thought she heard Armando call her name, ignored him, and dashed into the stable to grab a bridle. She ran to her hut.

When she reached it, she found Dezba holding the burro by its halter, patting its nuzzle, and whispering in its ear. She thought she heard the word, Dayish. Mount tossed his head at the sight of Yahzi as if ready for a ride.

Yahzi replaced the halter with the bridle, wrapped the pail in the frayed blanket that she and Pablo used, balanced it with the canteen, and strapped the roll onto Mount's back. She slung two hides over the burro's back and turned to Dezba.

"I'll help you up, Auntie."

Dezba looked around. "What will you ride?"

"I can walk. We'll have tonight and all day tomorrow before they start after us." Yahzi lifted the old woman onto the burro's back.

"Won't Diego's friend be angry? How will I do my weaving?"

"Armando has his sheep to worry about." Yahzi glanced around the ramada and hut one last time, decided she had everything she owned, and turned to Mount. She cooed into his ear that they were heading home. He started out as soon as Yahzi took a step.

"Won't Diego want your help? What will he do when he finds us?"

"We'll be on rocky ground. They'll never find our tracks." Yahzi took a deep breath. Perhaps they were headed for Canyon de Chelly. Wherever they were going was better than staying on the ranch.

"What will we eat?"

"I brought food. We're going to a river where there's lots to eat. Jemez isn't far from it. Dayish is in Jemez." Yahzi tried to estimate how many days it might take—if she knew the direction to take.

"I'll be glad to see Dayish. Will he meet us at the river?"

"Maybe." Yahzi didn't slow her gait until they reached unfamiliar territory. She wished the moon were a little brighter. "Dayish would meet us if he knew you were coming."

"How long will we stay at the river?"

"Not long." Yahzi felt her stomach cramp. Unless the baby comes, she thought. Then what?

For the first few days in the desert, Yahzi rarely stopped. Every night she swore she'd rest the next day, but each morning she managed to load Dezba and lead Mount off. She sensed going home even if they might be heading in the wrong direction.

She'd lost track of the days travelled when she knew they had to rest. Dezba's buttocks could take no more. And Yahzi's back rebelled. Dezba found grazing for Mount, returned wearing her old smile.

"What is it, Auntie?"

"I found that plant that has such good roots. The one I learned about after the Dinee took you away."

It was Yahzi's turn to smile when Dezba held out both hands with as many roots as she could hold. Yahzi started a fire to boil them and added the last of the meat. She decided they had to find the river soon or they'd face grave danger.

The dried beef soaked up enough moisture to release its meaty flavor. She and her aunt ate almost enough to feel full. They used Dezba's hides as bedding. Before Yahzi closed her eyes, Dezba was snoring. Yahzi rolled over, a streak of pain shot through her belly, and she bolted upright.

Dezba looked up. "What is it, my niece?" she said between yawns.

"The baby says she enjoyed your roots." Yahzi wasn't about to tell Dezba about the pain that had exploded in her groin. If we can reach the river before it comes, I'll be fine, Yahzi thought. She reassured Dezba before lying down. She didn't awaken until the sun was well up.

Dezba had started a fire and was adding water to the pail to soak the beans. When Yahzi sat up, Dezba brought her the canteen.

"We must be careful with the water, Auntie, until we reach the river."

"The burro found water," Dezba twittered. "It must have drunk its fill because I only had to kick him once to make him move away. I dug a little deeper and found enough water to fill the canteen."

Yahzi gulped her fill. "There should be more in a little while, Auntie."

"We'll let Mount drink too, won't we?"

"He can have all he wants. Mount's spirit must be Dinee."

"That's right," Dezba said. "He's generous like the Dinee."

That night the two lingered over the beans. Yahzi collected wood with caution, worried that more pain might overtake her before they reached the river. The next morning, Dezba insisted she'd lead Mount while Yahzi rode.

"The baby won't let me ride. If I did, she might want out to take the reins."

Dezba chuckled as she mounted, and the two headed for the river.

At noon they passed over a ridge to discover a streak of green snaking across the desert. Yahzi could not have been happier. She felt they were approaching home, whatever its direction.

They had enough daylight when they reached the river to construct a crude lean-to. Dezba told how she'd cover it over with cane the next day. Yahzi had time to set one trap while Dezba finished two beds. They hobbled Mount, dug a fire pit, and talked about the pack rats and rabbits they'd soon feast on. Yahzi didn't know if the rumbles came from her empty stomach or if the baby wanted to see daylight.

The next day Yahzi set more rabbit traps, caught two pack rats for dinner, and came home with a load of firewood.

Dezba had covered the lean-to and found more grass for bedding. In between their beds, Dezba had laid out matting for the baby. Yahzi grinned when she saw what her aunt had done, told her how happy the baby would be with its new home.

During the next few days, Yahzi taught Dezba how to trap rabbits. Soon Dezba was spending most of the daylight hours exploring for rabbit trails, setting new traps, and checking out old ones.

One morning when Dezba left early, Yahzi stayed in bed, breathing deeply. The pains had started again. She wished for a medicine person to hasten the birth. She rolled over, intending to go back to sleep, when she heard Dezba running toward her.

"We'll have roast rabbit tonight, my niece. Look!" Dezba held a rabbit by its hind legs.

"You've caught your first rabbit, Auntie. Good hunting. You'll catch many more."

Dezba stood over Yahzi, catching her breath. "We're going to have fresh meat—just like Christmas."

"Did the trap break its neck?"

"No," Dezba giggled. "The boys at Jemez made us girls break their necks when they caught rabbits. They knew we didn't like it, but we enjoyed their teasing."

That night the two women let the rabbit roast until the aroma set their stomachs rumbling. The anticipation of the meat made both anxious. The baby seemed ready to enjoy the meal outside the womb. Yahzi alternated between standing and kneeling while she ate her share of the rabbit. Her nipples oozed, and ripples of pain zigzagged through her.

She slept in fits, Dezba stirring beside her. At first light, Yahzi knew it was time. "Auntie," she said. "Are you ready to be a great aunt?"

Dezba smiled. "My new niece wants to taste my rabbit, is that it?"

"I think so." The contractions came close together.

"I found a good tree trunk to serve as a pole. It's not far," Dezba said. "You can hold onto it while you kneel. That's the way I saw it done at my mother-in-law's."

"That must be the best way," Yahzi said. "Diego had me lie down for my first birth. Maybe that's why Hokee had a club foot."

The two women made their way to the place Dezba had prepared. Yahzi kneeled before the pole, clinging to it. Dezba knelt behind her and massaged downward, urging the baby to come into their world.

"Augh." The pain was like Armando's whip, but lower in the back.

Dezba pressed harder on Yahzi's stomach. "Is the pain lower?"

"It's not like my first time." Yahzi gasped for a breath. "It's all in the back. Rub down my spine, Auntie."

Dezba relaxed her hug to massage Yahzi's back but soon returned to pressing downward on the baby.

Another bolt of pain shot through Yahzi's back. She suppressed the urge to scream so as not to frighten Dezba. Moments later another contraction racked her body. The pain no longer seemed so terrible because it spread throughout.

102

"I can see her head." Dezba was leaning over Yahzi's shoulder. "She'll see daylight soon." Dezba laughed in delight. "Keep pushing, my niece, keep pushing."

Yahzi slid her hands higher up the pole, leaned backward, and pushed as hard as she could. She felt the child leaving the womb. Dezba rushed around in front of her, reached for the baby, laughed the whole time.

"He's going to be a mighty hunter, a warrior. He'll take care of you in your old age." Dezba cradled the child in her arms, rocking it, cooing Jemez words in his ears.

"Can you get some thread from your blanket, Auntie? Tie off the navel cord. It's what Diego did." Before she could ask to see her son, another pain rocked Yahzi. She grabbed the pole and pushed with muscles she didn't know she had to expel the afterbirth. Instead, a second baby saw daylight.

Dezba's laughs ceased. Her eyes opened wide. Her jaw dropped.

"It's twins," Yahzi gasped. Is the second one a boy, too?" Dezba didn't answer. The effort was beyond her.

"What do we do?" Dezba's question was filled with anxiety. Her face was blank as she tied off the second cord.

"Don't you remember the Hero Twins born to Changing Woman? How they saved the Dinee from all the monsters."

"It's not what my mother-in-law told me. When I lived with her, twins were born to a neighbor. That's when my mother-in-law told me how Talking God fathered twins. One was born blind, the other lame. It's not good to have twins." She covered her face with her hands.

"Well, are they both seeing daylight?" Yahzi asked.

"The first one hasn't opened his eyes." Dezba pulled back the baby's eyelids. When she looked at Yahzi, her face was filled with sadness. She held her cheek to the child's mouth. "Oh, Yahzi. I can't feel it breathe."

Yahzi grabbed the baby from Dezba. It hadn't cried. She shook it. Nothing. Put her hand where its heart should be beating. She felt nothing. Moments later she felt relief. How could she ever return home with twins? One child threatened her escape, two made it impossible.

She asked for her other son. Dezba had him half hidden in her lap. "You must rest, my niece."

"I'll nurse him a little, Auntie."

Dezba made more excuses, her reluctance to hand over the baby obvious.

"What is it?" Yahzi demanded. "Is he dead, too?"

"No." Dezba hesitated but held out the child to Yahzi.

Yahzi gasped. Her son had her fine complexion and lustrous hair, but his legs extended only to the knees with what looked like a toe wiggling at the ends.

Yahzi took her son, dropped onto her back, held him to her chest. She couldn't stop sobbing.

SIXTEEN

Yahzi must have dozed. When she awoke the baby was doing its best to nurse. She smiled and positioned her breast for him. As she recalled what had happened, she did her best to avoid looking at her son's legs.

But her resolve lasted only moments. She glanced to make sure of the deformity, looked back to the baby's face so engaged with her breast. She smiled at the sucking sounds he made, then decided he wouldn't be harder to carry home than if he had full legs. Surely, a Dinee medicine person could help her son.

Before she could think further, Dezba stood over her.

"Look how big he is!" She held a rabbit by its ears.

"You've earned your name, Auntie. Mighty warrior and hunter."

"Do you really think so?" Dezba said. "At least you can rest while I skin and roast him."

Yahzi wrapped the baby in the hide they used for a saddle and built up the fire. She helped Dezba spear the butchered rabbit onto roasting sticks and propped them over the flames.

In the next few days Dezba's care giving became routine, watching over Yahzi and Mount, delighting in an occasional rabbit while providing a steady supply of roots.

The diet restored Yahzi's strength. She began gathering a few roots to roast with the rabbit while her aunt did most of the work. Yahzi's physical strength returned, but whenever she nursed the baby, her spirits lagged. She began to doubt that a medicine person could help her son. More important, would she ever find Canyon de Chelly without Nataalith to help? She wondered, too, why they had not encountered a Dinee. Anyone could at least tell her if the canyon was to the north or west.

"Ouch," Dezba cried. "I've cut my finger again." She sucked at it. "Old age is hard on the eyes. The joints, too." She stopped sucking and massaged the finger. "At least the rabbit will fill us up." Dezba had grown proficient at skinning and dismembering rabbits. She soon had its flesh roasting over the fire. She waved her hand at the smoke edging toward her eyes. "The wood is so green here," she whimpered.

"Scoot aside, Auntie, and rest yourself."

"What about my weaving?" Dezba frowned. "Diego is going to be angry when he sees how little I've done."

"We don't have to do any more weaving for him." Yahzi heard exasperation in her words. Would Dezba never realize they were free? "We're on our way to Dayish. To your home in Jemez!"

"Home? It's been so long. With my gray hair and wrinkles how will my relatives recognize me?"

"Dayish will know you. He'll take you to your relatives."

"There won't be any white men there, will there? No one to make me weave."

Yahzi grimaced as she recalled how the Spanish garrison at Jemez had slaughtered the Dinee peace envoys months earlier. But, Dayish could slip them past the Spanish garrison. If she could find Jemez. Or Dayish. She joined her aunt to turn the roasting sticks and forget her growing worry.

Days later Yahzi basked in an unusual warm sun. She had to force herself to think how the two of them could find Jemez and evade the Spanish guards. She thought they might stay on the outskirts of the pueblo until they found a friendly Jemez, but how would they know who was a friend?

Yahzi turned to her baby to forego further thought. She nursed him until he slept. She put him naked on the hide he was growing accustomed to.

Dezba returned with two pack rats and a handful of wood. She glanced at the baby, frowned before turning to build up the fire and skin the rats. Smoke drifted into Yahzi's face. She decided they must leave the river. Soon some one would be herding sheep into the lush grass of the river valley.

"Auntie, it's time we found Dayish." Yahzi's spirit lifted from the resolve she heard in her own voice.

"Dayish?" Dezba's forehead creased, then her face lit up. "Yes, Dayish, we're going home."

"Somehow." Yahzi rose, her head filling with plans but none of them concrete.

The sound of hoof beats interrupted. Dezba spotted the rider first. "It's Señor Baca. Or that new friend of his. Will he take us back to the ranch?"

Yahzi shaded her eyes and studied the man on horseback. It was a white man but a stranger. She thought hard to explain their presence.

The rider wore a fierce scowl on a face creased by the sun. His clothes were as worn as Diego's. The scabbard for his machete was frayed and torn at the top.

"What are you doing on my land?" He looked first at Dezba and then at Yahzi. "You must know you're trespassing."

Yahzi told him they were searching for a runaway daughter when they had to stop because she gave birth. She hoped for sympathy from the Spaniard, and her story should ease suspicion they might be looking for grazing land.

His scowl eased, but he showed no sign of sympathy. "Do the Jemez chiefs know you're here?"

Yahzi struggled for an answer. She couldn't guess if the man had been on the frontier long enough to recognize her as a Dinee of if she could pass for a Jemez.

"My husband might have told them. But we didn't know how far we'd have to come to find her. We never realized it might be this far."

The rider's expression gave no sign as to whether he believed Yahzi. Before he could ask another question, the baby's crying distracted them.

Dezba started for the baby before Yahzi, but the rider spurred his horse, knocked Dezba aside, and reached the infant first.

"My God," he exclaimed as he stared at the baby. "It's true." He yanked his machete from its sheath, leaned down in his saddle, and smashed the baby's head. Without a word, he jabbed his spurs into the horse's flanks and dashed away at a gallop. He never looked back.

Dezba's scream pierced the air. Yahzi stood striken, frozen in disbelief. How could even a Spaniard be so cruel?

Yahzi didn't know how many days had passed after her son's murder. She recalled Dezba urging her to eat, but she didn't recall tasting food. Her parched throat couldn't remember the feel of water. A bone crushing sound and spurting blood dashed in and out of her mind. She sat with her head between her knees, her body shuddering.

"Yahzi, Yahzi! You must eat. Smell this roast rabbit. It's so delicious." Dezba smacked her lips, held a bite size piece of rabbit under Yahzi's nose.

Yahzi took the morsel and chewed it, spit it out, and burst into tears. Dezba knelt beside her, cuddling her, mumbling her sympathy, wiping away tears.

After a while Yahzi ate more but tasted nothing. Dezba mixed roots with roast rabbit, urged Yahzi to continue eating, regretted that she had no corn or beans to restore Yahzi's strength.

Dezba's care and concern made Yahzi think of home, even consider how they might find Jemez. The pueblo couldn't be too far, she decided.

The next morning Dezba struggled with a fire. "All I could find was green wood."

"It's all right, Auntie. We only need to warm up the meat we roasted last night." Yahzi was so tired of pack rat flesh that it didn't matter to her if it was hot or cold. She'd give anything for a pot of corn and beans.

"Yahzi?" a male voice called from a thicket.

Yahzi jerked around, reaching for her knife. Dezba held her hands to her face and moaned.

A man stepped toward them.

"Nataalith? How did you find us?"

"From the smoke." He laughed. "I wondered if you were signalling me."

"We're lucky no one else saw the smoke."

"You were lucky to end up in this part of the river. It belongs to Jemez, but a Spanish rancher claims he bought it. I don't know why but both sides avoid it."

"I'm glad you found us. We were about to leave."

"Have you come to take us home?" Dezba interrupted.

Nataalith looked at Dezba, an eyebrow raised.

"She was born in Jemez, married a Dinee, and he brought her to Canyon de Chelly. We were taken as slaves at the same time. That Dinee we met just before the Comanche attacked us is her husband. He'll be at Jemez."

"He was a good man," Nataalith said. "We'll see if we can find him. She wants to stay at Jemez?"

"I believe that's what she wants. Can we take her?"

"I brought a horse for you and a pack horse. We'll manage."

"When can we start?" Yahzi said.

"Your fresh meat smells good," Nataalith said. "I've got corn and beans. Let's feast today, let my horses rest, and start in the morning."

That night around the dying flames of the camp fire, Dezba kept muttering "Dayish" and searched out other names in the Jemez language. Yahzi asked Nataalith why he had taken so long to find her.

"I went to the ranch for you. It took four days to make sure you weren't there. I guessed you might have come here." Nataalith looked into the embers. "Before that I had to take revenge."

Yahzi hoped her look told Nataalith that she wanted to know everything.

"In the fight with the Comanche two of my clan brothers were killed. They scalped the youngest one. Do you know what it means to scalp?"

Yahzi said she did.

"We got to high ground with half the sheep," Nataalith continued. "The Comanche were satisfied with the scalp and half the flock. I decided to herd the sheep home and raise a war party."

Yahzi nodded her understanding.

"We gave most of the sheep to the dead men's sisters, and started back. Tracked the savages to Santa Fe. Do you know Santa Fe?"

"I've heard it's a big camp with many Spanish."

"Many everything. Puebloans who want to live like Spanish. Rich and poor Spanish. Even Dinee. Some were slaves, but a few went there by choice. It took me two days to find a relative. My mother's brother claimed he remembered me when I was a child. I didn't remember him."

109

"Could he help you?" Yahzi asked.

"He's pretty old. He showed me Santa Fe first. The city stinks. Everyone buys their food. Can you imagine? They never share."

Yahzi leaned closer to urge Nataalith to continue.

"My uncle told me he had seen six Comanche ride into the city carrying sheep. They couldn't herd them with all those people around. Everyone knew they must have stolen them."

"No one cared?"

"The Spanish soldiers won't arrest Comanche. Besides, the men who buy livestock and butcher it to sell—do you understand sell?— they offered the Comanche some wine and then bargained with them." Nataalith had to use the Spanish word for sell. Yahzi assured him that she understood the strange behavior.

"Well, the Comanche left with flasks of wine. I knew they wouldn't go far before they started drinking."

"And did they?"

His lips snarled in a vicious grin. "We found them the next day. Too drunk to recognize us. We killed most of them, but two got away. We found a scalp on one of the dead men." Yahzi had never seen a face so contorted as Nataalith's.

He described in detail how his war party searched the bodies and what they discovered. He dwelt on how they had desecrated the bodies, customs unfamiliar to Yahzi. She felt sick at her stomach but determined to accept Dinee custom. Nataalith finished with a description of his war party's Blessing Way ceremony on their return, a protection against enemy ghosts.

He poked at the fire's embers, stirred a flame and added a few sticks. Dezba was spread out on a hide, a gentle snore rumbling from her throat. Nataalith gathered grass for two beds while Yahzi brought in fire wood for the next day.

As they sat on their beds, Nataalith spoke again of his need for revenge. Yahzi told him why she couldn't stay at the ranch and how she escaped.

"You did the right thing," Nataalith said. "This part of the river is never used for grazing, so no one comes to it."

"A Spaniard came to it," Yahzi spat out the words. "A murderer!"

"What do you mean?"

"He rode in on a horse. When he saw my baby, he smashed in his head with his machete. For no reason at all. Except he was Spanish." Yahzi saw no reason to tell Nataalith she'd given birth to twins or of her baby's deformed legs.

SEVENTEEN

When Yahzi awoke to the morning cold, she imagined a hurried trip into Jemez. Friendly puebloans would help them find Dayish or other relatives of Dezba. Then she and Nataalith would strike out for his hogan. She'd rest a few days before his brother-in-law took her with him to Canyon de Chelly. She even imagined being given a horse and leading Mount as a pack animal.

She was so eager to begin that she almost awoke Nataalith before remembering that he wanted a day's rest. Dezba's snores suggested her aunt could use more sleep. Yahzi gritted her teeth and waited, dreaming of her brother's horses—too many to count—and of his war exploits, so daring they were hard to believe.

When the sun edged over the horizon, Nataalith and Dezba stirred. The two women stood in the river, splashing themselves clean, while Nataalith plunged in, laughing his delight. The two women gathered wood on their way back. Nataalith stalked a rabbit but missed it with his throwing stick.

"We need more wood, don't we?" Dezba said.

"No, we'll leave for Jemez tomorrow. You'll return to Dayish!"

"Home," Dezba echoed.

Yahzi wasn't sure what the word meant to Dezba. But if she and Dayish failed to make a home in Jemez, they could go to Canyon de Chelly with Yahzi.

Nataalith reached their camp first and stirred the embers into a flame. They soon were heating the remains of yesterday's meals.

"What if the Spanish keep us out of Jemez?" Yahzi asked Nataalith.

"Considering how they killed the Dinee peace envoys, there's going to be some danger, but what threat is a man and woman accompanied by an old woman? When they learn the elder is Jemez, they'll surely let us pass."

"Hard to tell how white men think." Yahzi sighed. After years with Diego, he still reacted in unexpected ways.

"Let's circle the pueblo and enter from the east," Nataalith said. "That way we won't be suspicious, I can't pass as anything but Dinee, but if you don't say anything, maybe they'll think you're pueblo. Let Dezba do the talking. Make sure she says you're her niece."

"I'll do my best to make Dezba understand. But she's getting old, and I can't always be sure what she's going to say."

"Can you think of another way?" Nataalith asked.

Yahzi paused a moment but concocted nothing better. She walked over to Dezba, put an arm on her shoulder and explained how important it was to convince any Spaniard who blocked their way that they belonged in Jemez.

Dezba did nothing but smile while Yahzi explained a second time. "Can you do it, Auntie?"

"I am from Jemez. I'll tell them that." The tone of the words didn't encourage Yahzi. She didn't tell Nataalith about her misgivings.

Nataalith rounded up his three horses while Yahzi went in search of Mount. When she found him, she patted his muzzle at length while telling him of their plans to enter Jemez. The way Mount shook his head, Yahzi was certain he agreed.

When she led Mount into camp, Dezba was ready with her hide saddle. She also had tied together all the rabbit skins Yahzi had scraped clean as a way of keeping herself busy.

"Auntie, you don't need to take all those skins."

"After all that work you did? We can't leave them behind. The fur is so soft." She rubbed a hand over the bundle.

"The skins won't hold us back," Nataalith whispered to Yahzi. "To approach from the east will take time, but we can get there before the sun is overhead." He glanced up. "Or later."

Nataalith helped Yahzi mount. She still felt sore and was grateful they didn't have far to ride. Dezba had secured the hide over Mount and climbed on his back, forgetting her bundle of skins. Nataalith tossed the skins in front of her. She rubbed the top one, exclaiming how soft it was.

Nataalith returned to his horses and smiled at Yahzi. "We're putting our lives in her hands."

Nataalith was sweating when the three of them reached the east entrance to Jemez. Yahzi hoped it was merely the overhead sun. Dezba smiled at the sight of her pueblo, but she had smiled often and at many things along the way. A red cliff setting reminded Yahzi of her own home even if it lacked the canyon's magnificence.

An armed Spaniard and a Jemez guarded the east entry. Nataalith turned to Yahzi who rode by his side. "You and I will say as little as possible. It's up to Dezba."

"May she live up to her warrior name!" Yahzi muttered.

Nataalith smiled his agreement while he wiped sweat from his forehead.

When the three pulled up before the guards, Nataalith greeted the two men in Spanish. Yahzi hoped they could contend with his accent.

The guard flourished his weapon. "Dismount while we question you." The Spaniard sneered at Nataalith's appearance. He studied Yahzi's features, apparently unable to determine if she were Dinee or pueblo. He merely glanced at Dezba, not ordering her to dismount.

Without any questions, he asserted, "No visitors are allowed in Jemez."

Yahzi choked. She thought they'd have at least a chance to explain who they were.

Dezba raised her voice and out rushed a torrent of her native Towa. The Jemez guard got in a few words, but Dezba cut him short in another outburst. The man slouched as if being lectured by his mother-in-law. He would not interrupt again. The Spaniard lowered his weapon, staring at his companion, waiting for the translation.

Dezba sat erect on Mount, delivering her final oration. Her hands gestured emphasis and disdain for being held up from entering her home. Mount whinnied his support for whatever she was saying.

When Dezba stopped, the Jemez guard translated. "She says that she and her niece have had to travel to Santa Clara and beyond to find rabbit skins for her grandbabies. They got terrible rashes from the woolen cloth their parents used to swaddle them. A medicine woman said that rabbit skins would prevent the rash. She kept asking, do we want her grandbabies to suffer? What kind of Christians are we? Don't we believe in turning the other cheek?"

"What does turning the other cheek have to do with it?" the Spaniard asked.

"I don't know," the Jemez said. "I'm just translating."

"What else did she say? She went on forever."

"She kept asking why a Spanish garrison is afraid of two Jemez women, one an old grandmother. The Dinee was on his way home when he saw how tired and hungry they were. He gave them water and food. If he hadn't helped, they'd still be on the trail or maybe dead."

"Perhaps we should let the two women enter, but not the Dinee." The Spaniard licked his lips, obviously not relishing the idea of making a decision.

Dezba broke into another scolding torrent of Towa.

The Jemez translated. "She says something about a good Samaritan. I don't know what that is. How it's her Christian duty to host the Dinee after all he did for her. He won't stay long."

Nataalith slouched, sucked in his belly, limped a step. Yahzi hoped he wouldn't overact.

The Spaniard shrugged, moved close to Nataalith and spoke slowly and distinctly. "You can stay two days in the pueblo. Then you must leave. Do you understand—two days?" He held up two fingers, then pointed at the sun and made a sweeping motion.

Nataalith nodded and repeated haltingly, "two days."

"Don't mount up," the translator warned. "You can't ride horses in the pueblo. Well, I guess your aunt can stay on the burro."

Yahzi walked over to Mount and took his reins. "What's a Samaritan, Auntie?"

"The priest told a lot of Bible stories. I liked the one about the Samaritan. The Samaritan only did what any of us would do, but the Spanish made him a saint for it."

"Santa Samarita," Nataalith muttered. "The name has good sounds."

"But I think the Samaritan was a man," Dezba's forehead wrinkled. "Maybe they didn't make him a saint. Because he belonged to a different tribe." Dezba shook her head. "Many of the priest's stories were confusing."

Yahzi had no idea how they would find any of Dezba's relatives, but she guessed the most difficult part of their entry had been accomplished. The three circled around the central plaza pausing at different doorways into the multi-story pueblo homes. Children paused in their play, two older boys approaching them to pat Mount and to admire Nataalith's horses. Neither answered Dezba's questions. A few women knelt over metates in front of their rooms grinding corn. They pretended to take no notice of the three strangers. Dezba dismounted and the three continued to circle the plaza.

A squat, grizzled man came out one of the doors. His scowl was forbidding. He glared at Nataalith. "No strangers are allowed in the pueblo now." He studied Yahzi's features. "How did you get past the guard?"

"We're bringing our relative home." Nataalith nodded toward Dezba.

"She's here. It's time you left. Navajo aren't welcome in the pueblo because there's a meeting among pueblos. Serious discussion we must keep to ourselves."

"The guards gave me permission to stay two days. My wife and I will leave then. Once we're sure our aunt is settled."

"I'm the governor here," the grizzled man replied. "I decide who stays and for how long."

Dezba started a harangue which exceeded her first one. Yahzi regretted she couldn't understand a word of it, and wondered how Dezba could recall her native tongue so well.

The governor answered Dezba with what sounded like respect, then switched to Spanish. He said he'd allow Nataalith to stay two days, but he must avoid the pueblo's meeting. The commotion Dezba had caused drew two elderly women to the plaza. They must have heard what Dezba said, and they questioned her further when the governor left. Dezba answered in soft tones, at one point her smile spreading wide. The women gestured to Yahzi and Nataalith, beckoning them toward a pueblo room. The two women stood outside a moment, speaking to each other in loud voices.

Their words drew another woman to the door who appeared to be Dezba's age. Yahzi noticed a resemblance between the two.

"Daughter?" the woman said in Spanish to Dezba, then repeated a word in Towa.

"Mother?" A flood of Towa followed. The two drew close to each other and held hands. Dezba's mother led the three into her home.

She stirred a flame from ashes in a small fireplace. "You must be hungry." Her glance took in the three of them. Dezba said they had eaten well in the morning.

"So they feed you well?" The woman's question was an invitation for Dezba to tell where they had been and what they had been doing.

"It's a long story, mother. Before I tell you, let me explain to my niece and her husband what I've been told."

Dezba turned to Nataalith. "I hope you don't mind that I have you married to my niece. They'll more likely accept you. I'll call you nephew from now on."

Dezba took a deep breath. "This woman is my mother's youngest sister. She's the only one of my mother's siblings still living. I was close to her because she watched over me when I was growing up. She was more like a sister to me than a mother, but she never called me anything other than "my daughter.""

"It's so good you've found a home," Yahzi said.

"There's more good news," Dezba beamed. "Dayish lives two doors down. He's shepherding today, but he'll be back tomorrow. I've found both a mother and a husband the same day!"

"Even if you ate well this morning, you must be hungry now."

Dezba's mother filled four bowls with beans flavored with meat. She patted out four large tortillas and spread them on a grill. In her limited Spanish, she urged her guests to eat.

When the four finished, they sat with their backs to the room's walls, enjoying the fragrance of the meal mixed with wood smoke.

"We haven't had corn and beans until recently," Dezba told her mother. "Before that we feasted on rabbits and pack rats." She laughed. "Have you ever eaten a rat?"

"Oh yes," her mother laughed. "I didn't want to but when I was a girl, the boys would hunt them. They'd bring them back and make us roast them, like we were their wives." She shrugged. "Maybe you don't remember. I tried to avoid that game."

"Well, we found a wonderful place to hunt rabbits. It's along a river. We don't know its name. We needed a long rest after we fled that ranch I told you about."

"It was good you found the river empty. The Nuevos Mexicanos are occupying every place in the country. I can't believe they let you alone anywhere on the Jemez River."

"We didn't see another person the whole time we were at the river," Dezba said.

Nataalith cleared his throat. "It was the other river, the one the Spanish call Rio Puerco."

Dezba's mother glanced around. "You never saw another person the whole time you were there? No sign of any grazing?"

"We had it all to ourselves," Yahzi said. "Several moons ago when I rested there I saw no one."

Dezba's mother bit at her lower lip.

"What is it, mother?" Dezba asked.

"Best you not tell anyone else you were at that river. I know why no one was there."

"Is there some kind of danger?" Dezba leaned toward her mother to ask.

"Great danger. But maybe you escaped it."

118

EIGHTEEN

Dezba's mother told Yahzi and Nataalith they could spend the night there. She'd take Dezba to Dayish later in the evening. "It's been so long," Dezba giggled. "What do I do?"

After Dezba and her mother left, so little air stirred in the pueblo room that Nataalith took off his clothes. Yahzi lay down in a dark corner and slipped out of her dress. She slept fitfully and often heard Nataalith fidgeting. Toward morning she enjoyed a sound, but brief, slumber.

When she awoke, she reached for her dress only to find it gone. She wondered if Nataalith intended some joke, then noticed that his shirt and breechcloth were also missing. She sat up scratching her head, hesitating to wake her host who slept in the back room. Just then, the woman entered from outside, carrying her guests' wet clothing.

"I've washed your things. While they dry, you can wear one of my tunics and a skirt. You can pass for Jemez in them. Use them while you're here if you want."

Yahzi slipped into the tunic. It was snug but manageable. The wrap around skirt fit with no problem. "The cotton is so soft," she smiled. "The designs are beautiful." She hesitated to praise the clothing more, or her host would be obliged to give her the outfit. "Have you found something for Dezba? She'll enjoy being back in Jemez clothing."

"She's still sleeping. I washed her things last night. Maybe she can squeeze into the dress I've been saving for a special occasion." Her wide smile matched one of Dezba's. "How special to find a daughter. And without having to carry one inside." When she finally stopped laughing, she said, "As if a woman my age could get pregnant."

Nataalith awoke, sat up, and looked for his clothes. He frowned at Yahzi. She pointed at his wet breechcloth. Before he could reach for it, Dezba's mother said, "My husband's away. You can wear one of his breechcloths until yours dries. I don't think you could get into his shirt though." She took in Nataalith's broad chest as if she were forty years younger.

Nataalith nodded his acceptance.

"You'd have a hard time passing for a pueblo Indian whatever you wore," Dezba's mother said. "You best spend your time here in this room."

"We chose a poor time to arrive," Yahzi said. "And we can't stay long." She hoped they might leave tomorrow or the next day.

"Yes, but an interesting one. The Spanish don't want any outsiders to find out what's going on. Alcalde Mora, from Santa Fe, has called a meeting of Santa Clara and Jemez people. He won't tolerate any Navajo witnesses or other outsiders."

"We can stay until we find out what he's up to." Nataalith said.

"He claims the governor sent him to judge whether or not it was wrong for Santa Clara people to meet with Jemez people. As if those old men had enough courage to plot a revolt." She shook her head in disgust. "This Spaniard summoned the Santa Clara leaders to meet here. Some of them arrived yesterday."

With all the elders summoned, Yahzi gave up hope of a quick departure. She wondered if the Spaniard would drag out the questioning. She asked what the alcalde was like.

"Like all the Spanish. Arrogant. Thinks he knows everything. He'll conduct the meeting like one of their trials, I suppose. I remember watching one when I was young. Everyone talked a lot and said nothing, but they made the alcalde think he learned what happened. Or maybe he just gave up. I was too young to understand how the people fooled the Spanish." She held a hand over her mouth while she laughed.

"So the alcalde never found out what was going on?" Nataalith said.

"He never learned a thing. We were careful after that not to give the Spanish any reason to hold a trial. We were afraid of what they'd do. Maybe whip someone or put them in jail. Spaniards put people in jail for no reason."

"So what happened to cause this trial?" Yahzi asked.

"With the Spanish garrison here, they were bound to notice when something unusual happened." She shrugged. "But it took them a long while. They missed so much at first that the village council became careless. Everyone here knew that powerful Santa Clara medicine people had been invited to help Jemez. I suppose some woman living with a Spaniard told him too much. She'll be exiled if we find her."

"Isn't it possible one of the Nuevo Mexicano soldiers noticed strangers?" Yahzi said.

The old woman shrugged. "I hope that's what happened. I hate to think one of our people betrayed us." She turned to stir the fire, then mixed corn meal. Tortillas soon sizzled, the roast corn smell tantalizing Yahzi's nose.

After they ate, Dezba's mother grilled a few more tortillas for Dezba. She peeled four or five from the grill and wrapped them in a cloth, nodding an invitation for Yahzi to join her.

When the two reached Dayish's door, they heard laughing. Yahzi stood perplexed. Had her aunt become even more confused? Dezba's mother chortled, as if knowing the cause of the laughter. She coughed loudly, waited a few moments and then entered the room. Yahzi followed.

Dezba sat cross legged with a sash around her waist. Dayish was naked, poking Dezba in her ribs. "You're still so ticklish," he said before seeing her mother and Yahzi.

"It's so much like old times," Dezba exclaimed to Yahzi. "I never want to leave."

"You'll never have to," Dezba's mother said. "I think your husband wants to stay. He found a home here even before you returned. He dresses like one of us and speaks our Towa."

Dezba's mother and Yahzi gave the tortillas to the lovers and left. They saw soldiers erecting a tent on the plaza. Two of them carried a desk from the Spanish garrison to the tent. Three others struggled to plant a flag to symbolize Santa Fe authority. The hard ground of the plaza was reluctant to open itself for such a symbol.

"Let's get a head cover for you," Dezba's mother said to Yahzi. "Your hair style shows you're an outsider."

"Will they let women take part?" Yahzi asked.

"No. The Spanish won't question us, and the pueblo men don't expect us to say anything. But if we're careful, we can get close enough to hear what's going on." She led Yahzi to where the women had gathered. "Dayish and my daughter will find us. Dayish is getting good at understanding pueblo ways and Spanish custom."

"I'm glad he's not considered an outsider," Yahzi said.

"There's a Dinee woman married to a Jemez," Dezba's mother explained. "Dayish is close to her husband. He's become as much a part of the pueblo as any outsider has ever been."

"What about when the Santa Clara people speak," Yahzi asked. "Is their language the same as yours?"

Dezba's mother shook her head. "They talk funny. But between Dayish and me, we usually figure it out."

Everyone in the pueblo crowded into the plaza. Young people hung at the back. Children played on the outskirts, ignoring the adults but becoming part of the gathering.

A soldier raised a horn and made noise that hurt Yahzi's ears. Alcalde Mora left the garrison to take a seat behind the desk. Five elders stood at the front of the crowd. Yahzi guessed they were the leading men from Santa Clara. Twenty-five or thirty elders represented Jemez.

The alcalde rose from behind his desk. "You have been summoned here today because it is wrong to make plans behind the back of officials and your own governors. Do you not remember in the past how we uncovered your plans to join the Navajo? Do you want to suffer more whippings?

"Keep this in mind as you testify today. Prove your loyalty to us. Prove you are good citizens, faithful to the governor in Santa Fe who sent me here to find the truth."

There was considerable stirring in the crowd as a young man translated the alcalde's Spanish to Towa. More stirring among the elders followed while they digested the speech. Amid the murmuring, Dayish and Dezba joined her mother and Yahzi.

"Is that Spaniard with the loud voice another friend of Diego's?" Dezba asked Yahzi.

"I don't think so, but he's probably as cruel."

"He's certainly no friend of the pueblos," Dayish said.

"Send over the leading man from Santa Clara," the alcalde called out.

A stooped, one eyed man stepped toward the desk. He took his time, looking over the assembled soldiers. At the desk, he bowed to the alcalde, but from his demeanor Yahzi thought he'd never consider himself inferior to anyone.

"Why were you visiting Jemez?" the alcalde boomed. "What other pueblos have you been visiting?"

"I came to Jemez because I was invited. The Navajos offered us a mountain of corn if we would join them. The pueblos don't have enough food. We had to consider their offer to keep our children from starving. The Spanish took so much of our food, we went hungry."

"Did those Navajos who came here four or five moons ago invite you to join them? The ones who claimed to be peace envoys." The alcalde's face reddened as if he might be uncovering a plot he hadn't considered.

"Those Navajos came this spring," the one eyed man said. "They never made any offer to us. They wanted peace. I'm talking about that time when I was young. When I felt hunger year after year."

The alcalde rose from his chair, sweat covering his brow. "We are talking about this summer. What did you do when you came to visit only a few moons ago?"

While the one-eyed man thought through his reply, Dayish whispered to Yahzi and Dezba. "Before he's finished, the alcalde will be sweating a lot more than he is now."

"We talked about the Commandments," the elder began. "After the Jemez fed us, we discussed how Christians always share. We know you will want to share your food with us. Your garrison has more than you need. The priests tell us to watch your soldiers and follow their example. So we are waiting for them—for them to feast us with the bread and fish."

"You are not answering my question," Mora fumed. "Tell me what transpired at the meeting—when you came to Jemez illegally." Yahzi smiled at how often the alcalde wiped his brow as he spoke.

The elder asked for a further translation of "transpired" and then went into his understanding of what was meant by "trespass" in the Lord's prayer. It was more than Mora could take. He dismissed the man and asked if there were a more important elder. The Santa Clara elders conferred among themselves, one stepped forward and said the man who could answer Mora's questions would arrive tomorrow. Before Mora could say anything, the Santa Clara men dispersed to the homes of their Jemez hosts. Mora was left fuming.

Yahzi bit at her lip. She and Nataalith couldn't leave the pueblo before finding out what was going on.

The next day the elders gathered again. When the alcalde asked for the newly arrived Santa Clara leader, a man stepped forward who was as thin as anyone Yahzi had ever seen. Dayish whispered that his nick-name was Reed.

When asked why he attended the recent meeting with the Jemez, Reed touched on how they discussed the Commandments, but in his version he raised the issue that the most important commandment was to love one another. Had not Saint Jesus himself given this Commandment?

Mora tugged at his beard as if to gain patience from self-inflicted pain. "It is good that you discuss the priests' lessons among yourselves. But I don't believe you travel from pueblo to pueblo only to talk about the sacred scriptures. What other matters did you discuss? If you lie to me, you'll be disobeying the Commandments. Didn't you talk politics?"

The Santa Clara elders conferred among themselves. One stepped forward and asked for the meaning of politics. Mora struggled with a definition. Dayish laughed at his answer, clarified it for Dezba. "He wanted to equate politics with talk of rebellion. Then he realized everyone would deny that, so he gave examples of politics that cover everything."

Reed admitted that in their meeting they had discussed many things. He said he was sorry that he didn't know about politics at the time. One example of politics, he guessed, was how best to distribute irrigation water. After a diatribe about how Nuevo Mexicano farmers were taking Santa Clara water, and most likely Jemez water—though he couldn't speak for the Jemez—he described in detail the daily responsibility for cleaning and maintaining the ditches. He ended by quoting the Commandment not to steal.

When he finished, some of the soldiers wandered back to their garrison. A vein on Mora's forehead looked ready to burst. Dayish said to Yahzi, "Mora probably doesn't know the first thing about irrigation. Certainly his life doesn't depend on it the way ours does."

"Have you told the priest and your governor about this theft? If that's what it is." Mora wiped his brow again.

"We have gone to the governor many times. He says he told the Nuevos Mexicanos to stop taking our water. The priest says we should file a legal complaint to the governor in Santa Fe."

"You should be able to handle the matter without a lawsuit," Mora shouted his exasperation. "The governor is too busy to listen to every complaint about water from you people."

Reed countered with an assertion that he knew the governor wanted always to do what was right. Especially for the pueblo people. Perhaps it was the alcalde who didn't care about them.

Mora's shoulders sagged. He stared at Reed, his mouth working but not speaking.

"Looks like Mora may be through for the day," Dayish laughed.

The alcalde found his voice. "The governor has always wanted to do what is right for the pueblos. That is why it is so important that you stay in your pueblos. So the governor can watch over you. Do not gather to talk about going to the Navajo when they offer you a mountain where you can grow corn."

The elders murmured among themselves giving an appearance that they were voicing appreciation to the governor for watching over their lives. Four of them spoke at length to conclude the day's discussion.

The next morning, the meeting began with Mora pointing at one of the group who looked to be the youngest of the Santa Clara elders. The man glanced at the others as if for their approval. Mora commanded him again to approach the desk.

"When you were here for the meeting, what false idols did you see?"

"What are 'idols'?" the man hesitated after the translation.

Dayish whispered. "Mora's surprised him. The man is doing a good job stalling, but the elders may not have prepared him for idols. Years ago the priests talked of idols all the time when they were destroying the kachina masks, but now the few remaining ones have all been well hidden, I guess. My friend won't tell me about them."

Mora shouted out what he meant by idols, but he did little to clarify their meaning.

The man stammered. "We talked a little about them. How they were like witchcraft."

The word "witchcraft" sparked a buzzing among the remaining soldiers as well as the pueblo throng. The young man seemed to wilt while Mora's face burst into an even deeper shade of red.

"The priests have always told you witchcraft is evil," the Alcalde exploded. "For years you have denied anyone in the pueblos knows anything about witches. Are you telling me that you talked about witchcraft? The men of two pueblos? How can we ever civilize you people if you practice witchcraft?"

The Indian looked at the other elders for help. They appeared stymied, but the one-eyed elder made some hand gestures that could have passed for waving off gnats.

"There was someone at the meeting who knew Navajos practiced witchcraft," the young man replied. "That's what we discussed. How we should teach the Navajos that witchcraft is evil. Maybe the Utes, too."

The testimony seemed to satisfy Mora. At least, his vein ceased to throb so obviously.

"People wanted to know if a Navajo witch could keep people out of other peoples' land."

Mora's mouth dropped open, and the vein throbbed once more.

NINETEEN

Mora stepped from behind his desk. Dayish whispered, "The young elder may be dragged aside and questioned in secrecy. Maybe tortured. Let's hope he regains his wits."

Before Mora could summon a soldier to accompany him, a rawhide ball zoomed between the elders and Mora. Six boys came bounding after it, followed by ten or twelve dogs. The boys seemed in a contest to out yell the dogs's barking.

In the hubbub the young elder melted into the group of elders. By the time the boys and dogs had returned to the periphery, the young elder had time to be advised on tactics.

Mora must have seen the futility of questioning the man in privacy. He made a last public attempt. "These witches that you met with. What advice did they give you?"

"I never met any witches. We just heard that the Navajo, or maybe the Ute, know about witchcraft. How to use it against their enemies."

"Do you know what happens to witches when the governor finds out about them?"

"I guess he kills them. Isn't that what happened to those Navajos who claimed to be peace envoys? After you found out they were witches, you killed them."

The noise from the crowd reached pandemonium strength. Mora's hand went to his sword. He looked from the crowd to his soldiers. Four of them were running back to their fort. Dayish guessed they'd bring guns which wouldn't help the temper of the crowd.

Yahzi hoped Nataalith wouldn't be drawn to the plaza because of the tumult. She sensed that the mood of the crowd was changing. The presence of a Dinee could stir trouble. She studied the multitude but found no trace of Nataalith. She breathed a little easier.

"Maybe you and I ought to admit we're Navajos. See if Mora would kill us as witches." Yahzi frowned at Dayish's attempted humor.

"The Spanish seem so afraid of witches, they must believe in their power," Yahzi said. "A Spaniard I knew once told me that they used to have witch trials. Something they called the Inquisition. He claimed in modern times they no longer believe witchcraft is possible. But I wonder if a few don't still believe."

"They're not all fools, no matter how easily they let the puebloans mislead them," Dayish said. "They must realize there were witches in the past, there are witches now, and there always will be witches."

Dayish's matter-of-fact acceptance of witches reminded Yahzi of a conversation she overhead as a girl. Two uncles were discussing their loss of sheep. They argued bitterly about the witch that might have caused their loss, but it was clear neither of them doubted for a moment that a witch had caused their misfortune.

Her recollection was interrupted by the return of soldiers with weapons. Each carried two muskets and armed others of the troop. Mora signaled them to stay in place while he walked toward the puebloans.

"It is getting late," he told them. "The day has been hot. Tomorrow we'll rest since it's Sunday. A bugle call will summon you on Monday. Go back to your homes. Pray tomorrow for everyone to tell the truth on Monday. Remember what the priests said about hell's fire if you lie."

The youth along the edges were the first to disperse. They urged the children to return home. Yahzi guessed they were so excited over the talk of witchcraft they'd be slow to break up, but women were leaving to prepare an evening meal. Men moved away from the plaza, one eye on the Spanish, the other on their comrades.

Dezba and Dayish joined Yahzi and Nataalith at Dezba's home for dinner. Dezba's mother grinned. "My husband will regret missing the excitement. When he comes back from his trading, he always has stories about what's happening in the other pueblos. He'll have nothing to match what I can tell." She chuckled at length.

On Sunday, Dezba and her mother repeated all the ways in which the Santa Clara elders had evaded Mora's questions. Yahzi couldn't tell if they laughed more over the references to Christianity, or to how they stood each other's answers on end to sow confusion. They recalled and talked about everything that had transpired, Yahzi noticed, except witchcraft.

Yahzi sympathized with Nataalith about his banishment from the proceedings, but when the horn blasted across the pueblo on Monday, she teased him that if they needed a witch, she'd drag him into the plaza. He retorted that if she did, he'd use his powers to make all her hair fall out and boils to cover her face. She joked that she'd noticed her hair was falling out. Nataalith blanched before he laughed —a forced laugh.

At one end of the plaza, Mora was seated at his desk, his face fixed in a scowl. His men all carried arms.

"On Saturday," he began, "you told me many things about why you met without permission. I know you follow the ways of Christianity and discuss scriptures. You don't need to talk about such things this week."

Yahzi gasped, wondering if Mora intended to pursue the matter through the coming week. When would they ever leave Jemez?

The elders voiced their understanding.

"We'll begin today with the Jemez elders," Mora said. "Let the chief of your council begin."

The elders stood in front of the crowd, mumbling among themselves. Finally two of them stepped forward.

The tallest one spoke in a humble way. "We have no 'chief' your highness. So we don't know which of us should speak first."

"I am not 'your highness.' I am an alcalde, representing the governor." A drop of sweat rolled from Mora's brow. "Just select an important elder."

Both men stepped back and the elders conferred further. Yahzi noticed the soldiers tugging at their collars, fidgeting with their belts. Mora screwed up his face the way Diego did when he was impatient. Finally, an elder stepped forward supporting himself with a cane.

"You wish to question me, 'your grace'?" he said.

"You don't need to address me as 'your grace'." Mora raised his voice. "Tell me in your own words what happened when the Santa Clara elders came to visit Jemez?"

"You mean after we talked about how important it is to follow the Commandments?"

"Yes, yes, after discussing the Commandments." Mora choked with impatience.

Yahzi watched three Jemez elders grin.

"As I recall," the man shifted his weight on the cane, "we had heard that the Mexicanos had won a battle with the Spanish, and the Spanish all went back to Spain. But if that was true, why do so many Spanish remain along the Rio Grande? We decided that the rumor was not true." He paused, as if expecting a reply.

Mora obviously was considering what to answer. Finally, he said. "It is true that Mexico has won Independence from Spain. But it will do little to change things here in Nuevo Mexico. The new government will still protect the pueblo people. You have nothing to worry about."

The elder nodded. "Did the Mexicans kill the king of Spain? That was one thing we discussed. Does Independence mean there is no longer a Spanish tribe?"

Mora tugged at his beard, scratched his cheek. "The Spanish king still rules Spain. The Spanish tribe is one of the strongest in the world. But Spanish rule has ended in Mexico. The Mexican people will govern themselves. You need not worry."

"How will the Mexican people know who we are? Will they send their own governor to Santa Fe?"

"For now, the governor in Santa Fe represents the Mexican people. Obey his commands." Mora seemed to give second thought to what he had said. "And the commands of the Catholic Church. Listen to your priests and do what they tell you."

The man hobbled closer to Mora, then leaned on his cane. "Many priests order us to repair the churches our fathers built. Why don't the Nuevos Mexicanos help us? We've done our share. Isn't it the Christian way for everyone to share?"

"Listen to the priests," Mora raised his voice. "They'll explain how the Nuevos Mexicanos tithe to support the churches. How they give pesos. You do not have pesos to give."

A Jemez elder stepped forward. "A priest told us we should tithe. If we tithe, do we have to labor for no pay?"

"Discuss that with the priest." Mora shouted, tugging at his collar.

"If we rebuild the church, are we excused from the tithe?" the elder persisted.

"Ask the priest," Mora's face turned livid.

"I almost feel sorry for him," Dayish whispered to Yahzi. She covered her smile with a hand. "He won't survive if they go back to talking about the Commandments."

"We hesitate to ask the bad priests anything. They tell us to do wrong."

Mora's forehead furrowed. He paused, scratching his head.

"He's in a difficult spot," Dayish said. "He'll want to avoid discussing priestly behavior. On the other hand, the governor is often at odds with the priests. He could use priestly wrong-doing to undercut the power of the Church."

"I never knew the Church had such power," Yahzi said.

"Not over Dinee," Dayish said. "But priests settled in the pueblo villages, and forced the puebloans to support them. They were so cruel that the pueblos revolted. When the Spanish reconquered the pueblos, the governor and priests were kinder. At least, that's what my Jemez brother tells me."

"Things sound worse for the pueblos than the Dinee," Yahzi said. "The Spanish enslaved some of us, but at least we don't have priests living with us." Yahzi shook her head in disgust. "I think white men can't help but order other people around."

Mora stopped fidgeting and stared at the elder who had accused priests of wrong-doing. "What is the name of this priest and what did he tell you to do?"

"We went to that priest who left. I can't remember his name. We told him about the Nuevos Mexicanos who trespass on our land. That priest said they paid their tithes. It wouldn't hurt if their sheep ate a little grass and drank the water. What could it hurt if they just drank water?"

The elder with the cane started pounding it on the ground to call attention to himself. "That Nuevo Mexicano kept his cattle and sheep there all the time. We told the priest many times that he was using all the grass. There was no grass left for us. Do you think it did any good? The Nuevos Mexicanos all around us are taking our grass.

Who will stop it?" The elder was so angry he wavered on his feet, jabbing here and there with his cane. An elderly woman rushed to his side to support him.

"If Mora were smarter, he might find out why the Santa Clara elders were called to Jemez," Dayish whispered to Yahzi.

"You mean they came to help out in the land dispute?"

"That's right, but the elders won't want Mora to find that out."

"More Mexicans are coming to Nuevo Mexico every day," Mora said. "We must find room for their herds so the country will prosper. You can learn from them, but they don't have a right to your land. I'll report your concern to the governor." He approached the elders, a smile on his face. He pointed to an elder who stood at the rear. "I want you to tell me what went on at the meeting."

Dayish guffawed. "He's picked my Jemez brother. The shrewdest man I've ever met. I can't wait to hear his version."

"We worry about our land. The governor ignores us. That's why we met."

"I see," Mora said. "But exactly what did you discuss?"

"We heard that scouts from the American tribe came to Santa Fe. They brought trade goods that no one has ever seen. It is said, they have more wealth than the Spanish king."

"A few traders from the United States arrived in Santa Fe not long ago." Mora's eyes blinked rapidly. "They are not as powerful as the Spanish king. Nor the new government in Mexico. They may never again come to Santa Fe."

"But we have not seen any wealth from the Mexican government. We have heard the Americans are the wealthiest tribe anywhere. They may want to buy our land. What happens when our children are crying from hunger because we have sold all our land? It's said the Americans are more generous than the Nuevos Mexicanos so we'll have to listen to them." Dayish's friend had worked himself into such a feverish pitch that tears ran down his cheeks.

Mora seemed more uncertain of himself than ever. "You must not let a few American traders upset you so! The Americans are foreigners. They can never own Mexican land. Or your land. You can trade with them, but you must never sell them your land." Mora was shouting. "They'll never be more than visitors here."

"You'll protect our land, then?" Dayish's friend said.

"Yes, yes, that's why we're here."

"Then you'll make sure the Nuevo Mexicano ranchers keep their sheep and cattle away from our river?"

The trap was set. Mora stepped into it. "I'll report your concerns to the governor. I'll tell him you met to protect your land. But in the future you must get permission when you gather in other pueblos."

Dayish held his sides laughing, half controlling his guffaws. He explained to Yahzi that his friend had tricked the alcalde into pleading their case with the governor while he missed the fact that Jemez had invited Santa Clara witches to protect their land from the Nuevos Mexicanos.

"How do the witches protect the land?" Yahzi asked.

"They know curses and songs that poison the river water. If any big animals, like cows or sheep, drink there, their offspring will suffer stillbirth and deformities. The Nuevo Mexicano ranchers have all heard about the curse. They won't talk about it, but they discovered the hard way how well the witchcraft works."

Yahzi's stomach churned. Bile flooded her mouth. "And I found out the hard way, too," she thought.

TWENTY

That night when Yahzi told Nataalith about the witches' curse, he took her hands in his. "So that's why you lost your child," he said. "I told you to go to that stretch of river because it's deserted." He sighed. "It was my fault."

His concern made Yahzi feel better. "We didn't know. It's nobody's fault."

"You'll have another child," Nataalith said. "After you return home. I'm sure."

We could start home today, Yahzi thought, at least get to Nataalith's hogan and his brother-in-law's. The next morning Yahzi suggested leaving. She reminded Nataalith of the warning by the Jemez governor to be gone in two days although his warning hadn't meant much to Dezba's mother. She'd told them she'd host the two of them as long as they wanted to stay. Nataalith seemed interested in the invitation and commented on how he'd like to get to know Dayish and his friend better.

Yahzi liked being with her aunt. Dezba could talk of nothing but Dayish. She was happier than Yahzi had ever seen her, and Yahzi didn't want to intrude.

One morning Dezba and Dayish appeared at the morning meal with a basketful of tortillas. While the five of them ate, they talked of Mora's inquiry. Soon they were laughing so much they could no longer eat. Dezba's mother was so proud of how the Jemez leaders had misled the alcalde that she repeated their antics four or five times. Dayish couldn't refrain from recalling how his friend had misled Mora, describing his tactics innumerable ways.

When they finished with their amusement, Nataalith suggested it was time that he and Yahzi leave.

Dezba bit at her lip. "I knew you'd go, niece. But it's hard to accept."

Dezba's mother packed corn meal into corn husk packets and sliced dried meat for them. "I wish I had more food for you, but we're just beginning to harvest."

"We understand," Nataalith assured her. "I have to return my mares to a kinsmen. His hogan is less than two days north. His wives always have mutton. Maybe too much mutton. They're pretty fat." His guffaw infected Dayish, but Dezba and her mother only smiled. Yahzi didn't even grin because she was wondering if she'd ever get to Canyon de Chelly.

"I'll get my horses," Nataalith said. Dayish left with him.

"I'd like to see Mount one last time," Yahzi said to Dezba.

"I'll show you where he is," Dezba said. The two women strolled to the edge of the pueblo, a dry stream bed with struggling grass along its edge. They didn't have to go far to find a hobbled Mount, grazing contentedly.

Yahzi cuddled his muzzle, scratched his forehead, and whispered for him to care for Dezba. Mount nodded he'd watch over her. Yahzi smiled as she went back to the pueblo. She'd miss the burro but was glad he'd be in the care of Dezba and Dayish who'd provide a better home for him than Diego ever did.

She and Dezba arrived back at the pueblo at the same time as Nataalith. He packed the food and a few things on the third horse and saddled the other two.

"If we make good time this afternoon, we can reach my clan brother's hogan tomorrow. Then his wives can cook for us."

Yahzi took a deep breath when Nataalith kneed his horse to leave. She followed him without looking back, hating to leave Dezba but looking forward to returning home.

Nataalith kept a steady pace until dusk. He and Yahzi camped at a rock outcropping where a few holes in the stone slabs held standing water. They rationed what they drank as well as what they gave the horses. After a light meal of corn mush, the two found a sandy patch where they could sleep. In moments, Nataalith was snoring lightly. Yahzi fidgeted, thinking about her brother and sisters.

The next day they finished the corn meal and half the dried meat before mounting. Nataalith looked at the sun. "We won't have much time to rest, but we should make it to my clan brother's before they've eaten everything."

The two seldom spoke the rest of the day except when they walked their horses. Yahzi hadn't known any Mud clan members before she was enslaved and asked about the clan. Nataalith told her of Mud's origin and its founding grandmothers. He described where his clan brothers settled after marriage. Because most had stayed in the eastern part of Dinehtah, Nataalith seldom had trouble finding a brother to stay with when he traveled.

When Yahzi told him of Bitter Water origins and founders, Nataalith's knowledge of the clan almost matched hers. Two of his brothers had married Bitter Water women and both talked with pride about notable matrons and their distinguished brothers.

"Bitter Water women must be fertile," Nataalith said. "That's why the clan survives so well."

"I thought everyone knew we Bitter Water women were the most fertile," Yahzi said. "That Santa Clara witch may have hurt my offspring, but their curse can't last." Or can it? she asked herself.

Nataalith might have noticed the doubt in her assertion that the curse would be short-lived. "A Dinee medicine man can end any pueblo curse. I'm sure you'll have a child." He grinned. "Or two or three."

"We Bitter Water women are fertile, but we can't do much when we get too old." Yahzi intended to joke, but it fell flat.

"You don't look old," Nataalith said. "Don't speak of it again." He kicked his horse into a run on a stretch of hard-packed sand.

They didn't run the horses long, but the pace exhilarated Yahzi. When they slowed to a walk, she asked, "Have you raced your mares often?"

"One of the horses I left with Hosteen—my clan brother who owns these horses—is fast. His horses look to be good brood mares. You'll see for yourself soon."

It wasn't long until they rode up a gradual incline. At the top, Nataalith halted the horses. Four or five hogans lay in a wide valley below. Two young girls shepherded a flock on the edge of a stream. A corral full of horses caught Yahzi's eye. Five or six of them neighed a greeting to the three mares Nataalith had borrowed.

He slapped the flank of his horse, and Yahzi kicked hers. They trotted up to the nearest hogan. A man about Nataalith's age came out to greet them. He'd sprouted a thick mustache, unusual for a Dinee.

"My brother is in time to eat. I guess he has one of the best noses in the country when it comes to smelling mutton stew."

"It's the best mutton stew in the country." Nataalith got off his horse and held the reins of Yahzi's horse as she dismounted. He said to Yahzi, but for their host's benefit, "Hosteen knows how to find wives who cook. He gives extra horses to their brothers when he marries."

"I see you found the woman," Hosteen said. "Did you travel far?"

"Only to the Rio Puerco. Afterwards, we stayed in Jemez to watch the pueblo people make fools of the Spanish."

Hosteen seemed to know that Nataalith would tell the full story when he had a larger audience.

"Your horses eat like you do," Hosteen said. "I'll be glad to exchange them for mine."

"Yooee," Nataalith blew between his teeth. "There's a problem. I met this woman at a part of the river which is deserted. It's Jemez land, but a Nuevo Mexicano poached on it. Santa Clara witches cursed the land to drive him out. Animals that drink the water give still birth. Your horses may be cursed."

Hosteen fingered his mustache at length. "I've never held an Enemyway for a horse." He and Nataalith burst out laughing. Yahzi joined in, not sure of the joke.

Hosteen looked at Yahzi, shaking his head. "Did you drink the water?"

"For half a moon or more," Yahzi said.

"Yooee," Hosteen whistled through his teeth. "We'll decide what to do about the horses later. Now we have to think what to do for you."

Hosteen led the way to the corral where they unsaddled the horses and led them through the gate. Nataalith whistled and three horses separated from the others to gather around him.

"You've fed them well," Nataalith said.

Yahzi looked over the herd. A red stallion and a sturdy paint caught her eye. She admired both for her host's benefit.

Hosteen chuckled. "You found a woman with an eye for horses. She may know more about them than you do."

"Maybe I should have raced her here. We walked your mares most of the way."

"You're in time to see a race you won't forget in a long while," Hosteen said. "People are coming from all over. A lot of my kin have already arrived. You'll be crowded tonight."

"You racing another clan?" Nataalith asked.

"More important than that," Hosteen said. "A Nuevo Mexicano is grazing sheep on Dinee land. Claims to have paid some 'chief' for it. I've challenged him to a race. If I make him uncomfortable enough, maybe he'll leave. I can't run him off if I win, but my kinsmen and I hope to make him uncomfortable."

"Yooee," Nataalith said. "What if he wins?"

"No horse is faster than the red—unless it's the paint. If the paint is feeling ornery enough, nothing can come close to her."

"Have you talked the Nuevo Mexicano into betting?" Nataalith said. "If he loses, he has to leave?"

"I tried, but he's not like the Dinee. My kinfolk will bet everything they have on the red or the paint, but the foreigner wouldn't bet anything except part of his flock. I'll put up horses against his sheep. He'd like to build a horse herd, but he's tight-fisted when it comes to betting."

"Maybe he'll get the fever when he's surrounded by Dinee. Lose so many sheep he'll have to go back to Mexico," Nataalith said.

"He claims he doesn't have anywhere else to go."

"Why don't they all go back to Mexico?" Yahzi's tone carried such bitterness that Hosteen stared at her for a moment.

"Well, I'm going to enjoy however many of his sheep I can win first," Hosteen laughed. "Although I'm sure he'll bet his skinniest ewes."

The next morning Yahzi and Nataalith scrambled from a small hogan that had held far more people than its builders intended. Hosteen's wives and other women heated yesterday's stew and soon were feeding the multitude. Yahzi and Nataalith gulped their servings and then looked for Hosteen.

They found him in the corral, running the red and then the paint, talking to them, judging their reactions.

"How's the paint feeling?" Yahzi asked. "She looks to be in a racing mood."

"The woman knows horses," Hosteen said to Nataalith. "The paint is feeling ornery."

The two men joked about horse races they had seen in the past and how losers were put to shame. But Nataalith agreed with Hosteen that the Spanish—or now the Nuevos Mexicanos as they called themselves—could not be shamed. Strange people that they were.

When the paint picked up her ears and stared east, Yahzi turned to see what the horse had sensed. Riding down the ridge were three Nuevos Mexicanos. The leader sat bolt upright, his black pants tight on his thighs, the seams lined with silver buttons. His shirt had smaller matching buttons. His sombrero was decorated, too, though it had seen better days. Yahzi guessed the two who rode behind him were ranch hands, dressed in frayed skins she couldn't identify.

Hosteen drew a sharp breath. His eyes fixed on the black stallion led by the Nuevo Mexicano rancher. A patch of white blazed its broad forehead. Yahzi had never seen such a large horse. Its tail erect, the animal pranced more than it walked. It had the demeanor of a Spaniard who claimed royal blood.

Hosteen shook his head. "I've never seen that black stallion before. He was riding that nag he's on now. I thought that's the horse he'd race."

"Your paint's only half his size," Nataalith said. "Her legs will have to move twice as fast."

"As long as she stays ornery," Hosteen said. "You bet on her. The race course is over rough country."

"Maybe the black will step in a gopher hole," Nataalith said.

"Look at him prance. There's no way he can hold up in the rocks and brush. Probably break a leg in an arroyo." Hosteen never took his eyes off the Nuevo Mexicano's horse while he spoke.

Yahzi heard doubt in Hosteen's words.

TWENTY ONE

When the Spaniard rode up to Hosteen, the Dinee said in his halting Spanish, "You didn't bring your sheep? I've invited many people for mutton stew. Where will I get ewes to feed all of them?"

"Señor Martinez has no need to bring sheep. He's here to take your horses home." The youngest rider turned up his nose.

Martinez raised his hand to silence the youth. "My man does not know your ways, Hosteen. He did not realize you were joking."

Hosteen smiled, held the reins of Martinez' horse while the Nuevo Mexicano dismounted. "Look over my horses, señor. Perhaps you'll want to bet all your sheep against all my horses. With my herd you could quit raising sheep. They're always getting sick, or coyotes are killing their lambs. Horses are so much easier. So much more beautiful. Your wealth shows in your horses."

Martinez couldn't take his eyes off Hosteen's herd. He studied each animal as if memorizing its features. Yahzi felt certain he would succumb to the gambler's addiction, felt a twinge of fear that Hosteen might lose his horses.

"What do you say?" Hosteen asked. "All my horses against all your sheep."

"We don't have to decide right now, do we?"

"No, no. Let's wait. My friends will be racing today. My wives are preparing a special meal for you tonight. We'll race tomorrow on full stomachs. You'll be so heavy your horse won't be able to carry you." Hosteen laughed. "I can wait until tomorrow for your sheep."

"That's good of you, my friend. I'm glad to have this chance to know you better. I can use today to look over the race course. Will your friends race the same course as we will tomorrow?"

"You can never tell where Dinee will race," Hosteen said. "Some may use our course and we can watch, but we'll go over it ourselves so you'll face no surprises."

As the men talked of preparations for the race, Yahzi felt excluded and went to join the women. Hosteen's wives were curious about her, staring at the skirt and blouse that Dezba's mother had given her.

When Yahzi explained in perfect Dinee how she came to be dressed as a Jemez, the women asked about her clan affiliations, then let her decide what more to tell.

Yahzi related her capture at Massacre Cave. The women were astounded to meet an eye witness to the carnage. All had heard of the slaughter, and the renaming of the place as Canyon del Muerto. They were fascinated with her life as a slave. Yahzi continued her story as they worked, noticing that the women kept staring at her drab pueblo clothes. She longed for a typical ankle length skirt or two and a bright blouse.

Hosteen had tied a cow to a corral pole. One of Hosteen's wives called to a son to bring a gun. She led the animal to a tripod that had been erected the night before and waited. The women joked about how long it had been since they'd tasted beef. A few claimed they had forgotten how to butcher a cow so they could only watch.

While they waited, four or five more women joined the work party. Hosteen's wives didn't seem to mind the crowd since everyone was caught up in joking about the coming feast. In no time, Yahzi felt included in the group.

When a young man came out of a hogan carrying a musket, the joking and gossip stopped. The two wives each grabbed a cow's horn to hold its head steady. The young man shot the beast between the eyes. He helped the women hoist the cow to the tripod. Once they had its hind legs tied to the top of the three poles, a woman slit its throat while another held a battered coffee pot under its neck to collect the blood. When the pot ran over, another women substituted a clay jar.

Two or three women sharpened knives while waiting for the cow to be bled. They took turns skinning the animal. One motioned to Yahzi that she could help peel back the skin. Yahzi tripped on a woman's foot admidst jokes about the anticipation of beef making her dizzy. She answered that it was the thought of raw liver that sent her head spinning.

One of Hosteen's wives said Yahzi could have part of the tongue, too, if she'd help cut it out. A woman handed Yahzi a sharpened knife. When Yahzi hesitated, the wife poised her finger over where to cut. The tongue's muscle proved tougher than Yahzi had imagined. She stabbed and sliced until it was loosened. When she stepped back to straighten her back, another woman took her place to cut off the head. The woman turned to Yahzi and pointed to the brains.

"We use every part of a cow," she said. "Dinee never waste any of it."

Yahzi felt revulsion and held a hand to her mouth. The grayish pulp reminded her of the brains of the shepherd she had killed. A few woman laughed at her reaction, but one of Hosteen's wives put a knife in Yahzi's hand and directed her efforts to remove the last of the tissue. By this time Yahzi had recovered her composure, loosened the brain from its case, and lifted it onto a basket tray that a woman held for her.

The women stood back for awhile joking about each other's skills with a knife, soon making a transition to alleged skills in sexual encounters. Yahzi flushed at the jokes until recognizing Diego had influenced her more than she realized. She resolved to put Spanish ways aside.

Women who hadn't yet helped slit the cow's belly open to expose the entrails. They removed the delicacies first. The heart and the liver went into one clay bowl, the kidneys into another. A woman took the stomachs, walked downwind a few paces, and shook out the half-digested grasses. Another woman smiled her delight at the lungs and the esophagus. Two other women pressed out the contents of the intestines and cut the small intestine into pieces the length of a hand.

Before Yahzi could help more, the forequarters of the carcass were gone. The rest followed until only a rope hung from the tripod.

Yahzi turned to Hosteen's hogan, her nose caught by the wood smoke from three cook fires. At a fire pit, young men had laid a large fire and other men were bringing in logs they had chopped.

Most of the beef would be roasted. At the other fires she saw large clay pots boiling for the delicacies.

Nearer the hogan four or five women were stirring cornmeal into the blood. One of Hosteen's wives came up behind Yahzi and touched her arm. She explained, "I don't know what the Spanish do with the blood. We pour it into lengths of the intestines tied at the ends, and boil them a long time. They keep for moons. Good for our warriors and hunters when they travel."

Yahzi realized rations Nataalith had shared with her and Dezba had been these blood lengths. The taste was so much like beef that it passed for dried meat.

She doubted she could do more with so many women lending a hand, so when she heard shouting down in the valley, she headed there.

Nataalith and Hosteen, with their Spanish guests, stood on a rise overlooking a dust cloud. When the air settled, ten or so Dinee men were lining up their horses, but everyone else was staring into the distance. Hosteen pointed with an arm, Martinez shielded his eyes to look, and the Nuevo Mexicano youth exclaimed something Yahzi failed to understand.

She approached Nataalith's side. He said, "You're just in time to see the finish of the first race. I didn't think they'd ever start, everyone was so busy betting."

Hosteen added, "Young men are racing horses, many for the first time. No one knows what they're betting on. They just can't keep from betting." He turned to Martinez and spoke for his benefit. "A lot of men will go home rich today!"

"As many will go home poor!" Martinez replied.

Nataalith and Yahzi laughed. Hosteen shook his head but didn't conceal his grin. He tried again. "Horses don't eat every blade of grass and don't make supper for wolves."

"But they are ideal for horse thieves," Martinez said.

The Nuevos Mexicanos and Dinee laughed together.

Their laughter stopped as a dust cloud erupted on the horizon. Eight horses led the pack. Two or three horses were hidden in the dust. Shouting erupted among the spectators.

As the horses grew close, Yahzi saw a roan leading the pack, followed by a paint and two spotted horses. The bareback rider on the paint was a boy, but from the way he rode he appeared to be part of the horse. She regretted missing the start of the race. She'd have bet on the boy.

He gained on the roan, its rider glancing back, then whipping his horse. The boy leaned close to the paint's neck. Yahzi imagined him whispering encouragement in his horse's ear. The boy gained on the roan. If the race had been another hundred yards he might have won, but the roan crossed the finish line first amidst a crowd of cheering backers. When the roan reared and whinnied defiance, Yahzi saw it was a stallion. The boy reined in the paint alongside the roan, his horse a mere half the size of the roan.

The crowd broke away from the riders to settle bets. Men scurried around, looking for those who had wagered with them. The Nuevos Mexicanos must have wagered also. They went into the crowd looking for Dinee. The hubbub matched the cheering at the finish line.

While Nataalith and Hosteen exchanged opinions on the horses, a Dinee elder walked up behind them. He favored his right leg and stood upright with difficulty. He ran a finger over a gray mustache before plucking a nasal hair. When he was close enough to Hosteen to breathe on him, Hosteen jumped.

"My father," he said. "I was afraid you weren't coming."

"I don't have to see every horse race, but I wouldn't miss one of yours." He sneezed. "I might even bet on your horse. You gonna run that paint I gave you?"

"I won that paint from you. You made that foolish bet, remember?"

"I remember what a great horse you got." He scratched his head. "Well, maybe I lost a bet with you." The two chuckled. "So. What race is it that I can see?" the old man asked.

"It'll be the last one today but the best. The men are racing horses that everyone's seen run. They all have an opinion about who has the fastest horse," Hosteen said.

"I suppose they'll be forever wagering. You think they'll run before nightfall?" Hosteen's father asked.

Hosteen shrugged. He turned to Nataalith and Yahzi and beckoned them with a wave. Hosteen said, "This is Old Man Hosteen. He thinks he knows all about horses and women, but he hasn't had any luck with either."

They laughed. Old Man Hosteen glanced at Yahzi. "You remind me of my most beautiful wife." He stood a little straighter. "When she was a lot younger, of course."

Yahzi smiled at the compliment.

"What kind of Dinee are you?" he asked, a traditional way of inquiring about clan membership.

"I am Bitter Water, born for Towering House."

"Yooee," he whistled. "I guess I can't ask you to marry me, sister. I am Bitter Water, too."

Yahzi and Old Man Hosteen discussed relations, hoping to find relatives they both knew, but he had not visited Canyon de Chelly so the two were left with common clan membership.

Meanwhile, a growing clamor came from the horse racers. Yahzi noticed that some men had added finery to their outfits. One wore a red scarf around his forehead, the ends trailing half way down his back. Another wore a bright red shirt, another bright yellow. Two had donned purple shirts. One shirt had a black and white zigzagged pattern. The different colors and patterns dazzled Yahzi.

Two older men were in charge of the starting line although chaos appeared to be the major organizing principle. One or two aides goaded each horse toward the start while the riders tried to give the appearance of controlling their mounts without help. Other Dinee crowded in, perhaps hoping to smell confidence or doubt from the animals' sweating bodies.

When the fifteen horses were more or less lined up, one of the starters yelled something. One horse reared and almost threw his rider; fourteen dashed away. A rising column of dust marred a view of their progress as they raced toward a black flag atop a tall pole. The shiny purple shirts had fallen behind at the first turn. Red scarf led toward a second flag five hundred paces farther out. From that point the riders dropped into a wash, the only sign of the race being a swirling dust funnel.

Red shirt was the first to appear from the wash, on his heels red scarf. They'd come fifty paces before the other riders climbed the wash, bunched together. The cheering made it difficult for Nataalith and Yahzi to talk, but she teased him.

"Did you bet everything on red scarf? Or on one of those purple shirts?"

"I'm saving my bow guard to bet on Hosteen tomorrow," he said. "I don't have anything else. But I would have backed red shirt."

Yahzi laughed at him. "Sure. That's easy to say now. When he's in the lead on the last leg."

"And who would you have bet on?" Nataalith asked.

"Red scarf. His horse is all heart."

"It's legs that count."

"Heart."

The two gasped as red shirt's horse broke stride but quickly recovered. The pause was enough, however, that red scarf drew even. The change inspired the smaller horse, and it drew a neck ahead. After another twenty paces, it was a body length ahead. The cheers from the crowd were maddening. Yahzi joined in. Nataalith pumped a fist in the air. Red scarf raced across the finish line by a length and a half. Nataalith could do nothing but shake his head. Yahzi could do nothing but laugh.

The Hosteens joined Yahzi and Nataalith to watch the Dinee mob the riders, then turn to settle bets. They were about to leave when a new ruckus broke out. Two men screamed curses, then started shoving each other. Dinee circled the two, and the noise of the crowd died down.

"I'd never bet against that horse. The rider is a cousin."

"Most of the riders are your cousins. You did bet against him."

The two rushed at each other, exchanged a few blows, grappled and fell to the ground.

"Someone brought wine, I guess," Hosteen grumbled. "Only a drunk would refuse to pay up. Let's leave them to settle it with their fists," Hosteen said.

"Besides," Old Man Hosteen said, "We'll be first in line to eat."

TWENTY TWO

Although Old Man Hosteen bragged he would eat the hind quarters of the runty cow his son provided, he ate less than Yahzi.

"I'm thinking of all my relatives who have come," he said. "I can't let them go hungry." He rubbed his hand over his stomach.

"Your stomach's shrinking because you're getting old," his son said. "The only thing that keeps growing is your mustache. Or it may be because it's getting so gray it just looks larger." Hosteen poked his father's arm.

"Make fun of my mustache, will you? Just for that I'm not going to ride your horse in the race. When your kin see you mounted, they'll all bet against you." Old Man Hosteen pretended to be serious.

"What will you say if I tell you your grandson will ride my horse?" Hosteen replied.

"Yooee," Old Man Hosteen hissed through his mustache. "You mean Son of Hosteen is here? I haven't seen him."

"He said he'd come. He's been racing at the red rocks."

"Maybe you can win after all." Old Man Hosteen turned to Nataalith and Yahzi. "My grandson grows into any horse he rides. He talks to them, too."

"He says the horses trust him," Hosteen said. "Ever since you cured him of those dizzy spells, he has a way with horses." Hosteen looked with pride at his father. "Did he ever tell you that?"

Old Man Hosteen pretended not to hear, but Yahzi saw a gleam in his eyes.

"How about helping my horse win his race tomorrow?" Hosteen said. "Or making Martinez' stallion lose?"

"You be careful what you say." Old Man Hosteen glared at his son. "You want these people," he gestured at Yahzi and Nataalith, "to think I'm a witch?"

"I went too far, my father," Hosteen said. "But perhaps we could use your curing power, for my sister-in-law." He gestured to indicate Yahzi.

"Ahh," Old Man Hosteen muttered. "I thought she might be a widow. Too bad she's a clan sister."

"I am a widow," Yahzi said. "If you weren't my brother, how many sheep would you give for me?"

The men laughed at the question. Old Man Hosteen said, "I'd have to ask my wife how many sheep she'd lend me. I lost mine this spring betting on a horse that would have done better running backwards."

"Perhaps, I can give you some sheep if you'll care for my friend." Nataalith pointed to Yahzi with his chin.

Old Man Hosteen looked from Nataalith to his son. The three men drew close together to discuss the matter. Yahzi stood by gritting her teeth, irritated at being left out of a conversation that centered on her. She didn't feel any better when Nataalith told her afterward that Old Man Hosteen thought she needed an Enemy Way ceremony.

The first stars were coming out, and Nataalith touched Yahzi's arm. "Would you walk up the hill with me? It'll be darker there, away from the fires."

When they reached the top, they descended a short distance down the other side to block the fire lights from the valley. Nataalith pointed out the north star and two constellations that circled around it, reciting the legend about First Man and First Woman. His story resembled one she recalled from childhood, but details differed. Was it her memory or had Nataalith learned something different? How could all Dinee be related if their beliefs weren't the same?

"Was my story too long?" Nataalith asked.

"Oh, no." Yahzi said. "You made me think of my childhood. There are so many things I barely remember after all those years as a slave. Being taught Spanish ways and beliefs. I seldom had a chance to speak our language."

"You're speaking it well. I guess there are things that women learn that you haven't been taught. It must be difficult."

You'll never know how difficult, Yahzi thought.

The next morning was cloudy but devoid of thunder or lightning. If the clouds produced rain, they'd wait until afternoon. Yahzi and Nataalith found a vantage point for the race. A while later Old Man

Hosteen joined them to watch a few Dinee riders exercise their horses and challenge each other to short sprints. Everywhere the spectators were talking excitedly, waving their arms, making last-moment bets.

Yahzi saw Martinez and Hosteen ride over the course selected for the second race. The two men joined them when they finished. "It will do for my horse," Martinez said. "I suppose yours has raced it many times?"

"We seldom use the same course," Hosteen said. "That's why we mark off the course with flags."

The Spaniard nodded but said nothing.

"If we race before mid-day, we should avoid any rain," Hosteen said.

"That leaves us about two hours." The Spaniard said, studying the position of the sun.

Hosteen shrugged. Yahzi guessed he'd never understand the unnatural units the Spanish used to measure time. She recalled how difficult it had been for her to comprehend why the Spanish wanted to do so.

"Are you still going to bet all your sheep on the race?" Hosteen asked Martinez.

The Spaniard smirked as if anticipating the question. "Thirty of my best sheep for three of your mares."

"How about fifty sheep for five horses?"

The Spaniard shook his head.

"You've seen what good mares I have. You'll have more horses than you can count in another year with five of my mares." Hosteen gestured wildly as he spoke.

Martinez said, "I'll meet you half way. Forty ewes for four brood mares."

"That's the bet then," Hosteen said. "Forty sheep will barely feed this crowd. How soon can you get them here?"

"You can send your shepherds back with me. They'll need two or three days to drive the sheep here." He failed to hide a sneer. "If you should win."

Hosteen concealed his feelings. "We'll meet when the sun's overhead. Just our two horses."

Martinez touched his sombrero in agreement and left.

Yahzi turned to Nataalith and Old Man Hosteen. "Can you bet with his ranch hands? I'd like to see him wiped out."

"Some of Hosteen's relatives wanted to wager with them, but Martinez ordered his workers not to bet," Old Man Hosteen said. "When they've been talked into betting, they have little wealth to wager. They don't even own the horses they ride."

"Maybe they could steal Martinez's sheep." Yahzi's eyebrows arched. "Turn them against him."

Further talk of betting ended when a rider approached as if racing the dust cloud behind him. When the roan mare came to a halt close to Yahzi, the rider swung down in a swoop that reminded Yahzi of a hawk. The rider held his horse's neck. The yellow kerchief he wore on his forehead loosened to reveal a head of hair that failed to reach his ears. A mischievous grin dominated a boyish face.

"So, grandson," Old Man Hosteen chuckled. "The Comanche scalped you, I see. Did Son of Hosteen get caught seducing one of their women?"

"No Comanche is ever going to take me," Son of Hosteen bragged, avoiding an answer about his short hair.

"Do you want to tell your grandfather how you got your hair cut off?" Hosteen said. "Or should I?"

"It's a long story, grandfather. There's not time for it before the race." Son of Hosteen glanced at Yahzi and Nataalith from the corner of his eye. His grandfather nodded his approval that they be included in the story.

"You'll soon be a great grandfather," Son of Hosteen said. "My wife is large with a child." He seemed to need encouragement to continue.

"I don't know any custom that says you need to cut your hair because your wife is pregnant." Old Man Hosteen fingered his mustache.

"Well, she has three unmarried sisters who live in their mother's hogan, not far from ours. One day when I went to the river, I found them bathing. I hid their clothes and waited for them to come out."

He started laughing. "You should have seen their faces when they couldn't find their clothes."

"What else did you see?" Old Man Hosteen said.

His grandson laughed. "I stood up from behind the bush where I hid to tease them. But before I could say much, this bear of a woman grabbed me from behind and carried me down to the stream. She threw me down at the feet of my sisters-in-law."

Old Man Hosteen and Nataalith roared. Yahzi held her hand to her mouth to conceal a laugh.

"Those woman and the bear stripped me of my clothes."

"I guess they had a good time with you after that," Old Man Hosteen said.

"I wish," his grandson said. "But that bear had sheep shearers with her, and those women took turns cutting my hair. They all said they wanted a lock to remember me by."

The image was too much for Yahzi, and she bellowed her laugh. It was overpowered by Nataalith's and Old Man Hosteen's.

Son of Hosteen stood looking at his feet, embarrassed yet proud the way his story-telling captivated his listeners.

"Well, I'm glad they gave you your clothes," Old Man Hosteen said. "Otherwise, I'd have to race Martinez."

He turned to his son. "Which horse is my grandson going to ride?"

"The paint is as ornery as I've ever seen her. If that stallion of Martinez ever got in front of her, she'd chew off his hind quarters."

"I feel sorry for the stallion," Nataalith said. "With Martinez on his back, he'll be carrying twice the weight of Hosteen's horse."

"Martinez should have thought to have a son," Old Man Hosteen said. They all snickered before returning to the corral.

When the sun peaked, Yahzi returned with her hosts to the starting line. Martinez and his entourage rode up moments later. The haughty young Spaniard rode the black stallion. Martinez was mounted on the youth's mare.

"So the stallion is too much for you to handle," Hosteen said to Martinez.

"I heard your horse can't run with you on her," Martinez replied. "You have some boy to ride her?"

"I talked my son into it. He's never been in a real race before."

Martinez ran his tongue over his lips.

"Will you bet a hundred sheep for ten of my mares?"

"I don't bet everything I own, even on a sure thing," Martinez said.

"So. It's forty sheep for four mares," Hosteen said.

"Four brood mares," Martinez corrected.

"Four brood mares." Hosteen nodded affirmation.

As the Dinee crowded the starting line, Yahzi tugged at Nataalith's arm. "I can't see a thing."

"Let's get closer," he replied.

The two soon found themselves with others making two lines along the race course.

The two riders approached the starting line. The paint followed Old Man Hosteen. The stallion reared twice, almost dislodging his rider with the second lunge. When he settled at the starting line, the two men leading the horses stepped aside. A yell from the crowd started the race.

The paint and the stallion charged, both riders leaning close to their necks. Son of Hosteen whispered in the paint's ears. The Spanish rider used his whip. Yahzi lost sight of the two when they passed in a cloud of dust.

Nataalith coughed, then laughed. "The paint is edging ahead."

Yahzi stepped back from the dust, caught sight of the riders nearing the first flag. The paint led by half a length. Son of Hosteen guided the mare close to the flag marking the first turn. When the paint bore sharply to pick up the next leg, the saddle slipped. Son of Hosteen's left leg almost touched the ground, but he held onto the horse's neck. He swung his leg up, caught his heel on the paint's back, but then his foot slipped, and his arms gave way. He tumbled along on the ground head over heels. The stallion was half way down the second leg of the course before Son of Hosteen stopped tumbling.

Yahzi never hesitated. She dashed toward Son of Hosteen who stretched out in the sand and rocks, his left arm at an odd angle. When she reached him, she cradled his head in her lap, stroked his cheeks. In moments, Nataalith joined her, followed by Hosteen and his father.

Son of Hosteen shook his head, rose to his feet. He winced when he flexed his arm. He couldn't extend his left arm, and he grimaced when he tried to do so.

"It looks broken," Yahzi said. "You'll need a splint." She had to use the Spanish word for splint.

"He'll need a medicine man," Nataalith said.

"We can splint it until he gets to a medicine man."

"What's this thing you call a splint?" Hosteen asked.

"We pull the bone straight to set it, then strap it to a board to keep it in place. It'll hurt when we straighten it, but the splint is painless. It can't harm anything."

"I met a Dinee once who said a Spaniard had helped him with a broken bone by using a—whatever you call it," Old Man Hosteen said.

While Yahzi insisted Son of Hosteen sit for a while, Nataalith cut a branch with his knife, then whittled away at one side to flatten it.

"Will this do?" he asked Yahzi.

"It will have to," she said. "I saw a Spaniard straighten a broken arm one time, but I've never done it."

Old Man Hosteen stepped between her and his grandson. "I've straightened out breaks before, but I didn't have anything to keep them straight. You think this stick will work?"

"If he keeps it in place for a moon," Yahzi said.

"You hear that, grandson," Old Man Hosteen said. "You'll have to stay away from your sisters-in-law for a moon. And off horses. You think you can do that?"

"No more horses for a moon," Son of Hosteen said, stifling his pain.

When his grandfather straightened the broken arm, Son of Hosteen bit his lip.

Yahzi took the stick from Nataalith and wrapped it tight to Son of Hosteen's forearm with his scarf. Hosteen added a bandanna of his so the arm was well wrapped. Yahzi asked for Old Man Hosteen's bandanna and made a sling of it.

"You should keep it in the sling for a moon," Yahzi told Son of Hosteen.

The young man nodded that he understood, but Yahzi guessed he'd lose it by the end of the day.

"You are a good Dinee," Hosteen said to Yahzi. "I'm glad to have you as a sister." He drew closer to Yahzi. "Nataalith has told us how the pueblo people put you in danger. I've asked my father to protect you. It'll take a few days." He glanced at Old Man Hosteen. "If he can stop grooming his mustache long enough, he'll do a good job."

"The gods do the work, my son. I only coax them along." Old Man Hosteen looked at Yahzi while addressing his son.

TWENTY THREE

"I'll get the saddle," Son of Hosteen said.

"Don't carry anything with your broken arm." Yahzi spoke from concern, but the glances of the four men told her she shouldn't be giving orders.

"It's my saddle," Hosteen said. "I'll get it."

Son of Hosteen sucked at his lips, clearly uncomfortable, appearing to obey Yahzi. Yahzi sighed, wondering if she'd ever learn to control her tongue. She'd been too long with Diego and his ordering everyone. She must respect other people's independence in true Dinee fashion.

Nataalith interrupted the silence. "Not long ago I bet everything I had on my fastest horse. It was a short race, ideal for her. But she stepped in a gopher hole. Can you believe that?" He shook his head. "I'd gone over the course that morning. Not a hole in sight."

"You sure it was a gopher?" Old Man Hosteen asked. "They say Utes dig holes that look like gophers did it. They've won many races with tricks like that. Don't trust them any more than Comanches." He twisted the ends of his mustache into points.

Nataalith's mouth dropped open. "There were two Utes in the race, and one of them won."

Old Man Hosteen told of other wicked tactics he had encountered in his many years. He concluded with a story about a race down a canyon. When he described how his horse won by jumping onto the largest boulder in an avalanche, everyone burst into laughter.

Hosteen raised an eyebrow at them as he approached with his saddle, too late to hear Old Man Hosteen's yarn. "Grandfather's been telling one of his whoppers," Son of Hosteen explained to his father.

"Do his stories include cut saddle cinches?" Hosteen asked. He held the saddle to display the cinch. The tightly woven wool cinch was half ripped through, but the other half was clean cut so anyone could see it had been slit with a knife.

"Martinez be damned," Yahzi exclaimed in Spanish.

"What about Martinez?" Old Man Hosteen and Son of Hosteen asked at the same time.

"He must have cut the cinch. Who else would?" Yahzi's face flushed with anger.

"There were Dinee betting on his horse. That black stallion looks like a winner," Nataalith said.

"Only snakes do anything to win. My grandson could have been hurt worse than he was." Old Man Hosteen's eyes flashed as he spoke. "It must have been one of Martinez's ranch hands."

"Not much doubt about it," Hosteen said.

"What are you going to do about it, father?" Son of Hosteen used his broken arm as well as his good arm to gesture. Yahzi pantomimed to him to replace the arm in the sling. The young man slid his arm into it with a half smile. At least, she hadn't spoken an order.

"No need to confront him," Hosteen chuckled.

"What do you mean?" his father asked.

"It only cost me one brood mare."

"I thought the bet was four brood mares," Nataalith said.

"Three of them will be those mares you borrowed. How many foals do you think they'll have after drinking that bewitched water?"

Yahzi smiled, the men chortled.

"And the brood mare that isn't sterile looks strong but hasn't won a race." Hosteen heaved the saddle to his shoulder as he and his guests headed for the cook fires.

Old Man Hosteen dropped back to walk with Yahzi. "I understand you drank that water. No one knows if it affected you, but you don't need to chance it."

"What do you mean?" Yahzi asked.

"My son's gathered his kin. We can perform an Enemyway."

"I've lost a lot of what I learned as a child. I thought the Enemyway was a blessing for warriors who had killed someone on a war party."

"It's more than a blessing. It's to protect them from ghosts of their dead enemies. It also shields a person from the influence of other tribes." He nodded affirmation to Yahzi. "Besides, what could it hurt?"

"I have no wealth. Wouldn't we have to feast many people?"

"You helped my grandson. You've contributed your share."

Yahzi looked at her feet. "I did very little. The splint may not hold, and he won't use the sling long."

"You did what you could. My son's got plenty of sheep and a few old cows to butcher. We'll begin the ceremony soon because so many relatives are already here. I've spoken to my son, and he'll be glad to host. We'll make one of Son of Hosteen's brothers-in-law the stick receiver. That clan he married into lives a day's ride away. We want to know them better."

Yahzi flushed. "I don't know how I'll ever be able to return your generosity."

"No need to," Old Man Hosteen said. "Since you and I are Bitter Water Clan, you're a sister to me. I may be ill in your mother's hogan some day." He laughed. "I'll remind her of how I helped you."

Yahzi felt grateful but wondered when she'd ever get home. She recalled a ceremony from childhood that had seemed to go on forever.

Yahzi's worry did nothing to speed events. A few days later Yahzi found herself with Nataalith riding with Hosteen and his father on their way to Son of Hosteen's camp.

"Everyone's going to a lot of trouble for me." Yahzi said. "And no one knows if the Santa Clara curse harms human beings."

"Don't you realize there's other danger?" Nataalith said.

"What do you mean?"

"You killed that Nuevo Mexicano with my hammer. His ghost must be after you."

Yahzi's jaw dropped. How could she have forgotten how dangerous ghosts are? She hadn't given a second thought to Esquipulo's ghost pursuing her. "We traveled so far from where I hit him. Could his ghost have followed us all that way?"

"When we killed those Comanches, we were far past Santa Fe, but as soon as we got home we had Enemyway performed for us."

"Maybe too much time has passed for an Enemyway to help me."

"I took part of the Nuevo Mexicano's scalp," Nataalith said. "When I told Old Man Hosteen that I had it, he said it'd help."

"You've done so much for me," Yahzi said.

"Don't you remember," Nataalith said. "The ceremony helps everyone who attends. The Good that it brings spreads around. The ceremony does more than drive off ghosts and Evil, it invokes the gods to bring beauty and harmony."

Yahzi bent her head. "I've forgotten so many Dinee ways. I should have paid more attention to my grandmother."

"Did she teach you about *anai*?"

"Is that the word for scalp?"

"It's a word for anyone who isn't Dinee. Dangerous people wanting our land. The scalp is part of the anai."

"What will you do with it?"

"In the end we attack it. That's the final step to drive away any ghost that's after you." Nataalith reached over and touched Yahzi's arm. "You're going to be fine."

"Do you have the scalp with you?" Yahzi asked.

Nataalith cast a worried glance around him. "I carried it in my saddle bag when I traveled. I buried it while we were with Hosteen. I'll get it when the Enemyway begins."

"Do we start at Son of Hosteen's hogan?"

"Not exactly. Hosteen will ask someone in his hogan to be the stick receiver. I'm sure one of Son of Hosteen's brothers-in-law will serve. He'll inspect the stick to see that everything is proper, then sing Blessingway songs. There'll be all night singing and dancing. The young girls pick young men to be their partners, and the men pay the girls afterwards."

"I remember that!" Yahzi exclaimed. "We talked about why we picked the boys we did. I really liked Slim Boy—I don't know his real name—only that he wasn't Bitter Water or Towering House. He had a scar on his cheek that he said was from a Ute. Later, I found out he rode his horse into a thorn tree," she giggled. "I remember he gave me a shell."

"There'll be shells and beads tonight. Maybe centavos. The old people object to using Spanish money, but the girls like the coins."

After the all-night singing and dancing, Hosteen's kin returned to his hogan. Yahzi's lack of sleep made her dizzy and uncertain of what was around her. The following night, more singing and dancing increased the uncertainty. Yahzi wished to be on her way home to have her brother and sisters support her in any ceremony.

In the morning, Nataalith woke her to say that the stick receiver's group had arrived and camped on a ridge barely within sight of Hosteen's hogan.

"Do you remember what happens next?" he asked Yahzi.

Yahzi thought hard but did not.

"Son of Hosteen's kin will attack us. Well, pretend to."

"I don't understand."

"After they attack, Hosteen will take them to a place nearby to camp. That shows everyone we're at peace. Hosteen's group will present the visitors with gifts. Everyone feels close."

"We'll all walk in beauty." Yahzi guessed at the ceremony's meaning.

"Sing and dance in beauty." Nataalith agreed with Yahzi.

More nights of singing and dancing passed. Deprived of sleep, Yahzi became woozy, unaware of what had happened, what was happening, but eventually she was conscious of Hosteen leading her into a large hogan.

"It's time for the blackening," he said.

Yahzi nodded as if she understood and watched as the brother-in-law of Son of Hosteen rolled a ball of fat in the ashes of different kinds of leaves. He rubbed the blackened tallow over Yahzi's face and body, chanting as he massaged her with the ball. Everyone watched her. Even in her kinaalda, Yahzi had never been so much the center of attention.

The brother-in-law chanted a long invocation to the deities to focus their power on Yahzi, to bring hozho to everyone. More chanting followed, a deep, sure voice compelling Evil to leave. Yahzi's loins stirred as if something inside her were tumbling, then departing. She felt all eyes on her, felt the chanter directing his energy to her. Suddenly she knew something within her had departed.

She lapsed into nothingness, unaware of what was happening until the chanter called several women to help bathe her.

"We need more soapweed," she heard a women say. "Her hair is long and thick."

"It will be beautiful when we finish," another said.

Yahzi sighed. She was never so relaxed as when the women rinsed her hair, then bathed the rest of her. A young woman tittered while drying Yahzi with coarse corn meal. Yahzi had never experienced so much attention, never felt so much a Dinee. She was among people who showered their concern on her. People who expected her concern when they needed it.

Yahzi guessed most of the night had passed when she realized Nataalith was missing. Perhaps he didn't belong in the hogan. All the participants seemed to be Bitter Water.

Suddenly, shouting erupted outside. It sounded like an attack. The women who had bathed her rushed outside. Yahzi followed. Men were stomping on a blanket or a rag as if it were an enemy. Faces were contorted, shouts savage, legs flailing at the cloth. She realized Esquipulo's scalp must be bound in what had become a tattered rag.

Nataalith crowded out the young men kicking at the scalp, screaming a war cry, using a long stick as if it were a spear to jab at the scalp. His frenzy frightened Yahzi. She wondered if he had gone mad. Would he ever be able to find the man who knew the way to her home?

TWENTY FOUR

Despite Yahzi's worry, she fell into an exhausted sleep. When she awoke, the hogan was empty. She rolled onto her back to stare through the smoke hole. She basked in her feeling of peace. That no ghost held her in its clutches. She yawned as she slipped on the dress Dezba's mother had given her and stepped to the hogan's door.

Nataalith approached, leading his three horses that Hosteen had cared for. The mares looked to be excellent breed stock, and Yahzi wondered if he had other horses. Surely, not as much as her brother— if Ganado Mucho was her brother. When Nataalith turned to her, the sunlight caught him full face. A smile replaced yesterday's rage. For the first time she noticed a front tooth was chipped.

"I thought you might sleep until tomorrow morning," he said in jest.

"You tempt me to go back to bed."

"Well. Since you are awake, what if we left? I've been given tortillas for you."

"Can we reach your home today?" Yahzi tried to hide her anxiety, but she felt desperate to start for home.

"We can take our time. What's left of today and a long day tomorrow should get us there. I'll have time to hunt."

"Venison will taste good after all the mutton." The thought of food made Yahzi hope that Nataalith would offer her a tortilla. She didn't know what she last ate although she remembered feasting yesterday.

"Have you got everything," Nataalith asked.

Yahzi glanced around. She had nothing to look for and felt no need for anything. If Nataalith would only give her a tortilla.

"You want to eat while we ride?" he said.

"That would be good." Once she mounted, Nataalith handed her four tortillas. She took a large bite of one. The flat cake was still warm. She chewed slowly to relish its texture as much as its taste.

Nataalith turned his mount, leading the pack horse with a rope that served as its hobble. Yahzi's horse fell in behind. It jerked at its reins when her mind drifted, and she tightened them without thinking. She liked its spirit.

"We have high country to cross this afternoon," Nataalith said. "The deer should be abundant this time of year."

"With everyone getting guns, I'd think game would be hard to find."

Nataalith nodded his head. "It was easy when we first got guns. Now the deer and antelope are getting scarce. Of course, our sheep and cattle are grazing on more land."

"And the Spanish move onto our land." Yahzi sounded ready to wage war.

"Don't forget the Utes and Comanches, warrior woman," Nataalith sighed his concern.

"And what about that American tribe we heard of? They may invade us, too."

Nataalith scoffed. "Maybe in hundreds of years. If they live moons away from us, how can they be a danger? Anyway, they say the Americans have all the land they can ever use."

Yahzi decided Utes, Comanches, and Spanish were enough to worry about and dismissed the American threat. She settled into her saddle, letting her horse follow the pack animal, and imagining her journey to Canyon de Chelly.

When they reached the high country, Nataalith told her to rest her horse. He'd take the other horses to a meadow that deer frequented. It might be dusk before he found one.

Yahzi tied her horse to a tree and laid down to rest. Large cloud formations reminded her of when she and her brother imagined shapes in them. Was her brother a wealthy warrior or a renowned medicine man? She guessed it didn't matter as long as she saw him soon.

Yahzi tired of watching the clouds and gathered firewood. It was high enough in the mountains that the evening would be cold. They'd need more wood to boil mush or roast deer. The thought of roasted venison made her mouth water.

At dusk, Yahzi retrieved flint and steel from her horse's pack and started a fire to help Nataalith find his way. She found green sticks and trimmed them to use for roasting. Her stomach had only growled once when she heard a horse approaching. She spied Nataalith's familiar figure, waved, and he waved back, a Spanish gesture she'd learned to appreciate. She appreciated even more the sight of a buck atop the pack horse.

Nataalith had bled the deer and eviscerated it. Yahzi wondered about the heart and liver for a moment, until she saw them in the stomach cavity. Nataalith smiled at her. "Did you think I'd save none of the best parts for you?"

"We've been feasting on mutton for days. I'm starving for venison."

"Then you'll be glad to help me butcher."

Nataalith found a sapling he could bend. He swung from it for a few moments like a child. Yahzi joined him at the tree, and together they hoisted the deer carcass so he could tie its back legs to the top of the sapling. The tree stayed bent enough for the deer to hang free. Yahzi tugged at the skin while Nataalith used his knife to loosen hide from flesh.

"If you tan the skin, it will be yours," Nataalith said. "I shot him in the head so the whole skin is intact."

"What a great hunter you are," Yahzi mocked.

"I have to admit, I was close. He froze when he saw me, so it was an easy shot."

"It's been years since I've tanned a deer skin, but I've done sheep and cows."

"We'll roll it up for now. You can work on it at my hogan. What if we have some of the belly fat—after you finish your share of the heart and liver?"

Yahzi speared the organs and placed them to roast while Nataalith butchered the rib case. Yahzi stuck four ribs on two sticks. Nataalith propped them up with rocks close to the fire. Yahzi gorged on warm heart and liver.

The two waited for the ribs until the smell of roast venison drove Yahzi's taste buds crazy. While they sucked at the fattest ribs, they spoke of childhood experiences, times of hunger and times of plenty, and how they shared with relatives when food was short or when it was abundant.

A white flash interrupted. "The clouds had patches of gray in them this afternoon," Yahzi said.

Thunder followed the lightning. "This high country weather is hard to predict." Nataalith stared at a nearly black sky. "There's not much chance of rain, but I can never tell."

A lighting bolt struck nearby with a thunderous explosion. Yahzi jumped. Nataalith took a deep breath and glanced around.

"It's the time of year when the Hopi bring rain to their mesas," Nataalith said. "I'm surprised their clouds visit this far east."

He added more wood to the fire. "I have something to show you." He went to his saddle bags and tugged out pieces of cloth that were hardly discernable to Yahzi until he brought them close to the fire. He held up a blue velveteen blouse. "It's for you!" He shook out two skirts, one red, one yellow. "And these go with it."

Yahzi clapped her hands in delight. It had been years since she wore anything but tattered cotton dresses so worn the colors were nondescript. Now two brightly colored skirts! Before Nataalith could say more, she slipped out of her pueblo dress and into the blouse. She pulled up the red skirt and twirled around twice. "They're beautiful." She pulled the yellow skirt over the red one and spun in the opposite direction. "They fit perfectly," she said, pulling the waist of the yellow one closer to her. "Where did you get them?" she asked, forgetting to hide curiosity like a good Dinee would.

Nataalith raised an eyebrow at the question but answered. "I didn't bet my bow string guard on Hosteen's horse because an old woman at the races wanted it. She forced the blouse and skirts on me. I thought you should be dressed properly when you meet my mother-in-law."

Yahzi started to thank him but recalled Dinee custom. "I feel rich." She held her hand to her mouth to hide her giggle. Before slipping out of them, she admired the skirts again. Nataalith asked why she wouldn't wear them. As she pulled on her pueblo dress, she answered that she feared they'd get wet.

Nataalith spread the blankets from the horses by the fire's embers. Yahzi laid down. Nataalith joined her instead of spreading his blanket on the other side of the fire as usual.

Yahzi wondered if he intended to have sex with her because of the gifts—the way Spanish men bought sex. She struggled to recall Dinee custom.

Before she could recall anything appropriate from her grandmother's teaching, a lightning bolt struck the sapling that supported the deer. Lightning did such dangerous things that they both froze in terror. The ear-wracking thunder that followed reinforced the horror of what lightning can do.

Yahzi jumped up and raced to put her blouse and skirts in the saddle bags. Nataalith unrolled the deer skin and called Yahzi to him. They wrapped themselves in it just as a downpour started, counting on their body warmth to get them through the night.

When Yahzi awoke, she realized she'd had a second good night of sleep. The blanket under her was soaked as was her hair, but the deer skin had kept her dry, and Nataalith's body had kept her warm. She was stiff from having been bound in the skin. She tried to edge away without awakening Nataalith until she missed the horses.

"They're gone," she bolted upright.

"Who's gone?" Nataalith asked with irritation in his voice.

"The horses are gone."

"It was the lightning," Nataalith rose and looked around. "They'll be hard to track after this rain. They must have bolted when the lightning hit. At least, they're hobbled."

They both went to look at the tree and the deer. The trunk was blackened, and the deer smelled of burnt flesh. "I'll bury it after I find the horses." Nataalith stared at the blackened flesh with loathing. "It must be full of evil."

Yahzi stayed with Nataalith as he walked a circle around the camp ground, then a larger circle. "Look," he pointed to some horse hair on a shrub. "They really ran, even hobbled." He pointed to the ground. "That leg dug in so deep the rain couldn't wash away the track. If they kept going in that direction, we'll find them soon."

He was right. After a few hundred paces, they found the three horses grazing on a patch of thick grass. The three looked up when Nataalith whistled, and neighed a greeting as if ashamed at having run away. Yahzi opened the bags on the pack horse to make sure her skirts and blouse were all right.

"Not even wet," she said. "I want to put them on, but I think I'll wait until we reach your hogan."

Nataalith nodded approval. They led the horses back to the campsite, shook out the blankets, and used them under the saddles. Nataalith began burying the deer. When Yahzi led her horse close to the burnt flesh, it snorted and reared. She tied it to a nearby tree and returned to help. The rain soaked earth was easy to dig but left them covered in mud. Yahzi joked about how appropriate the dirt was for a Mud Clan member. Nataalith splattered her face with a handful of mud.

By mid-day the mud had dried, and the two rubbed themselves clean. As they came down from the high country, the land looked like Diego's ranch except in the distance, hills rose with horizontal layers of yellow, gray, and white—a pattern of beauty resembling that of Canyon de Chelly. The scene stirred her homesickness.

When they reached a rock outcropping with scattered holes filled with water, Nataalith stopped. They drank their fill, watered the horses, and washed away the last of the mud.

"Is there always enough rain for your crops?" Yahzi asked.

"Almost always. Two summers ago the harvest was slim. We had to travel high into the mountains to get enough game."

"To those hills with all the color?"

"Beyond them. Or we come back here. The country provides."

Nataalith mounted. "If we push on, we'll reach my hogan tonight."

They trotted a while, but Nataalith slowed the horses to a walk when they entered rougher land.

"Who lives in your hogan?" Yahzi wasn't sure her question was polite. She supposed she shouldn't show such curiosity, but she couldn't help herself.

"The mother of my wives is called Asdzaan. When her husband died a few years ago, she married a younger man. He still has sheep at his mother's." He wrinkled his nose. "So Asdzaan makes all the decisions."

Nataalith paused so long Yahzi thought he'd finished. She prompted. "And your wives."

"Tso and Little Tso." He stopped again.

He married sisters. If Yahzi remembered correctly, the custom was preferred by Dinee.

"Do you have many children?"

"No." He said nothing more.

"No others in the hogan?" Yahzi's throat tightened. She was counting on a brother-in-law from Canyon de Chelly.

"My wife's sister, Yoo'o. Her husband is Hog Nose." He paused. "I told you about him."

Yahzi cocked her head. "I don't remember such a name."

"He's the Bitter Water man from Canyon de Chelly. That's my nickname for him. Have you seen the Spanish animal they call a hog?" Yahzi nodded she had. "Besides his hog's nose, he's short and ugly."

Yahzi felt a flush through her whole body. No matter his looks, Hog Nose was her clan brother and knew the way to her home. He might even know her brother and sisters, and if they lived. She had refused to consider the possibility of their death before. Now her heart pounded, fearful of what she might learn.

TWENTY FIVE

The flat valley they rode into supported scattered stands of grass but few trees. A stretch of cliff sides in the distance displayed layers of bright yellows, grays, and browns in the setting sun. The beauty was a second best to the red, gold, and contrasting black of Canyon de Chelly. Still, as Yahzi took in the colors, she experienced an inner calm. It was a place of beauty.

Nataalith rode toward a large hogan. Three or four youngsters filled the east-facing entrance. Ten or fifteen other children raised dust behind the hogan, kicking a ball, while yelling taunts at each other. Numerous women busied themselves cleaning up the remains of a feast and stacking firewood. Many men gathered at the corral, pointing at different horses, their mingling filled with laughs and serious faces. Yahzi doubted anyone noticed her and Nataalith in the disarray surrounding the hogan until a young woman broke away and ran toward them.

Her smile welcomed Nataalith but managed to include Yahzi. Her black eyes sparkled to compete with the sheen of long hair tied in a bun. Her heart shaped face radiated beauty. A purple blouse contrasted with a green skirt, the hem of a yellow skirt showing under the green.

"My husband has been gone too long," she said to Nataalith.

"Long enough to rescue the slave I told you about," he nodded toward Yahzi.

The woman grinned at Yahzi, took the reins of the two horses when Nataalith and Yahzi dismounted, and led the horses to the corral where men stepped aside to let her pass, while following her with their eyes.

"That's Little Tso," Nataalith said. "She'll grow some more, but she completed her kinaalda this spring."

"When did you share corn pollen?" Yahzi hoped the question didn't invade Nataalith's privacy.

"Not long after." Nataalith changed the subject. "My mother-in-law must be hosting a ceremony. I seldom see so many people here."

The two walked toward the hogan. Before they could reach it, a woman stopped Nataalith to ask what he wanted to eat. Before he answered, another brought him and Yahzi bowls of soup.

The woman who served Yahzi asked her clan affiliation, and the two spoke of numerous relatives before they found one in common, though neither were sure it was the same person. The woman had no knowledge of Bitter Water people at Canyon de Chelly, and Yahzi tried ending the conversation so she could search for Hog Nose.

At the corral men glanced longer than customary at Yahzi. At least she felt as uncomfortable as when Spanish men stared at her. She decided it improper to ask if anyone knew Hog Nose but listened to hear his name. Close to the gate she spotted a man with turned up nostrils. The flare might be enough to earn him the nickname. She summoned up her courage and approached him. He stiffened as she drew near and crossed his arms over his chest.

"I am Bitter Water, born for Towering House," Yahzi said. "I thought I recognized you as a relative. From a long time ago," she lied.

"I'm not related to either clan, except in distant ways," he responded. He dropped his arms to his side. "Are you from around here?"

"No. I grew up in Canyon de Chelly. But after that I've lived in the south."

"I was in the south a long time ago. I've never been to the Canyon." He took a step closer to Yahzi. "Have you had something to eat?"

His tone in the offer of food seemed overly familiar to Yahzi. She wondered how long it would take her to relearn the subtle aspects of Dinee relationships between men and women. Had she been too familiar in her approach or was he just being polite? She had no way of knowing.

"I've eaten. As much as I could," she stammered as she backed away, eyes averted from the stranger.

So she gave up finding Hog Nose and looked for Nataalith's mother-in-law. Near the largest cook fire an older woman was talking and gesturing to three other women. She seemed in command so Yahzi approached her.

Yahzi stood beside the four women, listening. The older one was telling the others how to distribute the food they had been given and what preparations they should make in the morning when it came time to leave. Yahzi felt sure the woman must be Asdzaan and waited until she finished speaking.

"I just arrived with Nataalith," Yahzi said. "How might I help you?"

"Who's Nataalith?" the woman asked, squinting at Yahzi.

"I thought he was your son-in-law," Yahzi stammered. "Do you know Asdzaan?"

"Everyone knows Asdzaan," the woman answered. She glanced at another older woman stirring a large steaming pot.

One of the other women touched Yahzi on the arm and spoke in a soft tone. "What is your clan?"

Yahzi answered, trying to match the woman's friendly tone. She glanced for a moment into her eyes before lowering her gaze.

"Yooee," the woman whispered. "Not many Bitter Water people in this part of the country. But Ts'osi may be Bitter Water."

When Yahzi failed to respond, the woman continued. "He's Yoo'o's husband. They say he's from Canyon de Chelly."

"Ts'osi must be Hog Nose," Yahzi muttered under her breath. She was getting somewhere, but the progress was slow.

"I'd like to talk with my clan brother," she said.

The woman who dominated said, "I haven't seen him since we arrived. He must be off somewhere."

Another said, "I heard he's looking for stolen sheep."

"Someone told me that he went to trade at Santa Fe or with the Zuni," a third added. "As handsome as he is, Yoo'o shouldn't allow him to be anywhere near those Zuni girls. They can't resist Dinee men." Yahzi forced a laugh, disappointed she had not found her guide home.

One of the women said, "As beautiful as Yoo'o is, you'd think Ts'osi wouldn't want to be gone long."

Yahzi continued to listen to gossip about Nataalith's hogan, not always able to put a name with the chatter about persons. By the time the women finished, it was nearly dark and people were looking for a place to spend the evening.

Yahzi guessed the hogan would be filled, but Nataalith was nowhere in sight so she went inside. She thought she heard Nataalith's laugh to the far side. The smoke hole gave little light, and she almost stepped on several children sprawled on the ground. A woman tittered near where the laugh came from. She took a few more steps and saw Nataalith getting to his feet, adjusting his breechcloth and his belt. Still lying at his feet, Little Tso was reaching for her dress.

Little Tso whispered to Nataalith. "Did you give that slave much of your essence in all that time you were with her?"

"None. I saved it for you," Nataalith said.

"I feel it mixing with my blood. We'll have a child soon. Come back in the morning!"

Yahzi backed away, feeling behind her with a foot for any children. She reached the doorway just moments before Nataalith did. She pretended to be entering.

"I was looking for you," Yahzi stammered. "Should I find a place inside?"

"It's crowded, but it's up to you. Here's a blanket."

Yahzi took the offer as advice to sleep outside. She found a grassy place not far from the hogan. She made herself comfortable but tossed and turned under the stars. The Enemyway had made her realize how vital it was for a Dinee to be surrounded by relatives. She felt estranged now, alone in the night. She longed for her brother and sisters and the clan relatives she'd grown up with.

In the morning, people were packing to leave. A few were mounted and about to depart. The multitude of children was gone, but three boys were shooting arrows at a crude deer figure. A little girl stood watching, a finger in her mouth. A cradle board with a baby was propped beside the hogan. Yahzi guessed Asdzaan's hogan was returning to normal.

A woman, her back to Yahzi, was boiling corn meal in a large pottery jar. Smoke from the fire curled into the nearly leafless roof of the ramada. Yahzi went to offer help. She coughed softly at the fire as if from the smoke. The woman didn't turn. Yahzi coughed louder. Still no response. She must be hard of hearing Yahzi thought. She reached out to touch her. The woman swung around. Her pox marked face startled Yahzi.

The woman scowled. "Have you never seen what the Spanish disease does to Dinee skin?"

"Yes," Yahzi replied. "You startled me the way you turned. I had coughed. I...,"

"Their disease left me hard of hearing, too," the woman barked.

"I'm sorry." Before Yahzi could offer to help, the woman interrupted.

"You must be the slave Nataalith brought." Her words were more statement of fact than inquiry, more disapproval than welcome.

"I'm a Dinee. Bitter Water, born for Towering House." Yahzi's words were resolute.

"There are few Bitter Water people here," the woman shrugged. "Have you thought about returning home?" Again, she stated her question.

"Nataalith brought me here so his brother-in-law could take me home. Do you know Nataalith?" Yahzi spoke in anguish, giving little thought to her question.

"I am Nataalith's wife!" Tso filled her statement with contempt. Yahzi guessed she might be jealous but could think of no way to dispel the feeling. She realized she should have known or at least thought of the possibility that the woman could be Tso.

"Why haven't you returned to your mother's hogan before now?" Tso said.

"I was taken as a slave years ago. I don't know if my mother lives." Yahzi bit at her lip, swore not to be defensive again. She wondered if the woman was jealous of Little Tso. Perhaps the two were not sisters. "I was invited here. I may not have any wealth, but I am willing to work hard as long as I'm here. Until Nataalith's brother-in-law takes me home!"

172

The woman frowned. "Where's your home?"

"In Canyon de Chelly."

The woman shrugged as if she had never heard of it. "Ts'osi has been away. Before he can trade, he has to go to Santa Fe. Then he usually goes to Zuni. Seldom does he go beyond Zuni. Why would he trade with other Dinee? What do they have that we don't have?"

Yahzi's heart sunk. She couldn't imagine why Nataalith would mislead her, but Tso's logic made sense. What reason would Ts'osi have for trading with Dinee in Canyon de Chelly?

Tso turned her back and shrugged.

Yahzi took the gesture for a sign of truce. "Can I stir the pot for you?"

The woman handed her the stick, flattened at the end to serve as a spoon, and walked toward the hogan. "I'll find more roots," she said over her shoulder.

The words were devoid of emotion, but at least the confrontation seemed to have ended.

As Yahzi stirred, she kept an eye on the hogan's doorway expecting Tso to return. Instead, Nataalith walked out, blinking in the morning brightness, holding up a hand toward the sky, as if welcoming the sun. His breechcloth hung too low in the back, and he tugged at it. Nataalith did not even glance at the ramada. Yahzi longed to call to him to ask when Hog Nose would return but knew she must not show her concern.

A little girl near the door took her finger from her mouth and ran toward Nataalith, grabbing him by the leg, and saying "Daddy." Her words caught the attention of the three boys. They put down their bows and ran toward Nataalith. They didn't touch him but sought his attention, addressing him as "my father."

Yahzi drew a sharp breath. If Nataalith had lied to her about not having children, might he have lied about a brother-in-law? She shook her head to clear it. Would she ever leave for her beloved canyon?

Nataalith finally looked at her and nodded. His pace toward her suggested he was reluctant to greet her, but he smiled and complimented her on how she was making herself useful.

"I should be helping your mother-in-law, but I have not found her," Yahzi said. "I suppose she is tired from hosting so many people."

"Don't look for her now. She's in a bad mood. Her husband left with Hog Nose when all the work began. He claimed he wasn't needed since it wasn't his clan hosting the ceremony. Hog Nose made the same excuse. His wife is furious with him."

"And her name is...?" Yahzi asked.

"Yoo'o."

"I heard she's beautiful."

Nataalith stiffened, his face reddening. "Some think so."

Yahzi wondered about his confusion over his sister-in-law. The close quarters of a hogan led to complicated relationships.

"I haven't met Yoo'o, but I heard women talking about her. Did she go with her husband?"

"No. She's here. Her mother would have been furious if she left. Besides, she probably didn't want to go with a man as ugly as Hog Nose."

Yahzi could hardly wait to meet the man who might lead her home. Was he as ugly as Nataalith claimed or as good looking as the women said? Yet, it didn't matter, as long as he took her home. If no Zuni woman had seduced him into staying with her. If no Ute or Comanche had ambushed him. If...Yahzi shuddered, wondering how she'd ever get home.

174

TWENTY SIX

Yahzi kept busy helping Tso and Little Tso to card wool and to spin. Asdzaan continued to avoid her, causing Yahzi to wonder how Nataalith explained her presence.

Then one morning, Nataalith sought her out. "I must talk to my mother-in-law about herding the sheep. She expects me to help even though I have few sheep." He paused, seeming to wonder if Yahzi understood him. She shrugged her ignorance. "I thought you might do my share with the flock," he said. "Remember all the skirts and blouses I gave you?"

Yahzi swallowed hard. She'd accepted a blouse and two skirts as gifts, not payment. But, why not herd sheep, she thought. "I herded as a child, I can do it again," she said.

"Asdzaan is probably at her loom." Nataalith led Yahzi to a cottonwood back of the hogan where a loom was set up in the shade of the tree. Asdzaan kneeled before it, contemplating her work. Blacks and whites mingled in a design that took Yahzi's breath. Yahzi couldn't remember ever seeing such an intricate pattern, so different from what Dezba wove for the Mexican trade.

Nataalith squatted some distance from his mother-in-law, looking at right angles to her. "I heard you need help with the sheep," he said.

"Yes," Asdzaan answered. "That worthless husband of mine is bringing his flock here. He claimed he needed Ts'osi to help him because he had so many." Her nose wrinkled. "We'll see."

"Can't Ts'osi help?" Nataalith asked.

"He'll be off to Santa Fe or wherever. I can't count on him." Asdzaan scowled her displeasure.

"I've brought this woman to help you. She can care for my sheep."

"She won't have much to do," Asdzaan sneered. "The Utes stole that handful of scrawny animals you call sheep."

"What?" Nataalith's mouth dropped open. "No one told me my sheep had been stolen. Did no one go after them?"

"My husband and Ts'osi. And, a few would-be warriors." She turned a moment to almost face Nataalith. "A rain washed out the tracks, but they were nearing Ute land when our men lost the trail."

"Was that black sheep with the three white legs one of the stolen animals?" Nataalith said.

"They took all of yours, except for two we butchered. Never chewed such stringy meat in my whole life." Yahzi wasn't sure if Asdzaan's lips curled into a sneer or a grin.

"I'm going after them," Nataalith said. "I can recognize that black sheep, and I'll take theirs to be even."

Nataalith jumped up, his dark eyes flashing. Yahzi sensed anger in the tenseness of his body, the same anger that she had seen when he attacked the scalp. Since Nataalith had little chance of finding his sheep, let alone stealing them back, perhaps the anger would subside and reason prevail if he waited. However, he spent the rest of the day preparing for his foray. Not even a night with Little Tso changed his mind. Early the next morning, he was gone.

Yahzi yearned to be gone, too. The loneliness she felt in Asdzaan's hogan equaled what she felt on Diego's ranch. So she looked forward to joining the children to herd sheep and show them how to find shapes in the clouds. She prepared mush early, fed the children, and herded the sheep to pasture. Once the flock was settled, she showed the children shapes in the clouds, and they soon were discovering their own. She felt less lonely, but her anxiety about returning home remained.

One morning Little Tso joined Yahzi and the children. She and Yahzi gossiped about members of the hogan. Yahzi discerned that Little Tso resented Nataalith's departure, and the gossip turned to belittling him.

"He is good looking, but he goes into a rage over little things," Little Tso said. "He knows nothing about women. How to please them, I mean."

"I thought he was pleasing you lately," Yahzi said in jest.

Little Tso giggled. "Oh, yes, he's good that way. But giving little gifts, or saying the right thing—he's never any good at things like that."

"I know what you mean." Yahzi wasn't sure she did. Nataalith had been kind to her, she thought, but she had only Diego to compare him with.

"He's had bad luck with women," Little Tso continued. "A couple turned him down before he married Tso."

"Did you know any of them?" Yahzi asked.

Little Tso smiled. "Yoo'o is one. I think she made him crazy. I hear he gave her so many gifts you'd think he'd paid the bride wealth."

"You mean he gave her sheep before they shared corn pollen?"

"Sheep, goats. And a horse." She emphasized horse. "If she hadn't turned him down, he'd have given her more horses."

"Did she give anything back to him?"

"Well, they must have slept together, but Yoo'o would never talk about sharing corn pollen with him."

"And so he turned to her sister?" Yahzi regretted her words as soon as she spoke them, having forgotten Little Tso must be Yoo'o's sister, too. She wondered if she'd offended Little Tso, but the woman did not seem upset.

"I'm not sure he turned to her right away," she laughed, "since that was before my time."

Yahzi laughed to be polite, not knowing the reason for whatever humor Little Tso saw.

"I've always suspected that when Ts'osi came along, Yoo'o wanted him for a husband."

So Nataalith belittles him because he's jealous of Ts'osi, Yahzi thought. Ts'osi probably doesn't resemble a hog in any way. He's probably the handsome man that the women say he is, Yahzi thought.

"And Ts'osi fathered all the children that Yoo'o gave birth to?" If that were true, Yahzi realized, then they were also sons and daughters of Nataalith by Dinee custom.

"He not only fathered all of them," Little Tso tittered, "but Ts'osi teases Nataalith about not being able to father any children himself. He knows it's rude, but Nataalith must have done something to make Ts'osi say such things."

"It must cause trouble in the hogan," Yahzi said.

"When Asdzaan's first husband headed the hogan, he didn't tolerate any bickering. Ts'osi and Nataalith didn't dare show their hostility toward each other. But now Asdzaan must keep the peace, it's hard, but with Nataalith gone as much as he has been, it's made things easier."

"When both are gone, the hogan must have enjoyed peace." Yahzi smiled at the thought until she imagined that Ts'osi might not return.

"Ts'osi and our father-in-law will be back soon." Little Tso's words assured Yahzi. "And I don't see how Nataalith can get his sheep back, so he'll soon return."

A burst of thunder interrupted Little Tso. She peered upward and studied the fluffy clouds lined with dark patches. She pointed to an ominous one, darker than the rest. "Look at that bear chasing a goat."

Yahzi was hard pressed to make out a goat, but a snout and ears were deftly placed on a bear's body.

When Yahzi and the children arrived at the corral, Asdzaan avoided her, but Yoo'o drew her into conversation. Yoo'o showed more interest in Yahzi's life as a slave than anyone else in the hogan, and Yahzi felt an affection for the woman. Once the children went to sleep, the two talked of their lives, Yahzi discovering a source of warmth in the hogan.

Another evening Tso joined them. Yahzi welcomed her, hoping to know her better. But the conversation lasted only moments before Tso accused Yoo'o of gathering less than her share of firewood. Yoo'o promised to work harder at looking for wood, but Tso made other accusations. It was clear to Yahzi that Tso resented Yoo'o. She was glad when Tso retreated to her side of the hogan.

"Perhaps, I can bring firewood back when we return with the sheep," Yahzi said to Yoo'o.

Yoo'o laughed. "My sister always finds reasons to belittle me. I try to ignore her. Maybe you can learn to do the same. It's in her nature to quibble."

"Has she always been that way?" Yahzi asked.

"No. She was a good older sister to me when we were growing up. Took the blame when I let sheep wander away. Always gave me more than half the peaches we were allowed to pick in the fall."

"Did the Spanish skin disease change her?"

"You're wise," Yoo'o said. "That had much to do with it."

"Was she a child when she fell ill?"

"No. She'd married a good man. Handsome and healthy. He brought harmony to the hogan because he was so cheerful. He knew what hozho was."

"Did the Spanish disease kill him?"

"No," Yoo'o shook her head. "He had taken their daughter to visit his mother, but he left their son here because he was still nursing." Yoo'o paused. "The fever struck the boy first. A few days later it hit her. She was too sick to care for her son. Asdzaan called a hand trembler, but he couldn't help. I think she blames me for our son's death."

Yahzi was so shaken by the story that she didn't know how to reply. She'd heard rumors of the new diseases striking the Dinee, but this was her first-hand experience of their enormity.

"We mourned the boy longer than usual. It helped a little when her husband and daughter came home."

Why hadn't I thought to ask about the daughter? Yahzi asked herself. "What's happened to the daughter?" she said aloud.

Yoo'o arched her eyebrows. "What do you mean?"

"Did the daughter leave with the father? I'm guessing the father left?" Yahzi's mind raced for answers.

"Tso's husband tried to make the marriage work, but Tso's bitterness was too much for him. He stayed about a year, but then went back to his mother's. They say he remarried."

"So he took the daughter with him?"

Yoo'o raised an eyebrow. "No one's told you? You don't know?"

"Know what?"

"Little Tso is Tso's daughter."

Yahzi's mouth dropped open.

"You thought Little Tso was Tso's younger sister, didn't you?" Yoo'o said. "Nataalith didn't explain?"

179

"No, he didn't." Yahzi felt uncomfortable with the idea that Nataalith had married his wife's daughter. In the Spanish view of things it was an incestuous marriage, and she'd never encountered such a marriage in her childhood. Yet, she understood how the marriage fit Dinee ways of thinking. There was no chance of a blood connection since the daughter's clan would be the same as the mother's. Still, it didn't seem quite right to Yahzi.

Yoo'o chuckled. "It's so like a man. They tell so little but expect us to learn so much from what little they say." She shook her head. "He didn't tell you Little Tso was Tso's daughter, did he?"

Yahzi tilted her head in thought. "I guess not. I assumed the two were sisters."

"I've heard the Spanish consider such a marriage to be like two Dinee clan members marrying. Do they really think that way?" Yoo'o looked perplexed.

Yahzi nodded vigorously. "That's a good way to understand it. The Spanish would be outraged if a man married his daughter—well—his step-daughter, they'd call her. As evil as a Dinee man marrying his clan sister."

"The Spanish are strange. Everyone has clans. The Hopi and Zuni do. I don't know about the Utes. You can never tell about savages like them."

Yahzi had never considered the matter—Utes and the Spanish being alike. The idea wouldn't set well with Diego, she knew. She grinned from ear to ear.

"If a man didn't have clan mates, where would he get bride wealth?" Yoo'o frowned.

"The Spanish had something they called a dowry. A little like bride wealth, but can you believe it? The bride gave the dowry to the groom!"

Yoo'o gasped. "I'll never understand the Spanish."

Yahzi decided not to tell Yoo'o how wives went to live with their husbands.

After moments of silence, Yoo'o continued. "When Nataalith married Tso, he gave our mother a handful of sheep. He promised more, but the few others failed to satisfy our mother. She called them scrawny whatever their size. Other people criticized him, too."

"Has he never been generous?" Yahzi asked.

Yoo'o laughed aloud. "He'd won a horse race and bet a lot on himself just before he married Little Tso. He gave many sheep for her and talked his Mud Clan brothers into giving horses, too." Yoo'o shook her head.

"Didn't that make her mother happy?" Yahzi asked.

"No, it made her furious. He wasn't expected to pay much for a wife's daughter, but he had all that wealth. Tso, of course, was jealous. It didn't help that Little Tso has a beautiful complexion while Tso is marred by the Spanish skin disease. The only one he really pleased was Asdzaan. She made him feel more welcome, which is hard for my mother to do."

Late the next day, Ts'osi and his father-in-law arrived with twenty-five sheep just as Yahzi and the children returned with the hogan's flock. Yahzi ran to the gate to open it. She guarded one side while the two men struggled to herd the sheep into the unfamiliar corral.

Out of the corner of her eye, Yahzi found Ts'osi to be as handsome as Nataalith. In no way did he resemble a hog. When he dismounted, she saw that Ts'osi was as tall or taller than Nataalith. His back was straighter, and he walked with a determined step. No wonder Nataalith was jealous of him, Yahzi thought. She felt a surge of pride for her clan brother. Ts'osi no doubt had much in common with her brother, Ganado Mucho. Brave warriors to be sure. She could hardly wait to ask him about her family and others at Canyon de Chelly. But most important, how could she convince Ts'osi to take her home?

TWENTY SEVEN

Yoo'o walked to Ts'osi equally erect, greeting him with a smile. She took the reins of his horse, brushing his arm with hers as if accidently touching. When he returned her smile, his teeth flashed an even white row except for a missing top front tooth. Yahzi wondered if her brother was missing any teeth. She felt guilty that for years she had never considered he might have been injured.

"We have a new woman in the hogan, my husband." Yahzi barely made out Yoo'o's words. "She is a clan sister of yours."

"Is it the slave that Nataalith went south for?" Ts'osi's words were barely audible.

Yoo'o nodded. Their shoulders touched as they turned toward the corral where Asdzaan's husband was unsaddling his horse and slipping off its bridle. The last exchange Yahzi heard between them was mutual laughter. She sighed in regret as she recalled her marriage to Pablo and her days as a mistress to Diego.

But most important, how was she to convince Ts'osi to take her to Canyon de Chelly?

She followed the couple into the hogan where Asdzaan had brought in the kettle of mutton stew prepared for the evening meal. Its aroma filled the hogan.

Yahzi sat to one side while Ts'osi ate, Yoo'o watching him. Ts'osi must have related details of his trip; Yahzi couldn't guess what Yoo'o told him. While Asdzaan and her husband ate, they said nothing. After finishing, Asdzaan busied herself spinning wool.

Her husband muttered to her. "We brought only a few of my sheep. I fell in an arroyo on the way and scraped my foot and ankle."

"Don't you herd sheep from a horse?" Asdzaan's words rang with sarcasm.

"The pain made riding difficult. A few days passed before I could find corn pollen to put on it."

"Humph," Asdzaan's grunt was noncommittal.

"I fear a worm is eating the flesh."

"You're always fearing for your health."

The two had nothing more to say.

Yahzi thought she should go to sleep though her mind raced with ways to initiate a conversation with Ts'osi. She was about to give up when Ts'osi handed his bowl to Yoo'o, got up, and walked toward Yahzi. Her mouth went dry. Her tongue stuck in her throat.

Ts'osi's grin failed to loosen it. "My wife tells me you are Bitter Water, from Canyon de Chelly."

Yahzi managed to add, "Born for Towering House."

"She says you were taken as a slave by the Spanish."

"Yes."

"Were you in the canyon when the Spanish slaughtered all our people at what they now call 'Massacre Cave'?"

"Yes. They caught my aunt and me across from the cave." Yahzi's tongue found its proper place.

"Is it true that all the people in the cave were killed." Ts'osi's eyebrows arched.

"They were. The Spanish shot their guns until everyone died. Then the soldiers went into the cave to make sure everyone was dead."

"You had not joined them in the cave?"

"No, we were too late. We heard the Spanish coming and hid in a cave on the opposite side of the canyon. The Spanish would never have seen the cave with the people, but an old woman yelled insults at them. They dismounted and found positions where they could shoot into the cave. The ricocheting balls did the killing."

Ts'osi moaned.

Yahzi looked puzzled.

"I had a younger sister and mother in the cave. Not the mother who gave birth to me, but the sister and I had the same mother."

"I'm sorry," Yahzi said. "I'm sure they were killed instantly. We didn't hear cries of anyone wounded." It was a hard lie for Yahzi. She'd heard the wails from the cave for years afterwards.

"Were there many times as a slave when you wished you'd died in the cave?"

No one had ever asked such a question before. She felt Ts'osi must be truly concerned because she was a clan sister.

"I was so frightened at first. I don't know that I could have survived if my aunt hadn't been with me."

"Did either of you speak Spanish?"

"No. We both worked hard to learn it." Yahzi hadn't told Yoo'o about becoming the Spaniard's lover, although she did reveal that to her clan brother.

"After Diego's wife came back, he forced me to marry another slave, but I had a child by my master. I could think of nothing but escaping and returning to Dinehtah, but my son had a club foot. One time I tried to escape with him, but Comanches stopped us, and my son was killed. Before I could try another escape, the husband forced upon me made me pregnant."

"So how did you escape?" Ts'osi's question was breathless.

"A Dinee raiding party came by, led by Nataalith. I was on my way north with them until Comanches attacked us. I was forced to return to Diego's ranch."

Ts'osi sucked in a breath.

"Then Diego lost his ranch. A new owner came who was cruel. The first chance I got, I fled even though my baby was due. I was to meet Nataalith at a river. I waited there with my aunt."

"Just the two of you? And she was getting old?"

"Her mind wasn't working well. She was from Jemez pueblo so not a real father's sister, but I always thought of her as my aunt." Yahzi paused a long time, considering whether to tell the truth. Surely her clan brother would sympathize. She explained how confused she was over the meaning of twins, how the still birth of one must have meant Evil hovered over twins. Yet, she intended to bring the second child with her until a Spaniard killed it.

"What you did was right." Ts'osi's nod showed sympathy.

"Nataalith found us soon after and took us to Jemez where my aunt had a husband. We found out that the pueblos had cursed the river because of a land feud. Their curse must have caused my misfortune."

"Those pueblo people have strong witchcraft," Ts'osi's face grew pale.

"After we left Jemez, Nataalith stopped at a clan brother's where he had borrowed horses. The hogan held an Enemyway for me. I felt the ceremony lift the curse."

"You must be right," Ts'osi said. "You've suffered more than anyone deserves."

"So now I am here," Yahzi sighed. "Little Tso and your wife have been good to me, but the hogan has no need for a stranger."

"You're my sister, not a stranger."

Yahzi smiled, felt a surge of warmth.

"I have a brother—from the mother who gave birth to me—that I haven't heard of since I was enslaved. He had only a childhood name then, Nantai." Yahzi waited to see if the name meant anything to Ts'osi. When he didn't respond, she went on. "I've heard about a man from the canyon I think may be my brother. Do you know Ganado Mucho?"

"I met him once. He's from Canyon de Chelly where I lived as a child. Is he a much younger brother?"

"No. He was only a winter younger."

Ts'osi winced. "Ganado Mucho resembles you—a little."

Yahzi wondered. She remembered Dinee felt it proper to tell people what they wanted to hear. Perhaps, Ts'osi thought she was younger than she appeared. After all she had endured, she must look older than her years. She'd be glad to tell him her age, as Diego had taught her, but it would mean nothing to him. Besides, he had no way of knowing Ganado Mucho's age.

"Is it true that he's wealthy?" Yahzi asked.

"Yes, he's given away many horses and sheep. They say he still has a large herd of horses so he can mount his warriors to fight the Spanish."

"My brother was always kind. Has Ganado Mucho given to the widows and the poor?"

"Indeed," he nodded, then looked at Yahzi a second time. "In the fading light I didn't see at first how much you do resemble him."

Yahzi's heart beat faster, but in her mind she suspected that Dinee etiquette focused Ts'osi's words. Since he had just returned, she hesitated to ask him about visiting Canyon de Chelly, but she couldn't help herself. "They say you trade at Canyon de Chelly."

"I still go there, but I may have to find a medicine person for my father-in-law before I can leave. He has a cut that may be infected."

Yahzi felt helpless. She knew she must wait.

A few days later Nataalith returned without any sheep. Yahzi saw a scowl on his face even from a distance. Before she could walk forward to greet him, Little Tso ran by her.

Little Tso took the reins before Nataalith dismounted, asked if she could take the tether to his pack horse. Nataalith assented with a nod and climbed down from his horse. When he looked around, and saw Yahzi, he looked away. Little Tso walked behind him. "You must be hungry," she said. "I'll serve you stew."

"Did you unsaddle my horse?" Obviously, Little Tso had only time to turn the horses loose in the corral. She hung her head.

"Unsaddle her and join me in the hogan." He glanced at Yahzi. "You're still here."

Yahzi couldn't comprehend if his words were a statement or a question. What was clear was that his expression was devoid of emotion. Perhaps, he had failed to accomplish anything, perhaps he was growing weary of her company.

"Has Hog Nose returned?" he asked.

"He has."

"Probably he'll leave soon for Santa Fe. Pick up trade goods, then head for Zuni." He turned to the corral to make sure Little Tso was caring for his horse. "Maybe you could convince him to go on to Canyon de Chelly after trading with the Zuni."

Yahzi's mouth dried. What had happened to Nataalith's assurances that his brother-in-law would lead her home? How much time would Ts'osi need in Santa Fe? Among the Zuni? And would he have any reason to continue on to Canyon de Chelly?

TWENTY EIGHT

Yahzi refrained from asking about Ts'osi's plans since he was still uncertain. Every morning when she left with the boys to herd sheep, she looked for Yoo'o who might have learned something. But, Yoo'o was always busy helping her mother or tending her children.

One afternoon Little Tso joined Yahzi. She joked that it was good to get away from Nataalith because he had been so ill tempered. When she turned serious, it was to report that Nataalith had left in the night, furious with Tso. Apparently, she, like Ts'osi, had accused him of being unable to father a child. She had added to the accusation that he had spread his essence around so far he'd never be able to have a child, and he might even have caught the dreaded Spanish disease that came from intercourse with them. This final insult had sent Nataalith into a rage.

Little Tso sighed. "Ts'osi may leave, too."

Yahzi felt a chill. "Is he on his way to trade?"

"He's looking for a medicine person to help his father-in-law. Ts'osi thinks no one around here can do anything for him."

"I've seen little of your step-father. How is he?"

"It's hard to know. My mother says he claims the cut is much worse—that it's infected."

"Are there red streaks around it?" Yahzi asked.

"I don't know. He stays off by himself. Ts'osi is concerned, but he doesn't want to come between Asdzaan and her husband. Sons-in-law are outsiders in the hogan."

"Do you think Ts'osi will stay here until his step-father is healed?" Yahzi saw herself stuck in the hogan for moons.

"I heard him say to Asdzaan that there is a Zuni surgeon who could do the most for her husband. But Asdzaan thinks a Zuni would want too much livestock."

"Does your step-father have that kind of wealth?"

"No. But Ts'osi claims the surgeon is a friend of his. He wouldn't demand much."

Yahzi couldn't contain herself. "If Ts'osi takes his father-in-law to Zuni, would he take me? And go on to Canyon de Chelly? Ts'osi told me he would take me home some time."

"I'm sure he will. Some time." Little Tso made "some time" sound a long time off.

Yahzi's hopes wilted.

"Some one in Canyon de Chelly makes the most beautiful necklaces you've ever seen" Little Tso said. "Traders in Santa Fe pay dearly for them since they can't go there themselves."

Yahzi's hopes rose—a little.

"Ts'osi gets ammunition, even guns, in Santa Fe to trade for the necklaces, but now he'll have to bargain hard. He used his last necklace a few moons ago. Now, he has blankets my mother wove, but they aren't valued much in Santa Fe."

Yahzi felt despair.

"You look sad," Little Tso said. "Don't be. If Ts'osi said he'd take you to Canyon de Chelly, he will. Just not soon."

Yahzi forced a smile.

"That's better," Little Tso said. "Let's think about something else."

"What would you like to think about?"

"Do you think I'll have a baby soon?" Little Tso asked.

"If not this moon, then the next one."

"You see, you can be cheerful." Little Tso giggled.

"And after this one, many more." Yahzi put an arm around Little Tso. "The sun is getting low. Let's take the flock back to the hogan."

After the evening meal, Yahzi went outside with her raw hide bedding. It was warm enough that she did not need the protection of the hogan although she'd miss the companionship it offered.

She was sitting near the entrance contemplating which tree to sleep under when Ts'osi came to sit beside her.

"I may leave for Zuni tomorrow, my sister," he said. "If you can't be ready, I could wait a day."

Yahzi's mouth dropped open. She was too stunned to answer.

"I can't wait much longer. My father-in-law has a worm growing in a cut that he got on our return trip. He needs help soon."

"Won't he see a Dinee medicine person?"

"Asdzaan wants him to, but I have a Zuni friend who knows the most about wounds like this. He met my father-in-law the last time we went to Zuni."

"I'm sure it's the thing to do!" In Yahzi's elation, she forgot it was not her place to advise. But, she could be on her way home in the morning! She'd be with her brother and sisters in no time. If Ts'osi would go on to Canyon de Chelly.

"Tomorrow will not be too soon?" Ts'osi asked.

Yahzi swallowed the elation she felt. "I'll be ready," she said, as if the invitation were an everyday event.

The two sat in silence for a while. Yahzi tried to restrain herself but couldn't help asking, "Will you go on to Canyon de Chelly after Zuni?

"I hadn't thought about it because my father-in-law's wound worries me. I only have enough trade goods for the surgeon. A trip to the Canyon wouldn't do me any good."

Yahzi sucked in her lips.

"We'll see what happens after we reach Zuni. I haven't forgotten my promise that I'd take you home, my sister. But it may have to be some other time."

"It's not far to the canyon, is it? Perhaps you could tell me how to get there." Yahzi kept herself as calm as she could.

"You could probably find your way, but we never know about the Spanish. You wouldn't want to be enslaved again, would you?"

The thought sent a shiver down Yahzi's spine. It would be better to wait until "some time" than be taken a captive of the Spanish.

In the morning, Yahzi was awake before anyone else. She rolled up her skirts and blouse to pack, tucked her knife and flint and steel into a pouch that she tied to her waist band, then stirred the fire. Yoo'o joined her to prepare the morning meal.

Ts'osi joined them. Yahzi tried to jest. "I guess your father-in-law won't take any of his sheep for the surgeon." She remembered how Asdzaan had ridiculed the flock that her husband brought home.

Ts'osi chuckled to be polite. "His mother sent some gifts to Asdzaan that he's kept for himself. That's another reason Asdzaan is in a foul mood. She was expecting more than that handful of sheep we drove back."

"You think Asdzaan was expecting bride wealth?" Yahzi covered her mouth to hide her grin.

"She'd argued with a brother of her husband that his family ought to pay something. I don't know how serious she was. She was too old to have children when they married, so no bride wealth was expected."

"Was there more peace in her hogan than in this one?" Yahzi asked Ts'osi. "And I've added to the upset."

Ts'osi chuckled. "You don't do any more than I have done to stir up trouble. I don't know why I can't stop teasing Nataalith."

Yoo'o poked Ts'osi in the ribs. "Yes," she said half- joking. "Shame on you."

Yoo'o filled three bowls with corn mush, and they ate while others in the hogan stirred. "I've put dried meat in the pack sacks for your horse," she said. "There's room for any gifts you take."

"Not many," Ts'osi said. "And few from your step-father."

Yahzi put a hand on Yoo'o's shoulder. "You've been kind to me. If I don't return, perhaps you can come to visit me someday."

Yoo'o grinned. "I'd like that. Maybe when the little one is finished nursing. If another one doesn't arrive soon after," she laughed. "I've been to Zuni but not to Canyon de Chelly. Ts'osi promised to take me some day. He says the canyon walls are more beautiful than the ones at Zuni."

Yahzi felt a moment of longing. Yoo'o and Ts'osi made good companions. She'd miss them. She breathed deep and scraped the last of the corn mush from the bowl with her fingers. She handed it to Yoo'o and left for the corral to help with the horses.

She haltered the three they would ride while Ts'osi loaded bags on the backs of three pack horses. Yahzi joined him to lash one in place, guided by a few comments from Ts'osi. When his father-in-law limped into the corral, he grunted a greeting to Yahzi, then proceeded to tighten the cords she had tied.

Ts'osi led the way out of the corral, two of the pack horses tied to his. His father-in-law followed with a pack horse. Yahzi brought up the rear. Yoo'o carried her baby on its cradle board to see them off. Her other children swarmed around Ts'osi's horse, begging to go with him. Ts'osi replied with his widest grin and a waving of his arm.

The three kept a steady pace on the trail. Ts'osi examined his father-in-law's foot whenever they rested.

After three full days on the trail, they reached a village that Yahzi assumed was Zuni. The canyon behind a cluster of houses reminded her of home. It wasn't as wide but two bright red sides walled in a stream bed. She couldn't be sure that water flowed because at the canyon's mouth she saw only lush grass and shrubbery.

As they rode farther, they came to farm fields. Ts'osi handed the ropes of the pack horses to his father-in-law and rode back to Yahzi. "This is a Zuni farming village. The Zuni town we want is still half a day's ride. Maybe a little more."

"Some of these fields look like wheat stubble," Yahzi said.

"You've seen wheat?" Ts'osi was impressed with Yahzi's knowledge.

"It's a Spanish crop. It couldn't be grown on the ranch where I was a slave, but I saw it in a field near Cebolleta. Wheat flour is prized more than corn flour among the Spanish."

"It's becoming a favorite with the Zuni, too," Ts'osi said. "Sometimes it's a good alternative to corn. But wheat needs more water than corn."

"Does that stream offer enough water? It seems to disappear once it leaves the canyon and spreads over the open land."

Ts'osi laughed. "In a way it does disappear." He pointed to a large tree trunk. "You see that big log? It's hollowed out to carry water from the stream to the wheat fields. They've just started doing that."

Yahzi shaded her eyes to study the land. Ten or more logs carried water from the stream to various fields. The fields were surrounded by mounds of dirt two or three hands high. Preparing the fields must have required moons of work.

"I can't believe wheat flour is so much better that they'd do all this work." Yahzi said.

"They irrigated their corn fields before they turned to growing wheat. But you're right. It's a lot more work." He chuckled. "You should see them at harvest. They spend days husking the wheat kernels when that's no work at all for corn."

"I hope the Dinee still grow corn. I can't imagine anything better," Yahzi shook her head as she looked at more of the fields.

"Look at them," Ts'osi said as they reached the village. "That family is preparing wheat flour."

Yahzi looked for metates, but what she saw were wheat kernels scattered on an earth-packed surface. Boys were driving a few burros over the kernels. When they stopped, women scraped up the remains into baskets.

"Don't they mind the dirt that gets into the flour?" Yahzi asked Ts'osi.

He guffawed. "They'll take the baskets to an open space and toss what they have in the air. The wind carries off what they call the chaff —the light husks the burro and kids broke off. A good wind carries off the dirt too. We can watch them work if a wind comes up."

Yahzi didn't care if she watched or not. It was obvious to her that no self-respecting Dinee would go to so much effort to make flour. Grinding corn with a mano and matate was difficult enough. Besides, what could match the taste of a warm, fresh corn tortilla?

Ts'osi held up a hand as he reined in his horse. "We'll camp under these trees," he said. "I know the family in that house. We'll visit them first."

The sun was still up, but Yahzi appreciated an early stop if it meant she didn't have to find firewood. Smoke curled out of the mud covered house that belonged to Ts'osi's friend. It stood alone like other homes while a row of houses resembled the pueblo homes of the Jemez.

She hustled to catch up with the two men as they entered the house of Tso'si's friend.

"Come in, sit. What do you want to eat?" she heard as a greeting. The man had spoken in heavily accented Dinee.

192

"It's been many moons, my friend, since I tasted Zuni *hewe*. Such a wonderful taste is unknown among us." Ts'osi repeated himself in what Yahzi assumed was Zuni.

The man called to a woman who must have been his wife. Yahzi didn't recognize a single word of the weird sounding language. She had picked up a little of the Jemez language, but Zuni resembled it in no way. The new sounds threatened to rupture her ears.

The woman answered. Ts'osi translated for Yahzi. "She wants you to help her cook the hewe."

He half hid a grin with his hand. Yahzi wanted to kick him. How could she help with a food she had never seen.

The woman was kneeling beside a large stone resting on four legs of smaller stones. Heat radiated from it. The small fire must have burned much of the day. The woman spoke some meaningless sounds. Yahzi sat beside her and watched. Two bowls of a white paste lay beside her. The woman dipped her fingers into one bowl, then the other scooping out a fistful of runny meal, and spread it on the rock. A spiral of steam climbed from the substance. In moments, the edges curled. The woman lifted an edge and flipped it over. It was like a tortilla but thinner. The woman scooped it up and dropped it into a woven tray.

She looked at Yahzi and spoke. Yahzi didn't need words to understand that it was her turn. When she dipped into the first bowl, she found it cool while the mush in the second bowl was hot. She tried to remember how much the woman had taken, spread whatever her fingers held on the stone. Her cake turned out larger than the woman's had been, its sizzle louder, the steam thicker. Yet, the edges curled almost as rapidly.

When Yahzi lifted hers, she saw irregular black spots. When she flipped it over, parts of the cake stuck together. Yahzi realized it would not brown evenly. She picked at it, tore it, and ended up with four or five pieces.

The woman held a hand to her mouth, but Yahzi heard her giggle. The woman said something before she put the pieces in the basket. Yahzi reached for one, waved it in the air to cool it, and put it in her mouth. The consistency was not to her liking, and the taste was distinctive. She chewed slowly, trying to like it. While Yahzi was deciding on the taste, the woman spread four cakes on the stone. Soon she had a stack, and the two women took the hewe to the men.

The woman laughed as she spoke at length often glancing at Yahzi. Ts'osi translated. "She says making hewe is too much for you. She doesn't know how you'll find a husband."

Yahzi joined in the laughter. She didn't care if she never found a husband, but the words tied her stomach in a knot. Would she ever be a mother if her brother and sisters didn't have children?

TWENTY NINE

Yahzi and her two companions started early, yet the sun passed its midpoint before they rode into Zuni pueblo. Yahzi saw mountains in the distance, but the wide, flat valley did not display the beauty that the farming village possessed. Its numerous ditches and low walls surrounding the fields showed the people irrigated but not in the neat, precise patterns of the out-lying village. The remains of both corn stalks and wheat stubble filled the farm lands. Among the corn stalks, a few flattened squash that someone must have stepped on were beginning to rot.

The town had far more dwellings than the village. A few houses lay away from the plaza, but compact pueblo rooms showed most Zuni preferred close contact and valued proximity to the plaza. She'd never before seen pueblo buildings with an ambition to reach the sky. She counted at least four stories of rooms with an abundance of ladders, many jutting from what must be hard-to-reach entrances. Yahzi couldn't determine how many, if any, kivas there were. She wondered if Spanish brown robes had convinced the Zuni to give up their ceremonial chambers. From what Yoo'o had told her of Zuni, Yahzi doubted that they'd give up such a fundamental part of their religion as their sacred meeting places.

The plaza and narrow walk ways through the pueblo were crowded with men and women, scurrying antlike from place to place. Their calls to each other matched the barking of a horde of dogs.

When Ts'osi and his father-in-law dismounted near one end of the pueblo, Yahzi halted her bay and climbed down. The three led their horses toward an isolated building and tied them to a corral pole. A lone burro brayed at the strangers. Yahzi sniffed the air for a hint as to what was cooking since a dense cloud of smoke from a multitude of cooking-fires filled the air. Burnt wood smell crowded out any scent of food except for a hint of roasting corn. Her mouth watered despite the acrid smoke.

Ts'osi stood close to the door of the building and coughed. After a second, louder cough, a greeting came from within. "Our host bids us to sit and eat," Ts'osi chuckled. "The Zuni are as hospitable with food as any Dinee. They make a mutton stew as good as any I've ever tasted, and they'll offer us hewe. They can't get enough of it."

The three visitors ducked upon entering the low, narrow door. The two men remained bent over. Yahzi felt her hair touching the ceiling. A large beam of wood supported a higher roof. She heard a child jumping above her. A small, square opening in front and another on the side added to the light from the cook fire. The room looked to be about eight persons long and two or three persons wide.

A large stone slab rested in the ground at the entrance, level with a hard packed earthen floor. A slab of wood that somehow clung to the side of the door-frame served as a door. A curtain closed off an interior store room.

Firelight at the side of the room illuminated a large cooking stone supported by four earthen pillars. Two or three metates leaned against the wall behind the cooking place. Yahzi wondered if corn and flour required different grinding stones. Beside the fire, a woman poured flour from a basket into a clay bowl. Yahzi thought the woman smiled at her, but she did not beckon her to sit by the stone. So Yahzi kneeled near the entrance while Ts'osi and his father-in-law sat near their Zuni host. Yahzi noticed another man sitting to his left dressed in white leggings and a red shirt reaching to his knees. He'd wrapped his hair in a whorl tied at the back of his head.

The host spoke in a loud voice, enunciating each word. Ts'osi translated. "He says to his friend but for my benefit—this is my friend and brother—meaning me." The man continued. Ts'osi said, "He claims I am a great trader, known far and wide, that I have more wives then fingers—which he made up—and brags about how I came a long distance to see him. He exaggerates my generosity—for my benefit."

Ts'osi spoke at length in Zuni. Yahzi assumed he was praising the host's hospitality and generosity. The man beside the host tried to hide a yawn. Yahzi couldn't resist yawning herself, being unable to understand the conversation.

When Ts'osi finished, the host reached into a buckskin bag at his side and retrieved a necklace that jingled as he waved it above his head for all to see. Yahzi guessed it to be silver. She could see small pieces of turquoise among the metal beads. When Ts'osi reached for the necklace, the man pushed his arm aside and pulled his head forward to place the necklace over Ts'osi's head.

Ts'osi translated the man's words. "You'll not find such a beautiful necklace in all of Dinehtah." He laughed, "Not until you return with it!"

Ts'osi nodded to his father-in-law. He rose, went outside, and returned with one of the packs from the horses. Ts'osi withdrew a Spanish dagger with a flourish, held it up by the blade. Its handle had been decorated in silver and a piece of coral. Ts'osi lifted it high and twirled it until a beam of sunlight glittered onto the host's face. All the while he was speaking in Zuni.

The host spoke to the woman. Ts'osi summed up what he had said. "He told her to prepare a mountain of hewe for his dearest friend and companions. Kiau, his wife, makes the best hewe I've ever tasted. So thin, it's always crisp."

The woman added water to one bowl and took another from the edge of the cooking stone. Yahzi realized it was necessary to use a paste combining both hot and cold batters. The woman dipped her fingers into the first bowl, frowned, and reached for a bowl with flour. She added a few pinches, stirred the mixture, and judged it to her liking. She scooped out cool batter, combined it with the hot, and spread a circle on the stone. The host exclaimed something in Zuni when he heard it sizzle. A moment later he sniffed and exclaimed. Ts'osi didn't need to translate. The host's grin said that his wife's hewe was the finest in all of Zuni.

"Palowah's first wife taught this younger wife to cook." Ts'osi said in Dinee. "She knew every trick invented to turn corn meal and wheat flour into delights for the tongue. Palowah mourned his first wife's death for more than a year—until he realized this woman was as good a cook as the first wife." He covered his chuckle with a hand.

From Palowah's facial expressions Yahzi guessed he'd understood most of Ts'osi's words. He must be a trader, too, she thought. The man turned to his companion and spoke in Zuni. The man edged forward to where Yahzi could make out his features. He was slender and short, but what caught her attention was his eyes. They changed from gray to brown to black as he took in the three of them. When he looked at her, her spine tingled. His glance shot a lightning bolt down her back. Bumps erupted on her arms.

His other features were normal, but their combination made him attractive. From his smooth forehead and glistening black hair she thought he had to be close to her age, but a few streaks of gray suggested he might be older. All in all he simmered in an attractive mystery. For a moment, she imagined lying next to him, feeling his eyes as he fathered her baby. She shook her head to get the thought out of her mind. She'd never let a Zuni husband keep her from family and her beloved canyon. The man scooted back to his place behind Palowah. Yahzi breathed easier.

Kiau emerged from the next room with a serving basket piled high with thin circles of brown. Yahzi was surprised at how short she was. Thick lips exaggerated her grimace. The way Kiau offered the food basket indicated an insistence that no guest could evade. Ts'osi and his father-in-law each took a handful of the cakes. Yahzi lifted three of the hewe, careful not to break them. They melted in her mouth. It was as if she tasted the thinness and the coloring.

"Loosen your belts," Tso'si translated Palowah's words. "After the hewe delights your tongue, it fills your bellies like nothing else."

The three guests nodded in agreement as they finished eating.

"By custom, I should wait until tomorrow to begin our trade," Ts'osi said to Yahzi, "but my father-in-law needs doctoring. I'll explain the urgency to Palowah. Perhaps you could bring in the next pack, a small one on the first horse. I'll nod to you when I need it."

Yahzi nodded she understood.

Ts'osi turned to his father-in-law who retrieved an empty carrying bag from his pack and laid it on the floor. "Friend," Ts'osi looked at Palowah. "We have a long journey ahead of us. No friends or relatives to feed us. I've told everyone how generous you are."

Yahzi smiled to herself. She guessed Ts'osi intended to accumulate food for the surgeon.

Palowah examined the knife's handle, felt the blade, tossed it from one hand to the other, then said to his wife, "Bring them more of the toothsome hewe. The driest you have for their trip."

Kiau glowered at Ts'osi. The woman rustled in the storeroom a long time before returning. She had only a handful of cakes that she placed in Ts'osi's bag.

"Friend, it's a long trip," Ts'osi whined.

"Bring him more, woman." There wasn't much of a command in Palowah's tone.

Kiau scowled again, but she returned with two more cakes. "The bin is empty," she whimpered, loud enough for Tso'si to hear.

"On your next trip we'll be better prepared," Palowah said. "If the Kachinas have brought rain. It's been a poor year for our wheat."

"Kiau is like a chipmunk," Ts'osi muttered in Dinee but loud enough for Palowah to hear, "the way she hides her food."

"You are like a rat, eating everything in sight," Palowah bellowed in Dinee. "My wife has given you more than you need." Although Palowah had an accent, Yahzi understood him with no difficulty.

"Did I not give you the finest Spanish knife you've ever seen," Ts'osi barked at Palowah.

"Aren't you wearing a necklace that's more beautiful than any in Dinehtah." Palowah's voice rose to a high pitch. His cheeks turned red.

"Who always comes to you first with the finest goods made in Dinehtah?"

"And who killed my uncle's father?" Palowah looked directly into Ts'osi's eyes.

"My father's father killed him, but your uncle killed my grandfather. How can I forget?"

The man with the changing eyes crawled between Ts'osi and Palowah. "Friend of this house, we have no need to talk about events of long ago. Those grudges from the past do nothing for us now. Let us forget them. Our tribes are at peace. Harmony has brought us trade and prosperity."

"You're right, friend. I didn't come to trade but to show you how much I care for you," Ts'osi said. He nodded at Yahzi. She left to get the pack he wanted.

When she returned, Ts'osi opened it and took out a finely worked deerskin. He unrolled it in a flourish, flinging it before Palowah and his companion. "You see how much I like you, friend. This deerskin is without flaw. Your wife will have the finest dress in all of Zuni."

The man with the changing eyes edged to the deerskin and felt it with both hands. "It is a delight to see. And to feel." He seemed to reconsider. "There are these rough spots." The man rubbed his hands over two or three places as if trying to rub them smooth.

"Still, your gift is generous, my friend," changing eyes said. "We are fortunate to enjoy your friendship."

"He is right," Palowah said. "The Spanish knife is beyond comparison. I will treasure it. If only there were a sheath worthy of such a knife." He looked in vain at Ts'osi and his father-in-law.

"I will always wear my necklace with pride," Ts'osi evaded a response to the request for a knife sheath.

"Woman," Palowah called to his wife. "We forgot about those pinyon nuts, we found the other day. Bring them here." He glanced at Yahzi. "Two trees bore early. I'm sorry we don't have more to share."

"It's been years since I've tasted pinyon nuts," Yahzi's mouth watered. "I'm so glad you remembered."

Changing eyes edged closer to Palowah, partially blocking Yahzi's view. He brushed away a few crumbs of hewe that had fallen on Palowah's lap.

He looked over his shoulder at Yahzi. "Why have you been unable to harvest pinyons?"

"I was enslaved in a place where few pinyons grow. The Spanish took whatever nuts there were, expecting us to live on corn and beans."

"How awful," changing eyes exclaimed in a high pitch that showed his concern. "Did other Dinee rescue you?"

"I escaped on my own," Yahzi said. Her shrug dismissed further telling of her story, but the man looked at her wide-eyed. As his eyes changed hues, she again felt attracted to him but in a different way. The concern in his voice reminded her of how Yoo'o had responded to the story of her enslavement. For a while the six of them said nothing.

When Ts'osi broke the silence, it was to ask about the famous Zuni surgeon who treated open wounds.

Palowah drew in a deep breath. "We stopped using his name moons ago. A Spanish disease took him from us."

THIRTY

"Oh, no," Ts'osi groaned. "We have come a long way for nothing. We'll have to return to Dinehtah for a medicine person."

Yahzi couldn't hear everything Ts'osi said, but his glances at his father-in-law troubled her. Could the Zuni surgeon have died? Did Ts'osi intend to go home? Yahzi felt a chill down her back, her throat tighten as she waited for Ts'osi to translate.

Tso'si turned with downcast eyes. He stammered at first as he translated, ending with the Zuni surgeon's death. Yahzi choked on a anguished cry.

Palowah smirked before he spoke. "There is someone here who assisted our surgeon. They say he learned everything the surgeon could teach. A moon ago, a patient gave him twenty sheep for his help. They say his fingers are more skilled than those of the man who taught him."

When Ts'osi translated, his father-in-law asked where the man was.

"He's here," Palowah said.

"Can you take us to him?" Ts'osi raised an eyebrow.

"Yes," Palowah said.

"Can we see him now?" Ts'osi said.

"Yes." Palowah nodded as he spoke.

"Let's go, then," Ts'osi was losing his patience.

"There is no need to go," Ts'osi translated Palowah's words.

Yahzi wanted to scream "what do you mean?" but held her tongue.

When Palowah finished speaking in Zuni, Ts'osi guffawed as did the two Zuni. Ts'osi translated. "The man next to our host is Huseysena, whose fame as a surgeon has spread throughout Zuni and to the Hopi. He's already cured a few Dinee."

Yahzi grinned at the word play. Ts'osi's father-in-law failed to conceal a frown. After Huseysena and Ts'osi conferred, Ts'osi said to his father-in-law, "Huseysena will wrap your foot in a poultice to reduce the swelling. It must stay on all day tomorrow."

His father-in-law sighed. "What if the swelling goes down tonight?"

"There's an important dance tomorrow," Palowah said. "All the men of the pueblo must participate. You're invited to watch. The next day Huseysena will operate."

Yahzi and her two companions spent the night in a small room above Palowah's dwelling. She awoke to a penetrating cry making her fear an Apache attack.

Ts'osi reassured her. "It's a Zuni priest greeting the sun." He laughed. "I hope he's wakened Kiau so we'll have hewe soon."

Yahzi stretched and descended the ladder to help. Huseysena was blowing embers awake. Kiau was pouring water into a mixing bowl. She indicated with gestures that Yahzi could bring in firewood. With an ample fire heating the cooking stone, Kiau showed Yahzi the metate used for grinding wheat. While Yahzi pushed and pulled the mano, Kiau mixed batter and taught Yahzi a few Zuni words. Huseysena brought a basket of wheat kernels for Yahzi to grind while he rubbed the cook stone with a block of salt. Kiau poured batter on the stone. Within moments the toasting aroma of hewe filled the air.

After feasting on hewe, Yahzi and Ts'osi left to find roof tops for viewing the dance. Ts'osi settled into a place among elderly men. A group of girls invited Yahzi to join them. Two of the older ones greeted her in Dinee, curious about the language and wanting to learn more. Yahzi soon had them speaking basic phrases while they taught her Zuni words.

Everyone fell silent when drum beats sounded, and a line of men emerged from a narrow passageway. The lead dancer, dressed in ornate costume, must be a priest, Yahzi thought. All the dancers wore masks covering their heads. A reddish black substance on the masks suggested dried blood. Yahzi tapped one girl on the arm, gestured at cutting her finger and smearing blood on her face, then pointed at the masks. The girl nodded that the smears were indeed blood. She whispered in Yahzi's ear the Zuni word for it.

Yahzi wondered why the masks had long black beards with even longer black hair. If it were not for the Spanish, she would never have imagined hair on a man's chin. When the dancers flung the masks back and forth, the flowing hair added drama to the dance steps, and the dancers became more than human.

All the dancers stepped in unison to the drum beat until they neared the roof top where Ts'osi sat. Suddenly, they flourished stone knives to threaten Ts'osi. Yahzi broke into a sweat until the dancers passed him by.

The repetition of the dance and the unintelligible songs bored her. She studied the spectators. Except for youths and a few old men, women made up the on-lookers until she saw Huseysena sitting between Kiau and other women. When the drums ceased, the dancers retired to rooms adjacent to the plaza.

Four nearly naked men painted black with white horizontal stripes rushed in to replace the dancers. Their short breech clothes were held in place by twisted ropes of a black fiber. The same rope adorned their necks.

Yahzi thought the black and white performers wore masks, but a second look revealed a heavy black paint around the eyes and mouths with daubs of white in-between. Yahzi didn't know how to ask the girls about the caps they wore. Whatever the material was, it supported corn husks resembling ears or horns.

Yahzi pantomimed a question about what the men were doing. The oldest girl grinned and pantomimed, then forced a laugh. Yahzi guessed the men intended to break up the seriousness of the dance. She recalled a Dinee dance where clowns poked fun at the main dancers and ridiculed spectators.

Two young girls pulled Yahzi back from the roof's edge and crowded in before her. They irritated Yahzi until she understood they meant to hide her. She welcomed their concern when one clown passed out clubs to the others. They darted at two older children while maneuvering themselves to dance just below Ts'osi. They screamed war cries and jumped to slash at Ts'osi's feet. A boy handed him a short stick, and Ts'osi flourished it like a war club, swinging at the clowns. The spectators roared in laughter.

The drumming picked up when the ceremonial dancers reappeared. The clowns sought refuge in the vacated rooms. Yahzi stretched and studied the ritual dancers but then she dozed. She focused when the clowns again appeared and concentrated on the ceremonial drama.

Ts'osi joined Yahzi, and the two returned to Palowah's home. Tso'si asked if Yahzi had enjoyed the clowns and told her what little he knew of the dance, explaining the Zuni shared little of their religion with outsiders.

"As long as they're generous with their food, they can keep their secrets," Ts'osi joked.

Ts'osi's father-in-law greeted them at the door.

"The poultice must be making you feel better," Ts'osi said.

"I spent a lot of time sleeping."

Yahzi examined his leg. The swelling was reduced, but the skin around the cloth was a bright red with a streak of black.

Ts'osi put a hand on his father-in-law's shoulder. "Do you feel ready for the operation?"

"Do you think Huseysena knows what he's doing?"

Yahzi saw fear in his eyes.

"If he's as good as his teacher, there's no one better," Ts'osi said. "It may hurt, but he'll remove whatever worms gnaw at your leg."

The next morning, Yahzi awoke to the priest's calling the sun. Ts'osi was shaking his father-in-law.

"You must have dreamed of the operation," Ts'osi laughed. "I've never seen you so restless."

"I don't remember," his father-in-law said. "I feel like I never got any sleep."

"Maybe you'll sleep through the operation."

"I don't think that's funny," his father-in-law replied with a nervous grin.

Huseysena and Palowah joined them. "How is the patient?" Huseysena asked.

"He didn't sleep much," Ts'osi said. "His moans kept me awake most of the night."

Huseysena examined the infection, then gave directions for preparing the room. Kiau spread a blanket close to the cooking stone while Huseysena laid out his equipment. Palowah sang under his breath as he smoothed out the blanket. Ts'osi helped his father-in-law onto it while Yahzi joined Kiau in a corner to watch.

Ts'osi whispered to Huseysena. "The infection is worse. The poultice came off during the night."

Yahzi wrinkled her nose at a foul smell when the ill man moaned as Ts'osi rolled him onto his back.

"Come hold his head in your lap," Huseysena beckoned to Yahzi. He turned to Ts'osi and Palowah. "You'll need to hold his legs, maybe his arms."

Kiau brought in a bowl with a red liquid that held a hollow cane about a hand's length long.

Huseysena unrolled a buckskin pouch to reveal the glass bottom of a bottle with jagged edges. Yahzi wondered if the Zuni had found it among Spanish rubble. Huseysena fingered three fragments of black, shiny stone. He mounted two of them in the cleft end of a short stick so they stuck straight out. He mounted the other one sideways, securing the joints with sinew.

Palowah reached into another pouch and removed some shredded bark. Yahzi caught the scent of cedar. He motioned to Kiau, and she brought a bowl of water to set beside Huseysena.

Palowah and Huseysena put their hands to their mouths and blew into them, muttering what Yahzi took to be prayers. Palowah bathed the foot with water, wiping away corn pollen, then patted the skin dry with shredded bark.

The two examined the ankle, their patient moaning when they turned his foot to scrutinize the infection. Huseysena drew a horizontal line across the wound with his fingernail and a vertical line reaching to the first. Palowah nodded agreement.

Huseysena spoke to his patient. Ts'osi translated for him. "We're going to remove the black blood and any flesh where worms might grow."

The patient drew a deep breath while muttering a Dinee prayer. Palowah handed Ts'osi a short cedar stick to put between his father-in-law's teeth.

Palowah took the patient's foot in his hands and stretched the infected area. Huseysena reached for a black stone knife and cut along the lines he'd indicated, then peeled back the two flaps of skin. Yahzi held her breath at the stench while rubbing the patient's brow. He jerked in agony. Huseysena picked up another knife to make a deeper incision. Yahzi saw that he avoided a reddish purple tube embedded in the flesh, wondering what it was. He also pushed aside a whitish cord running up the leg.

Palowah squeezed at the knife strokes. Blood and yellow pus oozed out. Huseysena soaked up the liquid with a wad of cotton, then dipped a length of cloth in water and cleaned the wound.

Ts'osi's father-in-law took a deep breath and relaxed, but the stick stayed in his mouth. Yahzi saw that his upper teeth were embedded in the wood.

Huseysena sucked up red liquid with the cane tube and blew it onto the wound. Palowah tucked the flaps of skin into place and secured them with a cloth, pressing against the wound. Yahzi was impressed with how quickly the bleeding stopped. Palowah applied the last of the cedar bark. Huseysena wrapped it with a length of cloth and tied it in place with a cord of twisted cotton.

Yahzi wiggled the piece of wood loose from the patient's mouth and asked if he wanted water. He nodded and she lifted his head so he could sip from a bowl that Kiau provided.

"The poison is gone." Palowah looked at Ts'osi. Before Ts'osi could say anything, Palowah continued in Dinee, "Huseysena expects six horses for saving your relative's life."

"He knows six horses is all we have," Yahzi thought. "How will we ever leave here?"

THIRTY ONE

"Don't you remember the many gifts I have given you?" Ts'osi spoke to Palowah in Dinee he was so angry. "Without horses where can we go? Will you feed us the rest of our lives?"

"I've given you enough hewe that you could walk back to Dinehtah before getting hungry. Or you could run back alone and return with horses for those two." Palowah pointed his chin at Ts'osi's father-in-law and Yahzi.

"Huseysena expects too much. Tell him I'll have three horses for him the next time I come."

"Do Dinee bargain over the life of a relative?" Palowah pretended shock. "The worms would have filled his whole body if it were not for Huseysena. Your father-in-law would be dead within a moon if it were not for my wife."

"What does Kiau have to do with the cure?" Ts'osi asked.

"Not her. My other wife." Palowah showed surprise. "Didn't you know? I married Huseysena moons ago. He cooks and sews better than most women. Best of all, he gets along with Kiau."

"I suppose you need my six horses to help you pay his bride wealth? Is that it? Doesn't a Zuni husband supply the bride wealth? Does a wife work to pay her—I mean his—own bride wealth?" If Ts'osi was trying to shame Palowah, it didn't work.

"Huseysena's father and brothers were more than satisfied with the arrangements I made before our marriage."

"And now your new wife is making you wealthy." Ts'osi's face went livid. "While making your life-long Dinee friends destitute."

"Perhaps, you could satisfy my new wife with five horses," Palowah said. "I'm sure he won't bargain with you, but perhaps he'll do me the favor of taking only five. Since you're such a good friend, I'll ask him to take only five."

"What am I to do with one horse?" Ts'osi looked from his father-in-law to Yahzi. He quickly translated for them before confronting Palowah again. "Do you expect them to live here with you? Would you put them to work like they were slaves?"

"You could ride back to your mother's hogan and return with horses."

Yahzi could no longer hold her tongue as she saw a chance to reach Canyon de Chelly. "What if Ts'osi gave you three horses, and I traded my horse for a burro. Isn't that your burro we saw in the corral where we left our horses? The one so skinny, vultures would pass him by if he died."

"That is Huseysena's favorite burro. Its endurance is greater than any horse." Palowah flung his arms wide to suggest the animal's value. "It's worth as much as a horse."

Yahzi knew Palowah exaggerated, but before she could haggle further, Ts'osi took up the bargaining in Zuni. Yahzi failed to follow the details of the conversation, but from the scowls of the two men, she judged they got nowhere.

When a silence broke their exchange, she offered her solution. "Let Ts'osi take me to Canyon de Chelly on his horse while I ride the burro. My brother has many horses. Ts'osi will bring back twelve horses for Huseysena." She held up both hands, flexing her fingers, then jerked up her two thumbs. "Twelve horses!" A vein in her neck throbbed at making a promise she wasn't sure she could keep. What would happen to Ts'osi if her brother weren't Ganado Mucho? Or if he had no horses?

"Who is your brother?" Palowah asked.

"Ganado Mucho." Yahzi believed so strongly that he must be her brother it hardly seemed she lied.

"Ayhe," Palowah muttered. "I've met Ganado Mucho. He is a man of wealth." Palowah paused only a moment in thought. "He should send more than twelve horses."

"You'll take care of my father-in-law until we return?" Ts'osi said.

"We won't be long." Reasserting the possible lie gave Yahzi confidence that Ganado Mucho must be her brother.

"Huseysena will watch over your father-in-law. Your brother may want to send some sheep, too." Palowah wet his lips. "We'll feast on mutton stew when you return. Huseysena cooks the best stew in the pueblo."

Once Ts'osi saw that his father-in-law's infection was healing, he told Palowah that he and Yahzi would leave. Kiau prepared more hewe for them while Yahzi went to the corral to befriend the burro. She took a handful of corn meal with her and sang a Dinee lullaby in the burro's ear while it ate. In no time the burro was familiar with her smell and nuzzled her even after it had eaten all the corn.

By the time Yahzi returned to the pueblo room, Palowah and Ts'osi had finished their hewe. Kiau handed Yahzi two paddies, both burned on one side, but the meal filled her stomach for the morning. Palowah accompanied her and Ts'osi to the corral where Ts'osi saddled his horse. Palowah dragged out a rickety saddle for the burro.

"Do you expect her to ride on that bundle of splinters?" Ts'osi demanded of Palowah.

"It's the only saddle I have for the burro. Besides, you said nothing about saddles. Or bridles. You might bring back a cow as well as horses and sheep." Palowah spoke as forcefully as Ts'osi had.

"I can ride bare back if the saddle breaks up," Yahzi said. As she lifted it to the burro's back, she corrected herself. "When it breaks up."

"Huseysena never complained about the saddle," Palowah said. "You should follow his example if you want to be a good wife."

Yahzi shrugged her reply to Palowah as she mounted, then followed Ts'osi toward a trail north of town. Neither of them looked back. On the edge of the pueblo she rode beside Tso'si. "How soon will we reach Canyon de Chelly?"

"No more than three days. Kiau wasn't generous with her hewe, but we'll find Dinee who'll feed us."

"I heard her talking to her husband yesterday. I didn't understand much, but I think she called us vultures."

Tso'si chuckled. "Next time I'll bring him a necklace of glass beads. The Zuni haven't learned yet which of the Spanish trinkets are worthless. Guess what I'll give him."

"He'll get good horses from my brother." Yahzi wished she felt the conviction that she put into her words.

They rode that day without encountering any Dinee. They used their saddle blankets for warmth that night and were ready to start early the next day.

"We're sure to meet Dinee today. Chinle Wash isn't far."

"Could there be someone from Canyon de Chelly?" Yahzi's words rang with hope.

"We'll be at the canyon's mouth in two days if we ride steady. And if we find water for the horses." Ts'osi laughed. "Water for one horse and a burro."

Yahzi's lips cracked during the day. Ts'osi's horse whinnied a helpless sound in its thirst; her burro seemed oblivious to lack of water. Neither she nor Ts'osi had spoken since the sun passed its peak. A splinter had worked its way into Yahzi's thigh, but she hardly noticed it because of how dry her mouth was.

"Over there," Ts'osi pursed cracked lips to point.

Yahzi failed to note the direction. She searched the horizon and saw a whiff of smoke to their right. They turned their mounts in that direction. Yahzi's throat was too parched to speak.

The smoke issued from a large hogan with two smaller hogans close by. A wagon was half hidden by the larger hogan. The outfit's corral was larger than most. Yahzi's anticipation of water and food made her forget questions about her family.

Ts'osi's horse bolted when it spotted a watering trough outside the corral. Her burro stepped faster. When she got to the trough, Ts'osi and his horse were both drinking. She dipped her hands into the water and cupped enough to fill her mouth. Two more handsful and she felt she might survive. The burro edged itself between Ts'osi and Yahzi to drink.

"Looks like you're thirsty," a man's voice came from behind them. Yahzi turned. The man cradled a rifle.

"We've come all the way from Zuni without water," Ts'osi said. After a glance at the rifle, he named his mother's clan and the clan he was born for.

The man looked at Yahzi. "Your wife?"

"No." Ts'osi didn't offer further explanation.

211

Yahzi couldn't refrain from speaking. She gave her clan affiliations, explained how she had been enslaved, and asked a multitude of questions before the man could answer any of them.

"I'd guess you're Spanish from how much you talk. But you speak Dinee too well to be Spanish," the man replied.

He turned toward the hogan. "You must be hungry. My mother-in-law might have a few scraps to feed you." He glanced at Yahzi. "My wife and mother may know about your family. I'm a stranger here."

At the hogan entrance, the man cleared his throat and announced the presence of two strangers, then led Ts'osi and Yahzi inside. A young woman added firewood to smoldering ashes that had given off the smoke they had seen. She smiled at Yahzi, nodded at Ts'osi.

"You missed our noon meal," an older woman said. "Not much mutton left after filling up big belly." She glanced at her son-in-law. He crouched at the doorway as if to make an escape.

The smell of mutton stew wafted through the hogan. Yahzi felt hunger creeping up on her, but her cracked lips could use more water. The young woman approached her and Ts'osi, carrying two gourd canteens. She handed one to each. The two emptied the gourds in hasty swallows.

"Good to fill up on water," the old woman said. "You won't need so much food." She stirred the kettle, resting on the ground, surrounded by flames. "This will get you through the day." She dipped two large bowls in the kettle, and handed them to the young woman who served the guests. Yahzi stared at chunks of meat in bowls filled to overflowing.

"Sit. Eat." The older woman pointed to sheepskins on the floor.

Yahzi sipped at her broth. Ts'osi picked up a chunk of mutton but dropped it, sucked at his fingers.

"Did you want cold mutton?" The older woman chuckled.

"Cold or hot. It's the best mutton I've ever tasted." Ts'osi picked up a smaller piece and got it into his mouth before it burned his fingers.

"I'll take care of your mounts," the son-in-law said. He appeared anxious for an excuse to leave. Yahzi guessed he was still uncomfortable around his mother-in-law.

She looked around the hogan. A small window covered with a thin cloth let in as much light as the tunneled entrance. Most entered from the smoke hole. The floor was large enough for ten or twelve people to sleep on; most of it was covered by plain wool rugs and sheepskins. Stones lined a shallow fire pit.

Yahzi tried a bit of meat. It was delicious and the right temperature. Between sipping and using her fingers she finished the bowl in no time. Ts'osi had already handed his bowl back to the young woman. The old woman beamed and refilled his bowl but ignored Yahzi's.

"We heard you asking about relatives while you spoke to my husband," the young woman said.

Yahzi explained how she had been captured and where she lived before the Spanish raid. Her father had seemed an old man to her, but she realized everyone in the generation above her had seemed old then.

She gave her father's nickname and what she remembered as his real name. She described him as tall and handsome but realized she had no more than a young girl's impression of her father. She recalled her mother and her mother's sisters in detail but failed to remember the nickname of her mother's oldest brother who had moved to his wife's hogan when Yahzi was an infant.

"Do you mind telling us your real name?" the young woman asked.

It was a question Yahzi had dreaded being asked since her romance with Diego. She had loved the sounds in her new name, given to her upon entering womanhood, but the trauma of the Spanish raid had caused her to forget it. She was too ashamed to admit that she could not recall her name.

"I was captured before I got a real name." Blood rushed to Yahzi's face. It was not easy to lie to fellow Dinee even if they were unrelated.

Both women looked puzzled. The daughter put a hand on Yahzi's arm. "The Spanish stole your name, just like they steal our land."

The mother asked if she remembered who performed her kinaalda. Yahzi recollected the participants as a vivid picture of the ceremony flashed to her mind. When she named them, the older woman's smile filled with warmth. Two of the participants were relatives of hers.

"My mother moved from the canyon after the Spanish massacred so many of us," the older woman said. "Too many ghosts in the place, my mother said. We seldom went back."

"Did you ever hear what happened to my brother and sisters?" Yahzi asked.

"Your sisters married and stayed in the canyon—although far from where your mother's hogan was. I'm not sure where they located. They say your brother left the canyon when he married. I never learned his name."

"I think he was given the name Ganado Mucho after he became a warrior," Yahzi said.

Both women exchanged puzzled glances. The older one said, "It could be." The daughter added, "We hear he raised a host of warriors to raid the Spanish, but he returned for the winter."

"Can your husband tell us where Ganado Mucho is?" Yahzi begged the younger woman.

"No one knows for sure," the young woman said. "He keeps his men moving to avoid the Spanish. Won't you want to see your sisters first? You won't have any trouble finding someone in the canyon who can tell you where their hogans are."

The thought of seeing her sisters made Yahzi's heart leap with joy, and they would know where their brother was. But Ts'osi needed to return to Zuni with horses. She'd have to find her brother first to pay what Palowah demanded of Ts'osi.

THIRTY TWO

Their hosts insisted Yahzi and Ts'osi stay another day to rest. The older woman heard from a reliable source that Ganado Mucho was mustering forces in the Chuska Mountains. The young woman's husband had a brother living near Luchachukai, a watering place at the end of the Chuska Mountains. The husband agreed to lead them there. If his brother didn't know the whereabouts of Ganado Mucho, his wife would.

On the day they left, the two women provided gourd canteens and dried venison for two days.

"Make sure your horses drink all they can along Chinle Wash," the mother said. "Once you leave it, there's no reliable water until Luchachuchai. You may see a herder in between or you may not. Even if you do, she won't have water for the horses." She glanced at Yahzi. "Nor your burro."

"We'll be careful with the water," Yahzi said.

"Make sure that son-in-law of mine is careful, too," she whispered to Yahzi. "He doesn't have much sense."

Yahzi nodded she'd watch him. "All your venison you've given will feed us well."

Ts'osi's horse and the husband's were eager to start, each one trying to get the lead. Ts'osi reined his in while both horses pulled ahead of Yahzi's burro. She kicked its sides before letting it set its own pace, one that somehow kept the horses in sight.

The trail sloped gradually but steadily. Two vultures circled overhead. Yahzi could not discern what they were looking for, but the husband looked up and said something to Ts'osi that caused him to laugh. He must have joked in return because the husband laughed loud enough for Yahzi to hear.

When the sun was overhead, the two men dismounted and sipped from their canteens, waiting for Yahzi. When she arrived, she dismounted. She'd just unplugged her canteen when the two men started walking their horses. She hurried her drink and caught up with the men, lagging a few steps behind.

"My brother was with Ganado Mucho this spring when he raided the Spanish," the husband said. "My brother came within a fingernail's width of being killed."

"Is he alright now?" Ts'osi asked.

"Not exactly," the man answered. "A Spaniard knocked him out and tried to scalp him, but a cousin rescued him. Then my brother came to."

"So his spirit never left him."

"No, but half his hair did," the man roared in laughter. "Now we call him Half-a-Head. He wears his left braid as long as ever, but it's like he's bald on the right side."

"How's he like his new nickname?" Ts'osi said.

"He's good humored. He laughs as much as any one about it. Except he won't let his wife use it around their children. Knocked her down the first time she did." He laughed again.

Yahzi reminisced about joking she had heard at home. She realized her relatives would think the results of the half scalping were funny, but she no longer appreciated the humor. She wondered how she'd fit in with her family after absorbing so much of a Spanish outlook on life. She licked at parched lips, started to reach for her canteen, but resisted the impulse.

Like the two men, Yahzi drank no more water until they camped that night. A cold wind came from the north. The rawhide from under her saddle did little to keep out the cold, but it did protect her from the wind. Thoughts of how close she was getting to her brother kept her warm—warm enough to sleep a little.

In the morning, the young woman's husband told them they could reach Luchachukai by tomorrow night if they managed a steady pace. He looked at Yahzi when he spoke. She assured him her burro would keep up.

At mid-day a mountain range rose before them. Patches of snow showed in ravines. Yahzi imagined more snow under the pine cover. It had been years since she felt encompassed by the beauty of snow-capped mountains.

"I hope all the sheep are down," the husband said. "A deep snow could come any time. Means good hiding for the Dinee. The Spaniards could never find their way up there."

"How will we find Ganado Mucho?" Ts'osi asked.

"We're getting close to my sister-in-law's hogan. Her mother's hogan, I guess. They always have plenty to eat. And that mother has plenty to say. Never stops talking."

The three rode until afternoon. When they spotted a spiral of smoke, they saw the hogan had two large cooking ramadas, placed away from the east-facing entrance's view of the rising sun. A smaller hogan lay a hundred paces beyond, its entrance to the east.

When the three approached, two boys ran toward them, waving their arms. The two men dismounted and handed the reins to the boys. They led the horses to a corral behind the hogan. Yahzi followed. The boys took her reins at the corral and promised to unsaddle and feed her burro. She joined the two men at the entrance to the hogan. A woman with a wrinkled face appeared, followed by a woman of middle age. Yahzi missed the conventional greetings. The woman was caught up in answering what must have been an inquiry about her son-in-law.

"He was supposed to be here yesterday. Who knows? You can't count on him for anything, anymore. When they half scalped him, they took half his brain."

The other woman interrupted. "He'll be here later. He's due to go see Ganado Mucho soon."

"What are they up to?" the wrinkled woman said.

"It's man business. Who knows? Except they'll talk a lot and then go off. If they had any sense they'd stay put. It'll be a cold winter with deep snow. At least the Spanish won't come raiding us."

The middle aged woman left for a ramada where coals surrounded a large kettle. Yahzi joined her and helped build up the fire. The two worked in silence until flames leaped high.

"You can add water from the olla," the woman pointed with her chin to a clay jug hanging from one of the ramada's forked posts. "I'll get beans and meat."

While the two took turns stirring the stew, the woman explained how her husband had earned the nickname of Half-a-Head. She

217

complained about her mother's constant use of it and wanted Yahzi to know the man had a beautiful name, Keyannie. Yahzi agreed it was beautiful. Before she could say more, the woman left to tell the others that the meal was ready. After two days of dried meat, the three guests stuffed themselves.

Keyannie's mother-in-law was explaining where the guests were to sleep when hoof beats interrupted her. The middle aged woman ran toward the sound, stopped and waved. In moments, Keyannie reined in his horse and dismounted. Hidden by his horse, he greeted his wife. Yahzi wondered how the two spent their moment of privacy.

When the two joined the others, Keyannie was grinning and welcomed the two men in traditional fashion. He added a smile for Yahzi.

"How much does she want?" his mother-in-law asked, obviously skeptical that they'd get a fair bargain.

"I promised her three sheep," Keyannie said.

He turned to his brother and Ts'osi. "Since I lost my braid, I've had terrible headaches. A medicine woman has given me herbs to cure it." He held up a buckskin bag and waved it. "She gave me a dose when I was there, and I haven't had a headache on the ride back."

His mother-in-law snorted. "Probably it's the ride that stopped your headache. Wait until tomorrow."

"Can you ride tomorrow? If so, I'll return to my hogan," his brother said. "These two need to find Mucho Ganado. The woman is Ganado Mucho's sister."

Yahzi felt a momentary thrill as someone else confirmed her belief that Ganado Mucho was her brother.

THIRTY THREE

Keyannie and his wife were the first up in the hogan. She dressed quickly and left to heat the stew. Keyannie soon left, too. Yahzi knew she should get up to help but pretended to sleep. A place on her right buttocks ached, likely a splinter, and there was no one she could ask to remove it. The other side of her buttocks ached all over. She rubbed it while stealing a few moments more to rest.

When the head of the hogan sat up, Yahzi jumped to her feet and pulled on her dress. The woman looked to the sleeping place of her daughter and son-in-law. When she saw it empty, she stretched and laid back down.

As Yahzi cleared the hogan entrance, she glimpsed the rim of the rising sun. No wind greeted her, but frost coated nearby grass. She wondered how she'd survive the mountain cold, then joined Keyannie's wife under the ramada. She added sticks to the fire, warmed her hands, and turned to warm her aching buttocks.

"Keyannie says he can start today," his wife said. "The relief from his headaches has made him a vigorous man. We haven't been intimate since his wound, but he made up for it last night." She spoke in matter-of-fact tones. "You'd better watch out if you're ever alone with him." She giggled before dipping her finger in the kettle to test its warmth.

"He won't want anything to do with me when he has a beautiful woman like you for a wife," Yahzi said.

"You're beautiful, too. Have you many children?"

"No. I've been a slave of the Spanish until this spring. Glad I never had children to grow up to be their servants."

"I didn't know," the woman spoke in a hushed whisper. "Do you want children?"

"I'd like children, but I'm too old."

"You don't look that old."

"I've missed a couple of moons."

"It could be the stress you've suffered."

"Maybe," Yahzi sighed. "I'd like to be a mother."

219

"There are medicine people who can help."

"After I find my brother and my sisters, I'll look."

Keyannie's mother-in-law emerged from the hogan to ask when the stew would be ready. She urged her daughter to be generous.

After everyone had eaten, Keyannie said his sons would get the horses ready, and he'd lend Yahzi a horse and saddle. Yahzi almost thanked him until remembering Dinee custom. But when Keyannie's wife brought her a thick, woolen poncho, she burst out with, "Muchas gracias."

The woman raised an eyebrow. Yahzi said her words were meant to praise the beauty of the poncho.

Three horses stood saddled in the corral, their breaths fogging the air. After the three mounted, Keyannie turned his horse and kicked it into a run. Ts'osi followed. Yahzi hated the trot her horse decided on, gave it a kick, and felt her buttocks relax when it ran. The ride would be better than on the burro.

In late afternoon, Keyannie pointed to a canyon mouth where smoke curled upward. "Let's dismount," he said. "The guards won't be so anxious if we walk in."

"Is it Ganado Mucho's camp?" Yahzi asked. She gritted her teeth. She should keep quiet and wait to see what was ahead.

"It may be," Keyannie muttered, not looking at Yahzi.

Four men greeted them with rifles. Yahzi hung back and could not hear the exchange between Keyannie and the guards. Her hopes rose when a guard waved them on.

When they reached the camp, another guard met them. Yahzi was surprised to see how many men had gathered. They'd built numerous shelters. Three or four women tended fires and roasted haunches of what looked to be venison. The men were occupied with adding to their shelters, chipping away at arrowheads, or cleaning their rifles. No one paid attention to Keyannie's arrival.

When he asked an older man something, a gesture pointed the way to a group where one man appeared to be leading a discussion with five others. The leader looked to be Yahzi's age, maybe younger. More than a year younger, she thought. Her heart beat faster but slowed when she recalled her brother's life of freedom would not have aged him as her slavery aged her.

Keyannie stopped a few paces from the group, not looking at any of them while he spoke. "I have brought a woman who is searching for her brother. His Spanish name is Ganado Mucho."

"Is that the woman?" the leader asked.

Yahzi approached. "I haven't seen my brother since my kinaalda. He hadn't earned a man's name when I was seized by the Spanish, but I'm sure he became a warrior. He was very clever, very brave." Yahzi became more nervous when the leader failed to respond. "He is Bitter Water, born for Towering House," she stammered. "A clever man, a handsome man." She stared at the leader a few moments before averting her gaze.

"I am Ganado Mucho," the leader said. "You have found me. But I am not your brother."

A pit opened in Yahzi's stomach. When she first glanced at Ganado Mucho, she had convinced herself his features were those of her brother. She backed away, trying to hide her despair.

"Wait," Ganado Mucho commanded. "How did you became separated from your brother?"

Yahzi told about the massacre and how she had been taken into slavery.

Ganado Mucho reached behind him for a blanket and insisted Yahzi sit with the group. He motioned for the others to make room on their blankets for Ts'osi and Keyannie.

"We have been discussing the white man's religion," Ganado Mucho said. "You must have learned much about it."

Yahzi paused. The disappointment in not finding her brother made her hesitate. Ganado Mucho smiled and asked if she had been sprinkled with water or wine, or whatever the Spanish used in their curing ceremonies.

Yahzi explained baptism and how she had been given a Spanish name when sprinkled. She said with a hiss, "Besides our land, they steal our names." She fought back tears while muttering, "They stole mine."

221

Ganado Mucho looked puzzled. "But they claim their gods say it's wrong to steal."

One of the men looked at Keyannie and guffawed. "Was it the Spanish who stole half your hair?" Everyone, including Keyannie, roared.

"Does one braid appeal more to women than two? I might cut one of mine off," another man said.

"No woman can keep her eyes off me since I lost my hair," Keyannie boasted. "Of course, they always looked at me with even more hope when I wore two braids."

Ganado Mucho waved a hand to dismiss the joking and addressed Yahzi in solemn tones. "How is it the white man can be so powerful when they have only three gods?"

"They insist they have only one god," Yahzi said. "There's God, his Son, and something they call the Holy Spirit. Then they claim the three are one. I never understood how that could be."

"What about this Son? Is he anything like the Hero Twins?" Ganado Mucho asked.

"A little." Yahzi hesitated. She didn't remember much about the Hero Twins. "God made a woman pregnant. A woman who never had sex."

Several men in the circle chortled. One said, "She must have been a remarkable liar."

Yahzi ignored the comment. "They call her Virgin Mary. I often thought she must be their fourth god, but Diego said that wasn't so." Someone asked who Diego was. "The man who owned me. He told me that her Son was called Jesus."

"I met a Spaniard named Jesus. He still lives?" one man asked.

"No. This Jesus died a long time ago. The Jews nailed him to a cross." Yahzi explained what nails were.

"Where is this Jewish tribe?" a man asked. "Maybe they can help us. They must be powerful if they can kill a god."

"They live far away, where the Spanish came from. The other side of the world."

One man asked how many days' ride that was.

Before Yahzi could answer, another interrupted. "Tell us more about this Jesus."

"You may have seen a fetish of him in their churches. A dead body wearing a breech cloth hung to a cross."

Several of the men shivered. Yahzi heard muttering about corpse powder and witches.

"So they only have two gods, now?" Ganado Mucho asked.

"They believe Jesus' spirit lives. His body, too. It was missing from its grave."

"Yooee," several men murmured as their faces paled. One said, "A ghost with a body!"

"The Spanish say that if you believe in Jesus, then you will live in heaven with God after you die." Yahzi grew uncomfortable with the discussion, realizing that she mouthed what Diego Baca had briefly explained. She hadn't realized how little she had grasped of his beliefs until she tried to make sense of them.

Ganado Mucho nodded encouragement. "You know more about the Spanish than any of us. You can be helpful."

"I speak their language, but I'll never understand them. They do such strange things."

"They did a most strange thing this spring," Ganado Mucho said. "Three of my clan brothers were among a peace party on their way to Santa Fe when they were invited to feast with a Spanish garrison at Jemez. Then the Spanish killed them. I guess with the help of Jemez people."

"No," Yahzi said. "The Jemez didn't help them. The Jemez hate the Spanish."

"How do you know this?" Ganado Mucho asked.

Yahzi explained her stay in Jemez and the Nuevo Mexicano intrusion on Jemez land.

"I must avenge the peace party," Ganado Mucho said. "Do you know any Jemez who would help us get inside the pueblo."

"My aunt is there. She speaks Dinee—lived among us because her husband is Dinee. He now speaks the pueblo language. He suffers poor eye sight, but his mind is as good as ever. His name is Dayish. He has a close Dinee friend there, married to a Jemez woman. He's become something of a Jemez leader!" She went on to explain how easy it would be for one or two Dinee to enter the pueblo and find Dayish.

Ganado Mucho's eyes gleamed. "You can't know what a help you've been."

The Dinee asked Yahzi more questions until Yahzi had told them everything she knew of the Spanish garrison. She felt elated but exhausted by the time they finished.

"Rest now," Ganado Mucho said. "Unless you want to know what Dinee are doing to drive out the Spanish. We're been talking about it."

The words charged Yahzi with energy. "I'll stay."

"Several war parties have tried to avenge the peace envoys slaughtered at Jemez."

One man described what his war party did. "We went south after we heard about the treachery and raided ranches around Socorro. Took many horses."

"They joined us at Belen," another said. "We killed three ranchers and raided the town. We went on to Alburquerque where we met other Dinee. The town is small, and we burned its houses." He looked around for approval. The others gestured encouragement. "We headed north and killed a rancher between Alburquerque and Santa Fe. Santa Fe is too large to attack."

Another man said, "When we headed north, Apaches joined us. We attacked Taos and killed two Nuevos Mexicanos outside the town."

"It's a step toward revenge, but we must do more," Ganado Mucho said. "Governor Melgardes has raised a war party in Santa Fe and is heading west."

"We'll wipe him out," a Dinee exclaimed.

"Or we can let him wander in the land. He may take men from the garrison at Jemez. Now that we can find a spy in the pueblo, we'll know the best time for revenge."

The men growled their approval of Ganado Mucho's plan.

Despite the excitement, Yahzi yawned.

"We have talked enough tonight. We all need sleep," Ganado Mucho said. The war leaders rose and left. Ganado Mucho signaled Yahzi, Ts'osi, and Keyannie to stay.

"Why did you think I was your brother?" he asked Yahzi.

"My hopes ran away with my reason," Yahzi said. "I heard much about you while I was a captive. I convinced myself you were my brother."

"Have you asked for him in Canyon de Chelly?"

"Not yet." She nodded at Keyannie. "When he volunteered to bring me to you, I couldn't resist."

"The three of you can rest here tonight. I have blankets by my shelter." Ganado Mucho pointed to a brush shelter, covered with a sheet of canvas.

The four walked to the shelter. Ganado Mucho pointed to a space where they could keep out of the wind. He asked Yahzi to join him alone for a moment.

"You are a strong woman. An intelligent woman. I would like you for a wife."

The proposal jarred Yahzi awake. "But we hardly know each other. Our relatives haven't arranged anything."

"I know it's not the Dinee way, but it's a desperate time."

"Do you have other wives?"

"Yes. They'd make life easy for you. I have moved them to my mother's hogan so none is favored by her own mother."

"It sounds like a good arrangement."

"I can give many sheep and fifteen horses for you. How many sheep would satisfy your family?"

Yahzi felt overpowered. She wouldn't have to ask her brother for help. Ts'osi could return to Zuni with payment for the surgeon and three horses for the help he gave her.

But she had doubts. "Why do you find me so attractive? I may be past the time when I can have children."

"Your knowledge of the Spanish is invaluable," Ganado Mucho said.

Yahzi's heart sank. Had she been among the Spanish too long that she needed an expression of desire from a suitor? Ganado Mucho hadn't even said he liked her, only that he valued her knowledge. Yet, life with him would be better than any prospect she'd yet had.

"You don't need to answer tonight," Ganado Mucho said. "I can wait until morning."

THIRTY FOUR

It took Yahzi forever to fall asleep. When she woke, she rolled over, determined to sleep longer. Then it hit her. She had to tell Ganado Mucho if she would marry him.

Yahzi thought about how wealthy he must be, the prospect of other wives to help with hogan chores, the likelihood of his wives having children who would be her sons and daughters. The prospect of instant motherhood was appealing.

But what of her family and clan? Marriage wasn't just between a man and a woman, her mother once told her. Marriage was an exchange between families, a way of joining forces with another clan. Ganado Mucho hadn't even told her his clan. His proposal had nothing to do with forming an alliance between families. It would be a mere union between one man and one woman. How improper! It was no way for Dinee to marry.

Yahzi dressed and went outside to help with the cooking. When Ganado Mucho arrived, she told him how honored she was to be asked to become his wife. Then she explained why she thought it would be unsuitable for her to marry him.

"You are more intelligent than I first thought. You're as shrewd as my oldest sister," Ganado Mucho said. "I never thought of marriage the way you describe it, but you are right. I had overlooked your Bitter Water people. That's not right."

Both sat in silence for a while before Ganado Mucho said, "I intended this as a marriage gift, but I want you to have it anyway. You've shown me how to avenge the Dinee peace party." He handed her a turquoise stone that filled her hand. Its beauty excelled its size. Black spider webs crisscrossed the blue-green gem. Specks of white glistened. The color and pattern stole Yahzi's breath.

When she squeezed the stone, a tingle shot up her arm. Her palm grew warm. Her arm quivered. She tightened her muscles to quell the sensation.

"It's magnificent," she gasped, glancing at Ganado Mucho. "I can feel its power." Her palm heated, her arm began to quake.

A wry smile spread across Ganado Mucho's face. "I see the stone is meant for you," he nodded. "It never revealed its power to me." He handed her a buckskin pouch to carry it in.

Yahzi felt urged to thank him but held the thought. Instead, she said, "I must find my brother. I'm not sure where to look."

Ganado Mucho stroked his chin a moment. "An old woman here joined us from Luchachukai. She knows the canyon people as well as those living along the west side of the Chuska Mountains."

"Where can I find her?"

"I'll show you."

Ts'osi and Keyannie were sitting up and stretching. Yahzi told them where she was going. The two laid back down.

"I only know the old woman's nickname, Many Medicines," Ganado Mucho said. "She helps cure our sick and wounded."

The two walked into a grove of pine trees where an old woman was boiling something in a pottery jar. The aroma filled Yahzi's nostrils with a strange smell, pleasant at first like pine needles, but when the smell became stronger, it turned bitter. Yahzi's nose twitched.

Ganado Mucho had to cough a third time before Many Medicines looked up from the pot she was tending. She squinted twice before acknowledging him.

"This woman is looking for her brother," he said to her. "It's been many years since she last saw him."

Many Medicines cupped a hand to her ear. "Eh?"

"This woman has not seen her brother since her kinaalda," Ganado Mucho's shout made Yahzi jump. He explained why they had been separated for such a long time, why she didn't know his present name, but that the two had grown up in Canyon de Chelly.

The old woman nodded all the while he spoke, acknowledging she heard him with a broad grin.

"Why don't you tell her more," Ganado Mucho turned to Yahzi.

Yahzi shouted her clan affiliations. She described her brother's physical features as best she could before adding that he must be a brave warrior and a wealthy man.

The old woman wrinkled her nose. When she relaxed it, the furrows around her eyes and across her forehead were as deep as any Yahzi had ever seen. The woman had much white hair, but a few streaks of black contrasted with it like the feathers of a magpie.

Many Medicines shook her head. "I don't know."

Yahzi refused to give up. She described the location of her mother's hogan and told all she knew about her mother and father.

The woman smiled. "Could be...What else can you remember?"

Yahzi recalled as best she could her other mothers and their children they had. She didn't do as well with her father's sisters or his brothers, but Many Medicines' smile turned to a chuckle.

"It has to be...But we can no longer use the names of your mother and father. Your father died long ago. Your mother lived to a good age." She hesitated in thought. "I'd almost forgotten you." She glanced at Yahzi a few moments. "I can't believe it's you." Her grin showed missing teeth.

"And my brother? You remember my brother?" Yahzi's words were breathless.

"Eh?" Many Cures muttered.

"My brother," Yahzi shouted. "Where is my brother?"

"He lives in a hogan not far from here. Half a day's ride north. Their hogans are nestled in a canyon mouth." She lowered her voice. "I suppose you don't know his adult name." She looked around and lowered her voice. "His name now is Nakai. He collects turquoise and other valuables."

"Do you think he'll appreciate this?" Yahzi couldn't help showing Many Medicines her gift from Ganado Mucho.

Many Medicines squinted, reached to take it. When Yahzi put it in her hand, the old woman's hand trembled. "It's powerful. Do you cure or do you look into the future with it?"

Yahzi stammered. "I don't know what I'll do with it."

"Does it feel warm when you hold it?"

"Yes," Yahzi said. "And it makes my arm quiver."

"You may have power you don't know about. Come back to me after you visit your relatives, and I'll teach you my medicines. It's time I passed on my knowledge."

Yahzi kissed the woman's hands. Many Medicines' jaw sagged, her eyes opened wide. The idea of becoming a curer was planted in Yahzi's mind. Many Medicines rubbed the stone four times before returning it to Yahzi.

After she told Yahzi how to reach Nakai's hogan, Yahzi raced back to the shelter to tell Ts'osi and Keyannie. Ts'osi was sure he could find the hogan. Keyannie decided to return home.

It was late morning when Ts'osi and Yahzi rode out of camp. A light wind struck them in the face as the trail north rose before them. Their horses kept a steady pace. Well before dusk, Ts'osi pointed to a cluster of hogans and corrals which he thought must be Nakai's. The two stopped their horses to study the layout.

The central hogan was large. To its north was one almost as large. Two girls drove a flock of sheep into a corral a hundred paces behind the large hogan. Twenty or thirty horses whinnied from the corral close to the large hogan which billowed smoke.

"It'll be a warm place to sleep," Ts'osi said.

"And plenty of stew," Yahzi added.

Ts'osi kicked his horse into a trot, Yahzi's followed. At the hogan he and Yahzi dismounted. The older girl ran from the corral to greet them with silent smiles. The other ran inside. A man came out, greeting them as he walked. He was too old to be Yahzi's brother.

Before Ts'osi could say anything, Yahzi explained who she was and why she was there. The man held his chin in his hand, his eyes half closed. He turned and called into the hogan. Two women came out, and he told them to prepare food and sleeping places for guests.

He sent a girl to ask Nakai to come. She raced to the other hogan and called into its entrance. A tall, erect figure emerged wearing a purple shirt with a green vest. Instead of a breechcloth, he wore a wrap-around skirt that came to his knees. His knee high buckskin moccasins were decorated with elaborate designs. Even from a distance, the pattern demanded attention. What was even more striking was the necklace he wore. Yahzi had never seen anything like it. Bone white beads of shell alternated with a pink rock, culminating to a pendant that glimmered different colors as it swayed with the man's walk.

The young girl skipped alongside Nakai, giggling at whatever he said to her. His graceful step reminded Yahzi of the way bobcats walk. When he reached Yahzi and Ts'osi, he cocked his head, looking from one to the other.

Yahzi's throat tightened. She couldn't think what to say.

Ts'osi spoke for her. "We've been told that you had a sister who was captured by the Spanish at Massacre Cave."

"That's right," Nakai said "Along with a woman who was like an aunt to us. Our men organized a war party to pursue them, but the Spanish fled before anyone could find them."

"My brother." Yahzi found her voice.

Nakai squinted, looked Yahzi up and down, and then glanced into her eyes. "It is you, Yahzi," he gasped. "Yooee. I had given up hope of ever seeing you again."

The two took each other's hands. Yahzi yearned to hug him, the way Diego had sometimes held her, but she resisted.

"Let us go to my hogan," Nakai said. His gestures made it clear his invitation was to Ts'osi and the man who had greeted them. Yahzi guessed some privacy with her brother could wait.

The sun was setting as they entered Nakai's hogan. Yahzi wondered why his wife had not started a fire. Nakai struck flint and steel to ignite the tinder he had prepared for the evening, and the flames' light played upon the hogan's interior. Ts'osi took a deep breath. Yahzi was astonished by the strings of necklaces that hung from racks made to display them.

"Where did you get all the shells?" Yahzi gasped. "Who makes the beads for you?"

"It's all my work," Nakai said. "I travel to a far west tribe. Partners give me the shells and anything else they have for my turquoise." His lips curled into a smile of self satisfaction.

Yahzi decided not to tell Nakai of the turquoise gem Ganado Mucho had given her until she retrieved it from her saddle bag.

Nakai showed off more of his necklaces.

"The yellow...or are they orange...?" Ts'osi was so awe struck that he couldn't complete his sentence. "I believe I have traded a necklace or two of yours in Santa Fe, but these are much more beautiful." He stared at the necklaces Nakai held. "They are orange? Or yellow?"

"It's something called coral," Nakai chortled. "An animal with a shell that lives in a far western sea, too wide to see the other side. The shiny beads, too, are ocean animals. The western tribe collects them. But they have nothing like our turquoise. They give me many shells in exchange."

"How do you make the beads?" Yahzi asked.

Nakai showed her his tool kit, mostly of stone but with a few pieces of Spanish steel. "I love the feel of cutting the shell, drilling is even more exciting."

The man from the large hogan put his hand on Nakai's back. "His real skill is the way he strings the colors and shapes together. Everyone tries to copy him, but none are able to make a necklace the way he does."

"You are too kind," Nakai said. Even in the scant light, Yahzi saw her brother blush.

"Enough of what I do," Nakai said. "Tell me, my sister, all you have endured."

"We should leave these two," the man from the large hogan said to Ts'osi. "You can tell me what Ganado Mucho is doing while my wives prepare dinner." He and Ts'osi stood up to leave. The man turned to Nakai. "I'll send a daughter to remind you there's a meal to be had. You can talk all day tomorrow, remember."

Yahzi relished every moment of telling about her captivity and recent journey because her brother never missed a word. She recalled what a rapt listener he was as a youth. He shed a tear when Yahzi told him of giving birth to twins and how one had died and the other was killed by a Spaniard who must have thought it was cursed by pueblo witches. He took her hand and reassured her that she had done everything she could.

When Yahzi finished, she realized Nakai had told little of himself. "And you, my brother. You live alone in this hogan?"

He laughed. "This is more like my workshop although I sometimes sleep here when I need my solitude." He pursed his lips to point to a sheepskin rolled up against a wall. A brown blanket was folded neatly on top of it.

"So you sleep in the central hogan?"

"Most of the time. It belongs to Holds Tight. That's his nickname because he seldom gives away sheep or horses. Indeed, some people think he must be a witch because he's so miserly."

"Do you think he's a witch?"

"No. He can be very kind. His father left him, and his mother had nothing. As a child he went hungry. That's why he seldom gives anything away."

"You don't mind living in his camp?"

"Oh, there are times I get away. My travels often require moons. In the summer, I accompany the shepherds to the mountain grazing fields." He cocked his head and smiled. "Do you remember how we herded sheep together? You'd make wonderful figures out of the clouds."

Yahzi laughed. "You imagined the shapes. And made up such wonderful stories about them!" She looked at her brother's expression longer than she should, but his face was characterized by such fine features she couldn't help herself. He is so handsome, she thought. "Do you still tell your stories to the girls who help you watch the sheep? When I first saw the two girls who brought in the sheep, I thought they were your daughters."

"No," he said. "My daughter lives in the canyon."

"But why not here?"

"She's my brother's child." He raised an eyebrow, then exclaimed, "Oh, you didn't know. Our mother gave birth to a boy after you were taken away. It's my brother's girl who is my daughter." Nakai frowned. "He's too young to share corn pollen. Imagines himself a warrior one day, a medicine person the next. But, he lives with an older woman in Canyon de Chelly."

"I have another brother! And I'll see him in the canyon?"

"Along with our sisters." Nakai told her of their marriages and where they lived. Several years after the Spanish raid, their sisters married, their husbands joining them. Their brother's hogan was in a side canyon some distance from their sisters.

Nakai concluded. "Our sisters found spouses who made them happy."

"And when are you going to marry, my handsome brother? Or have you had wives who sent you from their hogan?" Yahzi laughed. "I can't imagine that. An artist and so handsome."

"Oh, Yahzi."

Yahzi caught her breath. Why had Nakai addressed her by her name?

"You don't know?" Nakai paused. "I'm a part of Holds Tight's hogan. If I shared corn pollen, it would be with him."

THIRTY FIVE

Shortly after Nakai told Yahzi about his relation to Holds Tight, a young girl came to announce the evening meal. Nakai led Yahzi to the large hogan where the two sat next to each other but said little. Yahzi assumed it would be alright for her to be alone with Nakai so she asked to spend the night with him. Holds Tight suggested that he take Ts'osi to hunt the next day.

When Yahzi and Nakai returned to his workshop, they sat on sheepskins next to the small fire in the center of the hogan. Yahzi bathed in her brother's presence before asking more about their family.

"Our father never stopped looking for you," he told her. "One year he believed he saw you with a couple of Spaniards. He charged them, but they shot him before he got close. The three men with father brought him back to our hogan, but no one was able to cure him."

Yahzi sighed. "I didn't know."

"Our mother moved up the canyon beyond Massacre Cave. Not many Dinee travel beyond it. Even today, after all these years, many of our people fear its ghosts."

"Are you reluctant to visit our sisters?" Yahzi said, assuming nothing would stop Nakai from visiting their sisters.

Nakai half smiled. "I'm not comfortable near that cave, but more to the point, our sisters don't welcome me. When our mother died four winters ago, I gave my sheep from our herd to my sisters' sons and daughters."

Yahzi nodded approval.

Because our oldest sister, Kai, has seven children, and our youngest, Doba, four, I gave Kai's herd almost twice as many sheep as Doba's. I thought that was fair. But Doba felt cheated. She said mean things about me and about Kai. When I stepped in to make peace, they both turned on me." He laughed in scorn. "Now, I wish I had feasted everyone in the canyon on my sheep."

Yahzi's face darkened. "So, I've returned to a family feud."

"I don't know how they're getting along now," Nakai said. "After our mother's death, they left the hogan to avoid her ghost. Doba moved to a side canyon, upstream. Kai moved farther up and built a large place. Her husband works as hard as she does. I assume you'll go to see them both."

"Yes, of course."

"They can help you find our brother. The last I heard, he'd gone north to apprentice with a famous medicine man."

"I should leave soon to find my sisters," Yahzi said.

"Are you leaving because of Holds Tight?" Nakai said. "You seemed upset when I told you I lived with him."

"I tried to hide my feelings." Yahzi felt her face flush. "For years, I've imagined you as a wealthy warrior." She sucked in her lips. "I must tell you. I convinced myself you were Ganado Mucho."

Nakai chuckled. "I sometimes wish I were. But I don't want to head a war party. The Dinee have become as vicious as the Spanish. I couldn't scalp anyone or cut off their head." He looked at Yahzi. "Could you?"

Yahzi felt her cheeks flush as she recalled smashing the head of Diego's shepherd. "I guess so. After what the Spanish did to me."

"I've been spared that," Nakai said.

Neither spoke for a while. Yahzi added a few sticks to the fire. Finally she looked at her brother. "One reason that you had to be wealthy is that I promised a Zuni twelve horses." She laughed at the thought. "It's a debt that Ts'osi owes a Zuni surgeon."

"Ts'osi is the man with you? Is he not your husband?"

"No, he's a clan brother."

"Are you looking for a husband?"

"No. I was forced to marry two Spaniards."

Nakai raised an eyebrow. "I heard that they married only one person."

Yahzi smiled inwardly. "They only marry one woman at a time." She decided not to go into the details of her relationship with Diego. While he never considered their relation a marriage, she did. But she doubted she'd be able to explain such behavior to her brother.

After a pause, Nakai scraped his lip with his teeth. "Well, let's talk about the horses you need. I can't help with horses, but I want you to

236

have a necklace." He got up and lifted two from his rack. "You choose one."

It was a difficult choice. The pattern of one with pink and white shells took her breath away. The other, with bits of turquoise interspersed with gleaming bone-white shells, was unlike anything she'd ever imagined. She examined each one at length, turning them to catch the light until at last she made a choice.

Nakai laughed. "You like them so much, you must have both."

"Either one must be worth twelve horses," Yahzi said.

Nakai chortled. "If you can find Dinee to trade with, they're worth even more, but everyone's saving their horses for the war parties against the Spanish."

"Will Holds Tight go to war?" Yahzi asked.

"Probably not. His eyesight is failing. If he spares any horses, it will be for Ganado Mucho. He won't give me any." Nakai shrugged. "He's in more danger from Dinee who believe he's a witch than he is from the Spanish."

"I'll give Ts'osi a necklace. He can use it to pay his Zuni debt."

"I'm afraid not," Nakai muttered. "Zuni traders come here once or twice a year. They never show any interest in my work. They gave me four horses once, for a bracelet, but they want necklaces decorated with a fetish—a symbol of one of their gods. Only a Zuni can make a proper fetish."

Yahzi shrugged. "Perhaps Ts'osi can find a Dinee farther south who is willing to trade horses." She yawned, more in frustration than from want of sleep. Nakai claimed to be sleepy. He offered her a blanket and pointed to a second sheepskin if she needed it.

Yahzi stretched out to sleep but something in the back of her mind troubled her. Where would she find horses? But that was only part of her problem. She couldn't identify the other, falling asleep without an answer.

She awoke early to hear Nakai snoring. The sky in the smoke hole was as black as ever. She forced herself back to sleep.

Her dream began back on Diego's ranch when she and Diego were lovers. They'd gone hand-in-hand to the corral to watch the sheep being sheared. A ewe mounted another ewe. Diego's face flushed crimson. He dashed into the corral and beat the ewe on top, swearing curses that Yahzi seldom heard. He didn't stop until his walking stick broke.

"Why, Diego, why?" Yahzi had never seen his face so contorted.

"It's against God's law—one female making love to another— Only a man making love to another man is worse."

Diego wasn't finished with his sermon, but Yahzi ended it when she awoke bathed in sweat. Spanish beliefs were once again a problem for her. Their condemnation of homosexuality had stayed with her because of Diego's anger. Was there anything to his belief?

She recalled her grandfather's brother, a man she called grandfather. He had dressed differently. Her mother explained that he was a man-woman, a remarkable medicine person. He had diagnosed fifteen cases of witchcraft. One patient died before a healer could be found. The others were seriously ill but survived with his help. In two cases her grandfather identified the witches causing the illness even though they had died. Clearly, Yahzi concluded, there was nothing wrong with Nakai. It was the Spanish God who condemns the practice. She felt better.

Yahzi and her brother spent the next day reminiscing about their lives apart. On the following day, she decided to leave since Ts'osi had been away from his home so long. Nakai assured her she'd be welcome to stay with him if she didn't settle with a sister.

Ts'osi was eager to begin his return home although concerned they had no horses for the surgeon. When Yahzi assured him that he'd meet Dinee eager to trade horses for her brother's necklace, he accepted her word. She wished she were as confident of the trade as Ts'osi appeared to be.

Her concern diminished as they rode along the edge of the Chuska Mountains, their peaks capped in white. Snow sprawled under the thicker clusters of pine at the base of the mountains. To ride in beauty Yahzi thought—until she remembered her sisters' feud.

When they reached the mouth of Canyon de Chelly, Yahzi halted her horse, overwhelmed by awesome color. Ts'osi reined in his horse at the same time. The canyon's undulations and outcroppings of red and orange made Yahzi aware that nature had a life of its own. To walk in beauty, Yahzi felt the dazzling colors that surrounded her.

Ts'osi turned to Yahzi. "Are you happy to be in such beauty?"

She smiled her answer.

The two held a steady pace until nightfall when Ts'osi pointed to a hogan nestled in a niche of the canyon. A smaller hogan stood not much farther up canyon.

"I've traded here. She'll let us spend the night in the smaller hogan." He spurred his horse ahead with a backward glance. "Let me see what she has to say about the necklaces."

Yahzi waited a few paces away until Ts'osi appeared.

"We can use the hogan." He pointed upstream with his chin. "She'd give twelve horses for the necklace, but she's promised her herd to Ganado Mucho until he's finished fighting."

They'd hardly settled into the hogan before two young girls appeared at the entrance. They brought bowls of stew and tortillas with them, promising corn mush in the morning.

At daybreak, Yahzi was packing her horse when the girls came with the mush. While they ate, Yahzi told the girls what she had heard of the raids against the Spanish. As soon as Yahzi and Ts'osi finished eating, the girls dashed off with the gossip and the empty bowls.

It was past noon when they reached Massacre Cave. Yahzi pointed it out on the opposite side where she and Dezba had hidden. Ts'osi glanced in the direction of Massacre Cave before spurring his horse to a gallop. Yahzi gritted her teeth and urged her horse on. How many ghosts might still linger? Did they know their deaths had been avenged?

Yahzi was ready to camp and spend the night in the open, but the thought that her sister's hogan might be behind the next turn kept her going.

It was almost too dark to continue when Yahzi saw what must be her sister's place. The large hogan was half hidden by out-cropping. A corral disappeared up the canyon beyond the hogan. Echoes of unseen sheep bleated off the canyon walls. A few horses' whinnies answered.

Four children darted from the hogan, stood for a moment while their eyes adjusted, and then stared at the horses. A man followed them, carrying a gun. The children called a greeting. Ts'osi answered.

Yahzi couldn't wait. She bounded from her horse and raced to the hogan. The man shifted his weapon, unwilling to point it at Yahzi but disturbed by her behavior.

She called, convinced her sister must be in the hogan. "I'm a sister to Nakai, looking for my sister."

A young woman dashed out of the hogan. "What sister are you?"

When she saw Yahzi, she stopped and stared. Yahzi wondered if Doba recognized her by their common features—thick eyebrows, lustrous black hair, a complexion that Yahzi hoped she retained, at least some of it.

"Is it...Yahzi?" The woman obviously found it hard to believe it could be her long-lost sister.

"It is. I have just come from our brother. He told me where you live."

Her sister dashed forward, took Yahzi's hands. "I can't believe it. I do believe it. I never gave up hope."

"Neither did I. Many times it was only thoughts of you and my other relatives that kept me going."

"Come in." She looked at Ts'osi and bid him enter, too. "What do you want to eat? I suppose that brother of ours gave you very little. His hogan is greedy."

Yahzi did not want to confront Doba so she did not tell her of the two necklaces.

Doba glanced at Ts'osi. "Is he your husband?" she whispered to Yahzi. "He's good looking. Does he have many sheep?"

"I'm not married." Yahzi explained Tso'si was a clan brother, then added. "I escaped from slavery in the spring."

"You must tell me about being a slave. Was it awful? How did you escape?"

Yahzi sketched her captivity, omitting the children she had, touching only slightly on Diego and Pablo. She delighted in details of how the Jemez pueblo elders defied the Spanish with their pretended ignorance, explained how Nataalith had led her to Ts'osi.

240

Then, Yahzi asked about Kai and their younger brother.

"Our brother lives three days away. He's pursuing whatever his present dream is, I suppose. If he had any sense, he'd share corn pollen with that woman who gave us a niece."

"And our sister?"

"Kai lives a half day's walk up the canyon. We had lived in one large hogan until she died." Yahzi understood that Doba meant their mother. "After her death, Kai changed. Some people probably think she's a witch."

Yahzi lifted an eyebrow at such an accusation from a sister.

"And she tells everybody what to do. She told me how to shear sheep. Can you imagine? I don't know how her children put up with her. How will they learn if they don't do things on their own?"

"I'll have to visit Kai sometime," Yahzi said.

"A few days is soon enough. You must eat now. How is the handsome one called?" she whispered.

"Ts'osi," Yahzi said under her breath. "He's done much for me."

"I'll feed him well."

"Besides guiding me here, he's in debt to a Zuni surgeon who cured his father-in-law. I promised the surgeon twelve horses because I thought my brother was wealthy."

"I can give you two horses. My husband had more, but he lost many in a horse race a moon ago. What about Nakai? Holds Tight has more horses then he can count." Before Yahzi could speak, Doba added, "But he's so stingy, he'd refuse to help."

"He didn't give me any. Ganado Mucho is organizing a war party, and people have promised him their horses."

"I'll talk to my husband, but I doubt he can help."

"Perhaps Kai has horses."

"She has as many as Holds Tight. But she's so greedy she won't give you any either. You'll see."

Yahzi realized it would be futile to argue. She nodded to Ts'osi, and the three of them went inside. The oldest daughter passed bowls of stew, the next oldest made sure everyone had tortillas.

Yahzi spent the rest of the evening listening to Doba tell all that happened after Yahzi's capture. During the telling the youngest of

Doba's children crawled onto Yahzi's lap. The girl's thick eyebrows made Yahzi smile.

"Who is she?" the child whispered to Doba.

"She's your mother," Doba said.

"Mama," the girl looked into Yahzi's eyes.

"My daughter," Yahzi murmured, then sang part of a Dinee lullaby.

"Did you have to leave children behind?" Doba asked.

"No. I'd never let children grow up to be servants of the white man."

"Did the master force himself on you? I've heard the Spanish do that to our women."

Before Yahzi could answer, two of the children came to stand beside her. They looked to their mother. Glancing at Yahzi, they asked, "Is she our mother?"

"Yes. Another mother. Think of all the mothers you'd have if anything happened to me."

"You won't let anything happen to mama, will you?" The girl in Yahzi's lap asked. "No one will take her away, will they?"

"Your fathers will protect us, little one," Yahzi said. "You go to sleep now." Yahzi expected the girl to cuddle in her lap, but she got up and joined her sisters who spread out sheepskins along the hogan wall.

"It's good to have guests," Doba gestured toward Ts'osi. "Will he tell us stories?"

"If the men ever stop talking," Yahzi said. "What do you suppose men talk about?"

"They brag about all the animals they own or the ones they gave away. Maybe about races they've won. Who knows? Some are good story tellers."

Yahzi walked over to the two men. Doba's husband was gesturing and seemed to be mimicking a horse. Ts'osi turned to look at Yahzi.

"Doba asked if you'd tell a story."

Ts'osi nodded and the men moved closer to the fire to make a circle with the children. Ts'osi began with a Zuni adventure, told another about Hopi, and then made up a story about outlandish features and weird behavior of the Spanish. The night passed quickly. It was a night of beauty for Yahzi despite little hope of acquiring the horses she needed.

THIRTY SIX

In the morning, Yahzi was the first to wake. Her first thought was of the horses she'd promised the Zuni surgeon. Where would she find them? She rose, pulled on her dress, and stirred the fire, then looked for a kettle to heat. Before she found it, the oldest girl was at her side, addressing her as mother, and showing her where ladles and pots were. Being called mother warmed Yahzi as much as the flames springing to life. Her daughter said she'd get water. Yahzi had the kettle in place and heating before Doba woke.

When Doba did sit up, she said to Yahzi, "Our daughter likes helping you. I can tell by her smile."

"You have a wonderful family," Yahzi said.

"You can stay here," Doba said. "Where would life be better? Certainly not our older brother's hogan."

"You may grow tired of me," Yahzi said.

Doba's other daughter came up behind Yahzi. She hugged Yahzi and said, "Sleep near me. I have a warm place in the hogan."

Yahzi swallowed to keep back a tear. Home was better than she imagined.

The girl added. "And when you marry, we'll make room for your husband, won't we mother?"

"If she finds a man with many sheep," Doba joked.

Their laughter woke the others, and soon everyone was standing around the fire with outstretched hands. When the kettle boiled, the daughters served bowls of mush. Yahzi fed the youngest from her bowl.

Over the last of the corn meal, Yahzi said she must go to Kai's hogan to see if she had horses for Ts'osi.

"Perhaps she'll lend you horses," Doba said. "I know she won't give you any."

Doba turned to Ts'osi. "You won't want to stay long with my sister. She'll be telling you what to do. As if you couldn't think for yourself."

When they finished eating, Yahzi prepared to leave. She was uncomfortable with her sister's jealousy of Kai, wondered if Kai might be jealous of Doba. She wondered most of all where she'd ever get horses for Ts'osi.

The oldest boy had saddled horses and tied them to a post near the hogan door. The other children stood by Yahzi's side, making her promise to return. She hugged each in turn. Ts'osi mounted and waited patiently. As he and Yahzi rode off, the youngest called, "Come back soon, mama."

The early morning light intensified the colors of the canyon. When the sun struck a wall, reds and orange dazzled the eyes. At one point, Ts'osi dismounted, cupped eyes with hands, and stared up a side canyon with vivid lightning streaks of black on red. Yahzi watched from her horse, her mind absorbing the colors.

It wasn't long until the two reached a large hogan close to the river but protected from flooding with a steep slope. A natural corral composed of river and cliff side ran upstream. The pasture was still green. A touch of spring-like grass contrasted with a patch of snow caught in a cliff side depression.

Yahzi trotted her horse to Ts'osi's side. "I may not go home," he said to her. "Such a place of beauty."

"I am home, my brother." Yahzi smiled. She knew she could make a place for herself as a medicine woman. She'd build her own hogan and be with her own family at last.

An aroma of roasting lamb greeted their noses as they rode to the hogan. Yahzi saw two young women and an older boy in the corral with three rams, inspecting their ears. Four younger children chased a dog, or each other, around the hogan. At the side, a man grooming a horse worked his way behind it so he could watch the approaching couple. He called to whomever was in the hogan.

By the time Yahzi and Ts'osi reached the man, a woman about Yahzi's age waddled from the hogan, holding a swollen stomach with one hand and her lower back with the other. Her plain, square face was framed in bangs and thick, black braids, one of which was unraveling. She shaded her eyes with an uplifted arm.

Yahzi called. "Sister, I have come from our brother, Nakai."

The woman cupped a hand to her ear. Yahzi climbed down from her horse, handed the reins to Ts'osi and ran to Kai.

"It's Yahzi, little sister."

Kai blanched, then felt Yahzi's arms, ran fingers over her face. Covered her mouth with a hand to hide her amazement. "Yooee, older sister. I thought you must be a ghost."

"Oh, I've missed you so."

"Come inside," Kai took Yahzi's arm. "What do you want to eat?"

"We can wait to eat. Tell me about your family."

"Have you heard about our mother and father?"

"Yes. I've seen Nakai and have just come from Doba's. They told me everything."

"Did they tell you about Bahe?"

"No. Who's Bahe?"

"My husband, the one grooming a horse. I wish he paid as much attention to me." She shook her head. The loose braid unraveled further. "You probably don't remember. He lived near our mother's hogan when we were young, a friend of Nakai's." Kai half grinned. "Do you remember how he teased you when you and Nakai herded sheep? When he first came around bothering me, he talked so much about you that I didn't want him as a husband. But he kept coming back. He tells good stories, and he's always laughing. And we couldn't refuse the bride wealth he offered. I wish Doba had received the bride wealth that Bahe gave for me."

"So now you have wealth," Yahzi smiled her congratulations.

"More important, the family has been healthy," Kai said. "No sign of the Spanish. Everything has been peace and harmony since I married. Our hogan is filled with hozho."

"I'm happy for you." Yahzi held her sister's hands. "Your corral looks full of sheep."

"Bahe says I've eaten half the flock the last few moons. He's roasting a lamb now. Says it's to tempt the little one to come join us." Kai laughed as she rubbed her pregnant belly. "Uh, she's kicking good. She wants to see you."

Yahzi put her hand on Kai's stomach, felt the baby moving.

"How soon?" she asked.

"It's been nine moons. This one's shy."

"Were your other children nine moons?"

"It's hard to remember. I had Doba around when they came. Now she's changed. Become so greedy, the rumor is she's a witch. I defend her, but if she gets any more greedy, I'll give up on her." Kai shrugged. "Maybe she is a witch. So jealous of my wealth she's made this one stay in the womb."

Yahzi scoffed at the idea their sister could be a witch. Kai shrugged her shoulders. "I don't know why the woman says mean things about me."

"You know our sister would never hurt you," Yahzi said.

"Oh, I know," Kai said. "Maybe after the baby comes, I'll make up with her. I miss her until I remember how she's always telling everyone what to do."

"We'll all get together after the baby comes," Yahzi said. She wondered, though, if Kai could be jealous of Doba's beauty.

"Will you and your husband settle in the canyon?" Kai asked. "There's room for another hogan between mine and Doba's."

"I don't have a husband. Ts'osi, is a clan brother. His wife's hogan is far off."

"What do you suppose he and Bahe are talking about?" Kai asked.

The two women listened. The voices from outside the hogan were muffled, but they heard the laughs of delighted children.

"They must be watching the children ride horse back," Yahzi said.

"That Bahe wants his children on horses before they can walk. He says horses were made so humans wouldn't have to walk."

The two women sat in bemused silence.

Finally, Kai asked, "When will Ts'osi have to leave? You know, he's welcome as long as he wants to stay."

Yahzi explained the debt owed the Zuni surgeon and how she felt obliged to repay the twelve horses.

Kai chuckled. "Twelve horses are nothing. All my mares had colts last spring. Bahe will want to give you horses, too."

Yahzi felt a serenity that she'd never experienced since being enslaved. She was home, secure, in a place of generosity, where one knew hozho.

It dawned on her she could obtain many livestock with Nakai's two necklaces. She'd build her hogan close to her sisters and raise a large flock of sheep.

Kai interrupted Yahzi's thoughts. "I've been so excited to see you, that I've left you hungry. What do you want to eat?"

"Roast lamb," Yahzi laughed. "If our daughter-to-be doesn't want it all."

"She'll get her share," Kai chuckled. "There's beef stew, too. Our older daughters do the cooking now."

Kai went to the hogan entrance and asked Bahe to bring in the lamb, and called the children to the mid-day meal. While she and Yahzi waited, Kai told Yahzi the names of the children. When they came in, she called them to her and told them Yahzi was their mother. She explained slavery to the older ones, to the younger ones she said Yahzi had returned from a long trip.

The children sat at the edge of the hogan, engaged in quiet chatter. The four adults sat on sheep skins near the fire. When they finished eating, Ts'osi waved the children to join them and told stories that led to legends touching on First Man and First Woman. Everyone was enraptured by his tales, no one thinking of sleep until the younger children dozed off.

The hogan slept late. After the morning meal, the children went outside to play. Kai asked Ts'osi and Bahe to sit close. She turned to Ts'osi. "My sister has explained your debt to the Zuni surgeon. I am giving you twelve horses so he can be paid. That man could be a witch as well as a doctor. Who knows with those Zuni? They seem generous when we visit them, but then we come back with nothing. They are clever people."

She nodded to Bahe.

He said to Ts'osi, "My wife told me last night how much you helped her sister. I give you six horses for your kindness."

"Yooee," Ts'osi answered. "I have seen your horses. Anyone would be proud to own one. The Zuni surgeon will feel ashamed when I give him such wealth."

"He should be ashamed," Kai said. "But more likely, he'll be happy he's cheated another Navajo." Kai used the derogatory term for Dinee expecting a Zuni to call them Navajo.

"It doesn't matter," Ts'osi said. "He saved my father-in-law's life so I'm glad to give him the twelve horses. I just hope to get there with all of them."

"He'll go with you to help," Kai pursed her lips at Bahe.

"The trip takes several days," Ts'osi said.

"Just send him home once you reach Zuni. I don't want him chasing Zuni women." She hid a smile while looking at Bahe. "Those Zuni women use love medicine. You stay away from them."

"I may bring back two as wives. You and your sister will have to teach them our language. Or else you two learn Zuni."

Yahzi smiled inwardly at the jesting. Warmth flowed through her. She was home.

THIRTY SEVEN

Woolly clouds filled the sky before Ts'osi and Bahe readied their horses for the trip to Zuni. The youngest boy patted his father's horse, the oldest one inspected the lashing of Bahe's saddle bag. The two men seemed reluctant to leave, Ts'osi circling his horse while waiting for Bahe to lead.

Yahzi sensed a sudden yearning. She might never see the kind and gentle Ts'osi again. She recalled how impassioned Diego's embraces were with his wife, and how a few times he had embraced Yahzi the same way. She wished to show her feelings for the man who had been so generous with his time but knew she mustn't. She half smiled, imagining the confusion Ts'osi would experience if she embraced him. She searched her mind for a Dinee word like gracias but found none. Dinee expected deeds rather than words.

Before she could muse further over Spanish and Dinee customs, Ts'osi and Bahe trotted onto the trail out of the canyon. A melody of whinnying signaled their departure. Yahzi tightened her lips to stop a tear. She pondered how Kai kept similar feelings to herself.

When Yahzi turned, she saw Kai looking at her with head cocked. The woman took a deep breath, massaged her stomach before stretching to press her waist. She breathed hard, then called to the older girls to take the sheep to pasture.

Yahzi followed Kai into the hogan. Kai gestured that they sit a while before preparing a meal. Without men to feed, they could keep things simple.

The two women cut up roots, Kai promising Yahzi to build her a loom once the baby arrived.

"Oh, sister," Yahzi said. "I wove a learner's blanket before I was enslaved, but I've woven nothing since except to help my adopted aunt."

"Well, you can card and spin. I'll show you the dyes I have, but mostly I use the natural colors of my wool."

"My aunt said the natural colors were best. But then, that's all she had."

"A few women trade for red dye from the Spanish. The people around here love its brightness. I say, stare at the fire to see red. Burn up your eyes that way."

Yahzi forced a laugh. Kai interrupted her with a muffled screech. She dropped the root she was slicing and grabbed her stomach with both hands. "I don't know why the little one won't come."

Yahzi stood behind Kai and pressed downward on her stomach. "Does this help?"

"Have you assisted at many births?" Kai asked.

"Watching the ewes and a cow give birth was the only instruction I got," Yahzi said.

"There's no woman close with experience," Kai said.

"You said Doba helped before. Can't she assist?"

"She's assisted many women. That's where her sheep come from. Gifts from the women she helped. But last winter's blizzard took half her flock."

"Shall I get her? Maybe she knows ways to entice the stubborn one."

"No. I'll manage with your help, big sister."

"For now, sit and rest. At least I can finish with the roots. Can you sleep?"

"The children will come in soon. Making too much noise for anyone to sleep." Kai did recline on two bundles of sheepskins to make herself comfortable. "Tell me more about your life with the Spanish."

Yahzi tried to explain the household chores of a Spanish rancher but struggled to describe things like a stove or knitting needles.

When she finished slicing the last root, Yahzi turned to her sister. Kai's mouth was open, her eyelids closed. An occasional soft snore highlighted her breathing. Yahzi smiled and turned to the kettle.

When the first children entered the hogan, Yahzi gathered them in her arms and told them a story so her sister managed a longer nap.

The mild weather persisted the next few days. While the children played outside, Kai and Yahzi carded and spun wool. Kai sat close to Yahzi to show her how to use the spindle. She seldom spoke except when Yahzi had a question.

One night a cold wind rattled over the hogan's smoke hole. Yahzi rose and added wood to the fire. She pulled up whatever covers the younger children had kicked off, then checked on Kai. She was shivering but seemed to sleep. Yahzi found a shawl and added that to Kai's sheepskin. She stirred the fire and fed wood to it before returning to her own sheepskins.

The morning sun hid behind thick gray clouds. The wind blew in fits, and cold air settled in to promise a stiff chill. Yahzi stepped outside to gaze at muted gold and red cliff sides, a different kind of beauty without the glare of sunshine playing on them. In the corral, sheep huddled, their breath like smoke. Late-born lambs bleated for their mothers.

When Yahzi went inside the hogan, Kai was rubbing her stomach. Her sheepskin and the shawl still covered her legs. The oldest daughter prodded the fire into life. Yahzi whispered to the oldest daughter to encourage Kai to lie still.

Yahzi and the daughter moved the kettle of corn mush off the fire before Kai roused herself. She was rubbing her back when the youngest child awoke. His chatter woke his brothers and sisters.

"You're going to make me lazy," Kai said to Yahzi.

"Your daughters will do that."

"Our daughters," Kai corrected.

"How could I forget?" Yahzi muttered to herself.

The family enjoyed a leisurely meal waiting for the sun's rays to work their way through the clouds. Without any urging, the older children donned their warmest clothes and left to care for the sheep and horses. Yahzi emptied corn kernels from a storage jar onto the metate and began to grind.

"It's good to have help with the corn," Kai said. "My stomach protests when I kneel to grind it."

"Your..." Yahzi corrected herself. "Our older daughters help without being told."

"Yes. But, they have ways of avoiding the metate. Always claiming it's someone else's turn."

252

"You were too young to help when I had to grind corn for the family." Yahzi grinned as she recalled their early life. "But you know what? Nakai helped without being asked."

"We must invite him to visit," Kai said. "I'm afraid he didn't feel welcome the last time he was here. Doba and I quarreled. When he tried to stop us, we both yelled at him for interfering."

"He'll want to see his newborn niece. Then, we'll make things right."

Kai grimaced as Yahzi spoke. "Maybe his nephew." She rubbed both hands over her abdomen. "This one is so stubborn coming out, he must be male."

Yahzi smiled at her sister, thinking of Nakai. She visualized the necklace he had given her. She could use it to reconcile him with Kai. Instead of trading the necklace for sheep, Yahzi would claim it was a gift intended for Kai. It was the perfect time to give it to her, she thought. She went to the pouch with the two necklaces and retrieved one.

"Nakai is as generous as any Dinee," Yahzi boasted. "He hasn't let Holds Tight change him. He instructed me to wait until you had your baby to give you this, but I think now it will tempt our daughter to come see it." She held the necklace to the light to let it sparkle before placing it over Kai's head.

Kai ran her hands over the beads, couldn't resist taking the necklace off to examine it. She gasped at its splendor. "I've never seen anything like it. I can feel its beauty," Kai swallowed hard. "I've seen other necklaces of his, but this one is unique. How could I have been angry with him?"

"The necklace looks as if it were made for you," Yahzi exclaimed. She added, feeling no guilt for her lie, "He said he wanted to undo whatever he did wrong. He takes the blame for whatever happened."

"He's not to blame. Doba and I were foolish. We'll welcome him back. I'll convince Doba, somehow." Kai kept running her fingers over the necklace.

"When I was with him, he told me of our younger brother's daughter, but he talked forever about his nieces and nephews. It's obvious he thinks of your children all the time."

"They miss him," Kai said, wiping away a tear. "He told them wonderful stories. We must invite him to see the new baby when she comes." Kai gasped and held her stomach. "If she comes."

After the oldest daughter served bowls of stew, the children begged Yahzi for a story. "One like your uncle Nakai tells?" Yahzi asked. The children nodded vigorously. Yahzi started with stories she remembered from childhood. The children started fidgeting. She asked if they were curious about Spanish custom. The younger ones seemed frightened, but the older ones showed they were eager to learn.

Yahzi related the Genesis story of creation. The younger children dozed off, but the older ones stared in disbelief as Yahzi struggled to explain how God drove Adam and Eve from their homeland. Even children knew it was essential to learn how people arrived at their homeland, not be driven from it.

The children sought their beds soon after. Yahzi piled additional wood near the fire since the evening was as cold as the one before. She laid down, pulled the sheepskin to her nose, and fell asleep in moments.

THIRTY EIGHT

A muffled scream woke Yahzi. A Spanish raid, she thought, berating herself for not knowing where Bahe kept his weapons. He took a rifle with him she remembered. She tried to recall if there were another. He must have left a knife. Muttering to herself, she dashed to the cooking utensils and grabbed the largest knife.

Nothing stirred in the hogan except for Kai who writhed and groaned. She must have screamed in pain, Yahzi realized. She stirred the fire and went to Kai's side.

"The baby is coming," Kai groaned. She punctuated her words with a muffled wail. The noise brought the oldest daughter. Water flowed from Kai's womb. Their daughter dried her with a wad of grass.

"Surely, it's time," Kai moaned. "You know where the rope is," she gasped to the girl. The girl disappeared for a moment, then returned to the nearest post and tied the rope to it. Yahzi and the girl helped Kai to the post. She knelt before it, holding to the rope, pulling hard to no avail. She lifted herself upright so Yahzi could examine her womb.

"It looks like a rear end, mama. Why isn't it the head?"

"She must be confused," Kai joked, then jerked upright to suppress a scream. She looked at Yahzi in desperation. "Get Doba. She'll know what to do."

Yahzi had time to think while the daughter searched for a blanket. Yahzi retrieved the second necklace from her pouch, and slipped it into her belt.

Her daughter came with a blanket. "Can you find the hogan?"

"There's only one way between here and there," Yahzi said.

"But it's so dark," the girl shivered. "And the ghosts—from the cave."

"It's too cold for ghosts." Yahzi could joke about ghosts in the hogan with its warmth and flickering light. Once outside, in utter blackness and biting cold, she wondered what harm ghosts might do to her.

255

As her eyes adjusted to the dark, a rising slice of moon gave sufficient light for Yahzi to find the path leading to Doba's. At times, she felt her way with her feet as much as saw the path. The distance seemed so long, she thought she must be lost.

Wood smoke tickled her nose before she saw a glimmer of red from Doba's hogan. At its entrance she coughed hard, then entered, guessing her greeting awoke no one. She poked at the fire and added sticks to it. In the blaze she saw where Doba and her husband slept. She shook Doba. Her husband jumped up, clutching a knife.

"It's me." Yahzi touched the husband. "Our sister, Kai, needs help."

Doba rolled over, blinked her eyes, yawned. "What is it?" she said.

"Kai is giving birth, but the baby's upside down."

"Not good." Doba sat up. "Why do you expect me to help?"

"You know more than anyone about childbirth." Yahzi smothered a growing anger.

"Maybe that witch is getting what she deserves."

"Doba," Yahzi used her name to jar her sister. "Think of mother and the hozho we grew up with. We must find that again."

"You don't know how Kai mistreated me. She has the sheep our brother should have given me."

"She wants to make up for it. She sent you this necklace."

Doba turned up her nose at the necklace until coral sparkled in the new-born flames. She gasped. "How beautiful! It must be one of Nakai's."

"He told me he was thinking of you when he made it even if he intended it for Kai. Our sister wants you to have it. Nakai will make her another one." Yahzi never expected to lie so much to kin, but she'd do anything to unite them.

Doba slipped the necklace over her head without a word.

"Remember how Kai helped you during your kinaalda." Yahzi guessed Kai had helped like any older sister would.

"Kai did prepare me well." Doba felt the beads again. "My brother, too. I must forget our disagreements."

Doba turned to her husband. "Saddle a horse for us. The reliable mare for my sister."

After her husband calmed the children, he slipped out of the hogan. Moments later Doba wrapped a blanket around herself and rummaged on a shelf for herbs. When the two women left the hogan, Doba's husband had the horses ready.

Her brother-in-law let his horse find the way so the three were soon back at Kai's hogan. A low moaning from the hogan greeted them.

"Not good," Doba murmured as she pushed herself off the horse. "Bring the bag of herbs," she called to Yahzi as she rushed inside.

When Yahzi caught up, she found the children awake, huddled around an older son telling them stories. The oldest daughter was massaging her mother's stomach.

"That's good," Doba said to the girl. "Now watch." She got behind Kai and grasped her waist, pushing downward. "Push," she said to her sister.

Kai muttered "push" in between groans. She held to the rope as if to life. She was bathed in sweat. Her lower lip bled.

Doba came from behind Kai to examine her womb. Yahzi looked over Doba's shoulder. The baby's buttocks protruded, and Doba tucked up its legs and gently twisted the body. Kai panted. Doba chanted under her breath, pausing to reassure her sister that all was well.

Kai pushed harder than usual. Doba manipulated the baby. The legs worked free. A boy. Doba whispered a prayer, pulled again. When all but the head emerged, Doba pushed it back, reached into the womb and did something to the head.

Doba prodded with her finger. "His chin is free. Push, he's almost out. Ah, a mighty warrior." Kai tugged once more and expelled the afterbirth. A daughter handed Doba moistened cedar bark to clean Kai. Another daughter took the baby and wrapped him in a doe skin.

"How are his feet?" Yahzi asked the daughter, pulling aside the doeskin to see for herself.

The daughter raised an eyebrow as Yahzi studied the feet. "They're normal." Yahzi breathed relief.

Yahzi turned to Doba. "You were wonderful, sister."

"Thirty sheep await you," Kai murmured to Doba. "I should have given them to you before."

"No. They belong to your flock. I was too ambitious for my children."

"They're yours," Kai's voice trailed off. "Our new son owes you his life." She closed her eyes and sighed in relief.

"We'll feast everyone when the weather gets better," Yahzi said to Doba. "We'll go to the mouth of the canyon so no one need fear Massacre Cave. We'll host our brothers and any one else who calls us kin."

Kai said nothing but her peaceful smile said she'd heard.

Doba laughed. "Everyone in the canyon will be there. We'll roast a cow, too. Our youngest brother will have returned and be ready to cure the sick."

With a turquoise gem stone to help him, he'll be prepared well, Yahzi thought. She felt wonderful at the idea of bestowing her wealth on relatives. Her family would know hozho.

Yahzi and Doba edged closer to Kai. Doba took the baby, and teased its mouth with her finger. The baby sucked. "You may nurse him a little. It helps you both. Then rest."

"Look," Yahzi said. "He's yawning. He'll be asleep in no time."

Kai put him to her breast. He made sucking sounds, was soon satisfied, and closed his eyes.

Yahzi took the baby and handed him to a daughter who swaddled her new brother to a cradle board.

Yahzi and Doba reminisced about their mother for awhile, how she and their father filled their hogan with hozho. No one was jealous. Kai breathed heavily in sleep. Doba tucked the blanket around her and added a sheepskin over her waist.

"Will you stay for a day or two?" Yahzi asked. "She may need you."

"Yes. I want to boil my herbs to make a poultice for her womb."

"I'm glad you came. I could not have done it alone," Yahzi said.

"Where is Bahe?" Doba tilted her head. "Guess he fled when he thought he'd have to deliver a baby."

Yahzi laughed. "He went to Zuni with Ts'osi to help with the horses. He should be back in two or three days."

"I should be gone by then. But our two hogans must see more of each other. We might build new hogans where we could all live together so our sons and daughters can see more of each other." Yahzi felt an inner glow.

Three days later, Kai was doing her usual chores except when nursing. The baby showed no sign of suffering from his protracted birth. Doba left for her hogan.

On the fifth day, Bahe returned. He delighted in holding the baby, letting it clutch his finger. "He'll be a strong one. Own many horses like his father."

"Be as generous with his horses as his father is," Kai said, taking the baby from him.

"Oh," Bahe muttered. "I need to save my horses."

Before he could say why he needed them, the older children came running into the hogan. They badgered their father with questions about the Zuni. By the time he finished answering, Yahzi and the girls had prepared an evening meal.

The family sat around the cook fire, joking and telling stories. Periods of silence did nothing to disturb the hozho of the hogan. Younger children drifted off to sleep, the older ones cleaned up after the meal, and Kai nursed the baby.

The fire was dying, a southern breeze promised warmer weather, and the oldest child curled into her sheepskin. Yahzi moved her blanket and skin in order to give Kai and Bahe more privacy. She could hear little of what they were saying until Kai laughed at something Bahe said. "I suppose you'd want to spend all your nights in her hogan?"

"Well, I'd have to protect the herd."

"They wouldn't be your horses. You'd have given them as bride wealth."

"Well, that young girl is pretty good looking."

"No she isn't. She looks like her mother. I've seen better looking goats." Kai must have punched a finger into Bahe's ribs. He snorted before he guffawed.

"Well, I can get along with only one wife." His voice took a serious tone. "You're a good woman. You're all I need."

"No," Kai said, her voice serious. "The hogan could use another woman. A proper wife for you and a companion for me. Someone to help me grind corn. To talk with when you're away."

"You mean Yahzi?" Bahe gasped his surprise at his wife's suggestion.

"Who else? She's brought back the hozho of our mother's hogan. She persuaded Doba to help deliver our son. We're over our differences."

"If I marry Yahzi, will I have to pay bride wealth for her?" Yahzi thought Bahe suppressed a laugh.

"As many horses as you paid for me."

"But you've given me eight children. She can never have eight. Maybe not even one." Yahzi couldn't tell if Bahe joked.

"She'll have one or two, at least." Kai didn't joke.

"She's been a strong woman to endure all she has, but how can you be sure she'll bring hozho to our home?"

"She's done so much in the few days she's been here. Besides, she was always helping mother. And look how healthy we've been since she came. A good sign of hozho."

"Well, I remember I liked her as a young woman." Bahe said. "Just before her kinaalda, my mother talked about her as a possible wife for me. I thought that wouldn't be too bad."

"You see." Kai almost gloated. "You'll get used to the idea."

Yahzi wasn't sure she'd get used to the idea. But as she looked at a star through the smoke hole and lingered on the verge of sleep, she knew she was home. She'd returned to beauty.